Yes Means Yes

Yes Means Yes

A NOVEL

Steven M. Wells

Published by Overlake Media
Copyright ©2017 Steven M. Wells
All rights reserved

ISBN-13: 9780692908884
ISBN-10: 0692908889

This is a work of fiction. Names, characters, places, and incidents are the products of the author's imagination or are used fictitiously. Any resemblance to actual events, locales, or persons, living or dead, is entirely coincidental.

www.stevenmwells.com

For my daughter

Cast of Characters

(in order of appearance)

Natalie Garcia—Former sorority member and student at the University of Colorado. Withdrew from school after a sexual assault and moved home to Pueblo, Colorado.

Katie Russell—University of Colorado graduate student of philosophy.

Justin Carter—Katie's undergraduate boyfriend. Attends Claremont McKenna College in Claremont, California.

Brian Taylor—Temporarily disbarred attorney and director of the No Sexual Assault Foundation (NSAF).

Morgan—A female law student of Brian Taylor's.

Teresa—Katie's roommate at Claremont McKenna College.

Mary—Wild companion of Katie's during an outing in Las Vegas.

Ryan—A graduating former classmate whom Katie meets in a bar in Claremont.

Paul—Cybersecurity director at the University of Colorado.

Professor Amanda Hatfield—Professor who teaches Katie's "Philosophy and Law" class at the University of Colorado.

Assistant Professor Mark O'Connor—Philosophy PhD who is working toward tenure. Advises Katie's "Philosophy and Law" class. Raised on a ranch in Durango, Colorado.

Ava Greene—Lives in Boulder, Colorado, in the apartment upstairs from Katie. Former girlfriend of football quarterback Drew Evans.

Drew Evans—Quarterback on the University of Colorado football team. Ava's ex-boyfriend.

Desmond Baker—Drew's teammate.

Sally Clark—Investigator and training coordinator for the University of Colorado's Office of Institutional Equity and Compliance. Enforces Title IX compliance.

Professor Molly Wilson—Law school professor who advises Katie on her research and encourages her to attend law school.

Julie Downs—Senior conduct coordinator at the University of Colorado who chairs a committee that investigates incidents of sexual assault by students.

Detective Alex Scott—Semiretired detective from the Boulder Police Department. Consults with the University of Colorado's sexual-assault investigations.

Peter Blake—Dean of students, college friend, and brother-in-law of Brian Taylor whose office funds the No Sexual Assault Foundation (NSAF).

Jim O'Connor—Younger brother of Assistant Professor Mark O'Connor.

Wendy Tucker—Representative of the University of Colorado's Office of Risk Management.

Landry Clarke—Quarterback Drew Evans's attorney.

Harriet Becker—Katie's attorney.

Commander Robert Bennett—Manages twenty detectives at the Boulder Police Department, including Detective Scott and Detective Colin Richardson.

Detective Colin Richardson—Young detective in the Boulder Police Department assigned to Katie as a security detail.

Addison, Emma, Bailey, Amy—Former and current University of Colorado students who share tales of acquaintance rape with Katie.

Contents

CHAPTER 1

Pajama Party at the Fraternity

Natalie Garcia reclined on her bed and leaned against its headboard. After wrapping a wool blanket around her legs, she opened her Colorado history textbook to an assigned chapter about the Sand Creek massacre of 1864. A printed textbook was rare; her other classes were all digital. The violent attack, undertaken by the Third Colorado Cavalry against a village of Cheyenne and Arapaho tribes native to southeastern Colorado, was gruesome and disheartening. How, she wondered, could men so brutally kill over a hundred women and children? Not just kill, but mutilate and dismember. What precipitated the hate in the hearts of those men, and why were they capable of such abhorrent behavior? That was the essay question she would answer later.

Abigail, Natalie's roommate in the sorority house, appeared in the doorway. "You studying all night?"

"Probably." Natalie laid the textbook facedown on her lap. "Why? What's up?"

"Come with me to the frat party. It's Saturday—you should get out."

"You know I'm not much of a party person."

"You haven't been to a mixer since you moved in. They're fun."

Natalie was a sophomore at the University of Colorado, and had lived in the house since the start of the winter semester. She stared out her bedroom window. Abigail was right. She hadn't been to a party since she'd moved in, and sorority sisters like her were expected to attend house-sanctioned mixers. "OK," she said, "but I won't have to stay long, will I?"

"You can leave whenever you want. Let's head over there around ten."

"What should I wear?" Natalie knew fraternity parties typically featured themes: cavemen, eighties disco, beach party. Her least-favorite-sounding of them all was the "Catholic schoolgirls and dirty old men" party.

"It's a pajama party. Wear something simple."

Natalie read her textbook for another hour. She was still troubled by the Indian wars when she headed to the shower. How could men be so cruel?

Back in her room, after toweling off and applying light makeup, Natalie searched through the bottom drawer of her old wooden dresser and found the pajamas she liked to wear when it was cold out. The pink-and-blue tartan-plaid flannels were comfortable. The button-down top featured a full collar, and the roomy pants had a long, corded drawstring.

Abigail returned from her shower and began her own search for something to wear. While Natalie slipped into her pajamas, she noticed Abigail pull a small bottle from her backpack and fill a tumbler halfway with clear liquid. Then she took a can of club soda from their mini-fridge and filled the tumbler the rest of the way. Abigail met Natalie's gaze. She held up the drink. "Want one?"

"No, thanks. I don't drink, remember?"

"I've always wondered about that. Why?"

Natalie thought for a minute. "I guess because I'm not twenty-one yet and my parents don't approve. It's just not something I've ever done before. But it doesn't bother me that other people do. I'm sure I will, too, someday."

"I probably drink a little too much. The house must have selected us to be roommates so you'll set a good example," Abigail said with a smile.

Natalie checked herself in the mirror. She hoped to avoid any unwanted attention at the party and was satisfied by her notably youthful appearance. Next, she put on a white terry-cloth robe, reached inside behind her neck, and extracted a long plume of thick black hair that cascaded to her waist. Out of habit, she fastened the gold cross and chain she wore around her neck daily; she mainly wore it out of devotion to the church and for good luck. Sometimes, she'd put it in her pocket so she could touch the chain as if it were a talisman. She finished her pajama-party ensemble with some shearling slippers. "How do I look?"

Abigail took a final swig from her glass and grinned. "Like a tall Selena Gomez. Guys will be all over you."

"I don't want guys to be all over me," Natalie said, crossing her arms.

"I'm just saying: you look really cute, so be prepared for the attention you'll get. Don't worry. I'll keep an eye on you. And any guys you don't want, just send them my way. Who do I look like?"

Natalie studied Abigail, who was wearing a camisole, sweatpants, and some fuzzy pink slippers. Natalie thought she looked sweet, but she also knew that Abigail wasn't afraid to hook up with cute guys. Natalie was conservative, but she'd learned to be nonjudgmental. Besides, Abigail was a good student and was starting to become a good friend. "I'd say you look like a younger Kate Winslet."

"Oh, that's good!" Abigail grabbed her coat. "Come on—let's go."

The frat house was only a few blocks away. As they walked, Abigail reminded Natalie of the rules they'd covered at the beginning of the year. "Remember, if you decide to drink—which you probably won't—don't have more than one per hour. And get it yourself. Don't let anyone hand you a drink or drink from it after it's been left unattended—like when you dance. The best idea is to drink from a container you open yourself, like a can of beer. Finally, don't go upstairs with anyone. Other girls from our house will be there, and we all try to keep an eye on each other. Just have fun and be careful."

At the fraternity, they found a line extending from the front door to the sidewalk. Since Abigail was friendly with some of the upperclassmen, the two proceeded to the head of the line. After a short exchange, they were quickly ushered inside.

The noise inside the house was an energetic mix of voices and music. Abigail and Natalie went to the bar, where Abigail poured herself a drink in a plastic cup. Natalie located a bottle of water in a tub, also filled with ice and beer, and opened it herself. Drinks in hand, they retreated to a wall and strained to talk over the thumping music. Natalie sipped her water and surveyed the roomful of students. She was surprised by what some of the women were wearing. One had on a silk romper, unbuttoned to the waist, with a sexy bra fully exposed underneath. Natalie would never show that much skin. A lot of men roamed around bare-chested and in pajama pants. Bare feet, too. Natalie began to wonder if attending the party had been a good idea.

It wasn't long before two guys approached her. One seemed to know Abigail and asked her to dance. Natalie was left standing alone with the other guy, who stood before her in a T-shirt and boxers.

"Where you from?" he almost shouted.

"Pueblo."

"Never been there. Hear it's ugly."

The comment irritated Natalie. Pueblo, in the southern part of the state, had a reputation as a working-class town and a place where lots of Latinos lived, including her family. "Beauty's in the eye of the beholder. It's my home, and I like it there."

The guy's face dropped. "I'm sorry—that was thoughtless of me. I should visit it first."

Natalie smiled, relieved that he seemed at least somewhat self-aware. "Apology accepted. Pueblo has that reputation."

He asked her questions about school and her major, what house she was in and how she liked it, as well as for a few details about Abigail. While they were speaking, he kept touching Natalie's arm, which she didn't enjoy. She remembered reading that unwanted touching was against the student code of conduct and was considered a form of sexual harassment. Every time he touched her with his hand, she gently pushed it away. After his third attempt and a firmer rejection, he finally seemed to take the hint and stopped.

"Would you like to dance?" He nodded toward the dance floor.

Natalie decided that she might as well. She removed her terry-cloth robe, laid it over a chair with her water bottle on top, and followed him to the dance floor. Several years of jazz dance in middle school had given her confidence as a dancer, but she kept it low energy and didn't make eye contact. She spotted Abigail across the floor and rolled her eyes to signal a lack of interest in her dance partner.

After a few songs, Natalie retreated to the wall. Her companion followed behind her.

"I like that you're wearing pajamas," he said. "You're more tastefully dressed than a lot of the girls here. I don't think a lot of them really sleep in Victoria's Secret, do you?"

Natalie laughed. "I think you're right."

"Thanks for the dance. See you later." He sauntered off toward the back of the house.

As the evening progressed, Natalie concluded that Abigail had been right: guys seemed to orbit around her, and she danced with several of them. Most of them seemed sociable, or at least benign. Others were enthusiastic and obviously looking to hook up. She'd heard rumors about frat parties and how there were always a few women who went upstairs for casual sex—something Natalie had yet to experience. Ever. She'd kissed a few guys, but her mother had taught her to eschew male intimacy. Intercourse was out of the question. "Save yourself for the right guy" was one of her mother's favorite precepts, usually followed by "Sex is for marriage and when you want to have children." Her parents were conservative and devout Catholics, and Natalie was their only child. Consequently, their devotion to her was only exceeded by their expectation of respect from her. She held what she had come to understand was a quaint perspective. Her parents deserved her abstinence—for now, anyway.

At some point after midnight, as the crowd started to thin out, Natalie noticed that she had suddenly become parched. She returned to her robe and the bottle of water. The robe remained on the chair, but the bottle of water was missing.

"Like to dance again?"

It was Mr. Wandering Hand. Natalie turned and studied his face. Now showing a wide smile, his face displayed perfectly white and straight teeth. He was radiant and looked like a model.

"I don't think so. I'm thirsty, though, and I can't find my water bottle."

"I'll get you one." He disappeared toward the kitchen.

While Natalie waited, Abigail approached her, her skin gleaming with perspiration.

"Having fun?" Abigail asked. Her glossy eyes and smile suggested that she was.

"Yes, but I think I'm ready to go. Will you walk back with me?"

"Can you wait a few minutes? I promised a guy I'd go down to the game room with him and play some shuffleboard."

"OK, but don't take too long." Natalie wondered what else went on in the game room.

Abigail winked and left. Natalie watched the dance floor and wished she could leave. The big smiler returned and offered her a bottle of water. Natalie studied him some more. His build and obvious agility suggested that he was an athlete. Natalie took the bottle and made sure it was full. She twisted the plastic top, confident that it hadn't been opened, and it came off easily. She didn't consider that without a typical hard twist and a snap, the seal might have been broken. She took a long drink of cold water. Then, she surprised herself and said, "OK, one more dance. Then I'm leaving."

The guy took her hand and guided her between a few other students onto the floor. She kept the water bottle in her hand and took occasional sips while she danced. The music had a perfect rhythm, and after a few more songs, she felt exuberant, aware that her face had relaxed and that her mouth had turned upward into an easy smile. Another song played, and they kept dancing. When it ended, she felt a little unsteady and took his arm for support. "I think I need to take a break."

"Maybe you need some air."

He guided her toward the rear of the house, where they passed through a doorway and out onto a deck. Natalie noticed other students outside, some kissing and embracing, others smoking blunts or drinking. She felt him put his hands on her shoulders and turn her body toward his. He slowly leaned in and kissed her. It wasn't a bad feeling—sort of tender. She gently pushed him away. "I need to find Abigail."

"I'll take you to find her. Come on." But instead of returning to the house, he walked her down a set of steps toward the backyard and into an alleyway. They stopped next to a parked a car. Natalie looked around and became confused. Things looked out of focus.

"Where're we going?" Her intonation signaled more disorientation than worry.

"To find Abigail."

Beams from the car's headlights flashed over tarnished trash bins and dilapidated fence posts as the car moved down the alley and turned onto a side street. That was the last image Natalie remembered of the party.

NATALIE SLOWLY OPENED HER EYES and struggled to comprehend her shadowy surroundings. A dull throb permeated her head as she pushed herself into a sitting position. Violently rumpled sheets and the sight of her completely naked body triggered a rush of fear. From the glint of a streetlight outside a curtained window, she was able to make out what she thought were clothes on the floor. She didn't know where she was or how she'd come to be there. She heard the distinctive sound of someone urinating coming from behind a door across the room. Was the door nearer to the bed possibly an exit? Her instincts propelled her to run. She jumped off the bed, but the motion almost sent her to the floor from the intense pounding it caused in her head. She picked up the scattered clothing she'd seen on the floor, thankful for the soft touch of flannel that greeted her fingers. As she struggled to pull on her pajama bottoms, the sound of cascading urine stopped, shortly to be replaced by the sound of a faucet running into a sink. As she fought to pull on her pajama top, the door to the bathroom swung open with a groan.

It was the guy from the frat party. His naked and athletic body was silhouetted against a bright light bulb suspended from the bathroom ceiling. He flashed the same beautiful smile as he had at the party, but it now repulsed her. Natalie swung open the door near the bed and was relieved to find that it led outside. She stepped onto a landing at the top of a wooden stairway and rushed down as quickly as she could. Her bare feet scraped over the rough wood of the steps.

"Hey, don't go! We just met." The guy chuckled and slammed the door behind her.

Once she reached the bottom of the stairs, Natalie's stomach began to float up inside her throat. Two steps later, she doubled over and vomited. She heaved a few times, wiped her mouth on her sleeve, and hurried down the street. At the next intersection, she turned right and continued to walk, hunched over against a stiff breeze. Each step on the hard, cold pavement hurt, and she stumbled frequently. She didn't recognize her surroundings; the streets seemed empty and eerily quiet. Her body began to shiver, but she kept on walking and wrapped her arms around herself for warmth. Her head continued to pound. Finally, she heard a car approaching her from behind. She turned to face it and frantically waved her arms. The car stopped. Natalie screamed, "Help me! Please help me!"

CHAPTER 2

Someone Always Gets Hurt

"'Human reason is troubled by questions that it cannot dismiss but also cannot answer.'"

"Immanuel Kant."

"'Let woman share the rights and she will emulate the virtues of man; for she must grow more perfect when emancipated, or justify the authority that chains such a weak being to her duty.'"

"Mary Wollstonecraft."

"'Friendship often ends in love, but love in friendship—never.'"

"Albert Camus. Nice try. He wasn't in my notes."

"Glad you're paying attention."

"That's enough review for tonight," Katie said. "How about a glass of wine?" She closed her spiral notebook and slipped it into her backpack. She wanted to relax and forget about the upcoming philosophy final—her last.

"Sure thing." Justin got up and headed for the kitchen of his small studio apartment.

Katie leaned back on the sofa and watched Justin move to the kitchen. He took a bottle of inexpensive-looking white wine from the refrigerator and twisted its screw cap. It was the best they could afford, but it did the job. He pulled a couple of tumblers down from a shelf and carried everything back to the sofa. During the preceding week, Katie had sensed that change was at hand, but she was unsure of what form it would take. The situation reminded her of the clouds ahead of a summer squall. And it was equally as foreboding.

Over sips of wine, Katie reflected on her four years at Claremont McKenna College in the LA suburb of Claremont. Hard to believe her time was almost over. Yet what was ahead? And what of Justin? More introvert than extrovert, Katie had always prioritized academics. During her freshman year, when she had gone out, it was typically with friends to house parties, or dinners on Sunday nights when the cafeteria was closed. At one of those Sunday dinners, she had met a handsome business major named Matt who lived in her dorm. After a couple of subsequent connections, Katie quickly ascertained that Matt preferred hanging out with friends to hitting the books. Though he was cavalier about learning, his abundance of charm put Katie at ease. It wasn't long before they began to hook up regularly—something he seemed to enjoy more than she did.

Katie generally considered relationships to be tenuous and didn't put a lot of faith in them. Right before the start of summer break, during what she liked to call the "age of Matt," she had met Justin. He was in her Western history class, and they were assigned as partners on a research project. He was a bit of a geek, but he was the funniest guy she'd ever met. If college didn't work out, then she knew he'd be destined for a career as a stand-up comedian. It was hard for her not to laugh at his jokes while they worked together in the library. A looming deadline injected some urgency, and after a few late nights they finished the project on time. When freshman year ended, their friendship continued over the course of the summer through occasional texts and phone calls.

As sophomore year began, Matt returned to campus with a new girlfriend. Katie was initially hurt but then recognized she'd been ambivalent about him from the start. Sure, he was a good-looking and fun guy, but he wasn't much more than that.

As Thanksgiving break approached, Katie reconnected with Justin at a house party. They shared a few drinks and then ended up kissing on the back deck. It was his personality that won her over. During discussions over coffee or beers, she found him to be more disciplined about academics than Matt had been—a characteristic she valued—and he displayed intellectual curiosity. The night before they departed campus for the break, they hooked up.

They dated for the next two years. It was during a summer immersion trip between junior and senior years to a high-mountain village in

Ecuador when Katie began to fully appreciate Justin. They'd each studied Spanish in high school and college, so their verbal skills were quite passable. Over the course of four weeks, Justin taught basic computer programming, while Katie worked on a farm. She initially struggled with her assigned housing: a small compact house made of patched stucco walls, cracked tile floors, and oil-stained beams for a roof. She lived with three generations of family members, including four children, their parents, and one set of maternal grandparents. Katie recalled the greasy and stomach-turning diet of refried plantains, boiled potatoes with roasted guinea pig, and goat stew. More troubling was when she first learned that one of the cute guinea pigs that roamed around the kitchen floor in the morning might become dinner later that night. But it was memories of Justin that made the trip remarkable. He was humble and gracious to the family who housed him, and he obviously scored a big hit with the local kids when he played barefoot soccer on a dirt field. He was a decent guy.

Katie returned her focus to the apartment. She took another sip of wine and studied Justin. He now sat upright and asleep at the opposite end of the sofa, snoring like an old cat. He'd removed his customary eyeglasses and suddenly looked like a little boy. Katie estimated that maybe fifteen minutes had elapsed during her reflection, maybe less. Still, she felt as if she were coming out of a trance.

Graduation was now only a few weeks away; Katie felt as if her life would be on hold until Justin decided where to start his career. His prospects were bright, thanks to his degree in computer science and a specialty in "big data," whatever that was. Katie had written each of his cover letters to accompany the résumés he sent to prospective employers. He was smart, but the time he'd spent taking technical courses hadn't enabled a good writing style. Yet he'd already received multiple job offers.

Since Katie was a philosophy major—a field not known for its lucrative job prospects—her best option was graduate school. She'd applied to several colleges the previous fall and had received acceptance letters from the University of California (both LA and Berkeley) and the University of Colorado. All the universities were located in areas with strong technology sectors, and Katie hoped Justin would take a job near one of them.

Justin stirred. He put his glasses back on and poured the last of the bottle of wine into their glasses. He looked at Katie with a lustful grin, clearly looking forward to what was next. "I'm so glad finals are over. I can't believe we're done with school."

"*You're* done. I have one more to go."

"Will you study any more tonight?"

Katie shrugged. "No. If I don't know it now, I never will."

"You'll nail it." Justin leaned over and kissed Katie's lips and ran his hand through her wild mane of loose auburn hair.

Katie half-heartedly worked her lips over his. True affection seemed elusive, held at bay by the uncertainty she felt about the future.

Justin slipped his hand under the bottom of Katie's hooded sweatshirt and gently pulled upward.

Katie considered simply telling him that she'd rather go home and get some sleep, but she went limp and let the sweatshirt slide up and over her arms. Katie instinctively removed her pants and wondered why she wasn't inspired by the prospect of sex that night.

Her first lover had been a high school boyfriend. They'd kissed, explored, and groped each other during a period of teenage discovery. Then, one night, after messing around and drinking a few beers filched from her dad, they agreed to have sex. Katie was totally surprised when, prepared like a Boy Scout, he produced a condom. Just like that, she was no longer a virgin. Next had been Matt. Their intimacy seemed routine. She enjoyed his sexy body pressed next to hers, but she never felt the kind of satisfaction her friends bragged about. When would she experience the building tension, the exploding pleasure, and the satisfying relaxation they'd described so breathlessly? She'd wistfully imagined what it would be like. So far, her experiences hadn't come close.

Then there was Justin. Something seemed lacking, but what? Her friends liked him. Her parents approved—especially her father, who appreciated his career prospects. But she didn't feel any—she hated to use the cliché—chemistry.

By then he was moving inside her, sometimes fast, sometimes slow, but never for long. Where was the magic? Was sex just something men wanted and women were supposed to provide? Her mother told her that with the right lover, sexual intimacy could be transcendent. At the time, the comment had made her squirm. "You'll experience feelings and pleasure you didn't know possible."

Katie encouraged Justin with an occasional gasp or clench of her thighs. After a predictable number of minutes—always more than five and fewer than ten—Justin clearly went to some special place Katie had never visited. He lay on top of her, regained his breath, and told her how beautiful she was and how wonderful making love had been.

KATIE WAS ALONE IN JUSTIN'S BED when she awoke the next morning. Her head ached. At least she didn't have classes that day, she thought. Her last final wasn't until later in the week. She got up and looked out the window. It was a bright spring day, and since the apartment already felt sticky warm, she pulled on a light scoop-neck T-shirt over her sleeping shorts. She found Justin, shirtless and in cotton pajama pants, in the kitchen scrambling eggs.

Katie filled the coffee maker with water and added ground beans to a paper filter. While she waited for the coffee to brew, she leaned against a countertop assembled of ceramic tiles and stained grout.

Justin grated some cheddar into the skillet and added a dash of salt and pepper. "Katie, there's something we need to discuss."

Katie's stomach clenched at the comment. "Like what?"

"Like about us."

"About after graduation?"

"Precisely."

That was always the kind of word Justin used. Words like parsimonious, or punctilious, or perspicacious. He'd no doubt aced the verbal section of the SAT, even if he couldn't write a grammatically correct essay.

The coffee maker finished wheezing, and Katie poured them both a cup. He took his black. Hers was with milk. "So?"

"It's about my job offers." He stirred the eggs. Steam hissed into the air.

Earlier, Katie's stomach had rumbled with hunger. Now it began to churn. "Did you get another one?" She tipped her cup of coffee to her mouth and took a sip. Her eyes went wide as she watched Justin over the top of the cup.

"I accepted one."

Katie quickly put the coffee down for fear she might drop it. "Where?"

Justin turned to her, a wooden spoon waving in his hand. "In Seattle. It's with the big online retailer. It's a great offer with a huge signing bonus, stock options, and subsidized relocation. They'll even help me borrow money to buy a house."

"Seattle? You never mentioned Seattle. You hate rain." Katie gripped the counter for support. "When do you start?"

He returned his focus to the eggs. "The end of June. I'll go visit my parents for a couple of weeks and then drive up."

Katie's mind immediately sensed that hurt was imminent. Her heart picked up speed and pumped blood to her face. She could feel the heat. "Why didn't you tell me?"

Justin gazed back at Katie. His face went blank. "I thought you'd want me to take the best one."

"We talked about this. I only applied to graduate schools in cities with lots of tech jobs. I thought we'd move together."

"I never said that."

"You implied it. You knew I was waiting on you." Katie put her hands on her hips. "I've been accepted to graduate school in LA, Berkeley, and Boulder. We never even considered Seattle. Now it's too late to apply. Do you expect me to just move up there with no plans?"

Justin spread his hands. Pieces of cooked egg dropped from the spoon and landed on the worn linoleum. "I assumed you'd be happy for me. Go to one of the graduate schools where you've been accepted. We can still spend *some* weekends together."

The comment pierced Katie's heart. Tears formed around her large brown eyes, and she swept her hands upward from the counter to her face. She hooked the handle of her coffee cup, which sailed off the counter and shattered on the floor. Black stains spread across the linoleum like a monochromatic sunburst, and shards of white porcelain careened across the room.

Katie dropped to her knees to pick up the pieces. Tears flowed. "I'm sorry."

Justin dropped to the floor opposite her. He placed his hands on her shoulders. Coffee soaked into the knees of his pajama pants. "Katie, look at me. Don't worry about the cup. I'm the one who's sorry. I've loved our time together. I really have."

They were words from a stranger. Katie assumed he'd want to live with her. It was obvious he hadn't even considered it. She'd read before that women will never have a better chance to meet successful men than during their college years. She felt ripped from her moorings and cast adrift in a turbulent sea.

The sound of the breaking cup still resonated in Katie's ears as she stood and carefully picked her way across the kitchen floor amid pieces of broken porcelain. In the bedroom, she grabbed her pants, shoes, and backpack. Her bare feet marched briskly toward the apartment's door, which she slammed shut on the way out. The rest of her things could wait until later.

CHAPTER 3

"Our Remedies Oft in Ourselves Do Lie"

Katie remained in Claremont after graduation and tried to make sense of her unanticipated breakup with Justin. She cried off and on for a week and struggled to show up for her job as a part-time barista at a family-run coffee shop and bakery in town. The money helped, and though she found the work mundane, it did give her time to contemplate where she should attend graduate school.

Katie had always been intrepid, but the loss of Justin reinforced her belief that happiness was fleeting. Unexpected events could dishearten her faster than critical comments written by a professor in the margins of a sloppy essay. She strove to be self-reliant; she knew it had been a mistake to weave strands of Justin into the fabric of her future. As she struggled to come to grips with the breakup, the psychological tool of rationalization did its work. One likely source of her anger, she knew, was Justin's decision to break up with her before she'd broken up with him. Did she really believe he'd be a reliable long-term partner? She'd harbored doubts all along. She concluded that it was time for her to move on, but she still thought he was a jerk for walking away.

Katie weighed the comparative merits of the three graduate programs that had accepted her; she considered academic quality a top priority, but so was livability. She'd spent most of her young life in Orange County, so she didn't find the idea of attending UCLA to be exciting. And even though the program at Berkeley was the strongest, she knew it was time to leave California. Just before the deadline, she accepted an offer from the philosophy department at the University of Colorado, or CU, as everyone called it, a public university with a liberal reputation and the splendor of the Rockies as a backdrop.

In August, several weeks before she planned to move to Boulder, Katie received a call from Justin. They spoke at length for the first time since their breakup. He wanted to see her again, which she couldn't believe. He enthusiastically described his work on a new social media application targeted at men. It would track their clothing preferences from their credit-card purchases and, after scanning the profiles of women in the men's social networks, recommend a personalized fashion strategy for them. The app would then select vendors and automate orders for pre-selected clothing of an exact size. The company even planned to guarantee favorable results with any women the men dated. Revenues would come from advertising and commissions. The company planned to pursue partnerships with various online dating sites. Katie thought the app violated people's privacy in some ways but was impressed by its technology nonetheless.

"Give me another chance," he said. "Come see me. I'll pay for your airfare." He sounded desperate—never a good thing in a man, she thought.

"Justin, you had your last chance that morning in your apartment."

"It took forever to clean up the kitchen."

"It took forever to stop crying."

"Katie, I love you. I was a fool not to see it. I was too hung up on my studies and my career. I'm lonely up here. Come see me."

"I can't. I leave for graduate school in Colorado later this month. Let's just agree that we both made mistakes and move on. You'll meet other women. You have a lot to offer."

"But Katie, it's you I want."

Katie thought she detected a tremor in his voice and the sound of sniffles. She'd never seen him cry. "Justin, I'm sorry. Good-bye." She ended the call and stared at her phone for a moment.

BY LATE AUGUST, KATIE HAD FINISHED her last day as a barista and had begun to pack. She didn't own much beyond clothes, books, and a few kitchen things, so she could squeeze most everything into her five-year-old Subaru, a high school graduation gift from her parents. She shipped a few remaining boxes to the school to be picked up once she arrived. At her mom's request, Katie convinced one of her roommates, Teresa, to accompany her on the drive to Boulder.

On her last night in Claremont, Teresa suggested that they go out for a farewell drink. Teresa drove her to a restaurant; when they walked inside, Katie was surprised to find six of her best friends crammed into a large booth in a corner. On the table were several gift bags surrounded by drinks from the bar. Tears and laughter came easily as she relived their many great memories from school. The enormity of her move began to sink in. She knew she'd really miss her friends and the comfort they brought her. Each of them had encouraged her after her breakup with Justin and now repeated what they'd told her earlier: she wouldn't have any trouble meeting other desirable guys.

Later the next morning, after only a few hours of sleep, Katie left Claremont for the last time. After a stop at the apartment's rental office to drop off her key and leave a forwarding address, Katie and Teresa drove northeast to Boulder by way of Las Vegas.

BRIAN TAYLOR WALKED DOWN THE HALLWAY toward the office of the dean of students in the historic Old Main building. It was a place he'd visited frequently during law school. That morning, as had been his custom, he'd reached into his closet for one of his many Italian suits. He was clearly overdressed for a campus visit. Old habits die hard, he thought. Until a month earlier, he'd been one of the most successful criminal-defense attorneys in Boulder—a fact that now seemed bitterly ironic, since it was the dean who had a year earlier given him the chance to teach a law class each semester as an adjunct professor. Brian loved law, enjoyed teaching, and hoped to give back to the campus community. How terribly it had all turned out.

"Hello, Mr. Taylor. I'll let him know you're here." The administrative assistant pushed a button on the phone console on her desk. "Go on in." She barely looked up as she said it, and Brian sensed her disdain. She had likely already heard of Morgan and the accident.

Two months earlier, Brian had received the email that had started it all. He'd struggled to remember Morgan. After searching various social media sites and finding a profile photo, he quickly remembered that she had been in his ethics class the preceding spring. She was a bright-eyed and smart first-year law student who asked thoughtful questions. She'd seemed older than the other students, and he'd suspected law might be the start of a second career.

In the email, Morgan referenced a comment he'd made during class about his fondness for Shakespeare and wondered if he'd like to join her for an upcoming performance of *Hamlet* at the Colorado Shakespeare Festival. A friend of hers was acting in the play, she wrote, and she'd given Morgan complimentary tickets. True, he did love Shakespeare's timeless prose, especially his tragedies. But he also recalled that Morgan was very attractive. Though he was intrigued by the offer, he momentarily considered the propriety of dating a student. He concluded that her past status shouldn't matter.

Brian enjoyed the student company's performance, and though the outdoor theater would never be confused for the Globe nor would the production ever garner a Tony, Horatio's lines spoken to a dying Hamlet brought tears to his eyes: "Now cracks a noble heart. Good night, sweet prince; And flights of angels sing thee to thy rest!"

After the play, Brian drove Morgan to a popular upscale restaurant located in the foothills above Boulder. The city lights shimmering below their window table provided a romantic backdrop. Over Bordeaux and chateaubriand, their conversation ranged from law to politics, from sports to literature. Brian liked that Morgan challenged him. When they had opposing opinions, she tested his facts and logic. Even though he had years of trial experience, she wasn't deferential. Her smiles and confident demeanor began to spark a flame of desire in him. But the fact that she had been his student bothered him. Since she'd asked him, that made it all right, didn't it? It was alcohol that had likely interfered with sound judgment that night. Two personal flaws conspired to propel him down a slippery slope of irresponsibility—a penchant for drinking and a gnawing insecurity that could only be fed by female intimacy.

Over a second bottle of the luscious red wine, Brian should have observed that he was outdrinking his dinner companion two glasses to one. Their inhibitions receded faster than water at ebb tide. Laughter came easily. Even the worst jokes seemed hilarious. As he filled their glasses with the last drop of wine, Brian suggested they go to his place and continue their conversation alone. Morgan quickly agreed.

Brian's mind foresaw a naked Morgan on his bed as they crossed the parking lot to his car. He wondered if anticipation was the experience best savored, perhaps more acutely than the sex he hoped for. That was the moment, stated later in a deposition, when Morgan claimed she'd asked if he was OK to drive. She testified that he'd said yes.

Brian retracted the soft-top on his sports car and eased it from the gravel parking lot and onto the blacktop road that descended toward his condo downtown. He slowly negotiated the first tight curve and then let the car pick up some speed. He glanced down to his right and admired the tanned leg flowing from underneath Morgan's short skirt. Unfortunately, he admired it for a second too long and missed the double-hairpin turn in the road ahead. Morgan's beautiful leg was the last thing Brian remembered until he returned to consciousness in the holding cell of the Boulder County jail.

Brian, for his part, was treated by medics at the scene, who determined that he was unharmed; they then released him to the police, who promptly took him to jail and booked him for driving under the influence. Blood tests confirmed an alcohol level of 0.16. The subsequent legal proceedings took months. The law firm in which he was a partner anticipated his disbarment by the Colorado Bar Association and suspended him immediately. Brian knew that only luck had prevented him from being arrested for DUI several times over the years. He'd routinely consumed a few drinks before driving; the power of denial had always assured him that he'd never get caught.

The words of the judge stung: "For committing a criminal act that reflected adversely on his honesty, trustworthiness, or fitness as a lawyer in other respects, Brian Taylor, attorney registration number 444055, is suspended from the practice of law for two years. You are sentenced to one year at the adult detention center with credit for time served and good time earned. Execution of that sentence is stayed for two years on the condition that you be on probation to the community-corrections office at a level of supervision they deem appropriate."

But it was the harm he'd inflicted on Morgan that Brian most regretted. She'd suffered a shattered tibia, and despite the best efforts of a top orthopedic surgeon, she'd never again walk without a limp. At least she'd lived, which he was thankful for. Brian would never forget seeing her in the courtroom during his appearance, seated between her parents and glaring at him with contempt. Racked by guilt, he was glad she'd filed a lawsuit and hoped his insurance company would be generous.

Brian entered the dean's spacious office. After a quick hello and a handshake, he moved to a tufted-leather chair across from the dean's massive desk. "Peter, thanks for meeting with me."

"I always enjoy catching up. You look different. Healthier."

"I've stopped drinking. And I'm back to running. I feel pretty good." Brian had been running each morning since the accident. He was surprised how much extra energy it gave him.

"It shows. How can I help you?"

"You came to my defense with the bar association. I'll never forget it. Suspension without disbarment was a huge break." Brian knew he'd never square things.

Peter's angular face remained slack. "We've been friends a long time," he said. "I have fond memories of our undergraduate years." Brian glanced toward a nearby bookcase and saw a familiar, silver-framed photo taken at a fraternity party. They each had an arm looped around the other's shoulder and wore smiles that were a little too broad. "But there comes a time when a man must grow up, Brian. After graduation, I focused on law school and my career. Thanks to you, I found a wonderful woman who was willing to marry me. Your sister has been one of the true joys of my life. You might want to think about settling down yourself."

Brian relaxed a bit. "My priorities have been a mess, but I'm ready to turn things around. I owe you an apology. You arranged for the adjunct-professor position, and I embarrassed you. I'm truly sorry."

"Just promise me you won't drink and drive while your law license is suspended—or ever. In less than two years, you can petition the bar for reinstatement. Don't screw it up."

"I won't. On the advice of my attorney, I've started therapy. It's been helpful." Brian thought he detected a hint of acceptance on the dean's face. But he also understood that if not for his sister, the dean wouldn't have agreed to meet with him.

The dean crossed his arms and leaned back in his chair. "I have an idea for you, but promise me you're serious this time. Some of your past promises have been as hollow as a politician's."

"Give me a chance to prove it. You'll see."

"Do you remember the woman we knew our senior year, the one who married the herbal-tea entrepreneur?"

"You mean the guy who used to get high and pick wild herbs and flowers up in the foothills? He sold them to health-food stores as herbal tea. I remember him but don't remember her. I can't believe he turned that idea into a multimillion-dollar business."

"They got married. After ten years building the company together, they sold it. She continued to run operations, while he kicked back and enjoyed life. Two years ago, he died in a diving accident off the Baja coast. She inherited his remaining interest. Even though she's still active with the company, she now spends most of her time—and considerable fortune—on philanthropic interests."

"What does this have to do with me?" Brian pulled out a legal pad and started taking notes.

"We have a problem at the university involving sexual assault. It's a priority of the education department, and the university is under investigation for its abysmal record of enforcing those Title IX regulations that prescribe a gender-neutral and nondiscriminatory educational environment. The DOE is serious, and I want a proactive response. I've discussed the problem with her, and we've designed a nonprofit foundation we plan to fund. We'd like you to lead it. You say you're ready to turn your life around? Well, here's your chance."

CHAPTER 4
Grad School

Katie and Teresa took turns behind the wheel and four hours later approached the urban oasis of Las Vegas rising above the sprawling Mojave Desert. The 105-degree heat of late August created an invisible lens that reflected the desert scrub, making it appear to float on a pool of water on top of the highway. The car's air conditioning couldn't fully counter the heat that was making their skin stick to the leather seats. The sight of the massive casinos towering like pyramids on the horizon triggered in Katie a memory of an earlier trip there with Teresa and a few other friends from school.

Katie said with a chuckle, "Remember that weekend in Las Vegas?"

"I recall you had a bit of a scare. Wasn't that the interfraternity council's fall rodeo party our sophomore year?"

"Sure was. With a name like that, I should have expected trouble."

"What happened? I don't remember a lot about that weekend—just a debilitating hangover on the drive back."

"We started out at a pool party at one of those massive casinos." Katie wondered how much detail she should share. "I think there were four or five of us from Claremont. I remember thinking the place was full of too many men who spent all day at the gym, women with the most perfect breasts money could buy, and students like us who were just looking for fun. We met some guys in the pool, and late in the afternoon, when things had cooled off and the pool was clearing out, two of them suggested that Mary and I join them in their room for a drink and then go out dancing afterward. It sounded like fun, so we agreed."

"I remember Mary. Kind of wild, right?"

"That's her." Katie wasn't sure why she'd ended up with Mary that night, since they hadn't been that close.

"What happened?"

"After we arrived at the door to their hotel room, one of the guys unlocked it. I walked in, assuming the others would be right behind me. Then Mary said she and the other guy were leaving for a minute and would be right back. I was suddenly alone in the room with this guy I'd just met. I don't even remember his name. I wondered if they'd planned it."

"What did he do?"

"He poured each of us a rum and coke. Heavy on the rum, as I recall. He started drinking his pretty hard. I just sipped mine while he tried to make small talk. I think he was a college baseball player. I wasn't exactly sober, but I recall he was slurring his words and stumbling a little. Then he put his drink down on the nightstand, spilled it all over the place, and started to grope me. I pushed him back and said, 'Whoa, cowboy, I'm not ready to be ridden yet'—trying to be cleaver with the rodeo theme, I guess."

"Probably wasn't the best thing to say," Teresa said with a tepid laugh.

"Probably not. After that, he got up and headed into the bathroom. I should have walked out right then, but he seemed nice enough, so I decided to hang around a little longer."

"Then what?"

"He came out of the bathroom and wasn't wearing his shirt. He sat back down on the bed, drained the rest of his drink, and poured himself another one. Then he turned and starting kissing me. He was really drunk and sloppy. It was a big turnoff. He started grabbing at my breasts, and when he started running his hand up my leg, I decided I'd better get out of there. I gently pushed on his chest until he was lying on his back on top of the bed."

"Then what did you do?"

"I slowly rubbed the front of his swimsuit. It didn't take long before he got hard. I just kept rubbing and slowly worked my hand down inside the top of his waistband. He was really into it. After a little more rubbing and stroking, I slowly slipped his swimsuit down around his knees and gave him a hand job."

"Quick thinking. Then what happened?"

"I went to the bathroom to clean up and locked the door and waited. I took my phone with me and tried to call Mary, but she didn't answer. In a few minutes, I quietly opened the door and peered into the bedroom. Just as I had hoped, he was out cold on the bed and snoring heavily. His swimsuit was still down around his knees. Just for the heck of it, I pulled out my phone and snapped a photo of him, thinking I could use it for leverage later. After that, I dashed out of there."

"Wow, what a story. I want to see the photo! Do you think he would have forced you to do anything if you hadn't gotten away?"

"I don't know. He seemed like a nice guy. Maybe." Katie had downplayed the risk at the time, but she now believed that he might have gotten unruly had she not thought of a way to slip out.

"Did you ever see him again?"

"Thankfully, no. I doubt he'd have remembered me anyway."

Katie remembered the drive home at the end of that wild weekend. That was when she'd promised to start living by the rules her mother had taught her years earlier: keep your friends close, never take a drink from a stranger, and if it seems like a bad idea, it probably is.

They soon left the city behind them, and the drive northeast on I-15 gave Katie uninterrupted time to think. Her breakup with Justin suddenly felt final. She'd miss Claremont and her friends yet remained convinced that leaving was the best way to move on. Though her undergraduate education had been rigorous, she was now saddled with over $75,000 in student debt. And with a degree in philosophy, she knew it would be a slow process to repay it. She wasn't sure how pursuing an advanced degree was going to sustain her financially, even if it was in the subject she most loved. Money would be a problem. Late in the evening, exhausted after the long and hot fourteen-hour drive, Katie and Teresa pulled into Boulder, found a hotel, and crawled into bed.

LATE THE NEXT MORNING, AFTER SLEEPING IN, Teresa helped Katie begin her search for a place to live. She'd missed the deadline to apply for campus housing because she'd accepted the offer to graduate school so late, and with only a week to go until classes began, she expected limited availability around town. They looked in the daily newspaper, checked bulletin boards in the student union, and searched Internet listings. By the end of the day, they'd found a sparsely furnished one-room apartment within walking distance of campus, modestly priced at $1,550 per month. It was an old house that had been subdivided into four one-room apartments, each with a small kitchenette and bathroom. She considered finding a roommate to lower expenses but concluded that a shared two-bedroom apartment would cost around the same amount. She also felt ready to live by herself after living with roommates every year as an undergraduate. She signed a one-year lease and wrote a check for the first and last months' rent, plus a damage deposit. The check almost drained her bank account.

Katie and Teresa spent one more night in the hotel, and then Katie took Teresa to the Denver airport for her return flight to Los Angeles. During the return drive to Boulder from the airport, Katie fretted again about her financial situation. She'd borrowed money from her parents to make the first semester's tuition payment, and she'd been promised a graduate-assistant position with a stipend of $1,750 per month. She'd paid the minimum on her credit card bill the previous month, and another payment was due in a week. Fortunately, while she was enrolled in grad school, she could defer repayment of her undergraduate loans until six months after she received her PhD. Maybe she should get another barista job. Anything would help.

Back at the empty new apartment, Katie unloaded all her things from her car. After carrying the last box inside, she surveyed the living room and became aware of a unique fragrance. Not offensive or sweet, like the flowery scent from a cleaning product, but more like the stale air inside an old church, one rich in history. She wondered how many students had lived in the subdivided house over the years, starting new lives and immersed in academics.

Katie left the apartment and walked up to the Hill, a commercial area named for its elevated location on the west side of campus; she'd heard it was famous for its abundance of inexpensive bars and restaurants. She found a brewpub with outdoor seating, ordered a beer, and pulled her journal from her backpack. Writing was how she always considered difficult issues. She started by creating a budget and adding up all her assets. No matter how she manipulated the numbers, she would have only a month until her cash ran out. Since it was critical that she meet with her advisor and confirm her stipend, she started a list of questions to ask him during their meeting the following day. She put the stipend question lower down on the list lest she appear too desperate. She put her planned class load and the procedure for becoming a teaching assistant at the top.

After finishing both the beer and her notes, Katie left the bar and strolled around campus. The university's ivy-covered buildings, all adorned with the same red-tile roofs, evoked memories of an Italian village she'd seen during a summer trip with her family. The foothills of the Rockies provided a dramatic backdrop and the campus was replete with mature oak trees. Katie decided she was in the perfect place to rebuild her life but wished she'd asked Teresa to stay a few more days. She missed her companionship.

Back in her apartment, Katie started her job search. All university listings were online, and the local newspaper, the campus newspaper, and several dedicated career sites had postings. She didn't want to be a barista again. The money wasn't great, and the repetition of pulling espresso drinks over and over again bored her. She found two ads that stood out. One was from a single father looking for a part-time nanny. His five-year-old daughter needed supervision after preschool two days per week and occasionally on weekends to cover out-of-town travel. He stated that he lived downtown, which meant he'd be within walking distance of her apartment. The money sounded great, and the posting was well written. She'd done some sitting in high school and was comfortable with what was expected of the job.

The requirements for the position struck her as a bit odd, though. He wanted a female candidate with a college degree, preferably attending graduate school, who was at least twenty-one and no older than twenty-eight; the description said that applicants must be single, which Katie suspected was discriminatory of him to ask. She reluctantly decided to apply anyway.

A second job posting was more interesting. The wording of the ad was a bit cryptic; it seemed to be describing a nonprofit foundation that was dedicated to preventing sexual assault on campus. The managing director of the recently formed foundation was now hiring students to be "campus ambassadors." The primary responsibility of the position would be to attend training sessions on the nature and causes of sexual assault, learn the university's administrative procedures for responding to reports of assault, and to refer victims to organizations that provided counseling and support. After training, the ambassador would become a campus advocate and communicate with other students about the university's policies. The ad also mentioned a bonus plan of some kind, but it lacked specifics. It seemed like an interesting opportunity. Recalling her experience from Las Vegas, Katie understood how easy it was to feel threatened by sexual assault.

Katie grew tired of reading the endless list of restaurant and retail job openings and headed for the kitchen to get a glass of wine. She had to negotiate a maze of still-packed boxes to get there. She eyed her unmade bed along the way and, out of habit, almost stopped to make it. She resisted the voice of her mother and continued to the kitchen, where she opened a bottle of red wine and poured herself a glass. Back in the living room, she sat down in an old, upholstered armchair next to a bay window. The arms were worn, and oval shapes showed in the fabric of each one. Over a sip of wine, she admired the tree outside her open window. Songs of robins filled the room. The tree was covered in green leaves so lush and thick she couldn't make out the shapes of the birds, but their sounds were clear. A motorcycle's engine came to life down the street. She wished she had a view of the mountains, too. At least her place was cozy and she had a great view onto the street. She enjoyed witnessing the movement of the world outside her window.

After leaving the chair and returning to her laptop, Katie sipped her wine and completed applications for both jobs. It took several hours to assemble the required information and write professional descriptions of her skills. Each required a photo, so she searched for an appropriate image to submit. It didn't take her long to find a favorite from a friend's wedding that summer. She'd worn a simple blue dress with a gold necklace, her auburn hair brushed back behind her shoulders. She'd worn makeup and lipstick, a touch she seldom used. She preferred that photo because it made her look both natural and professional. After hitting send, she put away her laptop and made her bed. When she pulled back the sheet and climbed underneath, the old bed's springs creaked every time she shifted her body. Thoughts about the future and from her past filled her mind and convinced her that everything was transient in the world except for what we carry in our minds and our hearts.

CHAPTER 5
Make a Difference

Katie's meeting with her advisor went well. She'd take nine hours of classes in the fall semester and become a teaching assistant in the spring semester. She was to choose one of her fall courses and seek agreement from the course professor to help with assignments, grading, and students' questions. He confirmed her stipend, pending approval by the faculty board. Graduate school would be unlike what she'd experienced as an undergraduate, he warned. She was expected to take initiative, work independently, and produce results. If she needed help, then she must seek it. If she was serious about a research assistantship, then it was important to pick a topic early. Her advisors were there to offer guidance, but when it came to her research, thesis, and dissertation, she'd mostly be on her own. His tone was sober.

Katie explored the town and campus over the next couple of days and continued to set up her apartment. She unpacked the contents of her kitchen boxes and put away her dishes and cookware before shifting her focus to the living room. While she worked, she occasionally heard sounds from other apartments in the subdivided house. Four front doors at the top of the porch led to each apartment. Two were upstairs and two down. Hers was down. It felt comfortable, and she felt lucky to have found it.

When she came across her collection of framed photos, some taken with friends from college and others with her family, melancholy descended as unexpectedly as a rain shower from a blue sky. She'd once imagined doing this all with Justin—unpacking together in a place that was their own. At least here, she could make her own decisions; with Justin, he would have insisted that everything be done his way.

After several hours, Katie was satisfied with her progress and walked to the nearest grocery store. After returning with some basics for the kitchen, she threw her backpack on her bed and checked her email. It had been three days since she'd submitted her job applications, and she was thrilled to find responses to both. The first was from the man seeking a nanny, whose name was Paul. He explained that he was thirty-two and worked as a director of cybersecurity. He was smiling in an accompanying photo, wore fashionable eyeglasses, and had short cropped hair. Paul asked that she meet him for an interview. She accepted and asked where.

The second job-related email appeared to be a standard response, signed by Brian Taylor, executive director of the No Sexual Assault Foundation (NSAF). It said her qualifications met the foundation's requirements; as a next step in the hiring process, the message requested an interview. It included an email address and phone number for Taylor's administrative assistant and instructed Katie to contact him and schedule a convenient time to meet with Mr. Taylor at his office. Katie composed a thoughtful and pleasant response and thanked Mr. Taylor for his reply. She then promptly sent a note to the assistant requesting an interview.

Fifteen minutes later, she received a short email response from Paul, who requested that they meet the next day after work at six in the evening. He suggested the Bohemian Biergarten, located downtown and not far from campus and her apartment. Katie thought the choice seemed casual for an interview but felt safer meeting him in a public space than she would at his home. Just to be sure, she walked downtown to assess the restaurant. It looked fine, it was on a busy pedestrian mall, and it featured a large open interior. She agreed to the time and place. Katie then scheduled an interview with Brian Taylor for ten o'clock the following morning.

Katie entered the European-style restaurant and beer garden promptly at six. She wore jeans and a white button-down oxford shirt rolled up at the sleeves. The restaurant's interior featured rough-hewn wooden floors and long wooden tables. People sat scattered in small groups and singles, their tables laden with pints of beer and plates of cheese and charcuterie. The sound level in the bar was an energetic mix of laughter and conversation, and Katie immediately liked the place. She knew its lively ambience would also help keep their conversation private.

She walked to the restaurant's long bar and asked for a glass of water, then searched the room for anyone resembling Paul's photo. After about fifteen minutes, she noticed him enter the room. He wore a light-blue sweater and khakis, she noted: a style that suggested to her that he was fashionable and a bit conservative. He sported the stylish glasses she'd noticed in the photo.

Paul seemed to recognize Katie from her photo and walked toward her; Katie offered her hand and introduced herself. Feeling anxious and unsure, she stumbled over her first few comments. "Thanks for meeting me," she said nervously.

"Let's grab a table," Paul said, leading the way.

They sat down across from each other on opposing benches.

Paul put a notebook on the table that appeared to include a list of prepared questions. "Are you new to Boulder?"

"Just arrived this week. I'm starting graduate school in philosophy."

"Philosophy? Huh. What do you get when you cross a joke with a rhetorical question?"

"That's easy. Something with no punch line. There's no shortage of jokes about philosophy. I get it: the field's filled with theory and little substantiated proof. Maybe that's why I like it. I get to explore ideas." Katie turned her body slightly sideways. She always felt defensive about her major when discussing it with anyone other than another philosopher. She changed the subject. "Tell me about cybersecurity," she said.

"I'm a director who reports to the university's cybersecurity office."

A waitress came by and took their drink orders. Katie requested hard cider, Paul a beer.

"What does that entail?" Katie studied Paul's soft features and tried to imagine him as a husband and father. She assumed he was divorced, although he hadn't mentioned that in the job description.

"We manage several areas." Paul casually crossed his arms and rested them on the table. He leaned in. "Our primary goal is to ensure that all our students follow safe practices on their personal devices and minimize any malware attacks. Once a student loses a semester-long project without backup, she suddenly becomes aware of the problem. But we can help them avoid a lot of pain if they follow our guidelines. We also worry about security and protection of the university's intellectual property. Most university departments receive grants for academic research from corporations and the department of defense. Universities have been historically lax in their safeguards. My group acquires technology and establishes security protocols to stay ahead of cyberattacks. That's the quick answer, anyway." Their drinks arrived as Paul finished his description.

"That sounds really interesting." It actually sounded really complicated. Katie took a sip of the cold and crisp cider. It was warm in the bar, and she began to perspire, unsure if it was caused by the situation or the temperature. Once again, she was with another man involved with technology. Just like Justin. "So tell me about your daughter and the help you need."

"Her name's Olivia. She's five and a bit precocious." Paul showed Katie a photo on his phone. "She starts kindergarten this year."

Katie admired the girl's innocent smile and cascading and curly red hair. "She's adorable."

"She reads books, she's a good speller, and she knows simple math. School's never been a problem for her. She's very bright."

Katie remembered Paul's list of requirements. "You stated that the applicant should have an undergrad degree and preferably attend grad school."

Paul hesitated. "Someone with a great education will be better prepared to keep up with her. Education's important to me."

"I see." Katie took another sip of her cider. "And why do you prefer a woman over a man?"

"That's obvious: I think it's important for Olivia to be around someone who'll relate to her gender."

Katie considered his response. She couldn't decide if it sounded sexist or logical.

Paul referred to the list of questions in his notebook and asked, "Is your schedule flexible? I'd like you to help get Olivia to school in the morning. Maybe spend a couple of afternoons with her and have dinner with us."

Katie hesitated. "I'm not sure yet, I'm just starting classes. I think I can be available most afternoons and evenings, and part of the weekends when I'm not studying."

"Any chance you'd consider living with us? I have a spare bedroom."

Katie began to suspect Paul wasn't telling her everything. "Is her mom still involved in your daughter's life?"

Paul turned quiet and glanced briefly around the room. He fixed his eyes back on Katie. "She passed away."

"I'm really sorry to hear that."

"It happened in a cycling accident out on the Longmont Diagonal two years ago. Olivia was three at the time."

Katie remained silent and watched Paul idly spin his glass of beer on the tabletop.

After a pause, he went on. "She was training for a triathlon. Had a goal to complete an Iron Man. She had her timeline all mapped out. Her life was always on a schedule. It was early morning, and a car veered off the side of the road. Killed her instantly."

"Paul, I don't know what to say."

"I'd really prefer someone who will live with us."

For Katie, that was the end of the conversation. Her body stiffened, and she placed her hands firmly on the tabletop. She just about stood. "Look, I'm just getting settled into my place, and I'm looking forward to living on my own. I'm sorry, but living with you wouldn't work for me."

Paul smiled. "But you're perfect. You remind me of her."

"Are you looking for a nanny or a companion?"

Paul looked away, then locked his eyes on Katie's. "Life as a single dad is killing me. I want what's best for Olivia. I'm really struggling to make everything work."

"But aren't you looking for more than that?" Katie sensed his loneliness.

"I miss my wife terribly. I thought if I found someone who would live with us it would help. The house seems so empty now."

Katie looked at Paul and smiled.

"I understand, but that won't work for me," she repeated. She gathered her things to leave.

"I see that." Paul drained his beer and set his glass on the table. Katie finished her cider.

She asked, "Have you had much luck with this scheme of yours?"

"You're my first interview."

"I have a prediction."

"What's that?"

"It won't work. You won't find one person who can both care for your daughter and ease your pain."

Paul seemed to consider the comment. "You *are* a philosopher." He chuckled, which helped to defuse some tension.

"Told you. Let me give you some advice. Women don't like guys who seem desperate. You've suffered a tragedy, but you can't just jump back into your old life by hiring a surrogate as if nothing happened. Focus on Olivia. Hire someone who knows how to raise kids. Then worry about finding a companion. You'll meet someone."

"I like your directness." Paul grinned sheepishly.

Katie returned his smile and got up to leave. "Good luck, Paul. You'll be fine."

Paul stood and extended his hand. "If you change your mind, or ever need anything, let me know."

Katie left the bar and returned to the pedestrian mall. She didn't look back. Students milled about her as she strolled down the tree-lined and cobblestoned walkway. The late-summer sun, nearly complete in its descent behind the front range, warmed her face and raised her spirits. The town felt alive from staff and students returning to town after summer vacation. Fresh students. Fresh dreams. Though Paul had been a disappointment, she hoped for better luck with the nonprofit.

The next morning, Katie arrived at Brian Taylor's office in time for their ten o'clock meeting and took the elevator to the top floor office of the NSAF. The co-op office space housed several attorneys and shared a receptionist. The harried-looking woman explained to Katie that Mr. Taylor would be out to get her in a few moments. Katie took a seat and waited.

A man of average height dressed in a tailored suit and tie appeared momentarily. "Ms. Russell?"

Katie stood. "Yes, Katie Russell."

"Hi. Brian Taylor. Come into my office."

Katie followed him into a small and sparsely furnished room that included a desk and table with four chairs. He offered her a seat and something to drink. She took a seat but declined the drink.

Brian joined Katie at the conference table; a phone and legal notepad were neatly arrayed on top. "I have a great opportunity for you."

"I'm interested in hearing about it." Katie pulled out her journal and prepared to take notes.

"I represent a wealthy philanthropist who's funded a private scholarship foundation. I developed the organizational plan and I'm now hiring students who share our concern about campus safety and want to help us."

"Help you? How?"

"College campuses across the country are facing an epidemic of sexual assault against women. Recently, the president and vice president launched a task force on the issue. In response, the US Department of Education's Office for Civil Rights has released a list of higher-education institutions that are under investigation for possible violations of federal law because of their poor handling of sexual violence and harassment complaints. The government has threatened to pull millions of dollars of funding away from this school—a matter it's taking very seriously."

"But I've never been involved in sexual assault, nor have I known anyone who has."

"Are you sure about that?"

"Yeah, pretty sure." Katie thought back to the incident in Las Vegas. Realistically, had the man she'd met not been so drunk and had she not thought to give him a hand job as a pretext for getting out of his hotel room, she might have been assaulted.

"In January, the White House released a report titled 'Rape and Sexual Assault: A Renewed Call to Action.' That report clearly stated that while they're in college, one in five women will be sexually assaulted. And only twelve percent of student victims report their assault to law enforcement."

"Look, Mr. Taylor, I don't condone any kind of violence against women. I'm lucky that I haven't experienced any myself, nor have any of my friends. I think that any man who uses his power or authority to coerce a woman into having a sexual relationship against her will should be severely punished. But the numbers you just cited don't stand up to scrutiny."

"What do you mean?" Brian looked surprised by her challenge.

"We studied the data in one of my undergraduate classes. We looked at the actual crime statistics from Ohio State from 2009 to 2012. During that period, there were around a hundred reports of sexual assault on or near campus. If all the sexual-assault victims who were reported were female, and if you assume the White House claim that only twelve percent of campus sexual assaults get reported, then there would have been about seven hundred unreported sexual assaults. That implies the total number of reported and unreported sexual assaults to be about eight hundred. The Columbus campus has a total female student population of about twenty-eight thousand. If you do the math, only three percent of OSU women would have been sexually assaulted. That's still too high, but not even close to the White House claim that one in five female students are sexually assaulted while they're in college."

"I agree that the numbers are open to debate—especially if you consider the definition of what constitutes sexual assault—but I have an inside view of campus reports, and we have a big problem. Once the 'one in five' statistic got out there, it's been repeated everywhere. I agree that multiple and conflicting studies exist. One by the Bureau of Justice Statistics even predicts that women aged eighteen to twenty-four who don't attend college will have an even higher incidence of sexual-assault victimization. If parents believed there was a twenty percent chance of their daughter being caught up in a drive-by shooting while in college, do you think they'd enroll them? Probably not. We plan to put an end to the rape culture that is so prevalent on this campus." Brian sat back in his chair and took a sip of water. "Katie, are you ready for some coffee yet?"

Katie studied Brian and shifted in her chair. She noticed that his belt was fastened in the last notch, and the trousers' fabric was bunched together underneath as if he'd recently lost weight. "No, thanks. I'm still not sure I understand what you're looking for."

"We want you to act as an ambassador on campus. During your normal routine of study and social activities, we'd want you to look for any signs of sexual assault among students and faculty. We'll instruct you in the administration's code of student conduct policy for reporting and investigating sexual assault. We also expect you to staff our kiosk in the student union one afternoon on alternating weeks. For that, we'll put you on a consulting contract and pay you fifteen hundred dollars per month."

"And all I have to do is observe the activity of other students and faculty and report anything that appears related to sexual assault?" Katie knew he hadn't told her everything.

"That's about it. If any of your fellow students have questions about the university's sexual-assault policy, we'd expect you to educate them. Then there's the bonus plan."

"Which is?"

"If you report someone who's involved in a sexual assault, and you help bring charges against the assailant, then you'll be eligible for a grant from our foundation to be applied to your college expenses—even your past debts—so long as you're a student in good standing. The payment doesn't go to you directly, just to the university or the bank where you have student debt or expenses."

"Wait a minute—that sounds like you want me to be a campus spy."

"Katie, we're not asking you to put yourself in a situation where you could be at risk. The grant's only for indirect assaults. Otherwise, students might be tempted to get involved in a consensual sexual relationship, claim consent wasn't granted, and then try to collect the bonus. We're only concerned about student-based instances of sexual misconduct or harassment you witness or hear of. You'll file a complaint and provide testimony in any administrative or criminal proceedings that are filed against the assailant. If the complaint is upheld, then you'll be eligible for a contribution by our foundation toward your college expenses."

"Why are you so interested in encouraging women to report more assaults? Shouldn't your goal be to reduce the actual rate of their occurrence?" Katie noticed an infrequent tic in Brian's right eye as he spoke. She tried not to stare.

"This is a numbers game. Like baseball, we want to get our batting average up. Most college women are unwilling to report sexual assault. Why? Because they anticipate a weak and humiliating investigative process, one that will result in limited (if any) sanctions imposed against the assailants by indifferent university officials. Now that the DOE has instructed schools to adhere to the weaker preponderance of evidence standard in their Title IX enforcement, we think the door is open to more reporting. If more women bring complaints, and more men are subsequently punished, then men will wake up and no longer think they have a license to take advantage of young college women. Especially if they plan to use drugs and alcohol when doing so."

"I remember one of my law professors calling the preponderance of evidence standard the 'toss-up and a butterfly's wing' standard."

"What does that even mean?"

"When the scales of justice are perfectly balanced by the evidence, some insignificant testimony or even the smallest fact—something as lightweight as a butterfly's wing—could tip the scales in either direction. A guilty verdict by this standard can be so close that it can go either way, unlike the beyond a reasonable doubt standard." Katie bit her lip, wondering if she was making sense.

"We think it's a welcome change to adopt the lesser standard."

"But aren't you worried you might increase the number of men who are wrongly accused when the only evidence you have is hearsay? I mean, what if, after a night of excessive drinking, a woman lets her guard down and consents to a sexual encounter? She wakes up the next morning with regrets, maybe worried about a boyfriend who wants to know where she was all night, and decides to file a complaint, hoping to cover up her actions. Don't you risk deemphasizing personal responsibility and creating a culture of victimization?"

"Katie, I appreciate your questions. I'm also relieved you've never experienced sexual assault yourself. You've been lucky. But many men don't hesitate to take advantage of alcohol or drugs, or coercion, to achieve a sexual encounter. Trust me, I know." He paused a beat. "I've recently had my own epiphany on this subject. I think you will, too, someday." Katie was surprised by the sudden hint of frustration in Brian's comment. His tone up to then had been steady. "Are you interested in helping our foundation or not?"

"How much of a contribution are we talking about?" Katie was struggling to understand the full implications of the job.

"Fifty thousand dollars. Sounds better than working as a barista, doesn't it?"

"I'm not so sure. As mundane as that job was, your plan almost seems unethical." Katie slowly ran her hand over the back of her head and across her jaw. She returned it to her lap.

"Katie, what's unethical is these controlling men using their power and position to take advantage of women. We believe this isn't a case of well-meaning boys who are confused about the rules of consent. Instead, these are repeat offenders who know exactly what they're doing. It's got to stop. I want you to help us."

"Can I get this in writing?"

"Absolutely. I'll have the papers drawn up and emailed to you this afternoon. If everything looks satisfactory, and as I described, then you can stop by my office tomorrow and sign the documents. Until then, email me if you have any more questions. If you decide to go forward, then you'll join the other ambassadors in a Saturday-morning training session." Brian stood and offered his hand. It appeared the meeting was over. "Nice to meet you, Katie."

Katie stood and shook Brian's hand. After they said their good-byes, she left the office. Back in the parking lot, she realized she was well on her way to breaking Mom's third rule: "If it seems like a bad idea, it probably is."

CHAPTER 6
Classes Begin

Katie entered the classroom in Old Main a few minutes early and took a seat near the front of the room. She preferred to sit in the front because it helped her focus on the lecture and not succumb to daydreaming. Katie had signed up for three classes: "Self and Consciousness," "Contemporary Political Philosophy and Law," and "Seminar in the History of Philosophy: Aristotle's *Ethics*." The philosophy and law class was her only class of the day.

A few moments later, a tall woman strode through the door, stepped to a lectern, and opened a notebook. Katie knew from reading the professor's bio that she'd pioneered a curriculum in women's studies in the sixties. She was dressed in a blouse and sunflower-patterned skirt; long, charcoal-gray hair flowed down her back.

"My name is Professor Amanda Hatfield. I will be teaching this class with help from Assistant Professor Mark O'Connor. Dr. O'Connor recently completed his PhD in philosophy and will assist me with two lectures related to his dissertation on the philosophy of law." Professor Hatfield relaxed her tight face and showed a hint of a smile as she pointed in the general direction of the assistant professor. "He'll be available to help you with any questions you might have with the course materials. Mark and I both have our office hours posted in the syllabus. I encourage you to get to know Mark, especially those of you who are graduate students."

Mark leaned on a desk at the side of the classroom and made a tepid wave to the class at the mention of his name. To Katie, he looked like a poster boy for how a young college professor should dress. He wore jeans, a plaid flannel shirt, and a well-worn and rumpled corduroy jacket. He was tall, and his longish blond hair gave him a youthful look. She was surprised to see that he was wearing cowboy boots. Katie was immediately drawn to him.

"We'll be addressing several pertinent topics in this class: migration, self-determination, international aid, gender equality, state regulation and personal liberty, democracy and economic inequality, and responsibility for global poverty. We must consider many things when we discuss these issues: what's legal and what's politically feasible, but also what's moral. Political morality asks questions about the nature of justice, fairness, equality, freedom, and autonomy. It considers what a well-functioning democracy ought to be like; when, if ever, it's permissible to curtail individual freedoms to promote the public good; and what economic and international justice are."

She took a drink of water and continued. "Be aware that the required paper is mandatory and will reflect what you have learned from our discussion of these issues. I expect you to write at the same level that's required for academic publication. After your first draft, Mark and I will review your work and make any recommendations for revision. The final fifteen-page paper will count for a full twenty-five percent of your grade, so give it the attention it deserves. In your paper, you will explore the issue of informed consent in what are called amorous relationships on college campuses, as required by California senate bill 967, also known as the Yes Means Yes law. The law threatens college funding for state schools if they fail to implement an informed-consent policy. Your task is to either criticize or defend the law and to provide a thorough analysis to support your conclusion. Is it a good law or a bad law? Plan to look at the issue through the lens of feminism and paternalism, individual rights, the preponderance of evidence legal standard, and the dependence on administrative law versus criminal law."

Katie heard murmuring among the students, including a few chuckles from some of the males, who made up what looked to be about three-quarters of the class. Katie was immediately struck by the confluence of two seemingly independent events since her arrival on campus, events that seemed to intersect at the same topic—sexual assault on campus. It was then that she remembered that she needed to stop by Brian Taylor's office later that day and sign the required employment agreement.

Professor Hatfield reasserted control with a voice that sounded brittle. "Students, this is a graduate-level class; as such, I expect you to keep a respectful level of decorum during our discussions. We will be touching on several topics you will no doubt have strong opinions about. I ask you to honor the nature of intellectual discourse and respect the diverse perspectives that will be represented in this class. Also, as you may or may not know, there's been a trend on college campuses of students asking for trigger warnings on lectures, reading assignments, or class discussions that they might find offensive. I believe these requests have no place on a modern university campus. You're here to learn, you're becoming adults, and we can't protect your sensitivities forever. This course will cover topics that are mature and at times difficult to discuss. If you have any concerns, I suggest you drop this class and look for a different section or course that will satisfy your degree requirements. Now, please turn your attention to the syllabus."

Professor Hatfield then went through the list of weekly lecture topics and required readings, the schedule and range of exams, and her rules for the class, including a ban on phones, laptops, and side conversations. Katie noticed that on the class schedule, Thanksgiving was now called "Fall Break." Test-day protocol was even more explicit; it included a ban on wearing caps or hats that would prevent the professor from seeing a student's eyes; earbuds of any kind; and any visible phones starting from the time students walk into the class for the exam. Once an exam had begun, students were not to leave the room until they'd completed and turned in their exams. She closed with a warning that students were responsible for checking their email and her website for class announcements. Katie appreciated her rigor. Professor Hatfield wrapped up her introductory comments and dismissed the class with an expression of gratitude for the opportunity to teach them, assuring them that after a decade of teaching the course, she could promise them a profound learning experience.

Katie stood along with the rest of the students. As she followed the line out the door, she took a quick side glance at Assistant Professor O'Connor, who was speaking to Professor Hatfield. She looked forward to finding a reason to visit him during office hours.

The walk from class back to her apartment took Katie about fifteen minutes. She retrieved her car keys and drove to Brian Taylor's office.

Once she was inside, the receptionist gave her a stack of papers to review and sign. The forms included a standard term sheet and "hold harmless" and nondisclosure agreements. Katie hadn't remembered discussing confidentiality, but it didn't bother her, because she didn't plan to discuss the agreement with anyone. The payment amounts were exactly as they had discussed. Everything seemed to be in order, but how would she know? She wasn't a lawyer and was simply trusting Mr. Taylor at this point. She went through the documents again, this time signing or initialing where required.

Katie returned the forms to the receptionist, who thanked her, asked for a mailing address, and indicated that a fully executed copy would be sent to her once Mr. Taylor had signed them. The receptionist also gave her a set of instructions for filing her monthly reports, which were to chronicle her activities and observations while she was on campus.

Katie thanked the receptionist and turned to leave. When the receptionist addressed her again, she stopped and turned back around.

"Ms. Russell, Mr. Taylor wanted me to let you know that the training session for the Campus Ambassador Program will be held here next Saturday morning at eight. It will last until noon. And Katie, one more thing."

"Yes?"

"Here's your first month's compensation in advance." The receptionist handed Katie an envelope with her name on it. She looked inside and saw a check made out to her in the amount of $1,500. She stared at it. Why didn't she feel like celebrating? Who was she helping? The campus community, or a group of highly paid administrators avoiding cutbacks in government funding? She shoved the check into her backpack. She needed the money.

CHAPTER 7
New Neighbor

Katie left Brian Taylor's office and went straight to her bank to deposit the check. She only had a few days' cash on hand, and her credit card statement had arrived a day earlier. Because she only had enough money to make the minimum payment, she'd have to pay the ridiculous finance fees they charged. After making the deposit, she drove back to her apartment. While she stood on her porch and searched her backpack for her key, the door next to hers opened, and a young woman walked out. Katie smiled and introduced herself. "You must live in the apartment above me."

"I do. Ava Greene. Just move in?"

"Yes, I'm a new grad student. Hope I haven't disturbed you?"

"No worries. You get used to the noise from the other apartments in this house. The walls are pretty thin."

"Are you a student?"

"Senior in economics. Moved in last week. Come up and visit me sometime."

"Sounds good. When's a good time for you?"

"How about tomorrow night? Knock and come on up. I look forward to it." Ava stepped off the porch and headed down the sidewalk. Katie finally found her keys and unlocked her door.

Katie began work on the paper assigned in the contemporary political philosophy and law class. She liked to be proactive and start projects by breaking them down into concrete steps and building a timeline. She'd learned from her undergrad years not to wait until the last minute. Her first step was to read the text of the California bill. She found a digital copy online and printed it out. She read the bill's text several times and wrote notes in the margins.

The first clause of the bill stated that schools will adopt "a policy concerning sexual assault, domestic violence, dating violence, and stalking, as defined in the federal Higher Education Act of 1965." She opened her notebook and scribbled a reminder to look up the referenced act. Reading on, she came to the section of the law that seemed to get the most press: a requirement that this new policy must include "an affirmative consent standard in the determination of whether consent was given by both parties to sexual activity." The clause went on to state that "affirmative consent means affirmative, conscious, and voluntary agreement to engage in sexual activity. It is the responsibility of each person involved in the sexual activity to ensure that he or she has the affirmative consent of the other or others to engage in the sexual activity." She added to her notes and wondered how, in the absence of witnesses, one person could establish that his or her partner in a sexual act had given consent or not, especially when there were no physical indications of a struggle? She could see how either party would be concerned about this question in front of a university disciplinary hearing. Would the most credible participant win out?

That issue seemed even more relevant as she went on to read the pertinent language in the bill: a policy must ensure that "the standard used in determining whether the elements of the complaint against the accused have been demonstrated is the preponderance of the evidence." She wrote a note to look up the various legal standards for establishing guilt or responsibility and to compare their usage and application. She kept scribbling.

Her reading of the rest of the bill was straightforward; nothing else seemed exceptional. She felt confident that within a few days, she would have acquired enough background on the bill and formulated sufficient questions that she could justify setting up an office meeting with the alluring Assistant Professor O'Connor.

Katie cleared her bed of her books and notes and called her mom. Katie hadn't spoken with her since arriving in Boulder, and knew that she'd want to know how things were going. They were close, and Katie enjoyed her mom's emotional support and understanding. She didn't feel close enough, however, to mention the details of her employment with Brian Taylor and her recent $1,500 paycheck. They spoke for half an hour, during which Katie summarized her time in Boulder thus far. After finishing that call, she called her friend Teresa to thank her for joining her on the drive to Boulder. After the calls, she made an impromptu dinner from a can of soup, some pasta, and some barely fresh vegetables from her refrigerator. While she ate, she streamed a romantic comedy on her laptop. After cleaning up, she turned in for the night.

THE NEXT MORNING, KATIE WENT TO the first class of another of her courses, the seminar in the history of philosophy. Afterward, she found a comfortable and secluded carrel in the library to work and then wandered around the building to orient herself with the layout of its stacks. Even though most of the research she did was online, many of the journal citations she required were available only in the university's library. Following up on her notes from the night before, she searched for the referenced definitions in the California bill for "sexual assault," "domestic violence," "dating violence," and "stalking" as defined in the federal Higher Education Act of 1965. She found that the specific bill had been amended by the Jeanne Clery Act of 1990.

Officially known as the Jeanne Clery Disclosure of Campus Security Policy and Campus Crime Statistics Act, it had been named for Jeanne Clery, a nineteen-year-old Lehigh University freshman who was raped and murdered in her campus residence hall in 1986. The backlash against unreported crimes on numerous campuses across the country led to the act's passage several years later. Katie made a note to look up and review the most recent Clery reports (which the act required all public universities to publish) for CU.

It was late afternoon when Katie made her way back to her apartment. She stopped at a nearby liquor store on the way to pick up a bottle of wine for her visit to Ava's. After putting away her things and cleaning up, she changed into a fresh pair of shorts and a tank top. It was a warm summer night, and she knew the apartment above hers would be toasty. It was only a few steps from her door to Ava's. She knocked but didn't hear a response. She knocked again and tried the knob. It was unlocked, so she decided to open the door and head up the stairs. On her way up, she shouted, "Hello?"

When she reached the landing of the apartment, she heard water running from somewhere down a hallway. She waited by the entrance and again called out. "Hello?"

"Katie, is that you? I'm in the shower. I'll be right out."

She found the kitchen and placed the bottle of wine on a counter. She was impressed by how clean and neat everything appeared: not a single dish was in the sink. She found her way to the living room and sat down on a chair. Several pieces of well-worn furniture and lamps gave the place a dated but comfortable look, much like her own. She spotted a corkboard on the wall and got up to get a closer look. Large wooden letters, KKG, painted in light and dark blue, were mounted above the board. Kappa Kappa Gamma, she thought. She laughed out loud at a postcard pinned to the board: "If you're dating a Kappa, raise your hand; if not, raise your standards." She also admired a large wooden sorority paddle hanging on the wall. Photographs on the board included Ava with other sorority women and some of her with a very handsome man in a T-shirt and board shorts. In one photo, he held a football; in another, taken of him and Ava together, he wore a suit and tie and she a stunning low-cut and tight-fitting black dress. It looked like a formal event of some sort. When the sound of the water stopped, Katie returned to the chair and sat down.

"Hi, Katie." Ava walked into the living area with wet hair and only a towel wrapped tightly around her body. "I'm really glad you came up. Let me put on some clothes, and I'll be right back."

In a few minutes, she reappeared in cutoff denim shorts and a T-shirt. Below the short crop of her shirt, Katie noticed a diamond stud in her navel. White pocket material appeared below the frayed cut of her shorts.

"I brought a bottle of wine."

"Great! Let's open it. I'll get some glasses."

Katie followed Ava to the kitchen. Ava pulled two glass tumblers of different sizes from a cabinet while Katie opened the wine. One was adorned with the letters KKG, and the other was from a fraternity. Trinkets from a house party, no doubt. She put them on the table, and Katie poured the wine.

Katie returned to the worn and uncomfortable chair she'd been on earlier, and Ava took a seat on a tufted fabric sofa.

"I see you're a Kappa Kappa Gamma."

"Yeah, I love it there. I lived in the house my sophomore and junior years. I graduate in June and decided I should experience life alone for a year. The house was fun, but I was ready for some privacy. I wasn't an officer, so I didn't have to live in the house."

"Still active?"

"I'm over there all the time. I'm required to help with rush, and I still go to some of the parties. I have a lot of friends there." Ava smiled broadly, which suggested to Katie that she felt the sorority was the happiest place on earth. "What about you? Where did you do your undergrad studies?"

"Claremont McKenna, in California. It's a small liberal arts college outside LA. We didn't have a Greek system to speak of. We had a couple of nonresidential fraternities, but no sororities." Katie noticed the hint of a frown appear on Ava's face.

"I can't imagine going to a college without a sorority. I've met my best friends there. My mom was a Kappa. I guess I always thought that's what I'd do, too. But I will admit, there are times when I look around at the sorority system and wonder."

"What do you mean?" The upper apartment was so warm that Katie had started to perspire. She wished for a breeze.

"I don't know. There's so much competition among the girls. Who's got the cutest designer clothes, who's the hottest? Who's got a boyfriend from a top-tier fraternity? Which sorority had members competing for Miss Colorado? Sometimes the whole sorority thing seems sort of superficial to me. I know a lot of our members are considered fraternity groupies, as the guys like to call them. I've never really been a party girl, but I know a lot of girls in the house who are." Ava and Katie both took sips of their wine.

Katie sized Ava up as someone who probably had her own closet full of nice clothes and was fortunate to possess a natural beauty, including a slim body and tall stature. Katie admired the length of Ava's legs, from the bottom of her cutoffs to the tips of her perfectly painted nails. "Speaking of cute guys, who's that on your corkboard?" Katie didn't mind admitting that she'd been looking.

"Oh, that's Drew. He's just a friend. We used to date."

"You're no longer together?"

"We still hang out occasionally. We met at a house party our freshman year. He's on the football team and on an athletic scholarship. He wasn't the brightest student, so I kind of became his little sister and helped him with his assignments. One thing sort of led to another. I fell in love with him."

"What happened?" Katie looked at Ava's glass of wine and noticed it was still almost full. Hers was almost empty.

"I caught him with another girl. Thankfully, it wasn't someone from my house."

"Do you mind if I pour myself more wine? Do you like it? I noticed you haven't touched yours."

"It's nice. I don't drink very often. I've never liked losing control."

Katie topped up her tumbler. "You're OK meeting with Drew, even now that you know he cheated on you?"

"It was hard. I still had feelings for him. I was crushed at first. I decided that I'd end up seeing him around campus anyway, and it probably wasn't healthy to hold a grudge. We agreed to see each other occasionally. Just friends." She took a sip of wine. "What about you? Do you have a boyfriend?"

"I'm giving guys a rest. I had a serious boyfriend at Claremont. He graduated and took a job in Seattle. I wasn't invited along." Katie took a long drink from the tumbler and savored the effect of the wine.

"You must have been disappointed."

"I'm learning that life isn't all about guys." The words probably didn't convince Ava—even Katie still struggled with her own advice. "Sure, I hoped we'd be together, but I'm focused on my studies right now. I plan to get my PhD and then find a job."

"I'll be looking for a job next spring after I graduate. I'm thinking of grad school, but my father insists I work for a couple of years first."

The two women discussed their families and who was where. Ava was the second generation to be born in the state, and she planned to stay there and have her own kids someday. Her brother worked as an accountant in Chicago. Katie described her family life back in California and the uncertainty she felt about getting an advanced degree in philosophy.

"Speaking of studying, I need to get back to it," Katie said as she drained her tumbler. "Thanks for having me up. Come down to my place next time." Katie and Ava shared phone numbers so they could text each other.

Katie stood. Ava followed, took a halting step toward Katie, and gave her a hug.

"It's been great to meet you, Katie. Let's get together again soon. I can introduce you to some great guys!"

Katie was silent on her way down the stairs. The idea of meeting some cute-looking frat guy failed to pique her interest. She had other ideas. But she was thankful to have met a new friend in Boulder. She stopped in the middle of the stairway and turned around. "That sounds great."

KATIE GROANED AS SHE AWOKE TO HER alarm at seven o'clock on Saturday morning. She boiled water and prepared a cup of coffee with her French press. She had nothing to eat at the apartment. She hoped they would have some food at the training.

She pulled up to the law office with five minutes to spare and found her way to the building's conference room. Inside, she picked a place to sit and took off her jacket and hung it over the chair. She said hello to some of the other students and then was pleased to notice a serving table against a wall packed with croissants, fruit, and yogurt, which she helped herself to. She counted two guys and three girls in the room. She saw copies of the presentation and a stack of name cards on the conference table. She grabbed one of each and went to get a cup of coffee. Just as she returned to her seat, a professionally dressed woman appeared, closed the door, and walked to a podium at the head of the room.

"Good morning. My name is Sally Clark. Please write your name on the placard and place it in front of you. I want to thank the NSAF for inviting me to speak today. I am the investigator and training coordinator for CU's Office of Institutional Equity and Compliance. Our department is responsible for the university's compliance with the department of education's civil-rights law known as Title IX." At that point she displayed the first slide of a PowerPoint presentation:

TITLE IX: No person in the United States shall, on the basis of sex, be excluded from participation in, be denied the benefits of, or be subjected to discrimination under any education program or activity receiving Federal financial assistance.

Ms. Clark spoke to the slide. "This law, passed in 1972, is used today as an enforcement tool to encourage colleges and universities that receive federal funding to respond to, investigate, and eliminate occurrences of sexual misconduct in the campus community. If a school or university fails to implement what the DOE defines as a compliant implementation of Title IX enforcement, then the educational institution will be investigated. Today, over a hundred active investigations of colleges and universities are under way."

She delivered the presentation in a rote monotone. "Over the next four hours, I will cover this outline." She advanced to the second PowerPoint slide, which showed a list of ten topics. "My goal is for you to leave here today armed with the information you need to explain our university's student-conduct policies and procedures to your fellow students and to help you recognize and report any conduct violations."

From a quick review of the slide, Katie concluded that it would be a long morning. She chewed on a bite of croissant and looked around the room. She wondered if the other students felt the same discomfort she did over their new position as paid informants. They would all blend easily into any campus setting. Like her, they were probably trying to earn their degrees and finding ways to pay for them.

CHAPTER 8

Due Process

Katie was more excited than apprehensive as she ascended the steps of Old Main. In the hallway outside O'Connor's half-open door, she heard two men engaged in earnest conversation. Katie caught a glimpse of Mark through the doorway; he was perched on the edge of his desk with his hands curled around its top for support. He wore jeans and cowboy boots, like those he'd worn on the first day of class.

Mark nodded at Katie and said, "I'll be with you shortly."

Katie paced in the hallway and waited. She used the time to recall the questions she'd formed after her week of researching and composing a draft outline of the paper. In a few minutes, a male student left the office, said a cheery hello, and departed down the stairwell. Mark appeared and welcomed her inside. He offered her a wooden chair next to a small round table. "How can I help you, Ms. Russell?"

Katie sat down and opened her notebook to a page filled with prepared questions. "Professor O'Connor, I've started working on the final paper for the philosophy and law class, and I have a few questions."

"Please, call me Mark. You've already started working on the paper during the first week of class? That's impressive. I don't recall another student doing that, especially when the late-summer weather is so perfect outside."

"Well, getting out in front of things has always been my strategy."

"Commendable. How can I help you?"

"I don't understand how, in a fact-finding procedure, a sexual-assault complaint can be properly evaluated. If there isn't a witness, or some obvious proof that an assault has occurred, then how can it be shown that an expression of informed consent was or wasn't proffered? How does the disciplinary procedure keep from devolving into an emotional 'he said, she said' standoff?"

"Others have raised that concern, too. The old standard of No Means No had the same problem: How does a complainant demonstrate that he or she signaled a prohibition to the offending act? It's not a new issue that was created by the language of the California law, but I think you can see the not-so-subtle difference. In the old law, the complainant had to prove that a prohibition was given. In the new language, the respondent must prove that consent was received. That's a big difference. I think you're right to raise that question. I encourage you to consider it as an issue in your paper. What else?"

"I've read the text of California's Yes Means Yes bill and the referenced language in the Higher Education Act of 1965. I've reviewed the key definitions of sexual assault, domestic violence, dating violence, and stalking. But I found the key section of the bill, the one that specifies affirmative consent, confusing."

Mark raised a quizzical eyebrow. "How so?"

Katie again referred to her notes. "The law states that affirmative consent means 'affirmative, conscious, and voluntary agreement to engage in sexual activity.' And that 'it is the responsibility of each person involved in the sexual activity to ensure that he or she has the affirmative consent of the other or others to engage in the sexual activity.' What I found confusing is that I couldn't find anywhere in the law where it specifies a definition of affirmative consent. So, when it comes to enforcing the law, how would anyone determine what constitutes a violation?"

"You're not the first person to have pointed this out. I don't think the answer to that question is at all clear, but you're right to ask it. What else?"

"I've never studied law, but I'm also curious about the use of the preponderance of evidence legal standard. As I understand it, in a civil case, the plaintiff has the burden of proving the facts and claims asserted in the complaint. When a party has the burden of proof, the party must present, through testimony and exhibits, enough evidence to support the claim. For most civil claims, there are two different evidentiary standards: preponderance of evidence and clear and convincing evidence. It appears to me that the preponderance of evidence is the weaker standard. Most criminal cases require a burden of proof beyond a reasonable doubt, the tougher standard. Why did California decide to implement the preponderance of evidence standard in the law?"

Mark smiled. "Ms. Russell, you're doing a very good job of raising the relevant issues. I'm impressed."

"Please, call me Katie."

"The due-process question is one of the most troublesome issues in the law. But I don't want to bias your research. I recommend reviewing several cases in which the preponderance of evidence standard has been used in a university setting and seeing if you can draw any conclusions. It's hard to find relevant data, though, since disciplinary hearings for sexual-assault cases are typically held in secret, and the records are kept private. The records have leaked out in a few cases, which you might find helpful. I also suggest that you meet with Professor Molly Wilson in the law school. I'll send her a note of introduction. She's given this subject some thought and I'm sure she'd be happy to talk with you about due process. We're about out of time. Is there anything else?"

"My advisor said I can become a graduate assistant for this class next semester. I'm hoping you might be able to give me some advice on getting prepared for that."

"Sure. Do you have any free time before or after class? We could meet once a week, for about fifteen minutes at the beginning or end, and I can go over the lesson plan and what you need to know. You should start building a weekly notebook of lectures, assigned reading, and assignments. Take notes about how we cover those things in class. You're probably doing a lot of that already. I'm happy to help."

Relieved of the pressure of making a good impression and no longer distracted by her notes, Katie closed her notebook and took the opportunity to admire Mark. She wished she could stop time and, undetected, take a proper inventory of his features. As Mark leaned against his desk, his lightness appeared to give him such buoyancy that he would just float upward had he released his grip. His demeanor and mannerisms gave him an air of modesty, yet he was obviously bright and she detected notes of whimsy lurking underneath. If only she could study his lustrous eyes and search for kindness, too. She screwed shut her own eyes and tried to imagine the form that ran inside his clothes. What would his body feel like, unencumbered by fabric and pressed against hers? Perhaps to create a familiar reference, her mind struggled to recall what Justin had felt like. It couldn't. Like coastal fog on a summer day, the memory of him had begun to burn away.

"Ms. Russell? I mean Katie?"

Katie snapped open her eyes. "Oh, sorry...I was trying to think of more questions." Regaining her focus, she added, "No, I think I've covered them all." She stood.

Mark said, "There's something I wanted to mention. Every Friday afternoon, the faculty and students have an informal gathering at the West End Tavern in the Pearl Street Mall. You're welcome to join us. We usually arrive around five. Sometimes we stay for dinner, but usually we just drink, argue philosophy, and snack on happy-hour food. It's a good way to meet other grad students and faculty."

"Sounds interesting." Even though Katie knew she'd attend that coming Friday, she didn't want to seem too eager. "I'll try to make it sometime."

KATIE'S MEETING WITH PROFESSOR WILSON OCCURRED on Friday, two days after her meeting with Dr. O'Connor. After introductions, Professor Wilson explained that she was a specialist in trial advocacy and lectured on the topics of *voir dire*, opening statement, direct examination, cross-examination, and closing argument. "I teach what you might call a lawyer's game plan to use when trying a case. The focus of the class is on both defensive and offensive strategy."

"I never quite thought of it that way," Katie said. "I always assumed a trial was about the collection of facts followed by the application of law." She had visited a courtroom once for a speeding ticket, but the perfunctory process had ended with her writing a check.

"That's true, but strategy and tactics help nudge facts into the sunlight. How can I help you, Ms. Russell? Mark O'Connor mentioned that you have an interest in due process."

Katie explained the writing assignment, her research to date, and her conversation with O'Connor. "We started to discuss the preponderance of evidence legal standard required by the California law, and Assistant Professor O'Connor mentioned that he felt the due-process question was an essential problem of the bill. That's when he suggested I speak with you. He said you've studied the issue."

"Several faculty members and I have held a few forums on this topic. We understand the university has a difficult job in providing a learning environment on campus that's safe from sexual harassment. It must also provide for balance and fairness in the procedures that are used to decide cases of alleged sexual misconduct. The Title IX office is responsible for investigation, prosecution, fact-finding, and appellate review. From my reporting on the university's administration, I believe it lacks impartiality. As faculty members, we feel these rules, required by the Office of Civil Rights, go against the fundamentals of due process, including the rule of law, administrative decision making, and the substantive laws that are already in place governing discrimination and violence. These are the rules we teach in our classes."

Katie stopped taking notes for a moment. "What's driving the adoption of these rules?"

Professor Wilson leaned back in her chair and paused. "I can't speak for the department of education, but they've been clear from their investigation of more than a hundred universities that loss of federal education funding, or penalties, are at risk if these universities don't follow these rules. I won't speculate about what's motivating them, but from my experience, politics plays a role. Some schools have talked openly about suing the government, but our school is so dependent on federal funding that we would never take the risk. Recently, twenty-eight members of the Harvard Law School faculty signed and issued a statement calling on Harvard to drop its recently adopted sexual-harassment policy, which was created in response to this federal pressure."

"Why are they concerned? Isn't trying to reduce sexual assault on campus a worthy goal?"

"They're upset about the procedures that are used to investigate and assign penalties in sexual-harassment cases. Many cases are heard by disciplinary committees composed of professors, deans, and students; these people often have no legal training. The procedures also lack the safeguards that are typically found in criminal courts. Often the accused has no right to a lawyer and no chance to cross-examine witnesses. The Office for Civil Rights issued a letter in 2011 that provides guidance to colleges and universities that receive federal funding. Euphemistically referred to as the 'Dear Colleague Letter,' it expands Title IX protections of sexual harassment to include acts of sexual violence, including rape, sexual assault, sexual battery, and sexual coercion. Some of the new requirements are unobjectionable and even welcome—for example, OCR's emphasis on making sure that students accused of sexual harassment and sexual violence are afforded the same access to hearing documents, counsel, party statements, and meetings, as well as the opportunity to present witnesses and evidence. But it also strongly discourages schools from allowing the two parties to an accusation of sexual assault to personally question or cross-examine each other during the hearing."

"What about requiring the preponderance of evidence legal standard?"

"That's one of my biggest concerns." Professor Wilson turned to a stack of papers on her desk and retrieved a document. She handed it to Katie. "Read this. I think it'll help you understand the legal issues involved in burden of proof. It's a discussion among lawyers who are reacting to this provision of the California bill. Lawyers want to ensure that the burden of proof is matched by the legal standards that are used to establish guilt. If you follow the preponderance rule that says that a finding of guilt will be reached when a violation was more than likely to have occurred, then the odds of a wrong decision being made in favor of the complainant are only slightly greater than the odds of getting the decision wrong in favor of the respondent."

Katie struggled with the concept. She'd think about it later. "But do wrong decisions affect each party equally?"

"That's an excellent question. Ever consider becoming a lawyer?" Professor Wilson laughed at her remark. "The money's better than in philosophy. As for your question, think about this. Which party is more aggrieved, a female student who was sexually assaulted and then watches as her assailant is found innocent, left to walk around campus, appear in classes, and generally humiliate her? Or a male student who is wrongly accused, found guilty, and expelled from school, a failure that will likely follow him the rest of his life? When considering a standard of beyond a reasonable doubt in criminal cases, we go by the old saying, 'Better that ten guilty persons escape than that one innocent person suffers.' Of course, this view anticipates possible incarceration in jail or prison, which is not the level of punishment that a university's administration will hand out."

Katie stopped writing and sat back in her chair. As her mind tried to process these new concepts, she realized how much she had to learn. That was why she loved college. Great teachers, like Professor Wilson, asked thoughtful questions and created a framework that then encouraged more research. Professor Wilson clearly expected Katie to form her own opinions instead of simply laying out the answer for her.

The professor broke the silence. "I assume you're aware of the Occidental College lawsuit?"

"I'm not."

"Jane Doe and John Doe lived in the freshman dorm. They met up on a Saturday night in September in John's dorm room with a few other friends. He had been drinking all day as part of his athletic team's hazing ritual. She had been out with friends drinking shots. They later admitted that they were each drunker than they had ever been before. After they'd all danced and listened to some loud music in John's dorm room, some of the others who were present decided to get Jane back to her room, because she was slurring her words and stumbling. They took her to the room, put her to bed, and watched her for a while. Then they left her alone."

"What happened?"

"After the friends left, Jane and John started texting. He asked her to come back to his room. She texted back to ask if he had a condom. He texted that he did. She texted to a friend in another city that she was going to have sex now. She managed to climb the stairs to John's room, where they did have what both agreed was consensual sex."

"Then what?"

"A week later, Jane filed a complaint with the college. After a three-month investigation, John was found responsible for sexual assault and nonconsensual sex and expelled. Even though they were both incapacitated, and their sex consensual, the adjudicator found that intoxication did not relieve John of his responsibility of ascertaining the complainant's incapacitation and obtaining informed consent. John appealed the finding and lost. He's now suing the college. The results of the trial promise to be interesting."

"How did the text messages and details of the findings get out? I thought colleges kept those things confidential."

"That's what makes this case unusual. It's one of only a few in which some of the written records from the hearing were published in court documents. Over two hundred pages' worth. The college still refuses to comment."

"What a mess."

"Ms. Russell, I think we've probably covered enough for today. Continue your research and keep an open mind. These are complex issues that will have an important societal impact." Professor Wilson stood.

Katie joined her. "Thank you for your help, Professor. I have a lot to learn. I do have one more question. Do you know an attorney named Brian Taylor?"

Professor Wilson's eyes widened. "Why, yes, he was one of my law students. Last I heard, he was running a nonprofit of some kind. I guess he decided to chase principles instead of dollars. Why? Do you know him?"

Katie demurred. "No, I met him socially a few weeks ago; I was just curious if you knew him." She said good-bye and left the office.

CHAPTER 9
Faculty Fridays

Katie left her apartment and walked toward the West End Tavern for the philosophy department's Friday-afternoon gathering. The air seemed neither hot nor cold as she strolled along residential streets and past manicured lawns of well-maintained homes that looked to be at least a century old. The sky was a palette of such deep blues that it looked as if it had been painted with a brush of thick oils. She wondered if high altitude and dry air permitted a more vivid light, unlike the air back home, which was filtered by Pacific mist—even the greens of the trees appeared more saturated. Climate and altitude might be why the town seemed not only healthy but also less stressful than what she was used to in Southern California. Feelings of tranquility and optimism floated over her, but she wasn't quite ready to embrace them out of fear that they might simply dissolve away.

A hostess directed her to an upstairs deck that was bathed in bright sun and offered an expansive view of the downtown skyline. Katie walked toward an enthusiastic-looking crowd at the far end of the deck; it didn't take her long to pick out Mark, who was talking with a woman dressed in a long skirt and a button-down blouse. Katie recognized her as another professor in the department. She spotted a table occupied by two young men, casually dressed in shorts and T-shirts. Each had a beer in one hand and was speaking animatedly with the other.

"Mind if I join you?" Katie put her hand on the back of an empty chair.

"Please do." Neither man stood. So much for manners. Katie pulled the chair out and sat down.

"I'm Katie. First-year grad student. I assume this is the philosophy department's gathering?"

"If you think it, then it must be so." Both men laughed. "My name's Ken, and this is Sam. We're undergrads."

Sensing that they were analyzing her and not yet finished, Katie said nothing. A waiter arrived, and Katie ordered her usual drink, a hard cider. She put on her sunglasses to provide shade from the bright sun and watched Mark to see if he had noticed her.

Finally, after a pause that began to seem awkward, Katie spoke up. "I didn't mean to interrupt your conversation."

"We could use a woman's perspective." Ken turned in his chair and faced her. "We were discussing the question of whether philosophy departments are hostile to women. We don't think so, but we're probably not unbiased observers."

Katie paused and studied both men closely. "I do think gender bias exists, but I haven't seen it firsthand. I just finished my undergrad degree in California. The department there is chaired by a woman, and several members of the faculty are women. The majority were men, though—maybe seventy percent."

"Where did you go to college?" Sam asked.

"Claremont McKenna."

"Great school." He seemed genuinely impressed.

"CU is amazing, too. Do you guys think there's hostility to women here?"

Ken said, "No, but I'm sure you heard about the scandal."

"What scandal?" Katie hadn't heard anything.

Sam outlined the details. "It was a big story on campus a few years back. Some female grad students claimed that the department frequently engaged in sexual harassment and bullying. The American Philosophical Association sent a team to investigate. After they wrote and published their findings, the department chairman was removed, and all grad-student admissions were suspended for a year. Since the university seals any charges of sexual harassment, no one ever mentioned specifics. There's a lot of speculation about what really happened."

"I hadn't heard any of this. Is it true?"

Ken said, "I don't know. It doesn't seem that different to me from other departments on campus. I think the big question is why so few women study philosophy. That's what we were talking about when you arrived. Is it because women just aren't attracted to the field, or is there something about the climate in the department that prevents women from believing they can be successful?"

"Well," Katie said, "if you believe that men and women are socialized differently, as the feminist philosopher Nancy Chodorow has argued, then from an early age, women are not generally encouraged to study math and science. In math, physics, and philosophy, seventy percent of PhDs are granted to men; alternatively, in psychology and anthropology, the number is about seventy percent female. Are math, physics, and philosophy departments hostile to women, or do women avoid those fields? Perhaps one is the result of the other."

Sam said, "I believe confirmation bias is a major factor."

Katie said, "Like employers subconsciously calling Howard over Heidi for an interview when their résumés appear equal?"

"Exactly," Sam said with a nod. "People will prefer what they know until there's enough diversity in ideas to discourage them from a predetermined bias. That bias will cause them to ignore any evidence that doesn't support their view and only focus on what they already believe to be right."

Katie said, "Some firms are starting to hold gender-blind résumé screenings. Studies have shown that when evaluators looked at candidate profiles in isolation, they were more likely to hire men for math-related tasks and women for language-related tasks. But when they looked at multiple candidates, their stereotyped preferences disappeared."

"At least we can do *this* again." Sam raised his beer.

Ken met Sam's glass with his own and made a clink. They both drank.

"What are you talking about?" Katie lifted her own glass and took a sip of cider.

"The department banned gatherings like this for a while," Ken said. "The report suggested that some of the sexual-harassment problems were a result of a casual attitude toward off-campus socializing between faculty and students. Especially when alcohol's involved." Ken and Sam smirked and clinked glasses again.

"What is it about you guys and beer?" Katie said with a laugh.

"I see you're meeting some of the other students." Katie hadn't noticed Mark approach. "Hi, Sam. Hello, Ken."

"Hello, Professor," they said in unison.

"Mind if I join you?" Mark pulled out the last chair and sat down.

"We were just going to get some food," Ken said. "Nice meeting you, Katie. See you around." Sam echoed the sentiment, and they both shuffled off toward the far end of the deck, where several plates of appetizers were stationed.

"Nice to see you again, Katie. I'm glad you came. How's your paper going?"

"It's coming along well, Professor. I mean Mark." Katie hoped he didn't mind her lack of formality. "I had a great meeting with Professor Wilson."

"I thought you would. Molly's opinionated."

"She didn't give me a lot of answers, but she did ask a lot of good questions."

"She likes to teach."

The waitress reappeared, and Katie ordered another cider. Mark asked for a beer.

"How do you like Boulder so far?"

"It's beautiful." Katie removed her sunglasses. "Everyone's so fit! Even compared to the people of LA."

"The campus recruiters cite a statistic that seventy percent of out-of-state freshmen stay in Colorado once they graduate. It's easy to see why."

"I'm lucky to be here."

"We're lucky to have you," Mark said with a smile.

They spent the next hour talking about a variety of subjects: current trends in philosophy, politics on campus, and life in Boulder in general. As Katie started in on her third cider, she realized how much she was at ease with their conversation. The alcohol was relaxing her, and she spoke freely. Perhaps it was Mark. He was very sincere, he listened well, and he seemed to take a genuine interest in what she had to say.

Katie, now free of inhibition, asked, "Are you married?"

Mark hesitated. "No. I came close once—engaged to a girl from back home. We were friends in high school and dated while we were undergraduates at the University of Denver. I'm the one who ended it."

"May I ask why?"

"I don't know. I loved her. But there was something that just didn't feel right. I've never been sure what it was."

"'Human reason is troubled by questions that it cannot dismiss, but also cannot answer.'" Katie smiled, pleased with her recall.

"Immanuel Kant. Nice."

"It's from a final exam I had last year. I've been looking for a way to use it ever since."

"What about you?

"Never been married. Not even engaged. I was once a bridesmaid, though." She smiled." I had a serious boyfriend in college, but he took a job in Seattle, and I moved here. Probably for the best."

"Relationships aren't easy. Marriage is a huge commitment. My parents have been married for thirty-five years, so I know it *can* work. I hope to find out someday."

"Did you grow up in Colorado?" Katie wanted to know everything about him.

"Yep, on a large ranch outside Durango. My life was a cross between *Little House on the Prairie* and *Dr. Quinn, Medicine Woman*. My mom started an animal shelter for cats and dogs, and my dad ran the ranch."

"How did you get involved in philosophy?"

Mark let out a deep-throated laugh. His blue eyes brightened. "I think it came from spending so much time on a horse. When you're riding flank on a cattle drive, other than having to watch for strays edging away from the herd, you get a lot of time to think."

"And you thought about philosophy?"

"I thought about how humans and animals interact in the world. Early philosophers, like Aristotle, believed that only man is endowed with a rational soul and that other animals have no cognition. I prefer to believe Darwin's views—in his *Origin of Species*—that a mental continuity exists among all species and that animals do have some degree of awareness."

The conversation stopped for a moment as Katie pondered his comments. Mark was an intriguing blend of Western ruggedness and intellectual rigor. She fondly recalled the only time she'd ridden a horse, during a week of vacation at a Montana dude ranch with her family. She was around ten years old at the time. At the ranch, she'd been assigned a horse named Snowfire for the week. Her butt had been painfully sore from day one. By the end of the week, when it was time to go home, she grew despondent. Her parents wanted to know what was wrong. She explained that she just had to take Snowfire home with her. It was an idea her parents gently dismissed, explaining that Snowfire wouldn't be happy living on a cul-de-sac in Orange County.

Katie's focus returned to the deck, and she became aware that the sky had grown almost dark. "It's getting late, and I should probably go. I plan to work on my paper tomorrow. I enjoyed hearing about your life and why you chose philosophy."

A server came and deposited a check. Mark wasted no time finding his credit card and putting it on the tray.

"I don't often talk about it. Maybe next time you can tell me about your personal journey. Are you going to stop by my office before class next week?"

"I'll be there. Thank you for the cider."

Katie pushed her chair back and stood. Mark joined her. Their eyes met, and Mark lightly placed his hand on Katie's shoulder. "I'm glad you came."

Katie returned the piercing gaze and studied his face. Everything peripheral to it became indiscernible, like a mirror in a steamy bathroom after the center has been wiped with a towel. Then she experienced a most amazing sensation, as though her emotions had started to flow directly from her body into his, like current through a wire. She was aware of nothing but his eyes and the flux between them.

After a moment, one likely measurable in seconds but seemingly endless, Mark released her arm and walked away. Katie's vision slowly cleared. She looked around the now-empty deck and let out a nervous chirp of a laugh. What had just happened? Katie felt certain of only one thing—a small part of her heart now resided within his.

CHAPTER 10
Road Trip

The morning after the drinks on the terrace, Katie awoke to the sound of a new message arriving on her phone. It was from her neighbor Ava, who wanted to know if Katie would like to join her and a couple of friends for an outdoor concert near Denver. Katie had nothing scheduled and thought it sounded fun, so she replied yes.

Joining Ava later that afternoon were her two friends and roommates, Jill and Stephanie. Katie had a car, so she drove. She suspected her car might have been behind the invitation to join them. They piled into her Subaru and headed south along the mountainous front range. The concert was at the famous Red Rocks Amphitheatre in the small town of Morrison. The girls explained that the outdoor theater was in a natural stone formation and had hosted many big acts over the years, including the Beatles, the Rolling Stones, the Grateful Dead, and Jimi Hendrix. That night, they were seeing Ed Sheeran, the Emmy-nominated British pop star, who was on tour with Taylor Swift.

Katie had been so immersed in the topic of sexual assault from working on her paper that she thought the scenic drive along the foothills was a perfect opportunity to explore the topic with the other girls. Since they'd just met, and it was an intensely private subject, Katie started with a few general questions about their perceptions of the issue.

"Can I ask you guys a question?"

"Sure," Jill said.

"I'm researching a paper for my graduate class in philosophy. We're discussing a new law in California that addresses sexual assault on college campuses. I'm curious what the atmosphere is like here in Boulder. Is sexual assault a problem on campus?"

"I think so, yes," Jill said. "Although I've never experienced it, I think most women believe that guys try to push the limits all the time."

Stephanie spoke up next. "A friend of mine knew of a sexual assault last year."

"What happened?"

"She had a female exchange student living with her. The exchange student became friends with a male student on social media. They got together for beers and pool a few times. Over Thanksgiving break, the exchange student and my friend couldn't get the guy to take the hint to go home after they'd done some serious drinking. The exchange student ended up letting him sleep in her bed. She woke up in the middle of the night and found him on top of her, having sex. She screamed and demanded he leave. He did."

"That's terrible. Did they catch him?" Katie glanced at Stephanie through the rearview mirror.

"She called 911. The police asked her to call the guy in a couple of days and said they'd record the conversation."

"What did he say when she called?"

"She said he knew that she'd passed out. She asked him why he'd done it. She even asked him if he'd planned it. He basically said that it had just happened. He hadn't planned it and was too drunk to know better. He said he was sorry."

"What happened to him?"

"They arrested him. Then things got more interesting. Another woman came forward after reading about the arrest. She was a hometown friend of the guy. She testified to the jury that they'd had sex one night during her freshman year. On another night, after they'd played drinking games in his dorm, she'd told him that she didn't want to have sex with him. She passed out, and when she came to, he was assaulting her."

"The guy's a serial rapist," Ava said.

"There were more," Stephanie said. "Another girl came forward and said that she was a high school pal of one of the suspect's friends. She'd just arrived on campus for her freshman year, and after getting extremely drunk on Long Island iced teas at a bar, she passed out in his off-campus frat house. She awoke to find him performing oral sex on her."

"I've heard guys can become predators," Katie said, "and they routinely use alcohol and drugs to take advantage of women."

"He was a bad guy," Stephanie said. "Yet he was an economics major, he was in the marching band, and he got great grades. No one would have believed it until five women came forward with similar stories."

"Was he punished?" Katie asked. "Did he go to jail?"

"He was tried for sexual assault of the exchange student. The others testified, but they only tried him on what they felt was the strongest case. He was found guilty and sentenced to eighteen years."

Katie said, "I read in a recent survey that ninety percent of sexual assaults are committed by men who've had multiple victims. I'm glad he got a long sentence."

When they arrived in the town of Morrison, they looked for a place to have a few drinks and some food. They ended up at a place called the Red Rocks Grill. Knotty pine paneling and wooden floors added to a Western theme. Several mounted heads of moose, steer, and cougar hung from the walls. Along with beers, they shared plates of chile rellenos, tacos, and a burger with fries. Katie had a great time laughing with her new friends and sharing stories of her undergrad days.

Jill looked at Katie. "Do you have a boyfriend?"

"Nope. Just me."

"She's giving men a break," Ava volunteered.

Katie said, "How about you?"

"I've got a friend I hang with," Jill said. "I met him dancing in a bar one night. In fact, Stephanie was with me. We became friends. We hook up sometimes. Nobody really dates anymore."

Katie was aware of the trend: dating was a thing of the past. "What about you, Stephanie?"

"I don't really have one serious guy. I don't see the point. There are so many guys out there to choose from, and I'm not ready to be exclusive. I like calling the shots. Sometimes I'll just sleep with a guy if I want to have some fun. I get to decide." Katie was pretty sure Stephanie didn't have trouble attracting guys.

"What about marriage?" she asked.

"Sure," Stephanie replied. "Someday. Maybe after grad school. I want to have kids. For now, though, I just want to have fun and focus on my education. When the time comes, I'll find the right guy."

Katie asked, "But what if you met a guy you liked during school and then got a job out of town somewhere? What would you do?"

Ava jumped in. "We were just talking about that at the sorority last night. Almost everyone said they'd take the job. It was more important."

Katie reflected on the conversation. Her views were certainly more traditional than those of the others. It was impressive how much things had changed in the past few years. "Do you think guys even know how to fall in love anymore?"

"What do you mean?" Ava asked.

"People always say there're more fish in the sea when it comes to breakups and men." Katie had heard the phrase more than once after her breakup with Justin. "I wonder if the sea has *too* many fish. Everything is immediate. Check out friends on social media. Use apps to find photos of men near you. Swipe right if you want to meet, or left if you don't. It's like one big marketplace. In the past, you could control what people learned about you and share whatever you felt comfortable with as your relationship evolved. But now, just search online and you can find out everything about anyone. Dating just seems different."

"And don't get me started on what men want in bed," Stephanie added. "Thanks to porn, there's a new normal for what guys expect. If you don't give it to them, they'll just move on. It's not that hard to find women who *will* do what they want."

Katie enjoyed the conversation over dinner. She was impressed with Ava's friends; they were confident and open to sharing their thoughts. Soon it was time to pay the bill and head to the amphitheater.

Katie enjoyed the concert, although the abundance of teenagers in the crowd made her feel beyond her years. She enjoyed Sheeran's songs; his soulful lyrics and elegant guitar spoke of love, hope, and commitment. It wasn't long before her thoughts meandered in Mark's direction—anticipation was much better than loss. Images of Justin had faded even more, like stains from a soiled dress placed in a washing machine. She saw her mind as being composed of many compartments, some interconnected, others not. She was immersed in a process much like that of a landlord: cleaning an apartment after one tenant has departed and before the next one has arrived. She'd pitched a closetful of memories down the stairs and swept the dust from the room's grimy corners into a bin. After mopping the floor, Katie would push open the windows and let rays of sunshine in.

The drive home after the concert seemed long, and everyone was quiet. Ava stayed awake, but Jill and Stephanie quickly went to sleep. At the curb in front of her apartment, Katie woke everyone and rallied them out of the car. The girls each said their good nights and went home to their beds.

The week after the concert, Katie mostly studied and went to class. On Monday morning, she walked to Mark's office for their weekly review of the lesson plan. Their interaction felt strictly professional. Toward the end, he mentioned that he was glad she'd stopped by for drinks on Friday afternoon and hoped she'd had a good time. She smiled and said yes, and though she was tempted to say more, she refrained. She would be patient.

CHAPTER 11

Ava and Drew

The following week, Katie received a text message from Ava with an invitation to come up that evening to meet her friend Drew. Katie wasn't inclined—she had reservations about frat guys like Drew—but she'd had such an enjoyable time at the concert with Ava and her friends that she decided to accept. They agreed to meet up at eight.

Before leaving for Ava's, Katie changed into shorts and running shoes and went for a quick run. She'd easily adapted to the mile-high altitude of Boulder and found a series of great running trails in the nearby foothills. She drove to one of the trailheads and enjoyed an exhilarating five-mile run on a hilly, dirt-lined trail above the city. In Boulder, everyone spent a lot of time outdoors, it seemed. It was one more positive attribute of the city.

After the run and a shower, Katie put on some clothes, grabbed a six-pack of beer from her refrigerator, and headed next door. She heard sounds of music and voices coming from above as she ascended the stairway to Ava's apartment. When she arrived at the landing, she found that the door to the apartment was open. She shouted, "Hello?"

She heard Ava reply, "Katie, is that you? Come on in!"

Katie rounded the corner into the living room and immediately recognized Drew, sprawled on the sofa, as the handsome man in the photo she'd seen on the corkboard during her first visit to Ava's. Another man, a leviathan who was easily the tallest and most muscular man she'd ever seen, dwarfed the wooden chair he was sitting in. Ava sat on the floor with her back up against a bookcase and her hand wrapped around a wineglass. A half-empty wine bottle sat on the coffee table, along with five—she counted—empty beer bottles.

Ava stared at her blankly. "Katie, meet Drew and his friend Desmond."

Drew didn't even bother to get up, nor did the oversize Desmond. "I brought some beers," she said.

"Good thing," Drew said. "We're about to run out." He extended his hand and waited, as if expecting Katie to put a beer into it. She did.

Katie studied Ava, who was clearly intoxicated. She looked nothing like the bright and bubbly girl she'd just met a few days earlier. She recalled Ava's comment about not wanting to lose control.

"I hear you're a quarterback?" Katie asked as she studied Drew's piercing blue eyes. Katie understood Ava's attraction.

"Yeah, I'm starting this year. I finally get my shot."

"Desmond, do you play, too?"

"Special teams and strong safety." Katie only knew that this meant he was fast and took a lot of punishment. Several bruises on his arms and a scar on his neck confirmed it.

"Nice to meet you." No one spoke for the next few minutes. Katie felt Drew's eyes move over her as if she were a piece of meat and it was feeding time in the savanna. Music continued to play: mostly popular hip-hop, a style Katie didn't particularly enjoy. She preferred the works of bands like the Red Hot Chili Peppers, the Foo Fighters, and Nirvana. She opened a bottle of beer with an opener from the table and sat down on the floor next to Ava.

"You OK? You look tired."

"I'm fine. Just relaxed. Isn't Drew great?"

"What are your plans for tonight?

"Don't know. We might go dancing. You should come."

"I don't think so. Not my thing."

"Come on, Katie. Join us." It was Drew. Claremont McKenna didn't have a football team, and the high school players she'd known were nowhere near the size of the two men seated across from her. They were intimidating. Desmond did have a nice smile, though.

"I should study. Ava says you're in a fraternity, Drew. Which one?"

"Omega Theta Pi. It's a pretty cool house. We throw great parties. You should drop by sometime. The guys would think you're pretty hot, for an older woman."

Katie chose not to respond. "What about you, Desmond?"

"What?"

"Are you in a house? You know, a fraternity?"

"No. I rushed freshman year. Didn't get the one I wanted. I lived in the football dorm. Now I live off campus. We have a pretty good time."

Drew said, "What about you, Katie? I don't see you as the sorority type."

Katie sensed that Drew was looking for a confrontation and took a sip from her beer. "We didn't have sororities at my school. I guess I missed out." She stood. "Look, it's been nice meeting you guys, but I think I'm going to finish my beer and go study." Katie grabbed Ava and helped her stand. "Can I speak with you in the kitchen for a moment?"

Katie spoke in a low voice after pushing Ava gently to the kitchen. "I'm going to head back downstairs. Are you sure you're OK? These guys look like they're getting pretty wasted. Do you trust them?"

"They're fine. Stick around and have some fun."

Katie studied Ava's eyes. She looked all right, but she knew she might be vulnerable if she drank much more. "Look, I'll be in my apartment. You have my number. If you need anything, call me."

Katie walked back to the living room, said good-bye to the men, and headed downstairs. She made a sandwich and listened to the beat of the music from Ava's apartment above.

KATIE WAS DEEP INTO READING A LEGAL BRIEF when she heard a loud thud followed by what sounded like a muffled curse. She looked at her phone and noted that it was ten-thirty. Then she heard the door to Ava's apartment open and slam shut. Good, she thought: the guys were leaving. Half an hour later, she decided to go back upstairs and check on Ava.

At the top of the landing, she found the apartment mostly dark except for some dim light that came from the living room, where they had all gathered earlier. She peered inside and saw a few burning candles scattered among the empty beer bottles on the coffee table. The room was empty. She then headed down the hallway to find Ava's bedroom. When she arrived at the doorway, her heart was beating against her chest in a steady rhythm. She cautiously peered inside the room. Illuminated by dim light from a small lamp on a nightstand, she saw Ava's prone body on top of her bed. She wore only a bra; a pair of panties lay on the floor. Rumpled bedsheets and the corner of a fitted sheet and pad had pulled free from the mattress. Ava's legs were spread, and she appeared unconscious.

"What are you doing here? Go back to your apartment and mind your own business." Katie jumped and saw Drew in a darkened corner of the bedroom. He had one leg in his jeans and what appeared to be a wet, bloody cut on his forehead.

"What did you do to her?" Katie sat down on the bed and put her hand on Ava's face. She was breathing, but when Katie shook her gently, there wasn't any response. "What did you do?"

"Nothing we haven't done before, and I guarantee you she enjoyed it."

Drew stumbled toward her. Even with his jeans on only partway, he still managed to quickly close the distance between them. He put his hand on Katie's shoulder and squeezed it with such strength that it caused her to cry out in pain. She didn't dare strike him, since she knew he would easily overpower her. She ran from the room and pulled her phone from her pocket. Drew managed to get his pants on and followed a few steps behind. "Who're you calling?"

"I'm calling the police if you don't get out of here right now."

"You better not tell anyone about this, or you'll regret it, you bitch." Drew finished buttoning his jeans and raced down the stairway. The door banged shut, and he was gone.

Katie returned to the bedroom and sat on the bed. She tried to revive Ava's listless body and noticed the surge of adrenaline in her own. She went to the kitchen to fetch ice, wrapped some cubes in a dish towel, and ran back to the bedroom. She placed the cold compress on Ava's pale forehead and with her free hand pulled the sheets up over her lower body. Ava began to moan.

Katie looked around the room and noticed an overturned chair. She surmised that Drew must have tripped over it while pulling his pants back on and then hit his head on the dresser or footboard. She examined the furniture and noticed some damp red liquid on the edge of the dresser. She assumed it was blood and knew not to touch it. Then she saw a familiar-looking piece of packaging on the floor and picked it up. It had once contained a condom. Scanning the room again, she hoped to spot its used contents, thinking it would make useful evidence. She crawled around on the floor and looked underneath the bed, repulsed by the idea of actually finding it. She didn't. He must have taken it with him or flushed it down the toilet.

"Katie?" Ava's voice was weak.

Katie returned to the bed and sat next to Ava. Her eyes were unfocused and barely open.

"What happened? Why are you here?" Ava struggled to lift her head.

Katie knew she had to decide whether to call the police right away or wait until Ava was coherent. She looked fine. It would be impossible to know if she'd had intercourse if they'd used a condom and there weren't other signs, like scratches or abrasions on her body. Whatever had happened, it was obvious that Ava had little memory of it.

After calling 911 and having a quick conversation with the Boulder police, Katie helped Ava get dressed and down to her Subaru. The drive to the local community hospital took only ten minutes. Once they arrived in the emergency room, it took another thirty minutes to locate a sexual assault nurse examiner, or SANE. The hospital staff included only one, and she was off duty at the time.

After the SANE arrived, she requested that Ava sign a release for the exam. Katie was permitted to provide personal support. The nurse collected Ava's general medical history and a detailed description of what had happened with Drew. She also collected the panties that Katie had picked up from the bedroom floor and brought to the hospital with the rest of the clothes Ava had worn before the assault.

Following the information uptake, the nurse collected samples for the rape kit: fingernail scrapings, hair samples, and oral swabs. And because Katie mentioned that Ava had appeared to be heavily intoxicated, the nurse also took blood and urine samples. She examined Ava's naked body for any signs of physical trauma such as bruises or cuts and then conducted a vaginal exam. After the nurse completed her work, she offered Ava optional emergency contraception and medications to prevent the contraction of sexually transmitted diseases. Ava chose to accept them.

Katie stayed with Ava throughout the exam. Clearly confused by the hospital setting, Ava seemed comforted by Katie's presence. Katie thought it best to wait until they returned home to discuss any details of the evening's events. By then, Ava would be more coherent.

The nurse provided brochures from several organizations that could offer victim assistance and counseling as well as a guide that explained her options for reporting the incident to the police. Ava was released from the hospital around two in the morning. As Katie drove back to the house, she decided that Ava should stay with her. They could talk in the morning.

Katie put Ava into her own bed and then went back upstairs to gather Ava's pajamas and toothbrush. She was surprised to notice that the bloodstains on the dresser were gone, and she detected a faint smell of bleach. Then she saw that the bed was devoid of any sheets. Katie went to the kitchen, where she found the counter and sink empty of glasses; the table in the living room had also been cleared. She thought to check inside the dishwasher and found that all the glasses were clean and still warm. She checked the washing machine and found it full of clean, wet sheets. Someone had returned to the apartment and sanitized the crime scene.

Once Katie had put Ava to bed in her own room, she found some extra blankets and a pillow and made up the sofa. She locked the door and made sure she had her phone nearby. Drew's threat unnerved her. She grabbed a beer from the refrigerator, sat on the sofa, and gazed around the darkened living room. She turned on a small reading lamp and perused some photos she'd unpacked recently and displayed on a bookshelf. She smiled at a small five-by-seven photo of her and two girlfriends taken her senior year.

They had been out for a hike near the Claremont McKenna campus. She couldn't make out the features on their faces due to the faint light, but it didn't matter. The memories of that day were still vivid, especially now that the negative side of the subject had hit so close to home. They'd all shared secrets of their first sexual encounters. Katie had told them of her high school boyfriend; the others had told of similar, mostly awkward, episodes. In the end, after some good-natured laughing and ribbing, they swore themselves to secrecy. Their experiences had been more monkey business than risky business, and none seemed the least bit romantic. But at least they'd all felt safe at the time. Katie thought of Ava and the football player who had simply taken what he wanted. As she took another sip of beer, it hit her: the evening's events could mean a bonus of $50,000. What had just happened?

An hour before she normally left for class, Katie delivered a cup of coffee to Ava, who she found awake in the bedroom and staring out the window. Sun shone through its old, warped glass and spread a prism of light across the bedspread. Ava turned to Katie. "What happened last night?"

"What do you remember?"

"You came up to visit Drew and Desmond. I think you left to go study. Then I remember they got into an argument. Desmond left. I think he was unhappy about something."

"Do you remember anything else? What did you do after Desmond left?"

"I'm not sure. I remember feeling light-headed. Drew offered to help me into my bedroom. That's the last thing I remember until I woke up at the hospital. You sat with me, and there was a nurse. What happened to me?"

Katie hesitated. "I think Drew had sex with you last night. I don't think you were conscious."

"That's what I thought. During the exam at the hospital, the nurse asked me if I'd had sex. I told her I didn't remember. I don't feel like I'm hurt or anything."

"I don't think he assaulted you forcefully. He didn't need to. I think you were intoxicated and didn't put up a fight. But that's still considered sexual assault, because you can't give consent if you're incapacitated by alcohol, drugs, or even lack of sleep."

Katie recounted her memory of the events after she'd left Ava's apartment and returned to her own to study. "Has he tried to have sex with you since you broke up with him?"

"He joked a few times about being friends with benefits, but I told him it was out of the question." Ava went silent for a moment. "Why would he do that to me?"

"Because he feels entitled to your body. Look, guys like that aren't concerned about what you want. For them, it's all about getting what they want, and exercising power. I think you need to report him. I bet he's done this to others, and he'll do it again."

"If I report him, I'll ruin his football career."

"Ava, if he's not guilty, then he won't have anything to worry about. But if he is, and he's done this before, then you have a chance to get him off this campus and make it a safer place for others."

"Do I have to go to the police?"

"No, you don't. But you should file a complaint with the university's Student Conduct Committee. Let them investigate. If you want, you can go to the police later."

"Oh, Katie, Drew will hate me. I know he'll try to make my life hell. He'll tell his friends about what happened. He'll probably even tell them that I'm lying about everything and that it's my fault."

"Ava, I was there. I have no doubt what happened. You have an opportunity to help put a stop to this. I promise to help you every step of the way."

"Let me think about it. Can I stay here again tonight?"

"Of course."

CHAPTER 12

We Knew This Could Happen

It was Brian's first visit to the dean's office since they'd finalized plans for the foundation. He sat in his usual large leather chair, stretched his stiff neck, and detected a headache coming on. "Good morning, Peter."

"Brian. Do we have a problem?" The words hung in the air for a minute while the dean finished some notes and finally put down his pen. "What's happened?"

"We suspect that a female student was assaulted in an off-campus residence last week. The student claims she never gave her consent to have sexual intercourse."

"And the guy probably claims she did, right?"

"We don't know yet," Brian said. "He hasn't been contacted. They had a prior relationship, which she ended several months earlier. I understand they still get together as friends."

"What's the problem? Isn't the goal of our foundation to uncover incidents like these and expunge these rapists from our campus? Pressure from Washington is worse than ever. The DOE has requested two years' documentation of all sexual-assault cases. Sounds like the perfect example of why we created the program."

"Maybe."

Peter gave Brian a quizzical look. "Are any of your—what do you call them—campus ambassadors involved?"

"Yes. I have a first-year grad student in philosophy who's under contract. She was with the woman the night of the assault and took her to the hospital for an exam afterward. The grad student filed a written report in my office the following day. She's encouraged the student to file a complaint with the university's Title IX office. The student's reluctant, though, because she doesn't want to ruin the guy's career."

"Any evidence?"

"The woman underwent a forensic sexual-assault exam at the hospital. The police won't receive the results from the state crime lab for a few weeks, though."

"Remind me, you'll give your ambassador a fifty-thousand-dollar grant if the respondent is disciplined, correct?"

"Correct."

"What did you mean about ruining the guy's career?"

This was the point in the conversation Brian dreaded. "That's the problem. He's a football player. And not just any player: he's the starting quarterback."

"What! Are you kidding me? He's the best hope our football program's had for over a decade."

"I know. I was expecting some entitled frat kid who deserved to get smacked. And we're undefeated after his first two starts this season."

"The coach will scream bloody murder to the president. He'll want this to go away."

"But isn't that the history with these sexual-assault cases? I thought our goal was to ensure that they don't just go away."

"It is—just not with this case."

Both men sat in silence. Peter stared through his massive office window in the direction of the giant sandstone slabs known as the Flatirons. "Any chance we can make sure the alleged victim files a Title IX complaint?"

"I don't know. She seems to have developed a friendship with the grad student, who's naturally motivated by the fifty-thousand-dollar bonus should the quarterback be disciplined."

"We talked about this possibility when we created the program: What do we do if we catch someone we don't want?" He paused. "What else? What's the name of the ambassador?"

"Katie Russell. She thinks the student was either drunk or drugged. If true, a defense of informed consent goes out the window. They took blood and urine samples. We should be prepared if they come back positive. And one more thing: another football player might have been involved."

"Great. This keeps getting better. I'll need to inform the president this afternoon. He'll come unglued. From what you've told me, I'll likely recommend that we get out in front of this one and sacrifice a player. With luck, maybe we can delay the findings until after the season's over. We can blunt the coach's concerns and still rack up a disciplinary finding of responsibility. You know what to do. Keep me posted on the lab results. I need to get back to work."

Brian nodded and left the room.

JUSTIN CARTER SAT IN THE STUDY OF HIS Seattle apartment and switched on his laptop. He located a folder titled "Katie" on his desktop and double-clicked it. It was filled with a directory of folders and file names. The folders were named with titles concatenated from descriptive words of their contents and the date they'd been created. He then created a new folder and named it "Photos," followed by the current date. Using the proper username and password—information he'd stolen from Katie, who hadn't thought to change them—he connected to Katie's cloud-storage account. He searched around for any new photos she'd taken and downloaded them to the new folder.

Next, he copied text messages from his phone, emailed them to his own account, and copied them into a new document titled "Messages" plus that day's date. He now received copies of any text messages that Katie sent because, when she hadn't been looking, he'd set that option on her phone. She hadn't yet noticed, so he still received all the messages she sent.

His last step was to log on to her email account and check for new ones. He only found a few that were interesting and copied those, too. Tracking Katie's communications had become a comforting habit, one he'd indulged in almost every day since starting his new job.

He got up from the desk and went to the kitchen, where he poured himself a glass of hard cider. Katie's drink. The one-bedroom apartment sat on the top floor of a large urban complex. It needed some decorating. Few photos adorned the walls, and most of Justin's books remained in boxes. He worked at least ten hours each weekday, five on Saturdays, and he hadn't yet met many friends. He socialized a bit with some of his coworkers, but he found most of them to be boring. He really missed

Katie and couldn't imagine being with anyone else. Why had he simply walked away from her? He'd been a fool, that's why. He'd assumed he'd start his career, make a lot of money, and have fun along the way. He hadn't anticipated that full-time software development would be mostly soulless and mind-numbing work. Sure, he was good at it, and he'd received strong praise for the clothing-based social app he'd developed, but now it was on to another project, one that was equally as invasive of people's privacy.

After a daily routine of collecting Katie's files, Justin patiently enjoyed opening an assortment of new photos. She'd taken many of them on the Boulder campus. Some included framed photos in the background that he recognized from her apartment in Claremont. One photo was a selfie of Katie standing with a tall blonde girl, both drinking glasses of wine. She'd sent photos from a recent mountain hike to her mom. It all looked beautiful. It was as if the photos had been copied from a freshmen-recruiting brochure for the university.

It was clear from her comments in some of her emails, however, that things weren't going as perfectly as the glowing texts and photos she'd sent to her friends and family would suggest. He'd read of the contract she'd signed with something called the NSAF. He'd also read the report she'd written about a suspected nonconsensual sexual assault of a student. Justin wondered if it might be the blonde girl holding the glass of wine he'd seen in the selfie. He looked forward to his daily research. What had started out as a technical challenge—almost a game, really—took on a more menacing tone after Justin had called Katie to ask for a second chance and she'd turned him down cold. That was the moment Justin began to think of revenge. He added a note to his journal. *She wasn't loyal or faithful. I made a mistake in thinking she'd wait for me if I moved. She refused to give me a second chance, ever. I deserved a second chance.*

He closed the files and ended, as he always did, by looking at the first photo he'd ever collected from her phone, early on in their relationship. It was of an athletic man, about his age, lying on his back on what appeared to be, from the rather utilitarian and plain-looking headboard and nightstand, a bed in a hotel room. He'd always wondered why Katie had taken and kept that photo. The man was naked, except for a swimsuit pulled down around his legs. He'd never asked Katie about it, insecure in the knowledge that she might have slept with him and reluctant to let on about his spying. He knew it was only a matter of time before he would find what he needed: something that he could use to get her attention. After closing all the files, he switched off the computer and went to make dinner.

CHAPTER 13
Ava Decides

Ava spent one more night in Katie's apartment after the assault. They went to a small Indian restaurant not much larger than either of their apartments.

"Ava, can we talk about Drew? Have you given any thought to reporting the assault to the Title IX office?"

Ava finished a bite of tikka masala. "I don't think I can."

"Why not?"

"It could end his football career. He'd know I reported it. Look, it's not like I'm hurt or anything. I haven't found a single bruise."

"But he raped you. I know it seems like a huge step, but it's one I think you need to take. You shouldn't let him get away with what he did. I know you loved him, maybe you still do, but I think he's guilty and I wouldn't be surprised if he's done this to others."

Katie took a sip of tea. The conversation was awkward. Sure, she'd benefit financially if Ava filed a complaint against Drew and he was found responsible. She knew it was the right thing to do with or without the bonus. Brian had called earlier in the week and pressured Katie to convince Ava to file. He also hinted that if she didn't, it might be possible to initiate an administrative review of the incident without a formal complaint.

"I'm not going to file. I don't want to go through the trauma of an investigation. I don't ever want to see him again. I just want it to go away."

"How are you going to avoid seeing him again when he's still on campus? That's another reason to file. If they find him responsible, then he'll likely be expelled. Especially if this isn't the first complaint against him."

"I can't. Katie, please, I really don't want to discuss this."

Katie decided to stop pushing. They finished their meal and left the restaurant. The weather since entering the restaurant had switched from balmy to cold and cloudy. A strong breeze picked up from the north, and only the wind, and an occasional car, interrupted their silence during their walk home.

OVER THE NEXT COUPLE OF WEEKS, Katie followed her typical routine of work-ing on her paper, attending classes, and staffing the nonprofit kiosk in the student union. She'd completed her research paper's outline and had finished a draft of the introduction. She planned to include inter-views and published data in the section on her research methodology. Although she hadn't yet decided what position she'd take on the central question of whether California's Yes Means Yes bill was a good or bad law, with a third of the semester behind her, she was confident she'd fin-ish on time.

After her emotional encounter with Mark over drinks that remarkable Friday afternoon, Katie frequently found it hard to concentrate. She could study, but while walking, reading, or even going for a run, her thoughts frequently wandered to Mark. Had his touch affected her alone? Their interaction since then had remained professional, both in class and at his office to discuss the weekly lesson plans. She hadn't detected any differ-ence in him, yet her life felt completely changed somehow. She longed to see him outside the university, but since she was making adequate progress with her research, she had no legitimate excuse to see him. She resolved that for him, their good-bye on the deck had been an innocent parting.

She quickly cast aside her doubts a few days later when she received a LinkedIn message from him. He must have found her profile. He asked, *Katie, how about joining me for dinner sometime?*

She considered the question for a minute. Goose bumps made the hair on her arms stand up. She replied, *I'd enjoy that. When and where?*

How about this Friday night? My place.

What can I bring?

Nothing, unless there's something you'd like to drink. He provided his address and suggested seven o'clock.

When Friday night arrived, Katie ran a bit late after a stop at a liquor store to buy wine. A friendly steward recommended a New Zealand sauvignon blanc and red Rhône blend. She parked on the street in front of Mark's apartment and checked herself in the mirror. Her makeup looked OK, and her hair, cut that day, never looked better. In a decision that seemed shallow at the time, she'd worn a sweater that emphasized the shape of her breasts. She appreciated the fact that men were visually stimulated, but all she could think about was gaining an emotional connection with Mark. Still, she wanted to make a great impression. She turned off her music playlist and got out of the car. Her heart pounded and her face flushed as she walked up the steps to Mark's front door.

She saw that the older residence, like hers, was subdivided into multiple apartments. She rang the doorbell and had only waited a few seconds before hearing Mark's footsteps on the stairs inside. The door opened, and Mark greeted her dressed in jeans and a rust-colored crew-neck sweater. She smiled at a white streak of flour on his cheek. She hoped for a hug. She didn't get one.

Mark escorted Katie upstairs to an apartment that was more like a large room. "Welcome to graduate-school austere." Mark let out a big infectious laugh as he swept his arm around the tiny apartment. "Come on into the kitchen." They walked toward the other end of the room, where Katie surveyed a tiny area of linoleum flooring. A long counter housed a stainless-steel sink that was dated but clean. Two small upper cabinets with peeling paint provided dish storage. An old refrigerator hummed loudly. The adjacent dining area was demarcated by an end of the kitchen's linoleum and the beginning of worn hardwood flooring. That room opened into the living area, which also served as the bedroom. A Murphy bed was folded up and out of the way. Mark demonstrated a roll-out desk he used to study during the day. The whole room was spotless and neat.

"Nice place. Looks like I won't need to worry about getting lost in here," she said with a laugh. "I brought some wine."

"Oh, sorry." Mark relieved her of the brown paper bag. "I see you covered all the possibilities. One white and one red."

"I told you, I like to be prepared."

"I need to finish some chicken pancetta and put it in the oven. How about a glass?"

"Sounds great. I like your apartment." While Mark opened the bottle of white wine and filled their glasses, Katie took a dish towel from the counter and wiped the flour from Mark's cheek. "A man who cooks—how irresistible."

Katie took her glass and wandered over to a set of bookshelves that held several framed photos. One of Mark was adorable. He looked to be around six years old and wore a Western shirt with a marshal's badge pinned to it, a cowboy hat, and a toy six-shooter in a holster. Katie laughed. "You're so cute."

Mark looked up from his food preparation. "Oh, that. My family took me to the rodeo that year and entered me in a costume contest. I won. It was all downhill from there. After that, I entered the Mutton Bustin' event. They put us on sheep, and we rode out of the bull-riding chute. I hung on for dear life and lasted about five seconds before I fell off and got a mouthful of dirt. It was embarrassing."

Katie returned to the kitchen and watched Mark finish the chicken. "Should be ready in about thirty minutes," he said. "Let's sit." They settled on his old sofa. "It's your turn to tell me about how you ended up in philosophy."

"Well, I wasn't sitting in the saddle, that's for sure. I grew up in Southern California, not far from Disneyland. In fact, I worked there a couple of summers as Belle. I had the right hair color for it. I liked seeing the excited faces of the little girls when they met me. They were convinced I was the real character. They were all so precious.

"It wasn't until high school that I began to grow interested in political philosophy. My dad's a city attorney, and he often discussed his cases over dinner. I liked to ask him about the process he used in deciding whether to bring a case. He'd consider two aspects: the relevancy of the alleged crime on a scale of normative behavior—yes, I knew what that term meant by the time I was eight—and the probability of gaining a conviction. He didn't like to lose, and he worked for a mayor who always saw things through the lens of political gain."

Mark took a sip of wine. "You ever consider a career in law?"

"I have, but I worry about the bureaucracy involved. It was a part of the job that always frustrated Dad. When I met with Professor Wilson, she asked me the same question. I think about it. Even when studying philosophy, I've been mostly interested in justice and law."

"You'd make a good attorney. The discussions we've had about your research paper suggest you have a very logical mind."

"Thanks."

Neither of them spoke for a moment. Katie used the pause to survey the room and sip her wine. His place was comfortable, and Mark had added a few obvious touches to give it some personality, like the photos and a roughly framed piece of Western art. She even noticed a pair of rusted spurs hanging from a hook on the wall.

Mark broke the silence. "Katie, there's something I've wanted to discuss with you. Something that's been troubling me." He reached over and took her hand.

Katie slid closer. "What is it?"

"Us."

Katie hadn't expected that. "Us?"

"Katie, I like you."

Katie gently squeezed Mark's hand. "That's a problem?"

"I'm afraid so. I'd like to spend time together, but the university has policies about this kind of thing."

"Mark, I—"

"Let me explain. The university discourages what it calls amorous relationships between faculty and students. Though not strictly prohibited, the university views them as unethical. If the faculty member is in a position of direct responsibility, then he or she is required to report the relationship to a supervisor. In our case, if we engage in an amorous relationship, then I'd need to report it to Professor Hatfield. She'd have to reassign me. I'd worry it might affect your grade or relationship with the professor."

"I know the university's worried about sexual assaults on campus. But we're both adults. Why should we be a concern of theirs?" Katie let go of his hand.

"A faculty member's judgment might be impaired by the relationship. Or other students might feel the student in the relationship has an unfair advantage over themselves." Mark got up and put on some light jazz. Katie recognized Charlie Parker and George Benson.

When Mark returned to the sofa, Katie put down her wineglass and retook his hand. "Mark, I think about you often. I was elated that you invited me to dinner. I'd hate to see a university policy stop us from exploring what we might have. Don't you want to hang out with me?"

"Katie, I'm worried about how this could affect both of us. You have a bright future. I don't want to tarnish it."

Katie slid along the sofa until she sat next to Mark, then leaned in. "I'm not going to tell anyone." She stared into his eyes and slightly parted her lips. Just as she hoped, Mark moved his head toward hers. Their lips touched. His were amazingly soft.

Mark put his hand up behind Katie's neck and drew her forward. He kissed her gently. His other arm slid down and around her back. He pulled her close and broke off the kiss. His lips moved to her neck. Then her ear. And back to her lips.

Katie's emotions surged. Just like that sunny afternoon on the deck, but stronger. Her heart pounded as she put her arms around Mark and kissed him back. Her feelings were as foreign as they were exciting. She thought to move her hand to Mark's chest. She wanted to feel him, to build an image of his body. She held off, aware his hands hadn't moved from her back or neck.

A shrill ringing sound came from the kitchen. Mark abruptly broke off the embrace and went to silence the alarm. Katie heard the oven door open and a baking dish land on the stovetop. Mark reappeared and took both of Katie's hands and helped her stand. As she rose, he used his grip to pull her hands back toward him and wrapped her arms around his back. He held her gaze as he wrapped his arms around her body and pulled her close. She rested her cheek against his chest. Mark pulled his head back and leaned down. Katie gave her lips to his and responded to every move with increased intensity. His erotic touches propelled her into a dream.

Mark pulled back. "Katie, this is exactly what I'm worried about. I find you irresistible, and I'm not sure I can hold back."

Katie smiled. "I feel the same." She paused for a moment. "If this is headed where I hope it is, I guess there's no need to rush. I'm a one-man kind of woman. I'm not going anywhere."

Mark grinned. "I think we should eat."

Katie smiled, leaned in, and gave Mark a light kiss on his cheek. "Let's go, Professor."

After dinner, Katie helped Mark wash and dry the dishes while they listened to more music. Then, after a hug and a quick kiss, she said good night and descended the interior stairway of Mark's upper-floor apartment. She was thrilled by his interest in her. He sure knew how to kiss. She'd never felt anything like it. But the amorous-relationship discussion nagged at her. She pushed those concerns aside and took joy in the knowledge that she wasn't alone with her desires.

Katie closed the entry door at the bottom of the stairway and stepped onto the porch. The scene before her was unexpected. Snow. Heavy snow. And it was only October. A blanket about an inch thick had already accumulated on the sidewalks and streets. Katie had never seen a real snowstorm before. She stopped and looked skyward. Snowflakes the size of quarters gently floated down. She closed her eyes and opened her mouth. Delicate geometric forms landed and tingled her tongue as they melted. She opened her eyes and watched the sky. A nearby streetlight illuminated a steady downward torrent of white streaks. Her heart felt as light as the snow. In the short moments since leaving the door, before Katie turned and smiled up at Mark's window, her shoulders had already become covered in a layer of white. She walked to the street near her car and kicked powdery snow into the air. She hardly remembered the cautious mile-long drive back to her apartment. It was late, and no one was about. She'd never felt so happy and optimistic. Ever.

Back inside her apartment, Katie peeled off her wet coat and boots and poured herself a glass of water. She was happy the next day was Saturday and she had nothing scheduled. She powered on her laptop and changed into pajamas. She looked in the mirror and studied her body as she changed. She thought about Mark's comment that he found her irresistible and smiled.

Back at her desk and in her pajamas, she skimmed through her email and found nothing too important—mostly junk and a few Facebook notifications. She read a short note from her mom, who wanted to know if she planned to come home over Christmas; she pointed out that her brother, Michael, planned to be there. Katie hadn't seen him since Christmas break a year earlier, when he'd come home during his freshman year of college in Michigan. They all wanted to see her, she wrote. Katie made a mental note to plan the trip. She was just about done with email when a subject line caught her eye: *Your presence is required.* The message had been sent by the dean of students. Its content was alarming.

Dear Ms. Russell,

Your presence is required as part of an Office of Student Conduct informal disciplinary hearing, scheduled for Thursday, October 22nd at 2:00 p.m. The purpose of this hearing is to investigate an alleged policy violation, which the university believes represents a serious threat to the security of our campus community.

On, or about, the evening of September 10th, you telephoned the Boulder Police Department to report a suspected sexual assault of a neighbor near your off-campus residence. The neighbor has yet to file a complaint with the university, or file criminal charges with the police. However, due to the serious nature of the alleged incident, the university is launching its own investigation of whether the incident represents a possible policy violation.

You are required to attend the investigative hearing and answer questions from the Hearing Officer about your knowledge of the incident. Your comments will be kept confidential, but should the university elect to hold a formal hearing, you will be required to present your testimony and answer questions in front of the Hearing Board, the respondent, and his representative, should he choose to have one present.

Respectfully,
Dean of Students

Katie stood and walked over to her window. Snow continued to stream down. The seriousness of the email ruined the magic of the beautiful winter landscape. It had never occurred to her that she'd have to testify. She'd incorrectly assumed that her duties had ended with her written report. Brian Taylor was obviously responsible. If only Ava had been willing to report the assault. The email suggested that Drew could be disciplined without any involvement by Ava. Realistically, Katie should have realized she'd be required to testify either way.

She returned to the kitchen, emptied her glass of water into the sink, and then filled it with wine from a bottle in the refrigerator. With a half-full tumbler in hand, she grabbed a throw from the sofa and curled up on the floor next to the living-room window. She watched snow continue to fall and considered her options. She didn't have many. She'd just have to meet with the hearing officer and tell him what she knew. She took solace in knowing Drew deserved whatever punishment he might get, but she was displeased by her involvement. Her mind turned to the $50,000. As much as she needed the money, the whole situation began to feel unsavory.

She put her immediate problem aside and turned her thoughts back to Mark. The evening had been amazing. She'd do anything to protect and nurture the possibility of being with him. Mark's sincerity, in discussing the university's rules on amorous relationships, had laid bare her own failure to disclose the sexual-assault incident. Her next step was obvious—be honest with him and tell him about Ava and Drew. The falling white snowflakes appeared distorted when viewed through her glass of wine. How much should she tell Mark about the arrangement with Brian Taylor? She was bound by the nondisclosure agreement she'd signed with the nonprofit, but her instinct was to tell him everything.

Katie finished the wine and retrieved a pillow. Sleep came slowly as she lay on the floor and watched snow swirl past her window. A single tree branch, buffeted by the wind, gently tapped on a pane of glass. She savored the memory of Mark's soft lips on her own.

CHAPTER 14
Truth or Dare

Snow piled up throughout the night while Katie slept. She awoke cold and stiff on the hardwood floor under the window the next morning. She wrapped the throw she'd slept with around her shoulders and shuffled over to the baseboard heater and switched it on. She put on the teakettle and gazed outside. A flat expanse of white, awash in golden sunlight, covered the street in either direction. Melting snow dripped from the roof of the house with a rhythmic *plunk* where the drops landed on the balustrade of the deck.

Katie smiled as her mind slowly awoke to memories from the night before. She decided to text Mark, eager to set up a meeting and tell him about Ava and the hearing. She found her phone on the floor and turned it on. Each night she switched it off in what she considered to be a luxurious indulgence that allowed for undisturbed sleep. One day she'd have a job that required her to be available around the clock, but until then, she liked her sleep. As the phone came to life, she saw a message from Mark: *I hope you survived the drive home in the snow. Thanks for having dinner with me. I look forward to seeing you soon.*

Katie began to appreciate Mark's understated personality. He had feelings after all. She tapped a reply: *The drive home was wonderful. As was your dinner. Can we go for a walk later today?*

As Katie waited for a reply, the teakettle emitted its first steamy hiss and then a shrill whistle. She returned to the kitchen, made coffee, and toasted a bagel. Her phone chimed as she poured her first cup.

I'd enjoy a walk. Let's meet on campus. Front steps of the library. One?

Katie was thrilled by the opportunity to see him, though her enthusiasm was tempered by the discussion that would follow. She'd have just enough time to shower and get dressed.

Katie arrived first and waited on the steps at the west entrance to Norlin Library, a centerpiece of the campus's Tuscan-village style. Students wandered past her on their way inside. She felt momentarily guilty that she wouldn't be studying that afternoon. She read the words etched in sandstone above the library's massive columns: WHO KNOWS ONLY HIS OWN GENERATION REMAINS ALWAYS A CHILD. She smiled at the quote from the Roman philosopher Cicero.

"Been waiting long?"

"Just got here." Katie turned and gave Mark a quick hug. "Thanks for meeting me. Where would you like to go?"

"Let's head up to Chautauqua. It's a park up by the Flatiron rock formations in the foothills. Looks like you're dressed for it."

Katie wore hiking boots, gloves, and a hat. She'd never worn traditional cold-weather clothes in California; her mom had sent them to her as a gift. The vivid autumn sun was angled low in the horizon, and the air was cold. She put on her sunglasses to shade her eyes from the bright reflection of the sun off the pristine snow.

They walked together through campus and up Sixteenth Avenue, a street lined with various older homes. Some she could tell were tired-looking rentals. Others looked to have been restored to their stately Victorian past. Katie eyed some of the large Greek houses and wondered if Ava's or Drew's places were nearby. Walking on snow reminded Katie of walking with shoes on a beach. The snow, like sand, grabbed her feet and made each step harder. They slowly made their way down the snow-covered sidewalks and eventually arrived at the park.

Katie said, "This place is amazing."

"It was built by a group of Texas educators as a cultural and educational retreat in the late nineteenth century. Today, it's run as a city park and includes the original ninety-nine cottages, a lecture hall, a dining hall, and lodge. They've all been restored, and are now used for cultural and educational events."

After ascending the steps to the deck of the two-story, restored dining hall of the original retreat, Mark put his arm around Katie, and they faced the Flatiron formations. The majestic red-stone faces, set against the cobalt-blue sky and rising up from a field of fresh white snow, created a stunning scene. Katie took a photo to post later. After a few moments, she suggested they go inside and talk.

They hung up their coats on a rack by the door and found a quiet table in a corner. When a cheerful waiter arrived, Mark ordered a pot of tea and some baked goods. After the waiter left, Mark asked, "What's on your mind?"

Katie had thought about what to say since they'd agreed to meet. "Well, you were so candid with me over dinner last night, I felt it was my turn to share a concern I have with you."

"You mean my thoughts about amorous relationships?"

"Sort of."

"You don't want to have one?" Mark said with a smile.

"I think you know the answer to that. I want to talk about that, too, but first, there's something else I need to discuss."

The tea and a plate of assorted pastries arrived. Mark poured each of them a cup of Earl Grey and offered Katie a pastry. "I'm listening."

"When I got home last night, I read an email from the university. It was about something that happened to a neighbor several weeks ago."

Mark finished chewing on a bite of his scone. "What happened?"

Katie picked her words carefully. "I met a woman who lives in the apartment upstairs from mine. Her name's Ava. She's a senior. We had drinks a couple of times. She invited me up to meet her ex-boyfriend one night. They'd dated until she found out he was cheating on her. She told me that after she broke it off, for some reason she decided to remain friends with him. That was a mistake, in my book."

"You know what Albert Camus said."

"'Friendship often ends in love, but love in friendship—never.'"

"Impressive."

"My ex-boyfriend taught me that one. Philosophy and irony in one tidy package. Anyway, her ex-boyfriend brought a friend with him. They're both on the football team. We had a few beers together, then I left to go study. Frat jocks aren't my thing."

"Relieved to hear that." Mark took a sip of tea and never took his eyes off Katie. She started to feel the effects of his piercing gaze and glanced away. She feared she would lose her resolve.

"Several hours after I returned to my apartment, I heard yelling upstairs. Then a loud thud, like a piece of furniture being struck. Someone yelped in pain. I also heard Ava's front door slam shut, so I assumed the men had left. I decided to go back upstairs and make sure Ava was OK. When I got there, I discovered her ex-boyfriend standing in her bedroom with his pants off. Ava was on her bed, naked. It was pretty obvious what had been going on."

"What was the thud?"

"I wondered about that, too. I think while he was putting on his jeans, he must have tripped and hit his head on a dresser. I think I saw blood on it. I confronted him about what he was doing to Ava. After he put his pants on, he threatened me and took off." Katie paused to drink some tea. She didn't feel like eating.

"Then what happened?"

"I called the police, and they instructed me to take Ava to the hospital, where she had a rape-kit exam. We've only spoken a few times since. She's a bit freaked out by the whole thing."

"Did she report the assault? Did the police investigate?"

"She decided not to talk to the police because she doesn't feel she was injured and doesn't want to get him into trouble. I think it's a bad idea to let him get away with it. I'm sure he's capable of assaulting someone else."

"I agree. Sounds like he's used to getting what he wants. To hell with the consequences. Tell me about the letter."

"It said I need to meet with a university hearing examiner for an interview. I think they're going to open an investigation without Ava's cooperation. I understand they can do that in cases where the university feels a safety concern puts the campus community at risk."

"It's all about Title IX and discrimination. The DOE Office for Civil Rights has found that sexual assault is a particularly egregious form of sexual harassment. If a university has reason to believe there's a safety concern of some kind on campus—one that discriminates against a class of people and prevents them from getting a gender-neutral and equal education—then they're required by law to eliminate it. Schools like CU are under increasing pressure to identify and discipline assailants. It's all good in my book."

"I wanted to let you know that I might be a witness if the university does decide to file a complaint against the assailant. I'm not sure what it all means, but it has me a bit worried about us."

"I don't see why. Taking Ava to the hospital was the right thing to do. You should cooperate with the university's investigation."

Katie decided to press ahead. "I don't think I have a choice. I'm sort of responsible for bringing the assault to the attention of the university."

"How?"

"When I first got to campus, I was desperate for money. Still am. I interviewed and got hired as a campus ambassador with a nonprofit foundation called the No Sexual Assault Foundation. I talk to students and raise their awareness of the risks of sexual assault on campus as well as the resources they have available if something happens. I work at a kiosk in the student union every other week. If I see a sexual assault, then I'm to report it to the executive director of the nonprofit. I'm the one who reported Ava's assault."

Mark pursed his lips and rested his arms on the table. "I don't see anything to worry about as far as we're concerned. Your efforts to help fight sexual assault on campus are commendable, and I don't see any connection to the issue of an amorous relationship. I'd say you should continue to support the university in any way you can."

Katie was relieved by Mark's understanding. She leaned back in her chair and took another sip of tea. Her body began to relax. She was sure the tenseness in her face had been obvious to Mark. She so wanted to tell him the rest, about the bonus. It would help to unburden her of the nagging feeling that she was somehow compromising her ethics for money. Though torn, she decided not to disclose the bonus payment. The language of the nondisclosure agreement restricted that aspect of her employment. Katie understood why Brian wanted to keep those details private—justifying a large payout from a public university, even if the benefits were obvious and the payout was done through a nonprofit, would be a sensational story the press would surely love to exploit.

"Thanks for telling me," he said. "Didn't you say you also wanted to talk about my comments?" Mark took a sip from his cup.

Katie relaxed, relieved to get the discussion about the investigation out of the way. She couldn't get over his eyes. Her face finally became softer. "I've been thinking about your concern about amorous relationships."

"And?"

"You're right to be cautious. Although I want to spend more time with you and explore what I think we might have together, I understand how much you've invested in your academic career. I can put things on hold if you can. I confess I've had a few fantasies, however."

Mark reached across the white tablecloth and took Katie's hand. "I've had some fantasies of my own. I noticed you the first day of class and wondered if we'd meet. I'm glad you came to my office. It would have been unprofessional of me to seek you out. We're worth the wait."

Katie didn't speak. She put her other hand around Mark's.

Mark leaned in. "Let's plan another dinner at my place after you finish your paper. How about the day of your oral presentation? Once I've graded your paper and the presentation, my supervision will be complete. I can't think of a better way to celebrate."

"Promise?" Katie leaned over the table and kissed him.

CHAPTER 15
Tell Me What You Know

Katie found it easier to concentrate after her walk with Mark to Chautauqua Park. Her life alternated between classes, the library, and occasionally the athletic center, where she went to swim when it was too cold outside to run. Every other weekend she did her stints at the kiosk in the student union. She continued her weekly meetings with Mark to review course materials and lesson plans for the following semester. They stuck to their plan of keeping their relationship focused on academics until after she presented her paper. Katie wondered about the term "amorous relationship." How was it defined? Did it require sex? She made a mental note to look it up in the university's code of conduct.

Katie occasionally met Ava for drinks, either in Ava's apartment or her own. They rarely spoke of Drew. Katie gently tested Ava's reluctance to go to the police. Ava remained firm and admitted she hadn't spoken with Drew since the incident. Katie was glad she'd kept him at a distance.

The day of the interview, Katie made sure to be on time. Punctuality was a courtesy to others, she felt; she was easily irritated by those who didn't reciprocate. She wore jeans and a cardigan over a long-sleeve blouse. After a short wait in the administration building's lobby, she was invited into the office of senior conduct coordinator Julie Downs.

"Katie, sorry for the delay. Please sit down. I was briefing Detective Scott here," she said, pointing to an older man seated in the chair opposite Katie's. "I was providing him with some background on the case."

"Hello, Katie. Please call me Alex." They shook hands. "Blame me for the delay; I was late getting here this morning." The detective had neatly trimmed gray hair and wore a rather rumpled wool suit set off with a white shirt and narrow black tie. He could have been an older version of her father.

"I'm confused," Katie said. "Why is a detective here?"

Julie nodded toward the detective. "Detective Scott recently retired from Boulder PD, who still employ his skills as a consultant. I've asked him to conduct the interviews for the informal hearing; if we think the facts justify a formal hearing, then I'll ask him to facilitate that process as well. Because we think this incident might involve criminal activity, Detective Scott is perfectly suited to bridge the protocols between the Boulder PD and my Office of Student Conduct."

"I see." Katie began to suspect that, once again, she was in over her head.

Detective Scott jumped in. "Katie, if you don't mind, I'd like to go ahead and begin our discussion. Julie gave me an office where we can have a private conversation. I can't imagine this will take much longer than an hour. Shall we begin?"

"Sure, might as well."

Detective Scott stood, and Katie joined him. "Follow me."

Katie followed the detective down the hallway to his small office. While not exactly an interrogation room, she was a bit nervous to find that it lacked windows.

"I think this once might have been a broom closet." Detective Scott let out a deep chortle that prompted Katie to laugh, too. It helped to defuse some of the tension.

Detective Scott seemed like a warm man, and Katie immediately trusted him. She looked down at the small table and saw a microphone connected to a phone, a stack of manila folders, and a legal pad.

"Please take a seat." He pulled out a chair for Katie and took the seat at the opposite end of the table. He flipped open the legal pad and pulled out one of the manila folders. He leaned slightly forward and placed both hands on the table. "Let me explain the procedure, then I'd like you to tell me what you know."

"Sure." Katie felt calm. She'd gone over the facts so many times that she was sure the discussion would be easy.

Detective Scott held up several pages of paper. "Here's a description of the events of September tenth, as transcribed from an anonymous report. As was explained in the letter you received, the university can, at its discretion, investigate any suspected cases of student-conduct violations if it believes those violations represent a legitimate concern for the safety of the campus community. In the case of alleged sexual assault, the university almost always launches an investigation, even if a victim declines to come forward—and especially if the assault is egregious. That's why we're here today."

"I understand. What would you like to know?"

Detective Scott switched on the phone's recording app and put on stylish tortoise-shell reading glasses. "Can you tell me, to the best of your recollection, what happened the night of September tenth in the apartment of Ava Greene?"

Katie recited the facts from memory.

Detective Scott interrupted her at one point. "OK, hold on. You say there was someone there with Drew named Desmond?"

"Yes. He claimed to be a football player; he was on the team with Drew. From his size and build, I didn't doubt it."

"Do you know his last name?"

"No."

"Do you remember what position he played?"

"Returning punts, or something like that."

Detective Scott flipped through his stack of folders and retrieved one labeled "Football Roster" that held a few photos. On the next page, he circled one of the photos and closed the folder. "If this were a criminal investigation—which is still a possibility in my view—then the police would ask you to identify him from a lineup."

"I see." The thought of attending a lineup at the police station began to erode Katie's comfort with the interview.

"I find it interesting that the anonymous report didn't mention another football player, only Drew. I'm curious, do you have any idea who submitted this report?"

Katie hadn't been prepared for that question. She found it odd that Desmond wasn't mentioned, since she'd included him in the document she'd prepared for Brian Taylor; she suspected that Brian was the source of the anonymous report to the university. "No, I don't." Katie started to feel anxious. She remembered back to a psychology class she'd once taken in which the professor had explained that anxiety arose when a person's actions didn't conform to his or her values: like two circles in a Venn diagram, with little overlap.

"That's odd. Go on." Detective Scott pulled aimlessly on his ear.

Katie recounted her suspicion that Ava had been drugged and summarized the conversation she'd had with her before she'd returned to her apartment to study. "I was concerned that everyone appeared to be getting more and more drunk, and I wondered whether Ava felt safe in that situation. She said she did."

Detective Scott stopped her again when she told him of the commotion she'd heard upstairs. "So you believed an argument had occurred between Drew and Desmond?"

"That's what it sounded like to me. Loud voices—although I couldn't tell what they said—followed by the sound of Ava's front door opening and banging shut and then footsteps crossing the porch."

Detective Scott continued to take notes. "Go on."

Katie went on with her description of the events; when she got to the part about finding the condom packaging, Detective Scott stopped her again. "Do you know where the packaging is?"

"Yes, I still have it at home. I kept it just in case."

"Good. Can you bring it to me sometime? Enclose it in a plastic bag."

"Sure."

"Do you know why Ava never called the police? It's unfortunate the apartment wasn't investigated as a crime scene. If there was blood, as you suspect, then it would have been important evidence."

"I don't think it would've mattered."

"Why do you think that?"

"Because after I brought Ava home from the hospital, I decided that she should sleep in my apartment. When I went upstairs to get her pajamas, I noticed that someone had come in and cleaned the place up. The sheets were in the washing machine and appeared to be clean. The glasses were clean in the dishwasher. And someone had wiped the blood from the dresser. I also smelled bleach."

"Have you mentioned this to anyone before?"

"No one's asked."

"So why didn't Ava report it to the police?"

"She wanted a few days to think about it, then decided against it."

"Tell me about the forensic sexual exam in the hospital, please."

Katie described as many details as she could.

"Katie, did the nurse say anything to you about gaining Ava's consent to have the exam done?"

"Yes, she explained that Ava needed to sign a consent form before she could start. If she refused, then the evidence couldn't be turned over to the police. Ava did sign a form, I'm pretty sure."

"Good, that's the correct protocol. But didn't you tell me that you suspected Ava might have been drugged?"

"Well, I sure thought so."

"Why?"

"After I arrived in her apartment that night, I drank a beer. The guys were drinking beers, too. I noticed that Ava was drinking a glass of wine, and the bottle on the table was more than halfway full. When I went into the kitchen later, though, I didn't see any other empty bottles, so I assumed that all Ava had had to drink was a glass or so from the bottle on the table. From my experience, people don't get that drunk from half a bottle of wine."

"Anything else?"

"Ava did say something odd once."

"What's that?"

"Well, when I first met her, we were drinking in her apartment. I'd brought along a bottle of wine. I was probably on my second glass when I noticed that she'd barely touched her first. I asked her if she didn't like the wine, and she said she didn't want to lose control, or something like that. I just found it a little odd."

Detective Scott scribbled more notes. "OK, so then you said you took Ava back to your place after the visit to the hospital?"

"Right."

Detective Scott reviewed his notes and the report before turning off the recording. "OK, I think we're about done here. I do have one last question, though. You said you've spoken with Ava only a few times since then. Have you discussed the events of that night with her?"

"Yes, I asked her if she was going to report it. She said she'd decided not to. I told her I thought she should, because I think Drew's a bad guy. I told her she needs to help prevent what happened to her from happening to some other girl."

"And she doesn't see it that way."

"No. I suspect in some way she still loves Drew, even after the way he's treated her. It's clear she doesn't want to ruin his football career."

"Do you think Ms. Greene feared Drew?"

Katie paused to think about that one. She tapped her fingers on the table. "Maybe. Based on a few of the conversations I've had with Ava, I think Drew needed to be in charge. But if she feared him, she never said so."

Detective Scott finished some additional notes and then took off his reading glasses. "Thank you, Katie. You've been very helpful. I'll be in touch. The office will prepare a written transcript of our discussion. Then you can come in and sign it. Do you have any questions for me?"

"Do you expect a formal hearing?"

"It's up to the Office of Student Conduct. But from what I've learned so far, yes, I'll likely recommend it. And if your friend Ava were to file a Title IX complaint, then I'd encourage her to talk to the police as well. The police might choose to investigate even if Ava chooses not to cooperate, but it's unlikely."

"Thank you, Detective Scott. May I go now?"

"Yes."

Detective Scott put his reading glasses back on and returned his attention to his notes and folders. Katie stood and left the room.

AS SHE WALKED BACK ACROSS CAMPUS toward her apartment, she called Brian Taylor, who answered in a few rings. "I just finished the interview," she said.

"How did it go?"

"Fine. I'll need to return to sign a statement at some point."

"Did you get any indication about whether they'll hold a formal hearing or not?"

"I guess it's up to the Office of Student Conduct. But the detective I spoke with seemed to think so."

"A detective?"

"Yes, a retired police detective interviewed me."

"Sounds like they're taking it seriously. Good."

"Mr. Taylor, when will I get paid? I really need the money."

"When the case is resolved and Drew is sanctioned. The investigation typically happens within sixty days, and the final report gets issued thirty days later. Then it's up to the standing committee and conduct officer to determine and levy sanctions. I'm just guessing, but I think this could all be wrapped up by the end of the semester—January at the latest."

"I hope so."

"Thanks, Katie." Brian ended the call.

Katie returned to her apartment an hour before her next class. She flopped on her bed and stared out the window. It was a sunny day, and the temperature outside was about sixty. She'd never been in a place with such consistently blue skies. The trees had lost quite a few leaves in the snowstorm weeks earlier, but swaths of yellow and orange streaked through many of their branches. Katie viewed herself as a hopeful person, but the interview with Detective Scott had left her deflated. She knew it was from the conflict she felt over being a paid informant as well as the questionable morality of her actions. Then there was Mark. She wished they could see each other whenever and wherever they liked. She knew taking caution was appropriate, but she found it hard to wait. She resolved to stay focused on her studies, get the paper done, and make it to the end of the semester. And she still needed to make plans to see her family over Christmas.

"Peter, it's Brian."

"What's going on with the quarterback case?"

"That's why I called. I spoke with Katie, my campus ambassador. She gave her statement this week in the Drew Evans case. They have a retired police detective running the informal investigation. I'm pretty sure they'll make it formal by the end of the week."

"That sounds promising. Is there another problem? You usually don't call me unless there is."

"It looks like they're going to bring Desmond Baker in for a statement. Katie told them about Desmond being there the night of the assault."

"I thought you said you didn't include that in the anonymous report you filed?"

"I didn't. Katie must have mentioned it."

"Look, my deal with the coach is that Drew will get investigated and any sanctions against him won't affect his player standing. But I told him we'd protect Desmond. He doesn't want to have both players involved. Any way to keep Desmond from being accused as an accomplice?"

"Yes, I have an idea."

"OK. Don't tell me, just do it."

"We have one more problem."

"Wonderful."

"I received some information from a friend in the Office of Student Conduct. When the victim went to the hospital the night of the assault for a forensic exam, she couldn't legally sign the consent form they require. The nurse on duty had to sign a statement that said that, in her opinion, the forensic exam would be in the best interest of the patient. This happens whenever there's suspicion that the victim is in what they call a transitory condition—such as being drunk—and can't legally give informed consent."

"Sounds like all the proper procedures were followed."

"Well, yes, but the victim has now decided against signing the consent form because she doesn't want to press charges. The nurse's signed permission only allows the tests to be performed, not the results to be transferred to the police. The victim must sign a release later, after she's no longer intoxicated. Only then can her evidence be used in the university's investigation, or by the police."

"I wasn't aware of that. Then without any hard evidence, we only have Katie's testimony? That certainly makes it harder to establish a finding of responsibility. We really need the victim to change her mind."

"I'm working on it."

"Figure it out."

The line went dead.

CHAPTER 16
"We'll Roll Up a Mighty Score"

After a morning class, Katie stopped by the Office of Student Conduct and reviewed and signed a statement transcribed from her interview with Detective Scott. As she was leaving the office, she almost collided with the charming detective, his arms full of legal folders and a large cup of coffee. Katie held the door for him.

"Hello, Ms. Russell. Nice to see you again."

"You too. I just signed my statement."

"I've been meaning to call you. Come with me."

Detective Scott led Katie toward his so-called office. It was exactly as Katie remembered; even the microphone sat ready to record another conversation. The detective set his things on the table and offered her a chair.

"The student-conduct office has decided to proceed with a formal hearing. You'll be asked to testify about your transcript before a hearing examiner and to answer any questions. You OK with that?"

"Sure. I won't have to face Drew, will I?"

"Actually, you will. But he won't be able to ask you any questions or interact with you. Only hearing-panel members are permitted to address you. It should be pretty straightforward."

"Any idea when it'll be?"

"Two to three weeks from now. All the required documents are being prepared."

"All right. I'm really looking forward to getting this behind me."

"I'm sure you are. I hope you appreciate the fact that you're doing the right thing."

"Nice to hear. I have something for you." Katie opened her backpack and produced a baggie with the condom packaging inside. "You asked for this," she said with a grimace.

"Thanks. That was on my list for follow-up."

Katie left the office and headed home. She noticed a text message from Ava on her phone: *Hey, want to go to the football game this weekend?*

She'd watched televised football games with her dad and brother and was familiar with how the game was played. It occurred to her that since Drew would play, she might have to confront him there. But she knew it was unlikely to happen in such a large stadium. And the weather was forecast to be nice that weekend. She texted back: *Sure, sounds fun. Just stop by and get me when you want to leave.*

Katie finished the first full draft of her paper in the days before the game. She'd followed the *Chicago Manual of Style* as required. She thought it was shaping up nicely, but she struggled with her conclusion. It had been difficult for her to arrive at a definitive yes or no answer to the question of whether the California Yes Means Yes bill was a good or bad law. She supported some of its elements but also found parts of the statute problematic. In her first draft, she took a distinctly nuanced view of the issue.

She thought to ask Professor Wilson to review her work, or at least her final chapter. Asking someone who wasn't her advisor to do so was a big request, she knew, but the professor's comments had been fundamental to her analysis, so she thought it made sense to ask. She planned to ask Mark for his feedback as well. She so longed to see him. Later that day, she gave her conclusion one more edit and emailed it to both professors with a request to meet.

The kickoff for Saturday's football game was scheduled for 1:15 p.m.; Ava knocked on Katie's door two hours earlier. It was a perfect fall day for a walk to the stadium. The morning air had some nip to it, but the afternoon promised to be warmer. They arrived at the tailgate area and joined some of Ava's friends: ten other students, all dressed in hats and gloves, their frosty breath visible in the crisp air. She noticed a keg of beer and a pile of grilled sausages arrayed on a table. A couple of drunk-looking guys were throwing a football around. Katie poured her own beer out of typical caution.

She enjoyed talking to Ava and her friends—especially vivacious Stephanie, who had seemed to be always full of energy during their Red Rocks trip. Still, she wished Mark could join them. She found herself thinking about their age difference. Would it feel awkward for a twenty-three-year-old like her to be hanging out with an older assistant professor? She didn't think he was that much older than she was, but she wasn't sure.

She'd done the math once before. If he'd followed a traditional schedule, then he'd likely finished his undergraduate studies when he was twenty-two; if she added on another six years of graduate work, then with research and teaching for a couple of years, he'd now be around twenty-eight or twenty-nine. Their age difference likely wasn't large, but would it feel awkward if they were there together as a couple? She already felt much older than most of the other students and had concluded that their ages weren't a big deal. The real issue was the one Mark had raised: Would other students assume she received special treatment? She recalled a conversation she'd had during a night of study in the computer lab with a woman from one of her classes. They hadn't spoken before that night. Katie was shocked when the woman casually confided to her how she'd slept with their teaching assistant, expected a better grade in return, and was disappointed that she hadn't received one.

About thirty minutes before kickoff, the students walked toward the stadium and drained the last of their beers from their plastic cups. The student section—probably because of the team's recent success, she surmised—was almost full. They found seats together and prepared themselves to enjoy the game.

The starting lineup of the home team was announced, and the crowd erupted in loud cheers when player 12, quarterback Drew Evans, took the field. Ava looked at Katie and shrugged her shoulders. Katie didn't fully understand football, but she'd read the sports section of the student paper most days and knew that CU's football team was undefeated following its first six conference games. She'd read that this was unheard of in recent years; everyone credited the turnaround to the team's star quarterback. He was so good, the pundits said, that they expected him to be drafted in the first round of the NFL draft the following year. That day's game was expected to be an easy win against a team from Oregon that was currently at the bottom of the standings.

On their first possession, Drew threw several passes and got the team to the twelve-yard line. After they were stopped for no gain on the next play, Drew handed off to a large fullback, who took the ball and ran, untouched, into the end zone for a touchdown. CU scored once again in the first quarter. Drew looked cocky on the field as he high-fived teammates and patted many of them on their butts, a move that always struck Katie as odd. By halftime, CU led by a score of 21–3. Katie enjoyed the screaming fans and the athleticism of the players, and the marching band in the end zone and cheerleaders on the sidelines added to the fun.

At halftime, Katie and her friends left the stadium and walked to a student refreshment area protected under a large canvas awning. As she sipped from a beer and spoke with Ava, Katie caught an unexpected glimpse of Mark on the other side of the crowd, deep in conversation with another man. She wanted to wave but thought better of it. She surveyed the crowd of happy and boisterous students, no doubt fueled by beer, and felt a profound and exquisite rush of hope. Instinct drew Katie's eyes toward the foothills, where she witnessed a stunning sight: sandstone buildings standing erect with crowns of uniform red tiles were ablaze in the golden sun. Nestled against the Colorado foothills and accented by a deep-blue and cloudless sky, the campus looked like an impressionist painting created with thick strokes of oil. On that brilliant fall afternoon, Katie gave thanks for whatever portent had led her to Boulder.

Back inside the stadium, Katie took her seat and waited for the second half to begin. She idly swept her eyes over the full-capacity crowd and then down onto the field when the players began to re-emerge from the locker-room tunnel. She studied the CU team; her curiosity was piqued when she observed Drew veer away from his teammates and linger next to the tunnel's exit. Soon, the Oregon team charged out and headed to their side of the field. Katie noticed an Oregon player stop next to Drew. They faced each other and appeared to be having an earnest conversation. Suddenly, Drew got very animated, grabbed the shoulder pads of the other player, and butted his own helmet into his. It looked playful. Oddly, they stepped back from each other then and shook hands. Drew slapped the other player on the back and trotted toward the CU bench. That was about the time the referee called the teams back onto the field, sent them to opposing end zones, and blew his whistle. A kickoff went skyward, and the second half was under way.

Halfway into the third quarter, after CU held the Oregon team on a fourth and one, Oregon sent its punting unit onto the field. CU's return unit lined up on the opposite end. The stadium announcer said, "Waiting for the return is number 43, Desmond Baker." It was the first time Katie had noticed Desmond in the game. After receiving the snap, the opposing team's kicker sent the ball spiraling high into the air at a perfect angle. Katie watched the Oregon defenders race down the field toward Desmond. The ball's high trajectory gave them plenty of time to cover the distance. Desmond waved his hand high in the air in what Katie knew was a signal for a fair, and unimpeded, catch.

Desmond stood with his hands outstretched and his feet firmly planted at the twenty-yard line. His eyes were locked on to the approaching ball. The nearest defender thundered forward in total disregard of the rules, which should have given Desmond a fair opportunity to catch the ball. When it landed in Desmond's hands, the defender struck Desmond with such force that his massive body flew backward for five yards before it hit the ground. The football skipped wildly away into the end zone. The crowd roared in protest at the infraction, and the closest official immediately threw down his yellow flag. When the defender slowly rolled off Desmond and stood, Katie recognized him as the same player Drew had spoken with before the start of the second half. Desmond remained still.

Ava placed her hands over her mouth.

Katie leaned over and whispered to Ava, "I think that hit was intentional."

The team's medical staff hustled onto the field and tended to Desmond's still form. A long ten minutes passed before he finally showed some movement. A small motorized cart arrived, and the staff loaded Desmond onto a stretcher and lifted him onto the cart's flatbed. While an attendant drove the cart toward the stadium tunnel, Desmond waved weakly with one hand; the crowd applauded in relief and to offer their support. The referee ruled the hit a flagrant personal foul, penalized the opposing team fifteen yards, and ejected the infringing player from the game for unsportsmanlike conduct.

Ava turned to Katie a few moments later. "Why did you say that? Why would someone hit Desmond that hard?"

"Come on, Ava. Let's get out of here. We need to talk about what's going on."

Katie took Ava to the Bohemian Biergarten, the place where she'd met Paul for the nanny interview. After a fifteen-minute walk, they arrived inside the airy restaurant and sat across from each other at the end of a long wooden table. The noise level inside the bar was moderate but would quickly amplify once the game ended, she knew. Katie ordered a cider, and Ava got a glass of water.

Katie cast about for words. Could she convince Ava to change her mind about testifying? Their drinks arrived, and Katie took a sip of the sweet cider. She took a second, longer drink. "I want to talk about Drew."

"What about him?" Ava slowly ran her finger around the rim of her glass.

"The school's investigating him for sexual assault. I think you should testify."

Ava's full lips pinched to the left in a hint of skepticism. "How do you know that?"

"Because I spoke with the Title IX office. It's part of my job as campus ambassador. The university's proceeding with a formal investigation."

"You talked to them?"

"I had to."

"What! Why didn't you ask me first?"

"We talked about this. He assaulted you. I think he should be investigated and that you should talk to them, too."

"I told you before, he didn't hurt me."

"Would you have had sex with him that night if you hadn't been high? You said he'd pressed you for it other times when you were together."

"I always thought we could be friends—you know, without sex."

"I always thought that if more women reported assaults, then they wouldn't happen as often."

Ava's body recoiled at the affront. She pushed her chair back. "Why did you say that?" She began to stand.

Katie pushed her own chair back a few inches, and its legs screeched across the floor. Curious faces turned in their direction. "Ava, I'm sorry. Please don't leave."

Ava paused before reluctantly returning to her seat. Her eyes narrowed and her face tightened in anger. "Look, you saw how horrible the medical exam was that night in the hospital. It was like being violated all over again." Ava dragged both hands through her hair and looked around the bar. She fixed her gaze back on Katie. "You think I'm somehow responsible for assaults on other people?"

"I'm sorry. I understand why you'd be uneasy about this. My comment was insensitive. You did nothing wrong. I'm just frustrated that he might get away with what he did. Women complain that the system is tilted toward men and that the process on campus is cumbersome and fails to yield justice. Only about five percent of campus sexual assaults are reported. Did you know that? I now understand why that number is so ridiculously low after seeing what you went through."

Ava relaxed her posture a bit, and her face began to soften. Katie quietly slid her chair toward the table and noticed a glisten in her eyes. Tears wouldn't be far behind, she knew.

"How can the university proceed with an investigation without my involvement?"

"They can investigate on their own. They don't need you to file a formal complaint if they have reason to believe the campus community is at risk."

"Katie, I chose not to make a big deal out of what happened with Drew. It's my business. Who gave you the right to get involved? Now the university's investigating?" A tear ran down Ava's cheek.

Katie looked around to see if anyone was watching. "Ava, I can't imagine what you've been through. But what about Desmond?"

"Desmond?" Ava put a paper napkin to her cheek.

"I don't think it's a coincidence that Desmond was hurt. In my statement to the university, I mentioned that he was there that night. I think the investigator probably requested a meeting with him, too, to ask a few questions. It's possible that Drew learned of it and decided to send Desmond a message that he'd better not talk."

"Drew wouldn't do that."

"Are you kidding? With his career on the line? You bet he would."

Katie emptied her cider and set it on the table. She *had* been insensitive. Was she motivated to prove Drew's guilt from the outrage she felt over his selfish assault? Or was it because of her role as campus ambassador and from possibly getting a bonus? Probably both. What she couldn't deny was her growing awareness that men routinely took advantage of women and were rarely held to account for their actions. Sexual assaults must have happened at Claremont McKenna, but she'd never heard of any if so. Her short time in Boulder had shown her the scope of the problem. She watched Ava gaze aimlessly around the bar, which had now become much louder from the increasing crowds. Katie overheard a passerby say, "It was a great win." That suggested to her that CU and its celebrated quarterback remained undefeated.

Ava took frequent sips of water and stared at the table. Finally, she fixed her eyes on Katie's. "If what you say is true—that Drew intentionally had Desmond knocked out of the game—then I'll cooperate with the university's investigation. But I won't talk to the police. I know you're concerned about the assault, but I wish you would have discussed it with me first before filing a report."

"I'm sorry. I should have. And I know my comment was hurtful." Katie hoped she hadn't destroyed their friendship.

Ava looked away. "This is really hard. I just want it to go away." After a moment, something above and behind Katie's right shoulder diverted Ava's attention. Katie turned to look. Mark and the guy she'd seen at the game were standing at their table.

"Professor O'Connor, hello," Katie said with a smile.

"Hello, Ms. Russell. I'd like you to meet my brother Jim."

"Nice to meet you, Jim. This is my friend Ava." Katie studied Mark's face to see if he'd link Ava to the story of assault she'd told him. His eyes did indeed widen in recognition. It didn't surprise her that he'd made the connection.

"Nice to meet you, Ava."

"You guys care to join us?" Ava made the offer.

Katie was impressed by how quickly Ava's face switched from a look of sadness to one of radiance. Her eyes brightened, and her mouth formed a broad smile.

"No, but thanks anyway. Jim's visiting from home, and we need to discuss our dad and ranch business."

"Oh yes, the ranch in Durango," Katie was probably too quick to remember. She caught herself. "I think I remember you telling the class that you'd grown up on a ranch."

"Jim manages it with our dad. He plans to retire in the next few years and wants us to carry on the tradition."

"Sounds romantic. Horses, cattle, big skies, that kind of thing." Now Katie was smiling.

"That and a lot of hard work. Katie, I received your email about your paper. How about we meet next Tuesday, during office hours?"

"I'll be there. How did you like the game?" She asked the question to keep him from leaving.

"I like that we won, but the hit on Baker was a cheap shot."

"Do you know if he's OK?" Ava's face displayed sincere concern.

"He has a cracked rib and a minor concussion. It was a dangerous hit. But he'll be OK. See you next week, Katie." The brothers said good-bye and headed for the bar.

Ava's gaze followed them as they wove through tables and people on their way across the room. "Is that one of your professors? He's cute."

MARK AND JIM STRUGGLED TO FIND A SPACE WIDE enough at the bar. After a few minutes, they edged in and ordered a couple of beers. Jim glanced over his shoulder to the two women back at the table. "She's one of your students?"

"Who?" Mark said, showing no expression.

"Katie: the one who was smiling like she'd just won the lottery."

"She's a first-year grad student in the philosophy and law class I assist with. She's very inquisitive."

"She seems enthusiastic. You have any interest beyond teaching?"

"There's a policy against that, unfortunately. The faculty's discouraged from having romantic relationships with students."

"Rules are made to be broken, bro." Jim said it dryly and with a faint smile.

Mark wasn't quite ready to concede to his younger brother the increasingly romantic thoughts he harbored for Katie. "Not by me. I'm on tenure track, remember? I wouldn't want to screw it up."

"How long since you broke off your engagement? Maybe you were out on the range too long. Don't you miss female companionship?" Jim chuckled.

"Three years, and hell yes, I do." Not only did Mark miss companionship, but his thoughts about Katie had become more pronounced lately. The strongest were from their dinner in his apartment, of her body pressed against his, of the supple softness of her skin when he kissed her neck.

"I'm not sure I could remain so disinterested."

"It's her mind that's attractive. She's mature for her age, and she grasps complex concepts quickly. She's quite exceptional. The way I see it, if it's meant to be, then things'll work out." Mark tried not to smile.

"You were always the romantic one in the family. Me, I'm more the here-and-now type."

Mark shook his head. "You're the 'guy who always unbuckles his belt before his mind is engaged' type. Now tell me about Dad and the ranch."

CHAPTER 17

Bad Reviews Don't Hurt—They Just Propel Me Forward

Katie's mind churned as she walked toward Old Main for her meeting with Mark to review her paper's conclusion. She'd called Detective Scott after the football game to request a meeting with him to share the conversation she'd had with Ava at the Biergarten. She felt unsettled that she hadn't heard back from him.

Another student was inside Mark's office, so she took a seat on a chair in the hallway. A few minutes later, a female student left the office and went down the stairwell. Katie gathered her things and walked in. "Hi," she said.

Mark smiled and offered her a chair. "Have a seat." He returned to his desk and picked up a copy of what she assumed was the draft of her paper.

Katie wondered if their meeting felt as awkward to him as it did to her. She wished she could throw her arms around him, but such a move would be risky in the event a student or another professor walked by the open door. And concerns over sexual misconduct on campus meant that closing an office door while a female student was visiting a male professor would be out of the question. "What did you think of my paper?"

"You've done a nice job. It's well structured, and your problem statement and review of the literature are both solid. The summary of your research is fine, but I think you could do a better job of setting up your conclusion—which is where I'd like to focus my comments."

Katie took notes. "Go on."

"I sense you're reluctant to take a strong stand on the question at hand. Don't be afraid to say whether Yes Means Yes is a good or bad law. You undervalued your excellent analysis by trying to take both sides, and your conclusion suffered from it. You've made strong arguments—use them. I see where you were headed but sense you were reluctant to take a stand. Just remember: there isn't a right or wrong answer. Professor Hatfield wants to make sure that you've applied the concepts we've taught in this class so that you can reach a logical and supportable opinion."

"My goal was to finesse my conclusion so I wouldn't antagonize partisans on either side of the issue. I was probably too cautious, though."

"You've done a nice job. With some minor editing, you'll be proud of your work in no time."

"Thank you." Katie put away her professional demeanor along with her notebook. "I miss you."

"Katie, I'm having a hard time following my own recommendation. I'm frustrated that we can't socialize freely, even if we only have a short while longer to wait."

"Can't be soon enough." Katie smiled, put her notebook into her backpack, and left the office. She felt good about the paper and even better about Mark. On the way down the stairs, she checked her phone and noticed that Detective Scott had finally returned her call. She called him back.

After an exchange of greetings, Katie said, "I want to discuss the football game last weekend. I'm worried about Desmond Baker."

"So am I. After I met with you, I sent him a request to come in and give us a statement. He agreed, but now he's in the hospital recovering from the injury he received in the game. The nurse said she doesn't know when he'll be able to speak to people."

"I don't think the injury was accidental."

"Why not?"

"Because I saw Drew, at halftime, having a conversation with the player who was charged with the flagrant foul—the guy who hit Desmond."

"Can you hang on a minute? I want to check something."

"Sure." Katie kept walking.

She heard the detective put his phone down. In a couple of moments, he continued. "Katie, I think you're right. I'm searching the Internet for the backgrounds of both Drew and the player from the other team. Guess what? They both played football at the same high school in Irvine,

California. Wait a minute—and it looks like they attended the same middle school. I bet they're old friends who just ended up on different college teams. Drew probably called in a favor."

"Now what?"

"I'll follow up with Desmond. Maybe the hospital will let me interview him there. Katie, thanks for being so observant. It's helpful."

"One more thing. I was at the game with Ava, and she said that if it's true that Drew somehow arranged for Desmond's injury, then she'll testify against him to the hearing board."

"That'll be important to the proceedings, but something's bothering me: I wonder how Drew might have known that I planned to talk with Desmond?"

Katie suspected how—Brian Taylor—but she kept it to herself. "I don't know. Sorry I can't help you."

PROFESSOR WILSON'S COMMENTS THE FOLLOWING day mirrored Mark's. Katie assumed that Professor Wilson had issues with the law and considered it to be poorly written, though she never explicitly said so. Like Mark, she recommended that Katie be more direct. "Take a stand. Don't be afraid to say what you really think. Sure, you'll upset some people, but no one can deny the well-reasoned logic you've used to reach your conclusion. Go for it."

After discussing a few more areas of feedback, Katie thanked Professor Wilson and stood to leave. The professor again suggested that Katie consider a career in law. "I recognize what it takes to be a good attorney. You have it."

Katie was satisfied by the feedback on her interim work and planned to finish her paper over the coming weekend. Work ethic and high standards were normally sufficient motivators, but there was something else: the palpable prospect of exploring her passion for Mark. A growing confidence led her to believe a relationship with him was not only possible, but inevitable.

After a weekend of revision broken only by intermittent meals and rest, Katie finished her paper on Sunday evening. Professor Hatfield had reserved the final two weeks of class for each of the twelve students to present their papers: ten minutes on the summary followed by twenty minutes for questions from the others. Katie chose to present early and signed up for the third slot the following Friday.

KATIE ENTERED THE CLASSROOM FEELING confident yet anxious. She'd memorized and rehearsed, in front of a mirror, a summary of the conclusion section of her paper for several hours. Following the advice of her professors, she'd made it stronger and subsequently anticipated some hard questions from her fellow students during the question-and-answer session afterward. She took a chair among the other students and noticed Mark seated in a chair next to Professor Hatfield. He barely looked her way.

Professor Hatfield reviewed the guidelines. "Class, as with the two earlier presentations this week, Ms. Russell will have ten minutes to present her summary. You've all received a copy of her paper, and each of you was to have read it before today's class. After Ms. Russell presents her summary, you will have the opportunity to ask questions. Remember, part of your own grade is based on your review of these research papers, demonstrated through the questions you ask. Ms. Russell, you are our first presenter today. You may begin."

Professor Hatfield seemed impassive as Katie stood and walked to the podium. Katie was sure she'd never heard her laugh. She opened her notes and began to read.

Is California senate bill 967, also known as the Yes Means Yes law—a law that threatens college funding for any state school that fails to implement an informed-consent policy on campus—a good law or a bad law? My comments today summarize my conclusion to this question.

The phrase No Means No was used to suggest that the lack of struggle, or absence of a verbal 'no' in a sexual encounter, do not imply consent, and that saying no is unambiguously nonconsensual. An assault victim judged by this standard was often required to prove that she had denied consent. Yes Means Yes, on the other hand, by specifying that affirmative consent must be given and remain ongoing throughout a sexual activity, has shifted the burden of proof in campus sexual-assault cases from accusers to the accused.

In evaluating this law, I've used a framework based on three principles. First, does the law promote gender equity? Second, is the law consistent with the Constitution's promise of due process? Finally, is the law consistent with this class's teachings on political morality?

SB967 was passed by the state of California and signed by its governor in September 2014. The law requires that all California postsecondary schools (public and private) that receive state money for student financial aid adopt a standard of unambiguous consent among students who engage in sexual activity. In addition to requiring training and access to support groups for victims of sexual assault, the bill contains two significant, and controversial, policy provisions:

- The first is an affirmative-consent standard in the determination of whether both parties have given their consent to sexual activity. "Affirmative consent" refers to affirmative, conscious, and voluntary agreement to engage in sexual activity. It is the responsibility of each person involved in the sexual activity to ensure that he or she has the affirmative consent of the other (or others) to engage in the sexual activity. Lack of protest or resistance does not mean consent, nor does silence. Affirmative consent must be ongoing throughout a sexual activity and can be revoked at any time. The existence of a dating relationship between the persons involved, or the fact that they have engaged in past sexual relations, should never by itself be assumed to be an indicator of consent.
- The second is a policy that the standard used in determining whether the elements of the complaint against the accused have been demonstrated represents the preponderance of the evidence.

I evaluated these two substantive provisions of the law against the aforementioned principles by conducting selected interviews as well as reviewing case history and scholarly opinion of both the law and the issue of sexual assault on college campuses. This methodology was not perfect, however, since it suffered from a lack of data. Many cases of sexual assault on college campuses (and the administrative procedures that are used during their investigation and resolution) are privileged, and their access is restricted due to privacy concerns. Understandably, the details of most sexual-assault cases on college campuses remain unpublished, thus preventing an analysis based on hard data.

Based on my research, I have concluded that broadly speaking, SB967 appears to fail the test of whether the law meets the goal of providing gender equity. Prior to passage of this law, several published cases of campus sexual assault demonstrated that when alcohol is involved—which occurs in a majority of the cases that are brought before campus hearings—and if the complainant and the respondent are each intoxicated and agree to have consensual sex, then the male is almost always found guilty of nonconsensual sexual assault. As one attorney who had experience with college campuses and their compliance with Title IX said,

> a good policy cannot make it a violation simply for a male student to have sex with an intoxicated person if he is completely ignorant of that fact. Otherwise, men are simply being punished for having sex. This represents gender discrimination under Title IX, because their partners are having sex, too, but their partners are not being subject to the code of conduct for doing so.

Next, in a consideration of due process, I conclude that the law fails this test and thus can be considered flawed. By implementing a standard of proof based on the preponderance of evidence, which is the lowest evidentiary threshold, the law strives to parallel the standard used in civil cases without the associated due-process provisions of judicial law. Clearly, it makes sense to use the "beyond a reasonable doubt" standard when contemplating the loss of liberty and jail time that may result in criminal cases, but equating the impact of a finding of guilt in a sexual-assault case to guilt in a fraud case (or other quasi-criminal wrongdoing in a civil case) seems inappropriate. A young man who is found guilty of sexual assault will pay a high price over his lifetime; most people would consider such punishment to be overly severe. In civil cases, hearings are conducted by impartial and experienced judges, while in university settings, hearings are often performed by administrators who may be biased in representing their employers. While in civil cases, either party may ask for a jury to determine findings of guilt, this is not the case in university hearings. The rules of discovery allow each party to gather the necessary evidence from the other side when requested, but this also is not the case in university hearings. Finally, hearsay and other forms of unreliable evidence are typically excluded from civil proceedings, and all testimony is given under sworn oath. This is not the case in university hearings.

In considering the principal of whether the law is consistent with this class's teachings on political morality, the answer has been more difficult to come by. The class considered political morality to comprise justice, fairness, equality, freedom, and autonomy. The state of California's motivation in passing the law was provided, in part, by pressure from the US Department of Education's Office for Civil Rights' "Dear Colleague Letter," which the office sent to university administrators in 2011. This letter contained a policy statement on sexual violence that was directed to college and university administrators nationwide. It was this letter that prescribed the use of the preponderance of evidence standard in sexual-misconduct cases. The California law's provision of an affirmative-consent policy follows from a belief that an assailant should not be able to use an excuse of silence on the part of the victim or a lack of protest as indication of consent. The consent must be affirmative and ongoing during sexual activity.

Minimizing sexual assault on campus is certainly a worthy goal. No parents want their sons or daughters to be the victims of such an egregious crime. But it is not clear that this law will help to achieve that goal. Several questions remain. Is there a practical, fair, or consistent way for colleges or universities to ensure that affirmative-consent rules have been followed? How can a student be required to obtain affirmative consent during each stage of a sexual encounter and then later prove that attainment in a hearing? How might an innocent student demonstrate that he or she did indeed receive affirmative consent? When asked that question, the bill's coauthor, Assemblywoman Bonnie Lowenthal, simply replied, "Your guess is as good as mine." A noted social columnist wrote in an 2014 editorial that "critics worry that colleges will fill with cases in which campus boards convict young men (and, occasionally, young women) of sexual assault for genuinely ambiguous situations. Sadly, that's necessary for the law's success."

In conclusion, I have found that California's "Yes Means Yes" law does have some well-meaning provisions, but it is a bad law. Promoting affirmed consent appears to be a difficult, if not impossible, policy to implement and enforce. As California's colleges and universities continue to implement this new law, further research will benefit from studying these institutions' experience. Great value is to be had in establishing an expectation among male and female students that in any sexual relationship, activity should occur only after both parties have established mutual consent. One partner taking advantage of another's impaired judgment by way of the prevalence of drugs and alcohol is a crime that should be punished accordingly. While implementing an informed-consent policy is certainly worthwhile, it is not clear that this law is the best way to accomplish that goal.

"That concludes my remarks," Katie said to the applause of her classmates. "Thank you."

"Thank you, Ms. Russell," Professor Hatfield said, still stoic. "We'll now hear from your classmates. I have a question, but I'll save it for the end. Does anyone have a question for Ms. Russell?"

A hand shot up. Sarah. "In support of your conclusion, you said that a young man who's found guilty of sexual assault will pay a high price over his lifetime and that most people would consider such punishment to be pretty severe. Well, what about a woman who's been assaulted but the accused is found not guilty: Won't she suffer a lifetime of emotional trauma from society's failure to bring her assailant to justice?"

Katie thought for a second. "The hearings that are held on college campuses are about violations of codes of conduct—they don't determine guilt but instead determine responsibility. Since I believe these hearings are weak from a due-process standpoint, I think we must worry about how little proof is required for someone to simply make an accusation. But I agree it's an important question to ask. Who's more wronged: an accuser who's been assaulted and then her assailant is found to be not responsible, or an accused assailant who's been wrongfully found responsible for a violation he didn't commit? This is an area that needs more research, as I noted in my findings." Katie knew she hadn't really answered the question, although she'd been ready for just such a question with her prepared response. She looked at Mark, who offered a smile of support. She felt no better than a politician must feel when ducking a hard question from a reporter on a morning news show.

Another hand raised, this time from Jason. "I don't understand how, in almost any scenario, I could prove in a campus investigation that I'd received consent prior to sexual activity. Isn't it my word against hers? Am I supposed to obtain a signed statement ahead of time? I understand there's an iPhone app on the market that claims to obtain affirmed consent by questioning a potential partner's level of sobriety. If the person's sober, then the app enables a response to a phone request to record consent for a sexual encounter. Do we really want this level of intrusion into the bedrooms of college campuses across the country? Is this just, fair, and autonomous? I'd argue that the law doesn't pass that test at all."

Katie wasn't sure if he was asking a question or just making a statement. "Realistically, I think hearing committees will determine responsibility for an assault by assessing which of the participants is more credible. Witnesses provide testimony and they can offer statements of character, but hard proof is elusive. Remember that while a university hearing may represent a low threshold of proof, the complainant is not restricted from also pursuing resolution in criminal courts, which follow the rules of due process and can impose criminal penalties."

The room grew quiet. After a brief pause, an older graduate student, Kerry, raised her hand. "If, as you suggest, the law discourages gender equity when drugs or alcohol are involved, why is that an issue? Isn't one of the biggest factors to contribute to increased occurrences of sexual assault on campus men who use drugs or alcohol to the point where a woman is unable to consent?"

Katie remembered her best presentation skills and looked around the room and made eye contact with the other students as she formulated her response. Kerry had asked about an area of the law that Katie found perplexing. "There's a basic difference between men and women. The philosopher Mary Wollstonecraft is credited with saying, 'Mind has no gender.' Perhaps that's true at birth, but by the time children are old enough to attend college, societal norms have established clear differences in most heterosexual males and females when it comes to sex. John Locke developed his theory of the mind as what he called white paper, a concept that John Money later advanced to suggest that gender identity is socially constructed. The reason that men assume the greater legal burden and are held responsible is because in almost all cases of rape, as found in an article in the *California Western Law Review*, women are the victims and men are the perpetrators. A supporter of the affirmative-consent law stated that 'the onus being put on men is not about gender bias, but about anatomy.' I believe there are fundamental differences between men and women, and I celebrate those differences. But I also think that students must take responsibility for their own actions while they're drinking. Be cautious. If there's any question of whether someone's intoxicated and unable to consent, wait."

After another moment of silence, Professor Hatfield asked the final question. "The Department of Justice, based on data from Clery reports, recently reported that fully eighty-two percent of rapes at universities occur in on-campus housing; furthermore, ninety percent of sexual-assault victims know their assailants. Those numbers suggest to me that university housing is a dangerous place to live. Yet most campuses portray their dorms as safe and secure places for their students. Why aren't universities more forthcoming with their female students and their parents about the risk of sexual assault in college housing? Especially since dormitory living is a product they sell and supervise?"

Katie thought for a minute and then offered a timid guess. "Because it would be bad for business?"

Professor Hatfield finally smiled. "Exactly."

CHAPTER 18

Transcendent

Katie couldn't have been more excited when she arrived in front of the door to Mark's apartment. The gloaming of the sky was a deep crimson, as if a speck of dark-red ink had been dropped into a bowl of clear water. She felt her own crimson blood flowing hot against a chill breeze from the north. Though dressed in a thick down coat and wool hat, she still shivered in the frigid air. She pressed the button next to Mark's door and heard a bell chime inside. Her hand clutched a reusable shopping bag containing a bottle of champagne and some flowers. Mark arrived and escorted her inside. They silently ascended the steps to his apartment. Katie beamed at the scene atop the landing. Several candles burned in different areas of the room: a pillar in the kitchen, tapers on the dining table, and a large tin on a small table near where the Murphy bed stood tucked up against the wall.

Mark took Katie's bag and hung her coat in the closet. Katie watched him intently as he returned and wrapped his arms around her body. She felt him plant his hands just above the back of her hips and pull her toward him, to the point where her body was firmly pressed against his. It was a moment she had often imagined. "Congratulations on your presentation today. You did an excellent job."

"I couldn't have done it without you, Assistant Professor O'Connor"

"You did all the work. I so wanted to stand up and cheer for you today. I thought you did a great job."

"Thanks." Katie hugged him.

"I just finished grading your paper, so I'm no longer involved in your evaluation. Professor Hatfield will deliver the final exam."

"I can't tell you how happy that makes me. Let's have a glass of champagne to celebrate." Mark released his hands, and Katie walked over to her bag and pulled out the bottle. It was quite expensive, and she'd paid for it with her credit card, counting on the next paycheck from the foundation to arrive before her next monthly bill.

Mark opened the bottle, handed a glass to Katie, and gently touched the rim of his glass to hers. "I don't have any champagne flutes—sorry. These should do. Cheers! To an impressive effort."

Katie proffered her own toast. "To a great night."

Mark led Katie to the sofa, where they sat and sipped their champagne.

"This is excellent." Mark took a second, longer drink.

"I also brought some flowers. Find me a vase, and I'll put them in water. I have one more present for you, but I'll save it for later."

Mark narrowed his eyes. Katie enjoyed his arched eyebrow of curiosity. She took another sip of champagne and studied his face over the rim of her glass. She wanted to savor everything. "Are you ready for this night?"

"Katie, I've been ready since you came to dinner. I'm sorry to have made us wait, but it was the right decision, don't you think? Now we can act normally and meet freely. I just hope you don't mind hanging out with an old college professor." His wink suggested healthy self-deprecation.

"Don't worry. I'm mature for my age."

"Mature beyond your years, I'd say."

"By the way, how old are you?"

"Twenty-nine."

"I'd say we're perfect."

Mark put down his glass and started a playlist on his phone. The music of Beyoncé and Sam Smith filled the room. He asked, "Are you hungry? I have a few things in the refrigerator, but I hadn't planned on cooking."

"I should probably eat something, but I'm fine here with you and drinking this." Katie raised her glass, and her heart beat faster, fueled by anxiety and anticipation.

Mark brought in a plateful of cheese, grapes, and crackers and sat, this time closer to Katie. They nibbled quietly and sipped their drinks. Katie closed her eyes and imagined a place that in her mind's eye appeared both foreign and familiar. Seated next to Mark, high on an outcrop of stone, she was admiring a sweeping canyon landscape. It must have been a place she'd seen, she thought. Wherever the location, its immensity suggested her own insignificance, yet its grandeur filled her with pure joy.

Mark took Katie's hand. She opened her eyes and watched his delicate fingers tenderly explore her skin and trace across her palm and around her wrist. As had occurred with his touch that sunny summer afternoon at the department's social gathering, a curious flux of emotions flowed once more from her body toward his.

Katie studied Mark's face. She tried to make sense of the sweeping vista she'd imagined. Perhaps it was a premonition of what was to come: that she would soon leap, her hand tightly gripped around Mark's, into an unfamiliar abyss. Confident. Fearless. Expectant.

"I think we should retreat to my bedroom." His words both pushed her toward the edge and beckoned her to jump.

Katie's eyes sparkled with mirth. "You don't have a bedroom."

"Observe." Mark walked over to the Murphy bed and lowered it from the wall. "Voilà: my bedroom."

"How practical." Katie put her glass of champagne on top of the nightstand next to the burning candle. She unzipped her boots and let them tumble to the floor. Mark switched off the lights. When he returned, Katie took his hand and pulled him gently downward onto the mattress. She wrapped her arms around his body and kissed him freely with nervous and pent-up desire. Suddenly, she pulled back. "I just realized: I didn't obtain your consent to kiss you."

Mark chuckled. "Good point. How's this: 'I give you my blanket consent for any increased levels of sexual intimacy you may care to pursue this evening, and such consent shall not be revoked under any circumstances.' Does that sound legal enough?"

Katie smiled. "Should I get my phone and make a recording?"

Mark rolled down onto the bed until they lay side by side. He stroked the side of Katie's auburn hair with his palm and fingers, as if to reassure her. He kissed her lips, and Katie observed a familiar sensation: everything peripheral to Mark's face slipped out of focus. Only his features remained recognizable.

While they were pressed together, Katie felt Mark's hand move to the bottom of her sweater. He gently inserted his fingers between its fine wool and Katie's skin until they came to rest on the cup of her expensive lace bra she'd purchased just for the occasion. Katie started to unbutton Mark's shirt at his neck. Patience had left her, and she fumbled with the closures. Mark rose to a sitting position and finished unbuttoning it for her. She'd imagined this moment, anticipating the first glimpse of his chest. Candlelight flickered across his body as he removed his shirt and tossed it from the bed. In the soft glow, she could see that his shape was even better than she'd imagined. His arm muscles were sculpted and firm, but not overly developed. Katie slid next to him and put her right hand on the left side of his chest. She kissed him. Her free hand found its way to his back. She explored his mouth with her lips and with her hand appreciated the firmness of his chest.

Mark broke off his kisses and grabbed the bottom of Katie's sweater with both hands. He gently coaxed it up and over her arms and head. After a few more tugs, he furtively tossed it in the direction of the chair. His aim was wide and the sweater tumbled to the floor. Katie leaned back on her arms and watched Mark's face. His eyes expressed the intense anticipation of a young boy unwrapping his favorite Christmas present.

"You're beautiful. I'm so fortunate to be with you." Mark took her hand and kissed it.

"I'm the fortunate one." Katie released her hand and reached up behind her back and unfastened her bra. She removed it slowly, carefully, and flung it casually in the direction of the chair. The look on Mark's face radiated pure desire. He carefully cupped her left breast in his right hand and bent over to kiss it. With his tongue, he explored the middle skin between her breasts, then followed a crease along the bottom and up the left side, where his lips gently surrounded her left nipple. Katie closed her eyes and concentrated on the sensation from Mark's soft lips on her skin.

Katie wondered if Mark could hear the beating of her heart, a beat that pounded steady like a drum as she reached for the top of his jeans. She unfastened the top button with one hand. Mark stood up next to the bed and worked his pants toward the floor. When they were free of his legs, he kicked them toward the chair and stood silently over her, covered by only his boxer shorts—she'd guessed this about him—with a rather large tent in the front.

Mark sat back down on the bed and reached for their champagne. After handing Katie hers, he said, as if in explanation, "I want to savor this night." He drained the glass and went off in search of the bottle.

Katie's gaze followed Mark, whose aroused form moved through the dark apartment like a sailboat with a bowsprit, parting a calm sea. She longed to touch him and briefly thought of following him to the kitchen. After Mark returned and refilled their glasses, they drank in silence for a moment. Katie stored sensory memories of everything: the taste of the champagne, the glow from the candles, Mark's body, the shadows of the apartment, even the scent of the sheets. Finally, Mark took their glasses and returned them to the nightstand.

Katie reclined on the bed while Mark turned his attention to her wool pants. After he unbuttoned and unzipped them, Katie lifted her hips, and Mark gently worked them down and off her legs. After the pants joined the rest of the discarded clothes on the chair, he reached down and carefully slipped his fingers under the fabric of Katie's thong. He began to slowly remove it, alternating with tugs on each side with such deliberation that Katie wondered if he were intentionally teasing her. He suddenly paused and stared. Katie knew why.

"Do you like your last present? I had it done yesterday. I'm still a bit sensitive."

Mark's studied the area intently, then raised his eyes toward hers. "I like it very much."

"Everyone's doing it. If you don't like it, it'll grow back."

Mark finished removing the thong and it, too, sailed toward the chair. He slowly touched his fingers to her newly bare skin. The look of hunger in his eyes foretold of his passion. She spread her legs slightly, making it easier for Mark to attentively stroke and caress the folds of her amazingly soft lips. She couldn't believe how gentle and relaxing his touch was. She closed her eyes and absorbed the intimacy of the moment. She wished his mouth would make company with his hand.

After several minutes of gentle exploring, Mark stood and removed his boxers. Katie had fantasized about this moment, too. She stared through wide eyes. He was perfect. Long and straight, no bends or crooks, just smooth hardness. She reached over and wrapped him in her hand. He emitted a quiet gasp as she gently slid her fingers along his whole substantial length. A thought came to her that she tried and failed to suppress: he was so unlike Justin.

Mark returned to the middle of the bed and sat with his legs extended. He lifted Katie up and over him so that she faced his upper body. She straddled him in a kneeling position, which allowed Mark to reach down and unfold each of her legs back and around his waist until she sat on his lap with her legs crossed behind him. He drew her close and kissed her slowly on the neck. Then he kissed her breasts, positioned perfectly across from his face. Katie felt Mark reach around her with one hand and lift her body up slightly. With the other hand, he slowly guided himself inside her. He then let her down slowly, using his thighs to keep her elevated, until she felt him slip inside.

"Slow," Katie said.

"I think you mean 'slowly,'" Mark said with a soft laugh.

"I mean 'take your time.'"

"Got it."

Katie's phone, located in her purse next to her coat, began to ring. She recognized the first few notes of her mom's ringtone. "Sorry. Ignore it."

Mark positioned one hand under Katie's bottom and wrapped the other around her back. He slowly lifted her body up, then gently let it back down. Each successive movement downward sent him deeper inside her. As his lifting and lowering struck a rhythm, his open mouth devoured her breasts. Then he stopped and simply let her body slide completely downward until she sat freely on top of his thighs. He wrapped both arms around her back and gently pulled her down with him as he reclined onto the bed. She pulled her knees up toward her chest to straddle him and pushed forward until she was leaning over him. She placed her hands atop Mark's chest and slowly began moving in a gentle rhythm. She pressed her nails into his skin. Mark placed his hands around Katie's hips and helped her move.

With her eyes closed and her head thrown back, Katie concentrated on sliding her hips back and forth at a steady pace. She felt Mark thrust in, then out, with each movement. Mark slightly lifted his chest upward. Something suddenly felt different, and she sensed physical pleasure in a new place, a place deep inside. It felt incredible. "Stay there."

She continued to slide back and forth, increasing her pace and her thrust. She wanted all of him inside her. The Murphy bed began to creak, and Mark increased the pace of his hands and arms. She glimpsed candle-light flickering over his glistening and flexed muscles.

Then it began: a pleasurable pulse that slowly built in intensity. Katie concentrated on that pulse. As with Mark's kisses, she felt a sensation of floating, of weightlessness, of suspension. She continued thrusting back and forth with a violent passion. She briefly worried that she might break him. But she wanted to consume him, to have all of him deep inside her. Then, slowly, imperceptibly at first, a wave began to crest and cascade over her, first deep in her pelvis, then explosively throughout her core. She thrust down on him once, twice, three times more as pleasure washed over her. She imagined an ocean wave crashing in a wild mixture of water and sand before dissipating in a surge of foam. She stopped her move-ments and opened her eyes, somewhat unsure of her location or what had just happened. After staring at the beautiful body lying underneath hers, she bent down and lay her head on Mark's chest.

"You OK?" Mark wrapped his arms around her back.

"I'm more than OK. This is the first time that's ever happened!"

"What?"

"An orgasm."

"Really?"

"Well, with a man." Katie looked up and reached behind Mark's head. She pulled him close and kissed him.

After several quiet moments, Mark sat up and sipped his champagne. He placed it to Katie's lips and poured. A dribble ran down her chin. He leaned over and simply kissed it away.

"I'm sorry about the phone call. I'm sure it was my mom. I'll check. Just a sec." Katie got up to retrieve her phone. Back in bed, she said, "Yep, it was her. I promised I'd call her after the presentation. She knew I was stressed about it. She probably wanted to know how it went."

"Do you want to call her now?"

"No, I'll text her and let her know I'll call her tomorrow." Katie tapped out a message.

"Do you have a photo of her?"

"Sure." Katie handed the phone to Mark. "That's the two of us at my graduation last June. It's one of my favorites."

"Wow, I can see where you got your beauty. She's a lovely woman."

"She's a great mom. I love her." Katie took the phone back from Mark and for fun decided to take a photo. She took a selfie of the two of them sitting side by side and smiling.

"Are you sure this is a good idea?"

"It's not like I'm going to post them online or anything. This is the happiest I've ever been. I always want to remember this moment."

Katie stuck the phone out as far out as possible and admired the image on the phone's screen. Amber light from the candle on the nightstand flickered softly on their bodies. She snuggled in next to Mark and framed the photo to extend from their heads down to their waists. Her breasts would never again be that firm—they'd surely succumb to age in time, she knew—so she was happy to capture them, too. She smiled and clicked the shutter again. She thought the image was perfect. Her face hadn't reflected such joy for a long, long time. She became playful and took another one, this time leaning in to give Mark a big kiss on his cheek. Mark then put his arm around her and kissed her on her lips. As he did so, she took one of his hands and cupped it over her breast. She took a third photo. After a few more, she put the camera down.

Mark reached over and took Katie's hand. "I think I'm ready for my turn."

Katie smiled, quickly perceiving what it might be his turn for. She knew it wasn't more photos. "You held back, didn't you?"

"I wanted to make sure you were happy." His sincerity was not lost on Katie.

She slid her hand between Mark's legs. "I think I can help you with that."

After some time, perhaps an hour, after Mark had had his turn and Katie her second, Mark unwound his arms from around her and got up from the bed. Katie pulled the rumpled bedsheet, still steamy from their sex, up around her body and inhaled. She rested her head on a pillow and watched Mark locate his boxers, pull them on, and head to the kitchen, a distance of only about twenty paces from the Murphy bed. The old refrigerator emitted a loud hum when he opened its door. Mark appeared light and graceful as he moved about the kitchen, exhibiting the same weightlessness she'd observed in his office. Katie felt wonderfully content. Happy. Hopeful. And sore.

Mark returned to the bed with a tray that held a sandwich, some vegetables, and two glasses of ice water. Katie was hungry again, and the food tasted wonderful. They ate in silence. Slowly, Katie began to succumb to the efforts of the past two days. Preparing for and then delivering her class presentation had been physically and emotionally exhausting. She could feel her body begin to relax, enhanced by the exertion and pleasure she'd just experienced. She knew sleep was on the way. "Do you mind if I stay here tonight?"

"I'd be disappointed if you didn't." Mark removed the tray to the kitchen and returned to bed. He pulled off his boxers and tossed them once more toward the nearby chair. Katie imagined a silent sentry at attention, a pile of discarded clothes draped over his fabric-covered arms. She heard a puff of air come from Mark's lips as he extinguished the candle; the room went dark. Then he slid under the sheet and down alongside her body. Katie pressed her back against his chest. The gears of her normally tireless mind began to slow from the simultaneous arrival of euphoria and exhaustion. Mark pulled her close and wrapped an arm around her waist, then kissed her on her neck. "Good night."

Katie's last memory before sleep that night was of a smile. It formed as she recalled the image of Mark pulling on his boxers before making their sandwich. It was a display of modesty that, even after they'd shared the most beautiful of intimacies, told her everything about his character and his charm.

CHAPTER 19
The Best of Times

The next week with Mark was enjoyed mostly in his bed. Intimate conversation gave way to hunger-filled passion interrupted only by classes, study, and important necessities like showers and trips to Katie's apartment for clothes, simple meals, and sleep. Mark's sheets appeared to be permanently unmade. One night, after a bowl of soup and a loaf of French bread shared over a bottle of wine, they squeezed into Mark's antique claw-foot tub for a candlelit bath. As they relaxed in the warm water, illuminated by candles scattered around the cramped bathroom's floor, Katie turned the conversation to her studies.

She turned around to look at him, with the flickering light illuminating his steamy cheekbones and chest. "Can we talk about philosophy, Professor?"

He leaned down and kissed her. "Assistant professor. As teacher and student, or as girlfriend and boyfriend?"

"Both."

"What's on your mind?"

"Oh, nothing major," she said with a grim chuckle, "just having doubts about philosophy as a profession. Value theory, metaphysics, and epistemology are interesting and all, but I don't see where they'll take me. Why invest years in the field if I can't make a living from it, or at least feel a sense of purpose?"

"You feel you lack purpose now?"

"Not right now." She slipped her hand beneath the surface of the water and between Mark's legs. She squeezed gently.

"Careful."

Katie returned her hand to Mark's knee. "I enjoy philosophy, but where will it take me? Professorship, maybe?"

"I hate to say it, but your chances of becoming a professor are pretty slim."

"Ouch. I wish you'd tell me what you really thought. Don't you think I'm capable?"

"Katie, you're as capable as any student I've met. But finishing a PhD program is more a matter of persistence than of intelligence. You have both, but the odds of success are daunting for anyone. Universities are hiring fewer professors, and the supply of doctoral candidates is increasing. You could spend another five to nine years preparing for a career that will leave you hundreds of thousands of dollars in debt and earning a lot less per year than people who started their careers right out of college."

His comments stung. The man she was falling hopelessly in love with had, in a few simple sentences, destroyed whatever hope she had for an academic career. She placed her hand in the water and propelled slow, repetitive ripples toward her toes. The waves reminded her of her first competition in an open-water swimming event near San Diego's Mission Bay. A cold and wind-driven standing chop made it almost impossible to make progress through the water on the outward leg. It had taken every fiber of determination not to quit. "I know you're right," she said, a steady rhythm of waves sounding against the cast iron, "but it makes me sad to think I've wasted my time."

Mark withdrew his right hand from the water and gently wrapped it around Katie's chest. He hugged her and then lingered in a gentle kiss on her neck. "I attended a Jesuit high school. Our goal was to master a small number of subjects, including literature, language, and history. Latin was most important, as was philosophy. All our teachings were done against a backdrop of Catholicism. 'You will develop the whole self,' we were told repeatedly. Only then would we complete our lessons."

Katie took Mark's hand from her chest and placed it against her lips. She held it there for a moment before putting it back. "Are you suggesting that I become a nun?" she said with a laugh.

"Time spent studying philosophy isn't wasted. You have a strong grasp of reasoning and logic. It's a tremendous investment. One of my favorite teachers said, 'The first step toward the power of moral action lies in the power we have to think morally.'"

Katie thought about the quote and turned on the hot-water faucet with her foot. Steam rose, and she turned her head back toward Mark's face. "You're very reassuring."

KATIE LINGERED IN BED WITH A CUP OF COFFEE one morning during that wondrous week and watched Mark sleep. She sat on top of the sheets and was dressed in one of his previously worn oxford shirts. Her back was against the wall, since the Murphy bed didn't have a headboard, and she'd wrapped her arms around her knees and pulled them into her chest. She so loved him. She'd never experienced such confidence in a person. And Mark seemed totally at ease about their new status as a couple. One of the few nights they'd ventured from his apartment, they'd gone out for a movie and drinks with one of Mark's colleagues and his wife. Mark seemed totally relaxed when he'd introduced Katie as his girlfriend and described her as one of his graduate students, though he was quick to add that she was no longer under his direct supervision. The couple's gracious comments and their outward acceptance of her status with Mark made the relationship feel natural.

One of the more charming stories Mark told during the week was from a time when he was around ten years old. He'd had a golden retriever named Lucy, and when she was old enough, Mark's mom asked him if he'd like to raise puppies. She explained that if he said yes, he'd have to care for them, including feeding, grooming, playtime, and trips to the veterinarian for health checks. Then, she explained, when they were eight weeks old, he could sell the puppies and keep one for himself. After reimbursing her for dog food, equipment, and veterinary bills, he could keep the proceeds. "That's your profit," she'd explained. Mark readily agreed to her proposal.

After the litter of eight puppies was born, Mark said he'd felt like a proud parent. He spent his extra time after school playing with and caring for the dogs. They each had unique personalities. He wanted to name them, but his mom insisted that he put a piece of different-colored ribbon around their necks and simply call them by their colors. She explained that she didn't want to give the dogs real names. They should leave that exciting moment up to their new owners. From then on, Mark always referred to them as Orange Girl, or Purple Boy, or Green Girl, and so on. As Mark cared for the puppies over the eight weeks, time seemed to fly by. All too soon, he had to put a for-sale ad in the local Durango newspaper.

Mark was crestfallen when it came time to say good-bye to all the puppies but one. He was so upset that he schemed with a friend to take them all by wheelbarrow to the friend's house, where they created a makeshift kennel in the barn. Every morning and every afternoon, Mark stole over to the barn to feed them. His mom, of course, had received an explanatory call from his friend's parents, but she decided not to let on to Mark that she knew. She asked him each day, "Where are the puppies?"

And each day, Mark repeated the same lie: "I don't know—they just disappeared."

Finally, on the fourth day, Mark could no longer take his feelings of guilt and confessed what he had done. After letting him cry for a short while, his mom calmly explained that if he didn't sell the puppies, he would deny seven other families the pleasure of owning one. "Do you really want to keep all those other boys and girls from having a great dog like you've had?"

Mark now believed that the experience was when he first learned the pleasure of giving to others. He and his mom were careful to only sell to families who offered them assurances of proper care for the puppies. Mark named the remaining dog Max, who lived a wonderful life of thirteen years.

Katie believed that a future with Mark was not only possible but perhaps probable. She observed nothing worrisome, like flashes of anger or glimpses of a dark past, and the more she understood him, the more comfortable she became. Yet a momentary lapse of self-esteem had visited her one afternoon that left her pensive and doubtful of Mark's inner thoughts. She was younger than he, deeply in debt, and suddenly unsure of her career. Why would Mark choose her over someone else? His comments that he admired her mind—which was most important to her, since the mind was the bond that could best withstand time—certainly seemed sincere. And she had no doubt that he found her attractive. Their activities over the week proved it. She sat on the bed and studied his long body, barely covered by a loose sheet, with his delicate feet hanging over the end of the bed. She trusted that he was sincere.

Over another sip of coffee, Katie thought about the passion they had shared. She could only describe it with a tired cliché: it was amazing. As her mom had foretold, intimacy with the right man was indeed transcendent. Mark rarely seemed to achieve orgasm before she did. It was as if he operated under some secret code of conduct—if Katie didn't come, then neither did he, however long it might take. Fortunately, it usually didn't take long before waves of pleasure crashed over her body like swells on a beach during a winter storm.

Not only was the standard repertoire of lovemaking techniques she'd experienced with other men suddenly more exciting and surprisingly fulfilling, but Mark had also inspired some exciting new fantasies. She imagined fastening his wrists to the bed to restrain him and then slowly and deliberately exploring every inch of his body until he'd beg to be let free. The passion they'd experienced together had inspired her—it was as if an idle part of her brain had been activated.

As Mark began to stir, Katie's thoughts inevitably moved to the sexual-assault hearing scheduled for the following morning. She knew its arrival would signal the end of a magical phase in their relationship, one filled with languorous and innocent discovery. Those nights with Mark were a dazzling turning point in her life. Though dreamlike, they were real to her. From her fumbling high school years to her disappointment with Justin, she had finally seen what was possible. Yet she always found happiness hard to trust.

"Good morning," Mark said, interrupting her thoughts. He pushed himself up with one arm and kissed her.

"Sleep well?" Katie returned the kiss.

"Perfectly. You exhaust me."

"Hope that's not a complaint."

"Consider it praise. Any coffee left? It smells great."

Mark got up and shuffled over to the kitchen and poured himself a cup. Katie admired his naked body, topped by wildly disheveled hair. He glided back into bed.

"That hearing I told you about is tomorrow morning," she said. "Back to reality I guess."

"It has to happen sometime. Christmas break is coming."

"I've been so focused on my paper and the hearing that I hadn't really thought past finals. I made plans to go visit my family."

"They'll be happy to see you." Mark shifted in the bed to look at Katie. "I've been wondering if you'd like to come meet mine."

"Your family? In Durango?"

"They'll be thrilled to know there's a woman in my life. I suspect they've been a bit concerned."

"Since the broken engagement?"

"They'll adore you." Mark took Katie's hand and squeezed it.

"Of course I'll come. How about after Christmas? We can ring in the New Year together."

"Perfect."

CHAPTER 20
Swear to Tell the Truth

Katie took a seat and felt something tighten in the pit of her stomach, like a hand forming into a fist. Senior conduct coordinator Julie Downs called the hearing to order. Seated with Katie in the university's administrative conference room were Detective Scott; Drew and his representative, a lawyer named Landry Clarke; Ava and her representative, the dean of women students; Ms. Ramirez, the nurse from the hospital's emergency room; and an older man named Mr. Bradley, whose nameplate read "External Adjudicator." He appeared to be in charge of the meeting.

After introducing the group, Mr. Bradley explained that he had no prior connection to the university, the complainant or respondent (or their advisors), the hearing officer, or any witnesses. He described the format of the hearing, including the requirements that neither the complainant nor the respondent could question each other directly and that their advisors were to remain silent throughout the proceeding unless questioned directly. Because the conduct coordinator had requested in writing to do so, a recording of the hearing would be created and made available to the participants within several days of its conclusion. He then turned the meeting over to Detective Scott for his opening statement and a summary of his investigation, including statements that had been taken from Katie, Ava, Drew, the nurse, and Desmond Baker, who had declined to testify at the hearing.

Detective Scott stood and addressed the group. "Based on my investigation, Ms. Greene and Mr. Evans had sexual intercourse on the night in question. Mr. Evans claims it was consensual, however, while Ms. Greene has limited recollection of the events leading up to the time when the sexual activity occurred with Mr. Evans. Two witnesses have provided written testimony that that both Mr. Evans and Ms. Greene had been drinking alcohol on the evening in question. About a year earlier, both parties were involved in a romantic relationship—one that had been subsequently terminated by Ms. Greene. These facts are not contested."

The detective coughed lightly and continued. "One witness, Ms. Russell, stated that Ms. Greene was intoxicated and was acting erratically during Ms. Russell's visit to Ms. Greene's apartment earlier that evening. The nurse who examined Ms. Greene at the hospital several hours after the incident was reported to police observed that Ms. Greene appeared to be intoxicated. The nurse also testified that during a forensic sexual examination, she found no evidence of sexual penetration or use of force. Since Ms. Greene has thus far refused to authorize the release of the results of her forensic sexual exam, I am unable to determine the level of blood alcohol or the possibility of drugs being present, or indeed any other lab results."

Katie noticed that Drew wore a smug expression as he watched and listened to Detective Scott. Ava stared at the floor.

"During my interview with football player Desmond Baker," the detective continued, "he stated that he was aware that Mr. Evans planned to engage in sexual activity with Ms. Greene that evening, a subject that prompted an argument between Mr. Evans and Mr. Baker prior to the start of sexual activity. As contained in his written statement (which has been distributed to all parties), Mr. Baker stated that Mr. Evans had asked him to participate in the sexual activity with Ms. Greene."

Drew jumped up from his chair. "That's a lie!"

Bradley cut in and said, "Mr. Evans, you will remain seated and silent until asked to speak. Otherwise, you will be asked to leave this room and the hearing will proceed without your participation. My instructions were clear on this. I suggest that you comply." Drew slowly took his seat while muttering something unintelligible.

Detective Scott resumed his summary. "Mr. Baker believed that Mr. Evans asked for his participation in order to secure Mr. Baker's silence and discourage his testimony, which would likely implicate himself along with Mr. Evans if the activity were to be reported. Ms. Russell stated in her interview that she heard an argument between the two men prior to discovering Ms. Greene. After the argument, when Ms. Russell returned to Ms. Greene's apartment, upstairs and above her own, she found Ms. Greene unclothed and in her bed. She also observed Mr. Evans getting dressed. Ms. Russell stated that when she confronted Mr. Evans and asked what he had done to Ms. Greene, he replied, 'Nothing I haven't done before, and she enjoyed it.' Ms. Russell later found an open condom package on the floor, but its contents were not recovered."

Detective Scott took a drink of water and added, "What can't be established by the witnesses' statements is whether or not consent was given prior to the sexual activity. That concludes my investigation."

"Thank you, Detective Scott." The external adjudicator then turned to Drew. "Mr. Evans, you may now make a statement."

"Thank you, Your Honor."

The adjudicator corrected him. "I'm no longer a judge. You may refer to me as Mr. Bradley."

"Whatever. Mr. Bradley, this hearing's a joke. Yes, I had sex with Ava Greene, just like we did many times before. She never complained then, and she didn't complain this time. I asked her, and she said yes. Then we did it. And as far as I can tell, she enjoyed it. It's as simple as that, and I hate to see so many people waste their time over two friends having a good time." Drew sat down. His representative glared at him and wrote a note on a legal pad and shoved it in his direction.

Katie imagined it had *Shut up* written on it.

Mr. Bradley disregarded Drew's impudent comments and said, "Ms. Greene, would you like to make a statement?"

"No, thank you, Mr. Bradley."

"Are you sure? This is your chance to be heard."

"I'm sure. Detective Scott covered everything. It's all in my statement."

"Thank you, Ms. Greene. At this point, I will read questions that have been submitted in advance by the representatives of both the complainant and the respondent. Please limit your responses to only answering the questions that are asked of you." He coughed and continued. "Nurse Ramirez, when you first spoke with Ms. Greene in the ER, was it your opinion at the time that she was intoxicated?"

"Yes, Mr. Bradley. I see many students who come into our facility in various states of mind. Based on my experience, I believe she'd either been drinking or had been drugged."

Mr. Bradley wrote some notes. "Why did you think she might have been drugged?"

"Her symptoms included drowsiness, some dizziness, and a state of relaxation, and she complained of feeling a bit queasy. These are all common effects of GHB, also known as the date-rape drug. It's a form of liquid ecstasy that causes euphoria and enhanced libido."

"But aren't these also symptoms of drinking alcohol?"

"Yes, they are, and without lab tests it's hard to tell the difference. But she was clearly in a state of diminished physical and mental function."

"Thank you, nurse."

Mr. Bradley next turned to Katie, who suddenly felt the spotlight turned on her. "Ms. Russell, in your statement, you also stated that you thought Ms. Greene might have been drugged. Why did you think that?"

"I had drinks with Ms. Greene on other occasions where I could observe her consumption: once in her apartment and another time in a social setting. She rarely had more than a full glass of wine. I'd never seen her appear drunk before that night. In my opinion, she didn't strike me as someone who drank very much."

"Do you have any professional education in toxicology?"

"I have a professional server's license for Class 13 restaurants that serve alcohol."

"On a scale of one to ten, ten being the highest, how intoxicated was Ms. Greene in your opinion?"

She eyed Mr. Bradley, who seemed to be studying her. "I'd say she was a six or seven. Her eyes were glazed, and she slurred a few words. We did have a conversation before I left, though, and she seemed to understand what I was saying."

"Thank you, Ms. Russell." Mr. Bradley scribbled more notes.

Katie was disappointed that Ava had refused to release the results of her forensic exam for the hearing. She was positive that Ava had been drugged; there was no other reasonable explanation. She was also surprised that no one mentioned Desmond's injury during the football game. Detective Scott, during a brief conversation before the hearing, had suggested that the injury was circumstantial and outside the scope of the hearing, so it was unlikely to be mentioned. Fortunately, Katie's conjecture that Drew had arranged the hit on Desmond had successfully prompted Ava to provide written testimony and attend the hearing. Desmond was scheduled to be released from the hospital before the end of the semester and was expected to make a full recovery. He'd be able to resume football the following season. Katie made a mental note to go visit him and drop off a card and some flowers.

Mr. Bradley asked a few more questions of Detective Scott before launching into a summary of the relevant code of conduct that the hearing members would review against the written record and the testimony. "At this university, nonconsensual sexual *contact* is defined as any intentional sexual touching, however slight and with any object, by any person upon another person that is without consent and/or by force. Nonconsensual sexual *intercourse* is any sexual intercourse, however slight and with any object, by any person upon another person that is without consent and/or by force. Consent for sexual activity consists of clear, knowing, and voluntary words or actions that create mutually understandable clear permission regarding the willingness to engage in, and the conditions of, sexual activity. Consent must be active; silence by itself cannot be interpreted as consent.

"After hearing the case, the conduct officer may find, by a preponderance of the evidence, that the charged student is not responsible for violating the student-conduct code, or the officer may find the student responsible for violating the student-conduct code and issue sanctions based on that finding. If the student is found responsible, then the charged student and alleged victim may provide an impact statement and character references for consideration during the sanctioning process. Once the hearing board has made its determination on this matter, the complainant and respondent will be notified in writing."

Julie Downs, the hearing officer, thanked Mr. Bradley and Detective Scott for their hard work. Katie was relieved when Downs said, "This concludes the hearing."

Everyone slowly left the conference room. Katie decided to linger in the hallway and wait for Detective Scott. The click of a latch caught her attention. She looked up and saw Drew and his representative come through the conference-room door and walk in her direction. Drew stopped and glared at her. "I told you to keep your mouth shut. You better hope this whole thing goes away." Drew's representative grabbed him by the elbow and escorted him toward the exit. Before he went outside, he stopped and wheeled around. "Why don't you come see me sometime—I can give you the same thing I gave Ava." The sounds of Drew's laughter trailed behind him as he continued through the double doors and out into the sunshine.

The color drained from Katie's face, and something snapped in her. Give her what, Katie wondered. Sex? Drugs? Shaken by the encounter, she peered through a door that remained open into the conference room. She spotted Detective Scott engaged in conversation with the hearing officer. The detective saw her and signaled with his hand that she should wait. After a few moments, he joined her.

"Ms. Russell, you OK? You look a little pale."

"I'm glad the hearing is over."

"You did well. Obviously, there's some conflicting testimony. In cases like this, the credibility of the witnesses is critical. Without release of the forensic report, it makes things more difficult." The detective stared at Katie with raised eyebrows. He chewed on his lower lip, as if biting back words. "There's something I want you to know. Can you keep it between us?"

"Totally."

"The police crime lab examined the evidence from Ava's forensic exam. The hospital assumed, after it acquired the nurse's preliminary signature, that the victim would follow through and provide her own signed release after a period of sobriety. The hospital wasn't concerned about getting the release, so it went ahead and submitted the kit to the lab, which then returned the results to the Boulder PD."

"What did they show?" Katie appreciated the fact that Detective Scott had trusted her with confidential information.

"You were right. Date-rape drug was present."

"I knew it. But why can't we use the evidence against Drew? He's dangerous."

"Katie, that's not the way the law works. Privacy and victim's rights are important safeguards we strive to protect."

"No doubt I'd want the same."

"I expect the student conduct office will release its findings within two weeks. Classes are almost over for the semester, and they'll want to wrap this up before Christmas break."

"Thanks for trusting me, Detective Scott."

"You did the right thing to testify. Sooner or later, Drew will get what he deserves. In my experience, guys like him always reoffend. So long, Ms. Russell. It's been a pleasure working with you."

Katie offered her hand. She appreciated Detective Scott's firm handshake in return. Outside in the cold sunshine, she zipped up her down jacket and watched as her cold breath vaporized into the still air. She wanted to see Mark, so she set out for his office in the Old Main building.

His door was locked, and the lights inside were off. Her visit was outside Mark's regular office hours, but she'd still hoped to catch him. She pulled out her phone and texted him: *Can I see you tonight? Your place?*

She headed back to her apartment, where she planned to study for her last two final exams, scheduled for the following week. She so hoped to see Mark that evening.

CHAPTER 21

Are Men Rational?

Back inside her apartment, Katie struggled to rid her mind of the scenes from the hearing. A text from Mark interrupted her thoughts: *Come on over. Just got back from a faculty meeting. I'll make dinner.*

She folded some clothes, packed a few things in an overnight bag, and headed out the door. After a twenty-minute walk, she entered his kitchen and was greeted by the fragrant smells of garlic and lemon; she saw the makings of shrimp scampi. She put her things down and wrapped her arms around his waist. "I'm so glad to see you."

Mark embraced her in a long hug. "I assumed you had a rough day. Tell me about it."

"It was horrible. Can I take a bath first? I don't think I've ever felt this grimy before. I had an upsetting encounter with Drew after the hearing."

"Sure. I'll bring you a glass of wine and then finish making dinner. You can tell me about it later."

Katie started for the bathroom but stopped and turned. "Where did you learn to cook? Most guys in their twenties don't have a clue."

"My father had a rule on the ranch. One Sunday each month, my brother and I gave our mom the day off, and we made dinner. We'd buy the ingredients, cook, and serve the meal, then we'd clean up afterward. He liked to say, 'If women can rope, men can cook.'"

Katie so loved him. Insecurity still visited her occasionally and spread over her emotions as easily as soft butter on warm bread, but those moments were arriving less frequently than they once did and didn't last nearly as long. She made her way to the bathroom and turned on the faucets of the tub. As she removed her clothes, a delicious feeling of confidence began to settle in.

"Here's your wine." Katie reached up from the tub and took a glass from Mark's outstretched hand. He stared at her for a moment. She could see the familiar look of desire glinting in his eyes. "As much as I'd like to join you, I imagine you need to be alone. Besides, I should finish dinner. When I hear you get out, I'll put the scampi in the oven."

Katie leaned back in the tub and took a sip of wine. She closed her eyes and thought of him—his empathy and awareness were gifts.

After she dried herself and drained the tub, Katie dressed in Mark's bathrobe and returned to the kitchen. Her skin was pink from water so hot it was just shy of unbearable, and her hair was piled high and secured with a clip. She found Mark setting utensils on the table; when she appeared, he paused to top up her glass of wine. "Dinner should be ready in about ten minutes."

Over bites of scampi, Katie recounted the details of the sexual-assault hearing. She began to tremble when she described the confrontation with Drew and his frightening comments. "I can't understand why guys commit rape. It seems so cruel."

Mark took a sip of wine. "You're talking about acquaintance rape?"

Katie thought for a moment. "Yeah, but rape is rape, isn't it? How can a man involved in acquaintance rape not fully understand the psychological impact of his actions? If he did, I can't imagine he'd commit that kind of offense."

Mark rested his knife and fork on his plate. "You assume he's at least mildly interested in his partner, not just his own self-gratification. The typical profile of a man who's involved in acquaintance rape includes being motivated by sexual dominance, being hostile toward women, and condoning the use of force in sexual relationships. Sure, some men are incapable of gauging social interactions, so they may not understand the impacts of their actions on their victims, but I wouldn't assume they don't do any gauging."

Katie finished a bite. "Drugs and alcohol are a factor in almost three-quarters of cases, which of course can confuse things, but I still don't understand why a man would press ahead with sex if his partner hadn't given him her full consent."

Mark hesitated for a moment and furrowed his brow, perhaps as he measured his words. "Some boys are raised to be sexually aggressive. It's how they affirm their masculinity. Men commit rape for the same reasons that motivate many men—even those who don't commit rape. They learn to initiate and persist in their actions during sexual encounters because they think they won't get rewarded with sex otherwise. Women set the limits. Pick almost any movie or TV show. The man always makes a sexual advance, and the woman always resists at first. That's how it usually went for me, anyway."

"I haven't been very good at resisting you," Katie said with a chuckle. "Maybe I should start."

"I'm just happy we both seem to want the same thing," Mark said, and squeezed her hand. "The point is that some men are taught to persist beyond a woman's protest, and don't believe a woman means no when she says no. Did you know that a survey in the eighties of female under-grads asked if they'd ever said no to sex even though they fully intended to have it? About forty percent said they had. Consent often becomes confused with submission. Which takes us right back to the Yes Means Yes law."

Katie poured more wine for them both and leaned forward in her chair. "I'll cut men some slack once they learn to act less like reptiles and more like humans. Have you ever been confused about where things stood with a woman?"

"Aggressive men are a lot like football players. Imagine you're carry-ing the ball from the ten-yard line toward the end zone. You manage to break a tackle at the five. You see a single defender blocking your path. At that moment, every fiber of your being is focused on getting across the goal line. You'll do everything in your power to knock that defender down and score. Some men, during sex, become like that running back, singularly focused on getting into the end zone. That's why I think the Yes Means Yes law, while it's definitely a well-intentioned law, has a problem. Remember your paper?"

"Every word."

"Do you remember the comment by one of the state authors of the bill that even she didn't know how they could enforce its informed-consent provision?"

"Clearly."

"So, imagine a normal college couple, one that's been dating for a few weeks. They've gotten physical but not to the point of discussing intercourse. They're attracted to each other, and the guy is passionate for the girl—testosterone and hormones are raging. He wants her bad. Then one night, they're alone and they've had a few drinks—but not so many drinks that she's drunk and can't give him her informed consent. He asks if he can kiss her. She says yes. A few minutes later, he asks if he can touch her breasts. Again, she gives her consent and says yes. Then, he asks if he can remove her sweater and bra. She says, 'I thought you'd never ask,' and takes them off herself."

Katie opened her robe and exposed one of her breasts. "Like this?" She puckered her lips as if sending a kiss.

Mark smiled. "Wouldn't have looked that perfect."

"Sorry, I'll be good." Katie retied the robe.

"Finally, they end up on his bed. The girl's given her consent every step of the way. The guy says, 'Can I go inside of you?' The woman doesn't hesitate and whispers, 'Please do.' He puts on a condom, and they start to have sex. But later she suffers a twinge of guilt and says, 'This is a bad idea—please stop.'"

"I'm guessing he doesn't stop."

"Some men will resist. Years of social conditioning are hard to break. For them, at that point, stopping isn't an option. As he explodes in pleasure, did their encounter go from consensual sex to rape? And how would you ever adjudicate that?"

Katie studied Mark's face. "I bet you'd stop."

"With you, it would be nearly impossible."

Katie locked her eyes on Mark's. A silent beat passed before Mark broke it.

"Let me tell you a story," he said.

"Will I like it?"

"Probably not, but it will help to make my point. One night, while I was an undergrad, I took my girlfriend home after a weekend together in Denver. She attended college in Greeley, and I'd promised to drive her back to campus. We were on the road around eight on a winter night. Very dark out."

"Go on."

"We were on a two-lane county road with little traffic and only an occasional stoplight. I was driving my Volkswagen Bug when, once we were about halfway there, she tells me she wants to give me a proper farewell."

"She didn't!"

"She did. I thought it was a fine idea and told her so. She reached over and started rubbing my crotch. A few minutes later, she unbuttoned the fly of my jeans, slid them down, and leaned over. It wasn't too long before—well, I'm sure you can figure it out."

"I don't like this story." Katie put on an exaggerated pout.

"It wasn't long before I reached the point of no return. It was a new experience for me, and I was young and foolish. It was hard to concentrate on the road. As I was about ready to explode, I looked down the road and saw a stoplight in the near distance. Unfortunately, it turned yellow well before we'd reached the intersection. I had to decide instantly if I should stop and ruin the moment, or keep driving and let things reach their natural conclusion."

"There's nothing natural about this story." Katie folded her arms.

"I wasn't close enough to the intersection to get through it before the light changed. I didn't stop—just kept on going—exploding at the very moment I entered the intersection and the light turned red. As we passed through, I looked to my left and was startled to see a state patrol car waiting at the crossroad for his light to turn green. I knew I was caught. Sure enough, he turned in behind me, switched on his lights, and pulled me over. My girlfriend was giggling like crazy."

"Serves you right! What did you do?"

"The first thing I did was button my jeans as fast as I could. He quickly arrived at my window. I pulled my license from my wallet and gave him the car's registration. I was afraid to look down into my lap out of fear of what I might see. I remember he pointed his flashlight at my face."

"He should have arrested you for stupidity," Katie said with a shake of her head.

"Probably. He didn't say much, just that it was obvious I'd run the light and that he had to write me a ticket. He even said he was sorry. He looked at me with a bit of a smirk, like he knew exactly what'd been going on. It was weird. My heart was pounding while he went back to his car. When he finally came back, he handed me the ticket and said good night. We had a very quiet drive the rest of the way to Greeley."

"Remind me of the point of your story?" Katie couldn't decide if she should be amused or not.

"That even intelligent, emotionally mature men like myself—" he bowed theatrically "—are capable of making dumb decisions when the promise of sex is at hand."

Katie laughed and jabbed Mark in the arm. "I understand your point of view. Men's social behavior is resistant to change and it's persistent. But that's not good enough. While we as a society promote a cultural shift in male awareness toward women, we also need strong laws and enforcement. These serial and predatory rapists must understand that they're beyond the pale. They can't commit rape. And if they do, they'll be severely punished for it."

"Wow. I'm impressed by your passion." Mark took Katie's hand in his.

"I've thought a lot about law school. Taking criminals off the streets is a good thing. I think I could be successful at it."

"Katie, you'll succeed at anything you try your hand at."

"Except for becoming a philosophy professor," Katie said with a chuckle. She got up and walked around to Mark's side of the table. After emptying the bottle of wine, she sat in his lap and rested her pile of wet hair on his shoulder and kissed him on the cheek. "Can we just clean the kitchen and go to bed? And no end zones tonight—I just want you to hold me in your arms."

"I can do that."

CHAPTER 22
A Digital Life

Katie remained asleep in Mark's bed when he left for campus to teach his introduction to philosophy class. He was five minutes into the day's lecture on "Logic, Critical Thinking, and Essay Writing" when two men opened the classroom door and walked inside. One of them, dressed in a suit and tie—something he rarely saw on a college campus—approached Mark at his lectern. Twenty-five students looked up from their notes to see what had caused him to abruptly stop speaking. Mark and the man spoke in hushed tones.

A few moments later, Mark turned toward his students. "Class, I've been asked to attend a meeting." He pointed to the younger of the two men, dressed casually, whom Mark recognized as a faculty member from another department. "Mr. Rozak will continue to lecture from my notes. I'll return as soon as possible." Mark and the man in the suit left the classroom while Mr. Rozak stepped to the lectern.

The walk from Old Main to the administration building took about ten minutes. During their brief exchange in the classroom, the man had explained that he was from the campus security office and had been asked to escort Mark to an important meeting with the dean of arts and sciences. He volunteered no more information while they walked. When they arrived at the administration building, they went directly to the dean's top-floor office, where the dean's administrative assistant motioned Mark inside. His escort remained in the lobby.

Inside the office were the dean, whom Mark knew only casually from faculty meetings, and a woman whom he didn't recognize.

"Dr. O'Connor, thanks for coming." The dean got up from his desk and walked around to shake Mark's hand. His smile was clearly intended to disarm. It didn't work. "This is attorney Wendy Tucker, from the university's Office of Risk Management. We have a few questions we'd like to ask you. Please, take a seat. Can I get you anything to drink?"

"I'm fine, thanks. What's this about?" Mark quickly realized that having someone there from the Office of Risk Management implied that the dean was worried about financial or legal exposure to the university of some kind. It wasn't a good sign.

"We'd like to ask you a few questions about a graduate student in one of your classes, Ms. Katie Russell."

"I know the student. But she isn't in my class. She's in Professor Hatfield's class. I'm assisting the professor with lectures and student advising." Mark's heart picked up its beat as he considered the direction the meeting might take.

"Professor O'Connor, are you aware of university policy regarding amorous relationships between faculty and students?"

"Sure. Such relationships are acceptable so long as the faculty member is not in a role of authority over the student. Why do you ask?" Mark noticed that the attorney was taking notes on a legal pad and smiling politely at Mark as she scribbled.

"We're wondering if you're having an amorous relationship with Ms. Russell."

There it was—that thing he had most feared. Weak rationalization, accompanied by acute physical desire, had convinced him that once his official class duties were over, he could indulge his passion for Katie at will. He'd been doing so almost continuously for over a week now and was still raw in places. His quiet pause in which he tried to buy time to think began to seem overextended. No reason he shouldn't be forthcoming. "Yes, we're having an amorous relationship."

"Can you tell me when it started?" Tucker asked the question.

"I can tell you precisely. It was last Friday."

"Are you sure about that?" She scribbled more notes.

"Yes, quite sure."

"Was that the date you first had sex, or was that the date your amorous relationship began?" Her pen hung suspended over her legal pad.

Mark looked toward the dean. "I'm not sure I'm comfortable answering that question. Am I being accused of anything?"

"Mark, just try your best to respond. This isn't a legal proceeding. We just need to understand the nature of your relationship with Ms. Russell."

Mark didn't trust the dean and assumed that the attorney was carefully trying to construct a timeline. He decided to lay out his version of events. "Ms. Russell and I met at the beginning of Professor Hatfield's class, at the end of August. I advised her during normal office hours, and it was last Friday that we first began at least what I understand to be an amorous relationship."

"Are your sure your relationship started last Friday? I trust you're aware that an amorous relationship doesn't necessarily include sex. A romantic relationship can be considered amorous. Isn't it possible that you've had feelings for Ms. Russell since earlier in the semester, feelings that could have influenced how you advised and evaluated her?" More note scribbling by Tucker.

"Yes, I'm sure." Mark wondered if he should refuse to say anything further.

As he listened to the dean, Mark observed that Tucker had put down her pen and opened a manila folder. "We have reports from several students that state you were seen with Ms. Russell at a downtown bar on a Friday afternoon in September, enjoying drinks and conversation. Nothing wrong with that, but it was also reported that you touched her arm."

"There's nothing wrong with that, either, is there?"

"Not unless that touch was unsolicited and unwanted."

"She seemed fine to me."

"We also have a report that you were seen having tea at Chautauqua Park early on a Saturday morning in November. You were holding hands and talking in a friendly way. Are you sure your amorous relationship didn't begin while you were advising Ms. Russell?"

"I'm sure. I just told you that. Look, I think I'm done answering your questions. If you plan to accuse me of any violations under the university's code of conduct, then you need to make a formal charge."

"Dr. O'Connor, I have one more question." Tucker pulled out a stack of eight-by-ten color photos from her manila folder. She laid them down in a row, one by one, on the desk in front of Mark. "Are these photos of you and Ms. Russell?"

Mark recoiled. "Where did you get these?" He immediately recognized them as the photos Katie had taken the first night they'd had sex together. In one, he and Katie sat next to each other, naked from the waist up. The look on his face was sort of dopey. In another, he was grasping one of Katie's breasts with his hand. Yet another showed her kissing him, again neither of them with any clothes on. And the last one he hadn't remembered her taking. It showed her mouth tightly wrapped around his fully erect penis; even though her face was recognizable, only a small mole gave him away.

"This isn't right. You shouldn't have these."

Tucker continued. "Professor O'Connor, we plan to launch a formal investigation into your conduct at the university for an alleged, and nondisclosed, amorous relationship with a student while in a position of authority to discipline, evaluate, or grade her. You are being suspended from all official duties while this investigation proceeds. You will be allowed to keep your office, but you are not to act in any official capacity until the investigation is complete. And you are not to discuss this matter with Ms. Russell. It is our guideline that such investigations be completed within sixty days, at which time the university will make its findings known, and a formal decision will be made on what, if any, sanctions will be applied."

Mark jumped up. "Why don't you write this down on your legal pad. I've done nothing wrong. I have not favored Ms. Russell, nor have I discriminated against any other student. I have not given her any special consideration, and I've evaluated her progress and performance based solely on her hard work and demonstration of her knowledge. You have this all wrong."

The dean said, "Professor, we take these issues seriously. If, as you say, you have not violated the policy, then you have nothing to worry about. Until the investigation is complete, I suggest you keep a low profile. You should be aware that the outcome of this investigation can also affect tenure decisions. You'll receive written notice of the charges and proceedings." The dean stood to signal that the meeting was over.

Mark stormed out of the office and into the reception area, where his leg accidently clipped the corner of the assistant's desk as he went by. The resulting pain in his thigh was intense, and the nervous yelp from the receptionist unexpected, but he didn't break stride. After slamming the door behind him, he quickly descended the stairs and hurried outside. It was bitter cold, and he was angry. How did the university get those photos? Could Katie have sent them? Surely not. She'd have no reason to do so. But who? More importantly, why? He stopped in the middle of the quad and buttoned up his coat. He walked across campus in the direction of his apartment. He didn't know whether to think himself a fool for getting involved with Katie or to conclude that someone else had set him up. Either way, he knew that his world, or the way he had imagined it, had just spun out of control.

KATIE STRETCHED LANGUOROUSLY IN MARK'S bed and opened her eyes. She vaguely remembered Mark's departure several hours earlier—he'd dressed quickly and hurried out the door for class. Dinner and wine the night before, enjoyed over Mark's insights into male psychology, had helped soften her angst from the hearing, and especially from the offensive interaction with Drew. She threw back the bed linens and smiled. Her growing confidence was as foreign as it was reassuring but was unmistakable nonetheless. She went to the kitchen and discovered that Mark had prefilled the coffeemaker with ground beans and water. He'd also left a note: *Good morning. Hope you slept well. XOXO.* She flipped to the next page of the pad and penned a response. When she was done, she poured a cup of coffee and leaned against his kitchen island. She felt truly happy. Not only were her spirits heightened, but the flavor and the earthy aroma of the dark-roast coffee also seemed more pronounced than usual. She straightened the apartment, packed her things, and finished her coffee. Then it was time to return to her place for a full day of study.

Sunset had turned the sky cobalt over the western hills when Katie closed her review materials and rubbed her tired eyes. She thought it odd that Mark hadn't contacted her all day. The evening ahead would be the first in a week she'd sleep by herself, and her apartment felt lonely. Maybe something unexpected had come up. After a dinner of soup, bread, and cheese, she climbed into bed and switched off her nightstand light. She tossed and turned and found it impossible to sleep.

Morning finally arrived after a fitful night. Katie got out of bed and started some coffee. The wind had howled all night outside her bedroom window, so she knew to dress warmly. After downing a cup of coffee and nibbling on a croissant, she put on her coat, hat, and gloves and went outside. The frigid air bit into her face as she walked toward Mark's apartment, her head lowered against the breeze. Over the three months she'd known him, he'd always responded within an hour or two to a message. Something wasn't right.

She arrived on Mark's porch and knocked on the door with her gloved fist. She tried three separate times, but the screen door simply rattled on its hinges. No answer. She thought to venture around back and into the alley where he normally parked his car. Not there. Her anxiety from the night before hadn't diminished, and she began to feel queasy. Back on the porch, she thought about what to do next. She decided to go visit Professor Hatfield. She didn't have the professor's class until the following day but hoped she might find her in her office. She pulled out her phone and checked the professor's website and confirmed that her office hours that day started in an hour. Katie went to the student union and sipped from a cup of hot tea while she waited.

An hour later, she found another student inside Professor Hatfield's office. Katie didn't wait long before the student finished his conversation and the professor invited her in.

"Hello, Ms. Russell. Nice job on your presentation. I found your analysis to be well reasoned, and you handled the questions well. How may I help you?"

"Thank you. It's an excellent class, and I learned a lot from it. Do you happen to know where I might find Assistant Professor O'Connor? I've been unable to contact him."

Katie didn't know what to make of Professor Hatfield's reaction. Her sullen eyes, recessed inside the bony structure of the professor's face, looked even smaller than usual as she narrowed them. They darted over Katie in search of something. She pursed her thin lips before she spoke. "I'm surprised you don't know."

"Know what?"

"Where he is, of course."

"How would I know? Has something happened to him?"

"You need to ask him."

"I'm trying. I can't reach him. I'm concerned."

"My dear, I can't help you." Professor Hatfield crossed her arms and leaned back in her chair. "He finished his teaching responsibilities for the term and then went home to Durango. He found a substitute for the other class he teaches."

Katie was stunned. She searched Hatfield's eyes for any additional clues. The professor's glare reminded her of the glares she'd received from her mother after returning home at four in the morning with a midnight curfew. "Can't you tell me anything?"

"You should speak with Mark. Is there anything else?"

"No, thank you." It was obvious that Hatfield wouldn't say more.

Katie left the office and headed downstairs to the building's small lobby. She pulled her phone from her backpack and called Mark. Once again, she got his voice mail. "Mark, it's Katie. Please call me. I need to speak with you. I'm worried."

Katie returned to her apartment and tried to study the rest of the day, but she couldn't concentrate. What would become of their plans for the holiday break? She'd already purchased her ticket home to California. Would she still go to Durango over New Year's?

She was in the middle of rewriting her class notes when her phone rang: it was Brian Taylor. What could he want? She knew it was too soon after the hearing for the dean to administer sanctions. She spoke haltingly when she answered.

Brian's tone was curt. "A source within the university told me about another sexual-misconduct investigation that's under way. I'm surprised I haven't read about it in your reports."

"What do you mean? As you know, I've been routinely submitting my required reports before the end of each month. I've assumed everything's been in order. I'm not aware of any other investigation beyond what happened with Ava."

"Really? I'm surprised, since you're named as a participant."

Her mind reeled at the comment. "Mr. Taylor, I don't know what you're talking about." As the words left her lips, her brain suddenly made the connection: Mark's disappearance, Professor Hatfield's odd comments, and now this…

"You and Assistant Professor O'Connor are alleged to have engaged in an amorous relationship. Is that true?"

Katie's first instinct was to avoid the question, but she knew she was under a contractual obligation to Brian. "Well, yes, but it didn't start until after he'd finished his teaching responsibilities with me."

"I understand he assists with your philosophy and law class. Are you aware that it's against the administrative code of conduct for him to have an amorous relationship with you as your professor? First, he's required to report it. Then, after reporting it and in consultation with his department head, he'll likely be reassigned to a position where he'd have no responsibility or authority over you. The university must avoid any conflict of interest and power differential between faculty and staff. My understanding is that he hasn't taken either of those steps."

"Like I said, nothing happened until after he was done with his supervision of me. I don't see why it's an issue."

"That's not the way the Office of Policy and Efficiency sees it."

She wondered if that name could be any more Orwellian. "How do they see it, exactly?"

"They contend that the relationship started early in the semester, at an off-campus party. I've seen the file. They've amassed a lot of information."

"Like what?"

"Emails, text messages, statements by other students and employees who saw you together—that kind of thing."

"What! Where did they get that?"

"I can't really say. It's the photos that make their case."

"Photos? What photos?"

"You're not aware of them?"

Her stomach churned. She recalled the selfies she'd taken with Mark that first glorious night in his bed. If the university had confronted Mark with them, he'd surely be outraged.

"Let's just say you make an attractive couple."

What an ass. Katie's voice went shrill. "What am I supposed to do?"

"Your contract stipulates that you must abide by the university's rules of conduct. If the university finds that you and Professor O'Conner have engaged in a prohibited amorous relationship, then I'll have to terminate your employment. We covered these rules in your training."

"Are you kidding? We didn't do anything wrong."

"That's not what's being alleged."

"You've caught me off guard. I need time to think."

"You'll hear from the university in the next couple of days. I'll be following this case closely and will keep you on the payroll until it's resolved. Until then, I expect you to cooperate with the university and to stay current on your reports."

Katie put the phone down and collapsed onto her bed. She rubbed her temples and swore a few times. How had the university gotten the information? Especially the photos. She picked up her phone and looked for them. They were still there. She hadn't done anything with the files but view them from time to time. She enjoyed seeing her expressions of happiness and the beauty of their bodies together. Mark would be beyond angry.

Katie rolled onto her back and stared at the ceiling. What would happen to him? What would happen to her? Guilt vied with outrage in a race of emotions. After several deep breaths, she thought to make tea and try to restore calm. On the way to the kitchen, she was so unsure of her steps that she kept a hand against the wall for support. She filled the teakettle with water and set it on the stove.

She switched on the gas and, after a hiss and a whoosh, blue flames began to lick the bottom of the kettle. She moved to the living room and settled into her favorite armchair next to the front window and waited. The tree on the street, the one that had been so verdant and lush in the summer, was now laid bare by fall, and its branches had hardened against a season of cold. Would her heart, like those branches, harden against the cold that Mark would surely blow in her direction? She closed her eyes and recalled the conversations she'd had with Professor Hatfield and Brian Taylor. She struggled to comprehend how the university had gotten the photos. It seemed so improbable. Then, like a ball on a roulette wheel, her mind bounced to a stop and landed on an idea. She smiled at the same time the kettle began to whistle.

THE BOHEMIAN BIERGARTEN HAD BECOME HER favorite bar. Her first visit had been with Paul for the creepy nanny interview at the start of the semester. Her next visit had been with Ava for their emotional conversation after the football game. After the shocking phone call with Brian Taylor and his comments about her having an amorous relationship with Mark, Katie remembered back to the end of her earlier meeting with Paul, and of his offer to help her if she ever needed it. She'd contacted him, and he'd agreed to meet her back at the Biergarten. His position as director of cybersecurity suggested that he would be in a unique position to help. She sat at an empty table and didn't wait long before a waitress came and took her order for a cider. The after-work crowd was thick and the noise level in the bar energetic.

"Hello, Katie." Paul appeared from behind her. "Good to see you."

Katie stood and gave Paul a quick handshake. "Thanks for meeting me. I need some help and didn't know where else to turn."

"I'm glad you called. Tell me about it." Paul pulled out a chair opposite Katie's and ordered a beer the next time the waitress came around.

Katie gave Paul a brief overview of her life on campus since they'd met for the nanny interview. She left out Brian Taylor, the sexual assault against Ava, and the subsequent hearing, but she did mention her strong feelings for Mark and how their relationship had developed.

"You think the university received, and has in its possession, emails, texts, and photos that belong to you?"

"Yes."

"And you have no idea how it got them?"

"None."

"Didn't you tell me that you have an ex-boyfriend somewhere?"

"Yes, he lives in Seattle. He works for a big Internet retailer there."

"Do you think he might hold a grudge or have any other reason to hurt you?"

"I don't know. He broke up with me, but later he said that he realized he'd made a big mistake and wanted to patch things up. I'd already moved on by then, though. I wanted nothing to do with him."

"Do you think he wishes you were still together?"

"Maybe. I guess that's possible."

"Would he have had access to your email passwords when you were dating?"

"I don't remember giving them to him, no."

"How about accessing your phone? Could he have done that?"

"Sure, I suppose. We were together a lot. He easily could have looked at my phone when I was out for a run, or taking a shower, or asleep."

"Do you have a log-in passcode on your phone?"

"No, I hate those."

"Mind if I look at it?"

Katie handed her phone to Paul and watched him study the phone's settings and options.

"Here's one problem. Your phone's set up to forward all your text messages to an additional phone number." He read off ten digits.

"That's Justin's phone number!" Her mind raced to consider all the information Justin might have seen. In addition to Mark, he probably knew about Brian Taylor, the contract, and her involvement with Ava.

Paul tapped the screen a few times. "There, that's disabled. You said you think he might've had access to your photos as well?"

"The photos the university has must have been taken with my phone. They're very private." Katie's face went crimson.

Paul tapped the screen a few more times. "Your phone's also set to copy all camera photos to your cloud-storage account. If he has that password, then he'd have access. Too bad you didn't attend one of my new-student orientation classes. This is exactly the kind of thing we warn people about in our topic on social media. I think you've been compromised. He could have put some spyware on your laptop and can probably capture any new passwords you create there, too. Let me do a clean install of the operating system. That's the only way to be sure. And change your passwords as soon as possible on all your sensitive accounts. Use your phone to do it, and don't log on again with your laptop until I've reinstalled everything for you. Do you have it with you?"

Katie reached inside her backpack. "Yes, it's right here."

"I'll work on it tonight and call you when I'm done."

"I'm surprised you're willing to help me after I turned you down. I can't thank you enough."

"I can think of a few ways."

"Paul."

"Just kidding. I'm happy to hear you found your guy."

"How about you. Anyone new?"

"I met a woman who lives and works here in Boulder. She finished grad school last June and seems genuinely interested in me and my daughter—who knows why. She's kind of a geek. We'll see. But you gave me some good advice. I appreciate it."

"Paul, you're a good guy. You'll do fine."

"Thanks. One more thing. Do you happen to have an old email from Justin?"

"I think so. I didn't delete them all, though one night I was tempted." Katie smiled for the first time during their conversation and began to relax. She flexed her tight shoulders and took a sip of cider. At least she had a better understanding of what had happened with Mark.

"Forward one to me. I want to look for something."

"Sure. Give me my phone." Katie took it back and scrolled through her emails. It took a few minutes to find one. She showed it to Paul. "Want me to forward it?"

"No, wait until you change your passwords. I'm going to my office now to work on your laptop. I'll text you when I'm done, and we can make plans for you to pick it up tomorrow. Until then, you can text, but don't send any more emails until after you change passwords."

"Thanks, Paul. I'll change them right now."

They stood, and Katie hugged Paul, who left through the back entrance. She took another sip of cider and got to work changing all the important account passwords on her phone.

When that task was done, she sat back and thought. She noticed how noisy the bar had become. It was packed now, and a couple of guys asked if they could sit at her table. The last thing she wanted was some idle conversation, so she said yes, finished her drink, and left. On the way home, she decided to walk back to Chautauqua Park to gather her thoughts. It was dark by then and very cold. She was amazed how warm Boulder had been in the summertime and how cold it had become in December. It was beautiful either way, but she missed the warmth of the sun. She had barely stepped into the park when she heard a unique ringtone on her phone, the one she'd picked for Mark.

"Mark, I'm so glad you called. I'm worried."

"I'm sorry I've been hard to reach."

Katie struggled for words. "Professor Hatfield told me you're back home in Durango."

"That's why I called. She told me you dropped by. I owe you an explanation."

"I think I know. I heard about the university's investigation."

"You did? How?"

Katie regretted not telling Mark about the whole messy business with Brian Taylor. She certainly didn't want to go into it now. "I heard they plan to talk with me."

"I'm not surprised. I don't think you have anything to worry about—it's me they're after."

"Mark, we didn't do anything wrong."

"That's not the way the university sees it." Mark sounded dejected.

"Did we make a mistake by getting together?" Katie asked, hoping for reassurance.

"Absolutely not. I was confident that if we waited, we'd be OK. Now, my tenure might be in jeopardy."

"I guess we could have waited longer. But we didn't, and I don't want to turn back now. I want to find a way to fix this."

"What can you do?"

"I don't know. I'll think of something. I know how they got the photos, though. That's a start."

"You know about those?"

"I'm pretty sure my ex-boyfriend sent them. I think he's been reading all my email and text messages since we broke up. He's probably been following our relationship from the start."

"But why? Why would he do that?"

"I suspect he's jealous. It seems unlike him, but he might have snapped or something. He acted weird once he took his new job."

"I'm sure he regrets leaving you behind."

"Something like that. Mark, I still want to come see you over New Year's."

"I'm not so sure that's a good idea. My teaching career could be over. I plan to help my dad and brother with the ranch until the university finishes its investigation. You should cooperate with them. For now, we need to be cautious. Let's talk again in a few days." He ended the call.

Katie stared at the sidewalk. Tears ran down her cheeks and fell onto hard cement, where they quickly glazed over on the frozen surface. She felt as though she'd been given a fragile figurine to hold and admire and instead had let it slip from her grasp to smash on the ground.

CHAPTER 23

"The Most Powerful Weapon on Earth"

Brian Taylor called Katie on Monday of finals week. "Do you have any more information about the investigation into Assistant Professor O'Connor?"

"I'm cooperating with the university."

"Smart decision. He's in trouble either way."

Katie remembered Mark's Jesuit-inspired advice: "The first step toward the power of moral action lies in the power we have to think morally." "Anything else?" She wanted the call to end.

"The sanctions against Drew Evans were announced this morning. You're now eligible for a fifty-thousand-dollar bonus for your testimony."

"What are his sanctions?"

"He's to perform eighty hours of community service and, beginning next semester and continuing for as long as Ms. Greene remains in school, he is not to contact her or register for any of the same classes. And he's required to write a paper and submit it to the Office of Student Conduct."

"Write a paper! Are you kidding me? He rapes a girl and that's his punishment? I bet he still gets to play football. No wonder people are outraged over the issue of sexual assault on campus. What a joke."

"Katie, if you hadn't reported the assault, he never would've received any sanctions at all. Look at it another way. These events are now on his record. The university knows it has a problem and will watch him more closely. If Ava had agreed to testify, or to release the results of her forensic exam, then it might have been a different story. You did your best to compel her, but without more evidence, I don't know how this could have come out any better."

"If that predator was sitting in jail, that's how. I guarantee you he'll reoffend with another unsuspecting student. Not only that, but I read that the football team's been selected to play in a major bowl game on New Year's Day. I'll bet the administration is proud of their star quarterback."

"Katie, I understand your frustration, but take my advice. Enjoy the win. I'll have your check waiting for you tomorrow in my office."

What was it about this money? She felt incredibly compromised. Her mountain of debt was about to be leveled by a payment that felt somehow dirty. She was nothing more than a paid informant. Think morally, Mark had said. It was time she started.

"PROFESSOR WILSON, THANK YOU FOR MEETING with me. I'm sure you're busy."

"It's a hectic time, but you sounded concerned. How can I help you?"

"It's a long story."

"We have an hour."

Katie told her everything: Brian Taylor and her contract with the NSAF, Ava's assault and hearing, her relationship with Mark and the accusations of an amorous relationship, and finally Mark's suspension and departure for Durango.

Professor Wilson raised her eyebrows several times and scribbled notes during Katie's retelling. "That's quite a story. I'm not a big fan of relationships between professors and students. Not because I believe they're inherently wrong—hell, I've had a few myself—but because they typically don't last. Worse, they often end badly. I have great respect for Mark. He's one of the brightest young professors we have on campus. He told me he thinks you're a gifted student. I'm not surprised there's an attraction between you two."

"I want to get Mark out of this mess," Katie said. "I'll never forgive myself if I keep him from tenure. It's insulting that the university can intervene in our personal lives like this."

"Don't get me started. It's as if the administration has become more concerned about Title IX's focus on sexual misconduct than the law's original intent of preventing gender discrimination. I hoped the freedom of speech and tolerance for opposing ideas would get us through this backlash of political correctness. Today, the university insists that we protect students from controversial subjects with trigger warnings and safe spaces. The president of UC Berkeley once said, 'The university is not engaged in making ideas safe for students. It is engaged in making students safe for ideas.' That notion seems almost quaint today."

Katie appreciated Professor Wilson's strong opinions but wanted to get her back on track. "How can I help Mark?"

"I'd like to help him myself, but it's too politically risky for me personally. Sure, I'm tenured, but they can still make my life very difficult. They could assign me classes at a remote campus somewhere on the other side of the state or increase my load of grad students. I think you should meet with a private criminal attorney."

"Criminal? Why?"

"Do you remember our first visit, when you asked me about Brian Taylor?"

"Yes."

"I've known Brian a long time. He was a very bright and charismatic student. I'm not surprised by his career success, nor was I surprised when I heard he was arrested for a DUI during a car accident that sent a woman to the hospital with a broken leg that left her with a permanent limp. She recovered, thankfully, but it was a serious offense. The Colorado Bar Association had no choice but to suspend him for two years while he completed counseling. He and the dean are close friends. They both attended this university, and I've heard plenty of rumors of wild behavior: excessive drinking, lots of women, even some backroom gambling. The dean put all that behind him in grad school when he married Brian's sister. His record in the administration has been exemplary."

She paused and looked out the window. "I'm speculating now, but I suspect that the dean set Brian up with this private foundation as a personal favor. I'd like to know where their donations come from and where the money goes. I've heard of a wealthy alumna who pressed the administration to become more proactive about reducing sexual assaults on campus. She was a practicing attorney before she married the founder of a local organic tea company that rolled out a successful IPO and hit it big.

Sadly, her husband died while diving off the coast of Mexico. She inherited twenty percent of the company. To her credit, she now gives most of it away to charitable causes. It wouldn't surprise me if the dean was somehow matching her gifts without formal authority from the university. It has to be off the books somehow."

"Why would the dean do something unauthorized?" Katie enjoyed listening to the professor and could easily imagine her presenting closing arguments in front of a jury.

"I think what Brian told you is likely true. The DOE is investigating more than a hundred universities for Title IX enforcement as well as those universities' failure to investigate and eliminate campus sexual assault and discrimination. The threat of losing federal funding is huge. Power is money on campus, and when the university president makes more than a million dollars a year, he and all the others who are below him want to keep it that way. It follows that the administration would want to appear proactive about the matter. An increase in investigations and sanctions against male students will go a long way toward keeping the DOE at bay."

"Do you think the university president knows about the private foundation Brian's running?"

"It sounds like we're talking about a sizable amount of money. I'd guess he does, but he'd also ensure that there isn't a paper trail to tie him to Brian, the dean, or the organization."

"What do you think I should do?"

Professor Wilson pulled a business card from her desk drawer and handed it to Katie. "Go see this attorney. Tell her I referred you. She's very aggressive. Once you set in motion legal action against the university, it'll be hard to turn back. If you want to help Mark, then I think she's your best option. If she believes she can help, then I wouldn't hesitate to have her represent you. I don't think she's ever lost a case."

"OK, thanks—I'll call her. But I don't know how I'll ever be able to pay her."

"Don't worry. If I'm right and she decides to take the case, then she'll find a way for the university to pay her fees." Professor Wilson paused a moment, which gave Katie a chance to think things over. "I need to wrap up," she said. "Keep your chin up: your life will be full of good things. I'm curious, have you given any thought to my earlier suggestion that you consider a career in law?"

"I think about it all the time."

KATIE WALKED TO PAUL'S OFFICE AFTER THE meeting with Professor Wilson and picked up her laptop, which was waiting for her at the receptionist's desk along with a note Paul had written.

> Katie, I've done some checking. I confirmed that the university received an email that was sent from the same laptop that was used to send the old email from Justin you gave me—the one that included the photos. I verified the email's hardware signatures. He didn't do a very good job at anonymity. Probably didn't care. If it's all right with you, I'd like to send a standard inquiry to his employer to verify the authenticity of the email and ask them if they're aware that one of their employees has been sending your personal and intimate photos—without your permission—through the company servers. It will teach him a valuable lesson.
>
> I also think I might have discovered why he's been trying to retaliate against you. I ran a search of his social media posts and those of some of his friends—something we do when we hire new employees. I found what seems to be a reference to you having a relationship with a professor at this university. I'm sorry if this all sounds very creepy, but I thought you should know. There's one more thing, but I prefer to discuss it with you directly. Call me when you have a chance.
>
> Best,
> Paul

That explained it all right. He must have learned about Mark through her emails and texts, then found the photos. She'd never really thought of Justin as being prone to jealousy, though he'd certainly been oppressive and controlling at times, but that didn't justify his creepy spying. She hoped Paul's email to Justin's employer would convince him to leave her alone.

CHAPTER 24
Not a Very Merry Christmas

Katie was demoralized and hopeless as she boarded the flight from Denver to Orange County. Nothing had prepared her for the pain of recent events. Her past life had been more blissful than melancholy, more successful than not. As she settled into her window seat, she eyed the crush of passengers struggling to stuff their items into overhead bins and squeeze themselves into undersize seats. Although surrounded by humanity, she became aware that for the moment, if not forever, she was alone.

After enduring an endless-seeming two-hour flight seated next to an older man who wouldn't stop asking questions, Katie arrived at the John Wayne Airport, where she was met by her family. As they drove her home, she struggled to maintain a pleasant demeanor and found that any conversation, no matter how easygoing, was unable to dent the impenetrable wall of defeat she felt.

After dinner that first night, when the dishes were washed and while Katie sat alone with her mother at the kitchen table, she slowly revealed the events of the fall semester. It was the first time she'd mentioned Mark, and she was careful with her words. Summaries were sufficient, she knew, and details, like the photos, were too risky. She'd obviously made a mistake and didn't need her mother's admonition on top of it. In a slightly awkward moment, Katie's mom asked her if Mark was passionate. Katie's sparkling eyes and wide smile confirmed that he was.

Katie took frequent refuge in her childhood bedroom, where she sat on her old twin bed with its familiar sheets and a herd of stuffed animals that placidly awaited her return, eyes open in seeming anticipation. She penned notes into her journal with a cup of smoky black tea nearby. On an unusually dark day as a gray and listless sky squeezed cold rain onto the neighborhood and the nearby beaches, Katie lay on her bed and listened to the rhythmic gurgle of rainfall running down the copper gutter outside her bedroom window. Though the day was cold by Southern California standards, she'd still dressed in shorts and an old Claremont McKenna sweatshirt.

She remembered something and got up off the bed and went to her closet. She moved some boxes of books around and located the one she'd thought of. It contained some of her favorite puzzles and brainteasers. As a teenager, when she wasn't with friends on the beach or helping around the house, she'd spent hours absorbed in those books. One of her favorite puzzles featured line drawings with hidden objects. They were designed to enhance children's observation skills. Birds and articles of clothing, like a robin or a sock, were often hidden, drawn into a tree or a yard. Katie frequently became so absorbed in the puzzles that she'd refuse to quit until after she'd located every missing item. Sometimes after her mother insisted she go to bed, Katie pulled out a flashlight to continue in secret, hidden under her covers. She suspected that her fascination with word games, puzzles, and brainteasers had eventually led her to philosophy.

Katie pulled from the box a stack of magazines and books and placed them on the closet floor. Toward the bottom, she found the object she'd recalled, wrapped in a soft chamois cloth. She stared at the framed photo of her with her father, taken the day she'd received her driver's license. Her raised hand held the freshly laminated card, and her father held his arm around her. He'd come from his office and so was dressed in a business suit. Katie remembered how, after the driving portion of the test, she stepped from the car and saw him waiting for her, tears in his eyes—the first time she'd ever seen him cry. He'd asked the examiner to take the photo. She studied it for a few more minutes, wrapped it back inside the protective cloth, and put it in her suitcase for the trip back to Boulder.

She adored her father. Because of him, her childhood had been boringly normal. Now that she was older and had some perspective, she especially appreciated her good fortune. He'd provided a comfortable life in a typical neighborhood with upper-middle-class values. The family bungalow, nestled among manicured lawns and gardens, sat only a few blocks from the ocean; seagulls frequently screeched in the blue skies overhead. The biggest risk to her health back then had been the threat of sunburn.

Her father loved their postwar bungalow and felt that it harkened back to a more honest time when people were judged by purity of heart and simplicity of purpose. As part of a generation of boys who were required to take wood shop in high school, he maintained the home with great skill for an amateur. Country clubs and Saturday-afternoon golf games were always less important to him than productive weekends at home making repairs or reading for work. Katie often helped him around the house, or at least watched him. She knew about miter boxes and circular saws, why screws were better than nails, and to always measure twice and cut once. She naturally compared every man she dated to her father, and he'd set the bar impossibly high. Though he'd usually been slow to warm to most of the guys she'd dated, she believed that Mark would be his favorite should they ever meet.

Christmas Eve, when Katie joined her family around their colorfully lit tree and toasted with glasses of champagne, her only thoughts were of Mark and how she could possibly undo what she'd done. It was perfectly understandable that he had cancelled their plans for New Year's Eve together in Durango, but she still wished she could have spent the holiday with him. The limited joy she felt during her visit home was provided by her grades, which her professors had posted online; she'd received all As. The grade for her philosophy and law class was the most gratifying, since it confirmed that Professor Hatfield hadn't penalized her for her relationship with Mark. That was something.

The day before her return flight to Boulder, Katie spoke by phone with Harriet Becker, the attorney Professor Wilson had recommended. During the hour-long call, Katie shared as much detail and as many important facts as she could remember. Though Becker sounded coolly professional, she became quite spirited when Katie mentioned the contract with the NSAF and her role as campus ambassador, especially the provision for payment of a $50,000 bonus should a reported student be successfully sanctioned for sexual assault. Becker requested a copy of the contract. By the end of the call, the attorney had promised to schedule a meeting with the Office of Policy and Efficiency once Katie had returned from California.

Over good-byes at the airport, Katie's mom expressed concern that Katie might be depressed and asked her to stay home a few more days and talk it over with the family doctor. Katie placed her head on her mom's shoulder and wrapped her tightly in her arms. They locked eyes after their embrace, and Katie wiped away a few tears.

"I think I messed things up with Mark." Katie struggled to maintain some composure.

"Sweetie, what happened?" Katie's mom took her hand.

"I did something stupid. But I'm going to find a way to fix it. Just know that I'm all right, and I'll tell you all about it someday."

Her mom had read Katie well, but what she didn't appreciate was the extent of Katie's resolve. Mark had shown her the possibility of a meaningful and healthy relationship. She loved him for that, unconditionally. She'd repair whatever damage she'd caused him by doing whatever it might take.

After boarding the plane, Katie sat back in her seat and stared out the window. By the time the plane lifted off the runway, its wheels had been tucked inside its fuselage with a solid mechanical thump; she felt her mind awakening, as though sloughing off the grip of some strange hypnosis. Her sense of purpose toward Mark had begun to relax her. A lugubrious week was finally over. She put down her tray table and anticipated a glass of wine once the drink cart arrived at her row.

New Year's Eve was three days away when Katie arrived back in her Boulder apartment. After turning on the heat and unpacking, she walked along the mostly empty streets to her favorite grocery store and shopped for food. As she cut through campus along the way home, she noticed that the Old Main building looked especially quiet. She surveyed Mark's office window and noted that the whole building was darkened for the holiday break.

Katie returned home and sent a text to Ava to ask if she was in town; she received a quick response that she'd be returning on January first. Katie made a pot of tea and retreated to her favorite chair next to the window in the living room with a plate of sandwich cookies. She savored the first sip of tea and, since no one was looking, separated the two halves of the cookie and licked off the creamy filling inside. She turned her attention to the tree outside the window, which seemed to be a living timeline of her life in Boulder: green growth in summer, paintbrush streaks of rust and gold in fall, and now barrenness in winter. She wondered what springtime would bring. Up and down the street lay scattered patches of leftover ice from a Christmas snowstorm. Katie smiled at the beauty of the scene and returned her gaze to the tree. It had likely borne witness to generations of students living in her apartment. If trees could speak, she wondered, what might it say of her idea? Katie took another sip of tea and closed her eyes. She'd considered the idea all week and couldn't let it go.

She opened her eyes, got up from the chair, and retrieved her phone. A mapping app showed that Durango was nearly a seven-hour drive through the Rockies and over several high passes—not a casual under-taking in the middle of winter. She'd never driven in snow before, other than the short drive home after dinner at Mark's, when the snow was only an inch thick and easily navigable. She checked the weather forecast; it looked promising until a few days after New Year's, when another storm was expected to arrive in the state.

On the morning of New Year's Eve, Katie loaded her car and was on the road by eight. The first couple of hours driving up I-70 toward Loveland Pass were uneventful. She was awestruck at the entrance to the Eisenhower Tunnel, which she'd read was the highest vehicle tunnel in the United States. The eleven-thousand-foot-high road was bare, but snow from plows and accumulated snowfall lay piled up all around her. She could see skiers traversing runs near the entrance to the tunnel. A mile and a half later, she exited on the other side of the pass.

After another half hour of driving, Katie pulled off the road in the small town of Frisco and found a gas station. She filled the car's tank and then thought to drive to a coffee shop across the highway and get some coffee and a sandwich to go. Inside, she sat down on one of many stools at a long counter. Energetic fry cooks moved around an open and noisy kitchen. A large clock on the wall read a little before noon.

"What'll ya have, darlin'?" A garrulous waitress, her face heavy with makeup and of an age that Katie guessed to be around fifty, held a small pad and pencil and waited expectantly. A gravelly voice and vertical creases in her lips suggested a lifetime of drinking and smoking.

Katie surveyed the menu for a minute while the waitress tapped her pencil on her pad. "Mmm, I think I'll have a cup of coffee and a turkey sandwich, to go."

"What kind of bread?"

"Whole wheat."

"Whatcha want on it?"

"Swiss cheese, lettuce, tomato. No spreads, thanks."

"Chips?"

"Sure."

"Okie dokie." The waitress—her name tag said Honey—put the pad in a front pocket on her apron. She brought Katie a porcelain white coffee cup and saucer in one hand and a glass decanter of coffee in the other. She filled the cup. "Where ya headed, darlin'? You don't look like you're dressed to ski."

Katie appreciated her interest. "Durango."

"That's a long way. You're lucky the weather's good. That's a treacherous drive in wintertime over Wolf Creek Pass." She put her hand on her hip and set the coffee carafe on the counter, as if she were prepared to stay a minute.

"Well, better to be lucky than good." Katie had no idea why she'd recalled that particular idiom. Funny how the mind worked sometimes.

"What takes ya to Durango?"

"A guy."

"Of course he does. Well, I hope he's worth it, because it's a long way to go."

"He's worth it. In fact, I need to get back on the road."

Evidently taking the cue, Honey picked up the coffee decanter and walked over to the kitchen window.

As Katie enjoyed her coffee, she surveyed her fellow patrons: everyone from trucker to skier was there. New Year's streamers hung from the ceiling. A Christmas tree adorned a corner by the door. A sign reminded everyone that the shop would be closing early in observance of New Year's Eve.

"Here you go, darlin'. I put plenty of napkins in there for ya." She set a brown paper bag on the counter with the check. "I'll get you a to-go cup for your coffee. Now you be careful out there. People around here have been known to start their celebratin' a bit early. Get off the road before dark."

"Thanks—I will." Katie left enough money on the counter to pay for the food plus a generous tip. Five minutes later, she was back on her way with her car full of gas.

The drive over Wolf Creek Pass, unlike Loveland Pass and its tunnel, required negotiating a series of switchbacks. It, too, was somehow over dry pavement surrounded by piled-up snow. Some of the switchbacks down the back side had small patches of packed snow and ice, but Katie had no trouble negotiating them. The mountains, including several majestic fourteen-thousand-foot peaks, were stunning, especially where the sunlight blazed on the craggy rock. The ski area's parking lot appeared full, and she could see small figures zigzagging down the white slopes.

It was late afternoon when Katie arrived in the authentic Western town of Durango and parked her car in front of the restored Strater Hotel. She'd read about its history before leaving Boulder. Built during the gold-rush years of the 1880s, it had been a second home for many residents, who moved into the hotel's rooms, most with fireplaces, during the cold winter months. It had fallen on hard times during the silver panic of 1895 and was forced into bankruptcy. During the Roaring Twenties, Western author Louis L'Amour frequently took up residence in a room above the Diamond Belle Saloon and wrote his novels. Now tastefully furnished with modern conveniences, the landmark hotel catered to tourists visiting the Rockies, Mesa Verde National Park, and the historic narrow-gauge railway to the old mining town of Silverton. Katie was impressed by the hotel's stately grandeur as she walked through its lobby and located the reception desk.

"May I help you?" A young man dressed in a white shirt and tie, overlaid with a black wool vest, looked at her with a smile so wide it suggested he'd been well trained in the art of customer service. Katie noted that his teeth were almost perfect. His name tag read Rob.

"Rob, I have a reservation under the name Russell."

Rob flipped through his reservation file, which really was a file and not listings on a computer screen. "Ms. Russell, I see you're only with us for one night. That's not nearly long enough to see all of Durango's attractions. May I please have your credit card and some ID?"

"Sure. I'd love to visit longer. Maybe during the summer so I can ride the train."

"Please, let me give you my card. If you do decide to return, I'd be happy to show you around." With a rather obvious wink, Rob handed Katie a business card with the title CUSTOMER SERVICE PARTNER printed on it. After a few minutes of paperwork, he handed Katie a room key and returned her credit card and driver's license. "Your room is up the elevator and left down the hall. I gave you a quiet room toward the back. Is there anything else I can help you with?"

"Yes, I'm wondering if you know where I might find the O'Connor ranch."

"Oh, you mean the J Lazy M dude ranch?"

"Dude ranch? I thought it was a cattle ranch."

"Oh, still is, but about ten years ago, they started taking in guests and offering horseback riding and other activities in the summer. It's quite popular."

"Well, then yes, I guess I'm looking for the J Lazy M."

"You won't find anyone out there now. They live in town during winter and maintain the ranch and manage the herd from here. Everyone moves back out in the spring and stays through the fall."

"So where can I find the O'Connors now?"

"At the family home about three miles away. Here, I'll write down their address for you."

"Thanks." Katie waited for Rob to write the address on a notepad. She estimated he was around twenty years old, probably working his way through college.

"Would you like me to give them a call and let them know you're coming?"

"No…it's a surprise, and I'd hate to spoil it. Thanks, though—you've been very helpful."

"You're welcome, Ms. Russell. And remember, if you come back, stay longer and give me a call." There was that wink again. "Happy New Year!"

Friendly town, Katie thought. She made her way back to the front door, where a bellman helped her with her luggage. He promised to watch her car while she went to find her room.

About an hour later, Katie returned to the lobby and, as promised, found her car waiting outside. She put the handwritten address for Mark's house on the passenger seat and a present and card she'd brought for him next to it. She punched the address into her phone, pulled away from the curb, and headed west toward the mountains. The sun had set below the horizon and had colored the sky in a palette of bright-amber hues that overlaid a jagged outline of mountains. Higher up in the sky, the amber hues transitioned into an inky blackness.

Three miles down the main road, Katie's phone directed her to turn onto what appeared to be a seldom-used road, one covered in patches of snow and ice. In a quarter of a mile, she gingerly pulled over next to a mailbox that displayed Mark's family's address. A split-rail fence—typical in the West, she'd noticed—ran between the road and the property line and on either side of a gravel driveway toward a large ranch-style home.

Katie switched off the car's engine and lights and surveyed the structure. The car's interior immediately started to cool, so she zipped up her jacket. She could see a large picture window that framed a Christmas tree decorated with small white lights. It looked like a painting. Next to the tree, a dog stood near the window and stared in her direction. Its tail wagged rhythmically, and it regularly looked to its right, toward another room inside the house. Following the dog's gaze toward another set of windows, Katie saw several adults standing around in what must have been the kitchen. She could see lots of movement inside. A woman placed a bowl on a counter, and a man appeared to be drying dishes. Katie was worried that the dog might bark and alert those inside to her presence, so she was relieved to see it trot off in the direction of the kitchen, probably in search of food. It must have decided that her car out front wasn't a threat.

Katie picked up the card and started to inscribe it with a quote from the book she'd brought to give Mark: *"Laws and principles are not for the times when there is no temptation: they are for such moments as this"* —Jane Eyre. She continued, *I'm sorry for the pain I've caused, but I'll never regret our time together. Unrestrained passion, unknown till now, smolders like a fire with embers that will never grow cold. My love for you is pure. Happy New Year, Mark. I love you, always. —Katie.*

She sealed the envelope and tied it to the book with a large length of white ribbon; it was her favorite way to wrap gifts. Once she had the bow perfectly shaped, she stepped from the car and walked to the mailbox, pulled open the lid, and placed the present and card inside. On the walk back to her car, she thought she saw Mark walk through the living room window and past the Christmas tree. Her heart picked up its pace; she was excited to see him but fearful that she might be discovered. He kept moving and went quickly out of sight. At least she got to see him on New Year's Eve. Sort of.

Katie retraced her route to the hotel. The thought of spending the night alone in her room at the Strater didn't appeal to her, but neither did venturing down to the Diamond Belle Saloon. She'd probably have a glass of wine from room service and call it an early night. With any luck, she'd be asleep before midnight and not have to face the New Year alone.

It was well below freezing as she turned her car back onto the county road. Near town, she approached a stop sign with a flashing red light, which marked the intersection of the county road with the main highway. Katie applied her brakes to slow the car. Nothing happened—it didn't slow at all. Katie pressed harder on the brake pedal. The wheels skidded on the pavement, unable to grip, and she continued toward the intersection. As the stop sign passed out of view behind her on her right, her attention was drawn to the sound of a horn and the glare of headlights on her left. She watched in horror as an old-looking pickup truck slammed into the rear quarter panel of her car. The impact spun her around so violently that her head hit the driver's-side window. Her car was too old to include side airbags, so she had no protection against her head hitting the glass. Fortunately, it didn't shatter. Spun around at 180 degrees and traveling backward, her car slammed into a utility pole. The sound of crunching metal was the last thing Katie remembered.

CHAPTER 25

A New Year

Katie opened her eyes and surveyed an unfamiliar room. The first thing she noticed was the sound of a slow and steady beep from behind her head, then the blood-pressure cuff wrapped around her arm and wired to an instrument panel. A clothespin-like device of some kind was squeezing the tip of her index finger. Her head ached, and when she lifted her hand to touch it, she felt gauze.

A cheerful-sounding nurse walked in. "Ms. Russell, how are you feeling?"

"Groggy. Am I in a hospital?"

"Mercy Regional, in Durango. You came in last night."

"What time is it?"

"It's eight thirty in the morning." The nurse checked a computer screen. "You're due for some pain relief. How are you feeling?"

"My head hurts."

"I'm not surprised. You suffered a mild concussion in the accident. Here, take this." The nurse offered her a paper cup with a tablet in it.

"Car accident?" Katie fought through her mental fog to recall the intersection.

"You hit some black ice. It was bad last night."

A man entered the room dressed in slacks and a shirt with a tie embroidered with party hats and streamers and the word *Celebrate*. He was older, with thinning gray hair and a wonderfully warm smile. "Happy New Year, Ms. Russell. Sorry you must spend it here with us."

Katie continued to struggle with the details. "Am I OK?"

"You're fine. You suffered a mild concussion in an automobile accident last night. Nothing worse, fortunately. What do you remember?"

"I think I slid past a stop sign and into an intersection." She paused for a moment. "Then I got hit by a truck."

"That's right. After the collision, you continued backward through the intersection and hit a utility pole. Fortunately, you didn't sustain any life-threatening injuries. I'd like to keep you here one more night for observation. I should be able to release you tomorrow. Not a very fun start to the New Year, I'm afraid. But you've got a TV if you'd like to watch some football games."

"I suppose champagne is out of the question?" Katie knew she'd need something to drink if she had to watch a bowl game featuring CU.

"I'm afraid alcohol is out of the question. Oh, I almost forgot: you have a visitor in the lobby. Would you like me to show him in?" Katie couldn't help but notice a rather obvious twinkle in the doctor's eyes.

The nurse and the doctor both left the room. Katie watched the door expectantly. In a few moments, Mark sauntered into the room, accompanied by his younger brother Jim, whom she'd met back at the bar in Boulder.

"Katie, I'm so glad to see you're OK." Mark approached the bed and took her hand. Neither of them spoke for a moment. "What are you doing in Durango?"

"I brought you a present. I was disappointed we didn't follow through on our plans to spend New Year's Eve together, so I decided to drive here anyway." Jim must have anticipated that this was going to be a private conversation and announced that he was going to find some vending machines.

"You drove here all the way from Boulder? That's crazy this time of year."

"How did you know I was here?"

"The police called the house last night. They searched your car after the accident and found my parents' address on a piece of paper. Either Jim or I have been here ever since, waiting until the doctor would let us see you. He said you suffered a nasty contusion on your head, but other than that, you came out of it fine. Not so for your car, though. The police think it's totaled."

"I was worried about that. My parents won't be too happy."

"Oh, I think they'll be happy to know you're doing well and in a hospital instead of somewhere much worse. Your car should be the least of their concerns. You brought me a present?"

"It's in your mailbox. I put it there and drove back to town. Beautiful Christmas tree."

"How long were you at the house?"

"About fifteen minutes. I think I saw you. It made me sad to see your beautiful home and face when I had to spend the night in the hotel by myself. At least the staff here in the hospital's friendly." Katie laughed, which caused her head to ache.

"The doctor gave me only fifteen minutes to visit you because of your condition. But he thinks he can release you tomorrow. I don't know if you've thought about returning to Boulder, but I'd like to take you out to the ranch and show you around."

"I'd love that."

"I'll get your things from the hotel and take them to the house. Why don't you spend tomorrow night with us? I'll arrange for a flight back to Denver for you the following day. Did you ever consider the fact that driving here on your own, during winter, was a bit impulsive?"

"Did you ever consider the fact that my love for you is a precious gift worth keeping?" Katie knew the pain medication was doing the talking.

Mark paused for a second. "I never stopped considering that."

"Why didn't you want to spend New Year's Eve with me?" Katie liked her newfound skill at directness.

"Because our relationship has put my whole career in jeopardy. I don't know what I'm going to do."

"I'm working on it. You should trust me."

"What can you do about it? The university seems hell-bent on making an example of me."

Katie so wanted to tell Mark everything, to explain why she thought she had leverage with the university, to explain her difficulty in telling uncomfortable truths. "Mark, I never intended for any of this to happen. The last thing in the world I want is to hurt you."

"I know this isn't your fault. But it happened. Everything I worked for might be undone. Even if I do get reinstated, everyone will know it was me. I'll never know how this will affect my career. Secret conversations will be held. Decisions will be made that will never be shared with me. That's the reality of this. Things will never be the same."

Katie's head started to pound harder, even with the pain medication. "I think staying with you here in Durango isn't such a good idea. I'm sure the doctor's going to ask you to leave any minute, and there's a lot I need to tell you. I think it's better if I fly back to Boulder tomorrow. I need to return for a meeting anyway. Can I come back and see the ranch in the summer? Maybe you can even get me onto a horse."

"Katie…"

Katie took Mark's hand and held it to her mouth. She kissed it, then dropped it to her chest and held it to her breasts. "Mark, let's plan twenty-four hours in your apartment with no interruptions, clean sheets, and a bottle of wine. Until then, all I ask is that you don't give up on us. Give me a chance to work this out. I feel horrible about what's happened, and I see how much pain I've caused. Someday, I hope you'll forgive me."

As Katie had anticipated, the doctor stepped back into the room. "Dr. O'Connor, I think you need to let Ms. Russell rest now. She looks fine, but she's been through quite an ordeal."

"Yes, Doctor."

"And say hello to your dad for me. Tell him I expect to see him on the golf course this spring."

"Will do."

Mark got up from the bed and picked up his coat. He walked to the door and turned. "Happy New Year, Katie."

"Happy New Year, Mark. And don't forget to check your mailbox."

Once she was left alone in the room, Katie turned her attention back to the sound of the heart monitor. Its rhythmic beeping reassured her. She was alive, and she had hope. She couldn't think of a better start to the New Year.

MARK FOUND HIS BROTHER WAITING IN THE LOBBY. Because it was New Year's Day, traffic was nonexistent on the drive home. Snow swirled around the pickup. Mark watched ice accumulate in the corners of the windshield and appreciated that Jim didn't ask about his time with Katie. When they arrived at the house, Mark asked Jim to stop the car near the mailbox. When Jim pulled to a stop, Mark got out and told his brother to continue up the drive. He walked over to the mailbox and retrieved Katie's present and card. He read the card while he stood on the gravel drive. He smiled at the *Jane Eyre* quote.

Back at the house, the brothers joined their parents, aunts, uncles, and two cousins for a traditional New Year's dinner. A fire crackled and occasionally popped inside the dining room. Mark didn't feel very festive as everyone dug in to the feast. The family golden retriever slept in a curl next to the fireplace and kept a watchful eye for any bites of food that might hit the floor. Mark felt guilty that he was enjoying a hearty meal with his family while Katie was alone in the hospital.

After dinner, Jim washed, and Mark dried, the dishes. It was a chore they had grown up with and still practiced when they were home together.

Jim handed a washed and rinsed baking dish to Mark, who examined it in the kitchen light. "You call this clean?" He handed it back to his brother.

"You're such a perfectionist." Jim put the dish back into the sink and scrubbed aggressively with a brush. A moment later he rinsed it off and handed it back to Mark. "That better?"

Mark looked closely, located a few spots, and polished them off with his dish towel. "Looks fine." He put it on a shelf.

"You were an impossible older brother growing up."

"Why?"

"Because you were always great at everything you did. I could never compete with you."

Mark took another dish from Jim. "Dad had mellowed by the time you came along. With me, it was always 'A job worth doing is a job worth doing well,' and 'Never walk past a problem.' I know I can be pretty compulsive."

"I sometimes think your expectations are too high."

"What do you mean by that?" Mark stopped drying and stared at his brother.

"I watched you break off your engagement. I know you had concerns, but she seemed like a great woman to me."

"She was, but there was something missing."

"Just like with Katie? You ever think you might have a problem with commitment?"

Mark returned to drying. "Maybe."

Dad walked into the kitchen. "Mind if I join you?"

Mark said, "Sure, we're just about done."

"What's this?" He looked at Katie's card and present on the kitchen table. He put down his bourbon on the rocks and examined the items. "Tell me about this girl of yours." He took a sip of his bourbon and leaned back in his chair. "I hear she's doing OK."

"Doc call you?"

"He did. Who is she?"

"She's a student from one of my classes. She drove here from Boulder and was in an accident near town last night."

"Sounds like she risked her life to bring these to you." His dad tapped his finger on the card and book.

"She did."

"Tell me about her, but wait till I get back."

His dad must have decided the conversation was going to take a while, because he left for the liquor cabinet and returned with the bottle of bourbon. He topped up his glass.

"Her name's Katie. She's a grad student. We met in a class I helped teach. We started dating toward the end of the semester. Then the university found out about it and suspended me."

"Is that why you came home early?" His dad stared at Mark, one eyebrow cocked.

"They have rules about professors dating students. I don't believe we started anything until after I was done with my supervision, but the university doesn't see it that way."

"She's hot." Jim leaned against the sink and folded his arms.

Mark glared at him. "She's very attractive. And for her age, she's amazingly bright. Her father's a city attorney. She's thought a lot about legal and social issues and has a very logical mind. I like her."

"Why didn't you invite her to come stay with us?" Mark knew he was failing his dad's measure of propriety.

"Because I'm not sure we're going to see each other anymore."

Jim said, "Are you crazy?"

"I may never get tenure. I have a hard time accepting that."

"Is it Katie's fault? Did she cause the problem?" With his eyes fixed on Mark, their dad swirled his glass on the table, and the sound of ice cubes clinked from inside.

Mark knew he could never explain the selfies. "No."

"Then it was a mutual relationship, and she didn't intentionally cause your falling-out with the administration?

"No."

"Do you love her?" His dad swirled his drink some more.

"I think so."

"Son, when it comes to love, either you do or you don't. If you have to think about it, you have a problem."

Jim pulled two beers from the refrigerator and handed one to Mark.

Mark took a sip and said, "Maybe she's too young."

"Do you remember Blaze?" His dad tapped his index finger on the table again.

"Sure. The brown and white Appaloosa I rode when I was a boy. He had a long white stripe down his nose."

"You loved him. What you don't know is that we had him for a year before it was safe to put you on his back. He was wild—had a mind of his own and wouldn't take a rope. We finally found a whisperer to train him. After a month, he could calm him down enough to take a rider. But a bridle was still useless. That horse always wanted to follow his own path."

"What happened?" Dad's stories tended to impart a dose of morality.

"After another year, Blaze finally understood how to follow a lead. He'd finally grown up."

"What's your point?"

"Katie might be young now, but if she's the one, might she be worth the wait? I bet she thinks you're the best thing to ever happen to her. When you get older, difference in age will matter less and less. I'm not trying to equate a horse to a woman—your mom would hit me—but I *am* trying to get you to understand that it takes time to grow into ourselves, no matter who we're meant to become."

Mark looked at his brother. Jim would follow his heart over his brain every time. And his dad made a great point. "My professorship means everything to me, and now it might be in jeopardy because of our relationship. I don't know what I'm going to do."

"Son, sometimes bad things happen to good people. That's life."

Mark chewed on his dad's comment and began to pace the kitchen. He couldn't imagine his life without Katie.

"One more thing."

"What?" Mark turned to his dad.

"No son of mine is going to let his girlfriend sit by herself in a hospital room while he's enjoying New Year's dinner with his family. Mom made her a plate and put it in the refrigerator. Now take it to her before we're all mad at you. I know Doc doesn't want her disturbed, but you've got to do the right thing, son."

Mark put down his beer and went in search of his coat and gloves.

CHAPTER 26
Junkyard Dog

When Katie arrived at the university's administration building, she was more exhilarated than anxious about the meeting. Once she was inside the reception area, her eyes were immediately drawn to a stylishly dressed woman seated on a leather armchair. A gray flannel suit and white blouse ensemble looked professional, but the knee-high, five-inch-heel, black-leather calfskin boots said all anyone needed to know about attorney Harriet Becker—she wasn't one to be easily intimated.

"Are you Ms. Becker?"

"Please, call me Harriet. Let's have a quick word in private."

They walked to a small chrome coffee table out of earshot of the receptionist and sat on a leather sofa.

"I hope you had a good vacation with your family."

"Not really, actually, but thanks for asking. I'm too preoccupied with this investigation into Assistant Professor O'Connor to have much fun these days."

"It's my job to worry. Your job is to follow my lead. After our phone call, I asked my best investigator to look into what you told me. On your recommendation, I also contacted your friend Paul in the cybersecurity office. You must have made a great impression on him, since he was more forthcoming with data from the university's computer system than I anticipated."

"I think he's hoping for more from me."

"He asked that you call him."

"OK, I will."

"I'm not sure how much progress we'll make today, but I can assure you that they won't be prepared for what I plan to say. Keep calm and don't volunteer any information. I'll give you cues if I want you to speak."

Katie turned and grinned when she saw the familiar face of Detective Scott enter the reception area. "What are you doing here?"

"Hello, Ms. Russell. I've been asked by the university to handle the investigation into Assistant Professor O'Connor. You must be Becker. I'm Detective Scott—retired detective, that is—from Boulder PD." The detective and the attorney shook hands. "The Office of Policy and Efficiency is aware that I worked with Ms. Russell on another investigation. They asked me to take this assignment, too. It's a little unusual, since there's no suggestion of criminal activity."

"Nice to meet you, Detective Scott. And please, call me Harriet."

"All right, Harriet. Come with me, and we can get started."

Detective Scott appeared to be wearing the same rumpled gray suit he wore the last time Katie had seen him. They walked from the reception area to the same conference room that had been used for Ava's hearing. All three took seats around the conference table. The detective sat behind his customary stack of manila folders and, as before, held a large cup of coffee.

They sat quietly for a few moments until a handsome man strode in, dressed in slacks and a blue button-down oxford shirt. Katie guessed him to be somewhere in his late forties or early fifties.

"Good morning, I'm Stan Humphries, Title IX coordinator for the university. Harriet, nice to see you again. I assume you've all met Detective Scott." Humphries sat down and looked at Harriet. "You called this meeting. How can I be of assistance?"

"Stan, nice to see you, too. I'll get right to the point."

"You always do."

"I'm representing Ms. Russell in the investigation into her amorous relationship with Assistant Professor O'Connor."

Humphries smiled. "Ms. Russell has confirmed to the university that such a relationship did occur. Our interest is with Professor O'Connor, however. He's the focus of our administrative investigation into whether or not a policy violation occurred. I don't think you, or your client, should be concerned."

"Stan, I hate to disagree with you so quickly, but I'm very much concerned. I'd like you to discontinue your investigation and reinstate Professor O'Connor at once."

Humphries's eyes widened. "Harriet, I agreed to meet as a courtesy. We have a long history of working together, but I'm under no obligation to discuss our ongoing investigation. You know I'm bound by the university's internal policy and by the federal Title IX policy and procedures. If a complaint has been raised, then we must investigate. I'm sure you understand."

Harriet thrust her chest forward and leaned in. "What I don't understand is the nature of the specific concerns expressed in the complaint. From my research, Professor O'Connor appears to be one of the most accomplished young professors on campus. I'm told he has a promising future. Ms. Russell has just received all top grades in her first term as a grad student, and other faculty members have described her as being extremely bright. I wonder who's been harmed by this stipulated amorous relationship—a relationship that we happily acknowledge. The only possible harm I can see are the sanctions and stigma that this university is about to inflict on two outstanding adults. Two adults who have enjoyed a consensual sexual relationship that you feel empowered to investigate. When did the university decide it should police what goes on in the bedrooms of its faculty and students?"

"Harriet, we don't need to show harm. This isn't a criminal investigation. We just need to show, by a preponderance of the evidence, that a policy violation has occurred. Our internal investigation is confidential. You know I can't disclose details from a complaint that was submitted under a promise of anonymity. Furthermore, while we're completing our investigation, Assistant Professor O'Connor won't be allowed legal representation other than in a role as advocate. If you'd like to act in that capacity, then I'm sure he'd like you at his side. As to Ms. Russell, since she's already confirmed the relationship, her participation isn't necessary and shouldn't concern you at all. Anything else?"

Katie felt like she was watching a tennis match, with volleys hit back and forth without any points scored, although she noticed Humphries's voice had risen in volume. She also observed that Detective Scott looked bemused. Maybe he was enjoying watching Harriet Becker take on the administration.

"I'll ask you again: drop the investigation into Assistant Professor O'Connor. It's a smart move."

"Why's that?"

"Because I'm prepared to sue the university on behalf of my client for violation of her privacy and damage to her reputation."

Katie hadn't seen that coming.

For the first time, Humphries appeared to lose some of his cool. Katie noticed his eyes dart toward Detective Scott and back again. "Based on what facts could you file such a lawsuit?"

Becker held up a file folder. "I know who filed the complaint. I also know that he submitted supporting documents—including several intimate photos of my client—that were copied from her cloud server without her permission."

Humphries instantly fired back, "We received those photos as supporting evidence to initiate our investigation. They can't be construed as a violation of privacy when used solely for that purpose." Humphries visibly relaxed and sat back in his chair. His smug look suggested that he felt confident in a successful counterattack.

"Perhaps, but a violation of privacy would have occurred if those photos were made freely available to university administration and staff. I have a log file showing access to a university server containing those photos. They've been viewed a total of 234 times and downloaded fifty-three times. Are you entertaining the administration with private photos of your students? I'd like to know. And if you continue to pursue this, I'll go through discovery and find, by name, which individuals viewed the photos and which ones downloaded copies. How do you think it would appear if the newspaper printed a story about secret photos of students kept on a university server for viewing by the administration and passed around by salacious employees? And if I go on that fishing expedition, who knows what else I might find? Perhaps information about a foundation funded by your administration that pays students to report sexual assaults?"

Katie was impressed by Becker's delivery. The attorney clearly knew how to take command of a room and spoke with confidence and conviction. Paul had earlier told Katie about his discovery of the photos on the university's server, but he hadn't mentioned how many times they'd been viewed. She was disgusted by the revelation.

"So, Stan, I believe we have sufficient grounds for filing a lawsuit. This university has knowingly violated my client's privacy and damaged her reputation, perhaps irreparably."

The conference room went silent. Katie was afraid to even look at Humphries. Detective Scott leaned back in his chair, cup of coffee in hand. His smile told Katie everything. Humphries stood and silently paced around the back of the room. After a full minute, he returned to his chair and stood behind it. He leaned forward, his hands at rest on the chair's back. "Harriet, I want to thank you for bringing this new information to my attention. I ask that you hold off on any action until I can discuss this within the administration. I promise to have a response to you by end of business tomorrow. Until then, let's all take a calm step back and reassess the situation at that time. Thank you all for coming." Humphries nodded at those present and hastily exited the conference room.

Katie, Detective Scott, and Becker were left alone. Katie finally began to relax. She'd loved Becker's display of negotiating style. It stoked some of the thoughts she was already having about pursuing a career in law.

The detective finally broke the silence. "That was an impressive performance, Ms. Becker."

Katie could tell he was genuinely impressed.

"It's always easier when you have the facts on your side, right, Detective?" Becker stood.

The detective stood with her. "As Arthur Conan Doyle said, 'There is nothing more deceptive than an obvious fact.'"

"Quite right, Detective Scott. I wonder if I might have a word with you in private?"

"Sure. We can go to my office down the hall."

Becker turned toward Katie. "Katie, feel free to leave. I plan to speak with Detective Scott about that other matter I mentioned. I'll let you know what I hear back from the university. Depending on what they decide, we might still need to consider the other plan we discussed."

Katie hoped it wouldn't come to that, but she was willing to take the step if required. "OK. I'll wait to hear from you." She said good-bye and left the room.

Outside the building, Katie pulled her phone from her backpack and called Paul.

"Thanks for calling, Katie. I have some news for you."

"What's that?"

"I heard back from Justin's employer in Seattle. After I sent them information about the email and its contents, they began an internal investigation. Justin was just let go from his job. They confirmed that your photos were sent from one of their laptops. They seized it and found that he had a long history of accessing your files. Their corporate policy prohibits the use of their systems for circulating pornographic photos or violating privacy. I thought you'd want to know."

Katie thanked Paul and said good-bye. Her first thought was to contact Justin, but she decided that would be a mistake. She only hoped he would finally remain in her past.

CHAPTER 27
A Tangled Web

Two days after the meeting with Stan Humphries, Harriet Becker called Katie with the Title IX coordinator's response: the university would indeed continue its investigation into Assistant Professor O'Connor. Becker believed they were stalling for time and were likely panicked about the meeting and its revelations. It was time, in her view, to turn up the pressure and take the next step. "You've read the draft of the story, right?"

"Yes. It's accurate."

"After it's published, your life as a relatively obscure grad student will be over. You'll become something of a celebrity."

"I prefer to remain unknown, but I understand your strategy."

"I'll give the reporter my permission, and they'll publish the story tomorrow. I can't emphasize enough that you must refuse any requests from the press. Refer any questions to me. I'll take it from there. Have you thought of anything else?"

"What about Mark. Shouldn't we tell him?"

"I don't think so. It's best if he can deny any prior knowledge. I appreciate the fact that it will cause some strain between you, but it's the best strategy. Believe me. You can explain it to him later."

The list of things Katie would have to explain later was growing longer by the day. "Well, if you think it'll work."

"I'm confident."

"OK, then. Go ahead."

Katie's anxiety began to ratchet up after the phone call. She walked to a local liquor store that catered to students. She found the wine section and bought two bottles of a cheap California chardonnay. Back in her apartment, she opened one and poured herself a tumblerful. She missed Mark terribly.

The next morning, Katie struggled to get out of bed. She made her way to the kitchen and started some coffee. She was surprised to see the empty wine bottle on the counter. She didn't recall finishing it. While the water for the coffee heated, she logged onto her laptop. The story was already on the front page of the Boulder daily newspaper's website.

GRAD STUDENT LEARNS HARD LESSON ABOUT INTERNET SECURITY

BOULDER, COLO. — A graduate student in the Philosophy Department has learned the hard way what can happen to those impromptu photos taken for fun while in compromising situations. This newspaper has learned that several photos, allegedly taken by the student in an intimate setting with a university employee, were sent to the university by an anonymous source. The pictures, known as selfies, had been taken from the student's online cloud account without her permission.

The university received the photos as part of an ongoing investigation into the relationship between the student, whom this paper refers to as Jane Doe to respect privacy, and the employee. The university considers the photos evidence in its investigation of an alleged and improper "amorous" relationship. So far, the university has declined to comment on this story, or to reveal the employee's identity. A spokesman for the student stated that she is cooperating fully with the administration in its investigation.

The university's Department of Cybersecurity advises all students to change their passwords frequently, use only secure Wi-Fi connections, and refrain from opening any attachments or links in emails from unknown sources.

Katie gently twirled her hair as she read the story. Mark would see it soon. She desperately wanted to contact him but appreciated Becker's advice against doing so. Now she'd have to wait to see if the story would have its desired effect on the university.

Spring classes started soon, and Katie was concerned about her looming notoriety. She'd registered for three more graduate courses and had signed up to work as a teaching assistant. The newspaper would soon discover the identity of the employee, which was likely common knowledge in the philosophy department. She hoped her attorney knew what she was doing. Would Mark ever forgive her?

After coffee, Katie decided to take a hike in the foothills to relieve the stress she was feeling. She texted Ava, who agreed to join her. Fifteen minutes later, they met on their common porch and headed toward the Flatirons. Katie halfway expected to look around and see reporters trailing them.

"What happened?" Ava put her hand gingerly on the large black-and-blue bruise on Katie's head.

"Oh, that. I was in a car accident. I'm OK, but my car was totaled."

"Wow, sounds like you're lucky to be alive. What happened?"

"I drove to Durango to visit a friend and lost control on a patch of black ice. I slid through an intersection and was hit by a pickup truck. It could have been a lot worse."

"I didn't know you had a friend in Durango."

Katie hesitated. She hadn't confided in Ava about Mark. It was probably time she did. "Dr. Mark O'Connor. He's one of my professors from last semester. He grew up in Durango, and I went to visit him there on New Year's Eve."

"Didn't I meet him at the Bohemian Biergarten after the football game?" Katie could tell Ava was impressed.

"He's the one."

"Sweet. Maybe I can get you to introduce me to that cute brother of his."

"Wow, you have a good memory! Remember, he works on a ranch."

"No wonder he looks so fit. I'm in."

Katie changed the subject. "So how was your vacation?"

"Nice. I was at home in Denver with my family. We spent a few days in Vail at our condo. The snow was great. Do you ski?"

"No. But I want to learn—it looks like fun. Maybe we could go together sometime."

"I'd enjoy that."

Katie hoped it would happen. They walked on in silence. It was about noon, and the radiant sun had warmed the air considerably.

"So how are you?" Katie wasn't sure she should broach the subject of Drew and the hearing, but as a friend, she felt it was important.

"You mean about Drew?"

"Yeah, and in general."

"I'm OK. Glad it's over. I haven't spoken with him. If he's guilty of what everyone said he did, then I just need to forget about him, I guess."

"I think that's for the best. No one doubts you loved him. And no one blames you for what happened. I hope you don't."

"I just hope he doesn't do it again to anyone else."

Katie was ready to launch into a lecture that Drew *would* do it again, that guys like him were unlikely to change, and that she wished Ava had filed a complaint with the police, but she didn't. She'd made all those points before and was happy to still have Ava's friendship. "Come on, let's go another couple of miles, and I'll buy you lunch."

After they'd stopped for a sandwich and walked home, Katie said good-bye to Ava on the porch and went inside her apartment. Instead of taking off her coat, she decided to head back outside and go for a walk to the bookstore. She found the study-guides section and bought a book on preparing for the Law School Aptitude Test. The LSAT was the key to acceptance at most accredited law schools. Sure, she'd heard that admissions officers looked at undergrad course work and grades, extracurricular activities, and letters of recommendation, but she knew a good LSAT score was critical.

Back in her apartment, she made herself a cup of tea, settled into her favorite chair, and started reading.

"HAPPY NEW YEAR, PETER," BRIAN TAYLOR SAID into the phone, trying to sound cheerful and expecting that the dean wouldn't be. The ensuing silence suggested Brian had been correct. He adjusted his earbuds, took another sip of coffee, and waited.

"Did you see the paper this morning?" Peter almost shouted it.

"I did. Sounds like Harriet Becker means business." Brian had followed the woman's career since his time in law school. She was tough but not necessarily a risk taker. If she took an aggressive position, it was because she held all the cards.

"The Office of Risk Management called," Peter said. "They're paranoid as hell. That's their job, of course, but if what this lawyer said is true—that they have records of the student's photos being accessed within the university community—then we're in trouble. Why the Title IX office decided to put her unsecured photos on our servers escapes me. She's one of yours, right?"

"Yes: Katie Russell. I have her under contract, and she testified in the hearing against the quarterback."

"You paid her, right?"

"The usual bonus: fifty thousand dollars."

"And now she's involved in this amorous-relationship investigation into the assistant professor?"

"Yes. But she's not culpable. Only the professor is. He's the one who's in violation of employment policy, not her."

"This is bad. The exposure we'll take if the foundation is exposed in a lawsuit will be a PR nightmare with students, parents, the DOE—everyone. I think you need to shut it down. I still consider it legal, but I don't want to defend it in the court of public opinion. Archive all your records in a secure location, off-site. Then go silent. I won't be able to communicate with you at all. Understand?"

"What do I tell my student ambassadors?"

"Thank them for their service, pay them their final fees, and remind them of their NDAs. Say we've made such great strides against sexual assault on campus that we no longer need their services. I don't know—think of something."

"I understand." Brian knew it had been too good to last. He was getting paid handsomely to run the foundation and worked fewer than twenty hours per week doing so. It was better than any deal he could expect to get after he was back in the private sector once his suspension was over.

"And Brian."

"Yes?"

"This is the last time I'm bailing you out. Even if you are my brother-in-law."

"Harriet, Stan Humphries here."

"Hello, Stan. Nice to hear from you."

"You surprised me with that story in the paper this morning. I thought you understood we're still proceeding with our investigation into Assistant Professor O'Connor's improper relationship with your client."

"That was merely a public-service story, Stan. We wanted to make students aware of the dangers of the Internet. Of course, I also wanted to make sure you were aware that, if necessary, we're ready to go public with the rest of the story. My client feels strongly about taking a stand. She's even willing to publish a few of her photos."

"I've had some internal conversations about this matter. We'd like to find a way to resolve it without involving the public."

"I'm listening."

"We maintain that your client and Assistant Professor O'Connor engaged in a consensual amorous relationship, one that is prohibited in the official code of conduct for university employees. We also believe that a hearing on this matter, using a standard of proof based on the preponderance of the evidence, would establish the professor's responsibility."

"I don't disagree, but I do maintain that the university has no reason to investigate the relationship, since you can't identify any harm that's been done. They were two consulting adults who became involved outside the classroom and outside their academic relationship."

"That may be true, but the employee did sign an employment contract that required him to abide by the code of conduct."

"I understand. Anything else?" Becker frowned slightly.

"Because no allegations of harm have been raised, the university's willing to drop the investigation, place a letter of warning in O'Connor's personnel file, and reinstate him to his position with no loss of pay."

"Will the university agree that the proposed letter of warning won't affect his future standing within the university, in any way, particularly as it applies to his consideration for tenure?"

"We will."

"That's a great start, Stan."

"What do you mean a great start? That's what your client wants, isn't it?"

"It is, but there's also the matter of compensation for damages. My client's privacy was grossly violated by the university. She's entitled to restitution. Her standing on campus has been irrevocably damaged. The public will find out about her relationship with O'Connor. Ultimately, her ability to receive an unbiased and nondiscriminatory education on this campus will be severely limited." Becker waited for Humphries's response.

After a pause, Humphries said, "Harriet, that brings me to a request we have. As part of this negotiation, we'd like your client to agree to withdraw from the university. We believe her ongoing presence here would create a distraction for our faculty and students. We want to avoid any future charges of favoritism."

"You can't demand that she leave campus. That's discriminatory."

"I never said demand. I said request."

"I'll need to speak with my client. We haven't discussed plans to continue her education at CU, but I do understand your point. I believe that her primary interest is in making sure Assistant Professor O'Connor's career is restored. I'll discuss it with her."

"It sounds like we have an outline of an agreement, then. When can you speak with your client?"

"I'm sure I can reach her quickly. How about we schedule a follow-up call for tomorrow. I believe Dr. O'Connor's due back in Boulder this week, and we'd like to get this wrapped up. When can you discuss compensation with the administration?"

"I'll run it past the dean and the Office of Risk Management tomorrow. Compensation will be prickly."

"I'm counting on you, Stan. Talk to you tomorrow." Becker ended the call and immediately dialed Katie's number.

Katie was just beginning a sample analytical-reasoning question from an LSAT practice exam.

Buses 1, 2, and 3 make one trip each day, and they are the only ones that riders A, B, C, D, E, F, and G take to work.
—Neither E nor G takes bus 1 on a day when B does.
—G does not take bus 2 on a day when D does.
—When A and F take the same bus, it is always bus 3.
—C always takes bus 3.

Traveling together to work, B, C, and G could take which of the same buses on a given day?

(A) 1 only
(B) 2 only
(C) 3 only
(D) 2 and 3 only
(E) 1, 2, and 3

She had just sketched a logic diagram when her phone rang. She saw it was Becker.

"I have some good news," the attorney said. "I just spoke with Stan Humphries. He said they'll drop the investigation into Dr. O'Connor and assured me that his eligibility for tenure won't be compromised. Also, he was open to compensation, but it may take some more pushing on our part."

"That's great news about Mark. What do you mean about more pushing?"

"I'm not sure yet. I just need to make sure they understand how explosive your knowledge could become if it went public. You're willing to publish one of the photos, right?"

"Definitely. There's worse stuff out there."

"True. I'll let you know if we need to use one. Which leads me to the bad news: they want you to withdraw from the university."

"What! They can't do that."

"Technically, no, but you can voluntarily withdraw as part of a settlement. Think about it. Would you really want to stay on campus once this gets resolved? Everyone will suspect you. I can't imagine that a single professor won't privately know what's happened. How can you be sure they'd evaluate you fairly? Especially if you plan to continue your relationship with Mark."

"It seems unfair to force me to leave. I'm thinking of going to law school anyway."

"Really? Professor Wilson thinks you should."

"She's encouraged me."

"You should consider it. It's a rewarding profession."

"Anything else about the agreement?"

"No, we're talking again tomorrow. I'll let you know. When does Mark return from Durango?"

"In another week, right before classes begin."

"I'm hoping to wrap this up in a few more days. Then you can give him the good news."

"Thanks, Harriet."

"Don't thank me yet—I need to pry some money out of them first."

CHAPTER 28
A Negotiated Settlement

While negotiations between Becker and the university continued, the concerns that had once weighed on Katie like a dull headache suddenly slipped away. She put her faith in her attorney and shifted her focus to the LSAT exam. One afternoon, after several hours of being immersed in a section on logical reasoning, she closed her workbook and fetched her journal. She began what one of her professors had called a "word trap." The technique required her to write down any words that spontaneously came to mind on a selected topic, look for common themes or meanings, and then eliminate any that were inconsistent.

Once the list was complete, she turned to another page in her notebook and began to sketch an arched bridge built of stones. The Norwegian fairy tale "Three Billy Goats Gruff" came to mind. She chuckled at the memory and decided to draw a troll under the bridge and goats crossing over it. The stones of the bridge were of different sizes and shapes, and she drew the bridge in perspective with an eddy and a standing wave, even a downed tree with jagged roots. Next, she labeled the larger stones of the bridge with words from her trap: *Trust*, *Love*, *Pain*, *Hope*, *Morality*, *Philosophy*, *Romance*, *Lust*, *Honesty*, *Passion*, and *Time*. She finished with a crude stick figure at the bridge's end in her own likeness, resolute with hands on hips. She labeled the bridge *Destiny*.

Katie leaned forward and studied the sketch. She only need look in a mirror to see what, or who, had changed. The New Year's Day encounter with Mark in the ER of the Durango hospital had nudged Katie away from worry and toward determination. She realized she couldn't control their relationship any more than she could (or would think to) control Mark. His painful departure from the hospital on New Year's Day, followed by an unexpected return with dinner later in the evening, had taught Katie the value of faith: faith in herself and faith in her future. Abetting her healthy transition from eager discovery to measured growth was her attorney's efforts to obtain restitution from the university. Perilous reefs and shoals still dotted the horizon, but Becker had added additional ballast to the growing stability of Katie's ship.

Although Katie eagerly anticipated attending law school and the opportunity to study justice, fairness, and equality, she fretted over the question of where she should go. If she did withdraw from CU, then the next-nearest law school was in Denver, a worrisomely short distance away. Even though her relationship with Mark was on hold while he remained in Durango, she embraced her growing confidence and trusted that it would survive Mark's troubles with the university.

Katie closed her journal and looked around her bedroom, not quite sure where she was. Had she fallen asleep? She yawned and blinked and moistened her dry mouth. She stepped to the kitchen and filled a glass with water from the tap, then opened the refrigerator and pulled out a bottle of wine. Over sips of the water, she acknowledged the fact that she'd been drinking more often since the accident. Perhaps too often. She put the wine back in the refrigerator.

Apart from Mark and law school, another topic that careened around Katie's mind was Drew. The feeble sanctions the university delivered seemed to be a miscarriage of justice if, as Katie believed, he was responsible for a series of sexual assaults. Could she prove it? It would be difficult to do without help. Becker could capably advise her, she knew, but she also knew that she couldn't afford her fees. The university certainly wouldn't help: Drew's case had been sealed, and they'd resist any additional investigation into their star quarterback.

Katie thought back to the meeting with Becker and the university's Title IX administrator. She'd always felt it peculiar that Becker, after the meeting had concluded, had requested a word in private with Detective Scott. Why? Maybe she should ask the charming detective. She found her phone and composed a text message with a request to meet. She wasn't sure he'd think it appropriate in his role as investigator, but she thought it was worth a try. After sending the message, she returned to the kitchen and opened the bottle of wine.

KATIE WALKED INTO THE BOULDER POLICE DEPARTMENT and asked for Detective Scott. He'd responded to her text within hours and suggested they meet the following day. She didn't have to wait in the reception area for long before he strolled in to greet her.

"Nice to see you. I'm glad you contacted me. Let's go down to the cafeteria, and I'll buy you a cup of coffee. It'll give me a good chance to show you off and watch a few heads turn when the young guys see an old detective like me sitting with you. How've you been?"

"Fine, thanks. But I'll wait until we sit down to explain why I'm here."

After they filled mugs of coffee at a self-service counter in the cafeteria, Katie followed Detective Scott to a table in an empty corner of the room. Sure enough, she felt casual glances from several uniformed police officers. The attention made her feel both a bit self-conscious and a little flattered.

Katie sipped her coffee and held the mug in her hands. "Thank you for your support in Ava's hearing and into the investigation of Professor O'Connor."

"Katie, I'm doing my job as a consultant on these investigations. I don't really have a position one way or the other. I just try to look for facts and apply common sense."

"True, but I always felt you were on my side."

Detective Scott smiled. "What brings you in?"

"I can't let go of this thing with Drew. I know what he did. It bothers me that his punishment wasn't much more than a slap on the wrist. I'm sure he's assaulted before, and he will assault again. Yet the university turns a blind eye. It doesn't feel right."

"A judge once told me that law isn't about justice, it's about conflict resolution. I think what you're witnessing are the effects of special-interest groups. The university's administration and powerful alumni want him out there on the football field."

"Is winning football games more important than keeping women safe on campus?" Katie set her warm mug down and slowly wrapped her long fingers around its circumference.

"Of course not, but college football's big business, and winning is a priority. I myself find it reprehensible. What do you have in mind?"

"Do you think it's possible to criminally investigate Drew?"

"Yes, but it's a decision that's made more difficult when the victim's unwilling to cooperate or to provide access to evidence that may be in the rape kit. Without Ava's cooperation in this case, I think a prosecuting attorney would find it difficult to prove that any criminal activity had occurred beyond a reasonable doubt."

"But what about other women? If I'm right that he offended before and will offend again, then maybe we can ask another victim if she'd be willing to cooperate?"

"Perhaps, but as you may or may not know, about seventy percent of most assaults go unreported, and of the remaining cases—those for which we do have records—I don't recall any similar incidents over the past few years that remain unresolved or are still open."

"Maybe we can find someone who didn't think it was worth reporting at the time but who might change her mind if she considered the risk to others."

"How would you find such a person?"

"I've been reading about untested rape kits, like the forensic exam Ava endured when I took her to the hospital. What if another woman was assaulted by Drew, received the forensic exam, and then, also like Ava, decided not to proceed with a complaint?"

"Sounds plausible, but it seems like a long shot. The Denver-Boulder metro area has hundreds of untested kits lying around in various places."

The detective got up from the table and took their mugs over to the cafeteria's big urn. Katie smiled when she remembered a similar-looking porcelain cup, one she smashed on Justin's kitchen floor. "So why don't kits get tested?" she called out as he filled the cups.

"Several reasons." He walked back with their cups. "Typically, most assaults occur when the victim knows her assailant, so identification's already been established. The prosecutor decides to proceed with a case after considering several factors. In some cases, DNA testing of the kit isn't necessary. Once in a while, kits aren't tested for the same reason as in Ava's case—she chose to remain anonymous—but many police departments have moved to testing all kits. If DNA is established, then it's added to a national database called CODIS—that stands for Combined DNA Index System. The FBI maintains it. It hasn't helped that there isn't a standard national policy on rape kits yet. The justice department's currently working on a specification that will prescribe how all kits are to be processed."

"I've heard money's an issue."

"In police departments, money's always an issue. But I've never seen a case where the prosecutor wasn't willing to apply every resource necessary to proceed with a successful prosecution. If a rape kit needs to be tested, then it will be."

"Didn't you tell me that Ava's kit *was* tested, even though she asked to remain anonymous and chose not to file a complaint?"

Detective Scott sat back in his chair and frowned. "Yes, that was a mistake on the hospital's part. They sent the kit over to us for testing with only the signed consent of the attending nurse. The staff's supposed to secure the victim's signature seventy-two hours after the exam so that any suspected intoxication has been eliminated. I understand the nurse was worried that any intoxicants in Ava's system might have gotten metabolized, and evidence lost, if she'd waited. Unfortunately, the nurse could've submitted the blood samples separately for toxicology testing and then retained the rest of the exam's contents until after she'd obtained the required signature. The hospital's implementing some remedial training because of the case."

Katie thought for a second and took a sip of her coffee. As with wine, she'd been drinking a lot more since her stay in the hospital. She was curious that Detective Scott hadn't asked about the bruise on her head. "You discussed this with Becker."

The detective smiled. "How did you know?"

"Just a guess. I wondered why you'd met with her privately after the hearing. She'd asked me about the rape kit, and I told her you requested that I not discuss it."

"Well, thank you for your discretion. Yes, she was very curious and wanted to know why the university didn't use the results of the kit as part of its investigation into Ava's assault. I told her I'd informed the university that it was available. I believe they feared that if the kit were to be entered into evidence, the university would be open to criticism of its failure to protect Ava's privacy, since she hadn't signed a release. In a similar incident that you may or may not have heard of, during an investigation of sexual assault at the University of Minnesota, a ninety-second video wasn't introduced because of privacy concerns for the victim. The video *was* used in a police investigation, however, and it was exculpatory to the football players who'd been accused of sexual assault, because it showed what appeared to be consensual sex. Regarding Ava's blood tests, I didn't agree with the university's decision not to use the evidence—an opinion I shared with Becker."

"That's convenient, isn't it? The university had access to evidence that showed the presence of GHB in Ava's body at the time of the assault, and they chose not to use it? That's bullshit—sorry, I didn't mean to say that."

"Funny, that was the same word Becker used."

"It seems to me that once the evidence is out there, it's out there. Why should Drew be protected to benefit Ava's privacy? I'm sorry the hospital screwed up, but the facts are what matter."

"Becker felt the same. I don't know how you ended up with her, but she's impressive. Good to have her on your side."

"I'm lucky." She took a sip of coffee. "Back to my idea of finding another victim who might be willing to charge Drew with assault. Could I examine sexual-assault case histories, including summaries written by the attending nurses and included in untested rape kits? Especially those with anonymous victims and known assailants but where the victim decided not to press charges."

"Accessing rape kits is almost impossible. They're protected by very restrictive policy. You'd need the permission of the person who was tested, or else an order signed by a judge."

Katie sat back and thought. If she could get access to police records, then maybe she could find leads from open assault investigations, or perhaps investigations that had been closed due to lack of evidence. "Can police records be obtained from a Freedom of Information Act request?"

Detective Scott perked up. "Sure, like any other public records, with some exceptions. Information that's described in police-related items may be withheld if it's determined that disclosure would interfere with pending or contemplated law-enforcement proceedings or endanger the lives or physical safety of law-enforcement or correctional personnel." He tapped his reading glasses on the table for a minute. "Do you have any experience with spreadsheets or databases?"

"Sure. I worked on a few projects as an undergrad. We mined data from several cloud-based databases and aggregated social-media information for a national study on the dating preferences of white males in their sixties."

The detective laughed. "You're very funny."

Katie smiled. "The study was actually directed at millennials. I'm comfortable, at least on a cursory level, with the technology."

"There's a part-time job open in the department as a public-records officer. The money isn't great, but it might be a way for you to review case files. From my experience, detectives don't like people looking over their shoulders. You'd need to tread lightly. If you came across something, you'd need to discuss it with me first. If I agree it's relevant, then we'd discuss it with the appropriate detective."

"What does a public-records officer do?"

"They respond to public-records requests—as you might expect," he added with a laugh. "People can request copies of written records, audio recordings, videos, or any other information so long as they certify that it's not for business purposes. The records officer takes the request, determines the availability of the appropriate records, verifies that the records aren't restricted, maybe redacts portions of the records, requests permission to release the report, and then collects the fees."

"Should I apply?"

"If you're serious about going to law school and studying criminal law, it might provide you with valuable experience. On the other hand, if you fail to follow the rules completely, you'll face some serious consequences. I know you're hoping to find other victims, but all these cases have already been examined. Some extensively. Prosecutors follow a rigorous process to decide whether they should pursue sexual-assault cases."

"What do you mean?"

"Prosecutors control the doors to the courthouse. In cases of sexual assault—especially in cases where the victim and perpetrator may be acquaintances, which is quite often—prosecutors like to minimize any uncertainty. They make charging decisions based on the seriousness of the offense, the strength of evidence in the case, and the culpability of the defendant. But the victim's character, behavior, and credibility may play an especially important role, because the likelihood of getting a conviction might depend primarily on the victim's ability to articulate what happened. The victim's testimony must convince a judge or jury that a sexual assault's occurred. If, as in Ava's case, a date-rape drug was present, then the victim will struggle to tell a credible story, and objective factors will become more important. A prosecutor will want to see evidence of harm—such as bruises or cuts—or the presence of physical evidence—such as semen, blood, clothing, bedding, or hair—that will corroborate the victim's testimony. All things that might be in a rape kit. When you look for other assaults, you'll need to make sure you can build a compelling case before we march off to a prosecutor."

Katie sat back and smiled. She was energized by the idea. Her father had taught her all about the power of setting goals. She admired Detective Scott. She liked the fact that he'd said "we." He reminded her of her father—smart and thoughtful.

"Will you help me apply for the job?"

"I can send you a link to the application and job description. And if anyone asks, I'll give you a favorable recommendation. But you must promise to only look at the information: no copying, no printing, and no contact with anyone you might discover in the records. You'll need to discuss your findings with me, and if I agree, then we'll go to the appropriate detective."

"How can I thank you?"

"Follow my rules."

"I promise." Katie's smile widened.

"What happened to your head?"

"I was in an accident over the holidays. Nothing serious." She was glad he'd asked.

"Are you sure you're OK? I don't remember those dark circles under your eyes."

Katie shifted her gaze and let out a short breath. "I've had a lot on my mind."

"Anything you want to share?"

"Probably not." Katie's eyes began to glisten. Her lips went tight.

"I understand. I'm available if you change your mind. Since I'm assigned to the case, I won't ask you about the investigation into Dr. O'Connor. I've heard they may drop the proceeding because of the hornet's nest you kicked up over in the admin building."

"Good. They deserve it." Katie stood to leave. The detective joined her. "Thank you, Detective Scott. I appreciate your support."

"Happy to help. You remind me of my daughter when she was your age. Though it's none of my business, I respect Dr. O'Connor. I think you're good together. Hang in there. He's worth it."

THE NEXT MORNING, AFTER SHE WAS ABOUT HALFWAY through an LSAT practice exam, Katie received a call from her attorney. "Good morning, Ms. Becker."

"Remember, call me Harriet. I just spoke with the university. I think we're getting close. They've offered $125,000—an amount I view as an opening position. I'm confident they realize that a lawsuit would be considerably more expensive, so I'd like to apply additional pressure."

"A payment of $125,000 sounds pretty good to me. I could pay off all my loans."

"But what about law school? I'd like to see you graduate after three years without any debt."

Katie saw her point. "Law school's expensive. At least $200,000, from what I've read."

"I want them to write you a bigger check. If we do what I'm about to propose, I'm confident they'll see things my way."

"Which is…"

"I want to you to pick one of the intimate selfies you took and send it to the newspaper. Don't worry that they'll publish it. Instead, I expect them to protect your privacy and only write that they have it. And if comes from you, then the university can't claim I released it." Katie remained silent as the idea sunk in, then quickly understood her logic. Becker continued, "If the newspaper risks a broader release of one photo into the public realm, then it would send a signal that they're willing to tell all."

"I'd have to let Mark know."

"This time I think you should. Can you get in touch with him?"

"I think so."

"Choose a photo you're comfortable with. We'll blur your face."

"I can think of one. You can see Mark's body and my breasts and face. I'd recognize a particular mole on Mark's chest, but that's the only way anyone would know it was him."

"Are you comfortable showing your breasts?"

"Is it possible to cover that part?" Katie was putting a lot of trust in Harriet. The last thing she wanted was for the university to walk away from negotiations and leave her in a protracted lawsuit instead. Her hopes for law school wouldn't stand a chance.

"Sure, we can add a black bar over your nipples. The newspaper will understand that the original photo's untouched. Send it to me, and I'll get it ready. Then I'll send it back to you, and you can forward it to the paper. And get in touch with Mark."

Katie ended the call and sent an urgent text to Mark.

She hadn't heard back by the time she read the story the following day. It was the lead article in the digital version of the Boulder daily newspaper.

EXPLICIT PHOTO OF GRAD STUDENT LEAKED ONLINE

BOULDER, COLO. — A nude photo of a University of Colorado graduate student has been received by this newspaper. As reported last week, the graduate student has been involved in an investigation of a university employee for having an inappropriate amorous relationship. Several "selfie" photos have reportedly been provided to the university as part of its investigation.

The student's attorney, Harriet Becker, said in a statement that "I can only confirm that the photo is one of several that were forwarded to the university by an anonymous source. The photo is the personal property of my client and I ask that it not be published and her privacy respected."

This paper continues to uphold its policy of protecting the privacy of the student and has chosen not to publish the photo, in which the student can be seen next to a partial image of a man who is, presumably, the university employee under investigation. The university had no comment for this story.

Katie's stomach started to churn. Then her phone rang with Mark's ring-tone. Katie stared at the story on her laptop and wondered how he'd respond.

"How's your head?" His voice sounded amazingly calm.

"It's fine. Still a bump, but it doesn't hurt and the doctor says I'll be as good as new in a few weeks."

"Great—glad to hear it. I got your message. I just read what was so urgent."

"Mark, I really wanted to tell you first. You've seen the story?"

"I have. How did they get the photo?"

"I sent it."

"What! Tell me what's going on."

"I need to do it in person. When do you get back to Boulder?"

"I drive back tomorrow. You should tell me now."

Katie didn't want to put him off any longer, but she also understood why Becker wanted to protect him from the negotiations with the university. Plausible deniability. "Mark, I've been working with an attorney to clear you in the investigation into our relationship. We've made a lot of progress that I can't disclose right now. If everything goes as planned, then you'll be reinstated by the university with no blemishes on your record."

"How?"

"I was involved in an operation by the university that would prove highly embarrassing if it were to be publicly exposed. And I've also found that the university was careless with my photos. I wanted to tell you, but I'd signed a nondisclosure agreement and couldn't discuss it."

"You're blackmailing them?"

"No, we're insisting that our romantic relationship is none of their business and hasn't harmed anyone. I believe that, and I know you do, too."

"I do, and I'll be eternally grateful if you get them to agree. But I'm as responsible as anyone that this has happened. I knew the rules about our relationship. I let you take the photos. I even took one myself. I was wrong to doubt our future because the photos leaked out. Spending time on the ranch has helped me realize what's really important in my life—it's you."

"Mark, I can't tell you how relieved I am to hear you say that. Trust me. I'll explain everything when you get back. When this is over, we can begin where we left off." Katie needed reassurance.

"Katie, I can't wait to see you again. Didn't you ask for twenty-four hours in my apartment with a bottle of wine and no interruptions?"

"Don't forget about the clean sheets!" Katie was thrilled he'd remembered.

"I haven't."

Katie thought back to the first night she'd spent in Mark's bed. "Mark, I love you." She didn't wait for a response and ended the call.

"Harriet, what the hell are you trying to do? Never mind. I know exactly what you're trying to do."

"Stan, I'm as upset as you are that the photo got leaked."

"That's crap. You leaked it."

"My client feels strongly about this situation. I've tried to control her, but I'm not sure how much longer I can constrain her. A motivated young woman seeking justice is a powerful force."

"So is a motivated older woman extorting a windfall for her client."

"I think 'extort' is a little strong. I prefer to think of it as 'restitution.' I just want what's fair. Have you discussed compensation with the Office of Risk Management?"

"I have. We agree that some level of compensation is warranted. We'll give you the $125,000 we discussed last time."

"That was just a starting point, Stan. I think the right number is more like $400,000."

"You're kidding, right?"

"No, I'm serious: $200,000 for three years of law school and another $75,000 for spending money. Then of course there's my fee."

Neither of them spoke for what seemed like a full minute. Harriet wondered how high Stan had been authorized to go. It would have been easy for him to estimate legal fees for a lawsuit. The accountants in risk management certainly would have done so. "If I can get you $375,000, would we have a deal?"

Harriet already knew she'd undershot the mark. He was too quick to agree and had likely been authorized to go higher. But it was still a generous amount for her client. "Yes."

"Your client will agree to withdraw from the university, without prejudice?"

"Yes."

"And she'll sign an NDA about the NSAF, the investigation into Assistant Professor O'Connor, the disposition of her private photos within the university, and her testimony regarding Drew Evans?"

"Everything but the matter with Mr. Evans."

"Why not?"

"She wants to see him punished for what he did. It's personal for her. She's not willing to let it go."

"Well, I have to agree with her, to be honest. I'm not a fan of how the university handled that one."

"Suppression of evidence, you mean?"

"How did you know?"

"I have my sources."

"Then you understand why we need to assure confidentiality with respect to the investigation."

"Stan, she'll balk, but I think I can get her to agree. It sounds like we have a deal. When can I get a draft to review? More importantly, when can you inform O'Connor?"

"I expect the dean will let him know of our provisional agreement in the morning."

"That's great news, Stan."

"Nice working with you again, Harriet."

CHAPTER 29
A Fresh Start

Katie endured several personal interviews, a lengthy aptitude test, and a criminal background check as well as having to provide written answers to background questions on multiple forms, all before she received an official decision from Boulder PD. She was thrilled to open the email and read the offer. A regular paycheck would keep her bank account afloat, while having a job in the department might help find another of Drew's victims. And once she withdrew from the university, a regular work routine would help occupy time that she otherwise would have dedicated to class and study.

Throughout her first week on the job, Katie compiled written reports from each of the police departments and the sheriff's office in Boulder County and created a consolidated quarterly report of any gunshots fired within each jurisdiction. It was a simple task that was designed to familiarize her with the data and tools the department used. Using a spreadsheet and the department's SQL database, she created a master table by joining the individual datasets and then creating a range of reports that indicated shots fired, location, and characteristic of the shot as well as whether death or injury was involved; this included citizen injury, suicide, officer involvement, or homicide. The goal of the report was to show any trends by the locations and total numbers of shots fired. She was disappointed to learn that the number of shots fired in Boulder County had gone up over the past three years. Fortunately, the number of homicides had gone down, even though the number of injuries had gone up.

Harriet continued to negotiate Katie's settlement agreement with the university, and Mark was provisionally reinstated for the winter semester. A sticking point in the negotiations was the requirement that Katie not disclose any information about Ava's assault, including the trip to the ER for the sexual-assault exam and the university's subsequent investigation into Drew's conduct. It was as if it had never happened. Katie worried the clause would derail her plans to search for other victims. Harriet said she understood Katie's reluctance but encouraged her to sign.

She did, and after all parties had approved of the agreement, Katie withdrew from graduate school as required. Mark resumed teaching and was obviously thrilled to be back on campus. She understood his passion for teaching. She was glad that he also had another passion. Her.

The weekend after she signed the agreement, just as they had planned, Katie and Mark spent twenty-four hours in his apartment drinking wine, eating food, and having sex on clean sheets. The sex was every bit as exciting, unexpected, and torrid as it had been during their first night together. Mark's touch varied from gentle, almost imperceptible caresses to firm, passionate strokes that delivered pleasure to Katie unlike anyone before him had done. She remained in a constant state of bliss. During Mark's occasional departures from bed, Katie adored the boyish smile he wore as he casually roamed around the apartment in pajama pants and a bare chest, or better yet, nothing at all.

During lulls in passion and while not sleeping or eating, Katie recounted the missing details of her time in Boulder. She put the final pieces of the jigsaw puzzle into place for Mark. She covered her financial insecurity, her agreement to become a campus ambassador, and the awkward first meeting with Paul and his invaluable help in uncovering what Justin had done with the photos. Katie closely watched Mark's facial expressions as she spoke and felt relieved as his looks of skepticism gave way to reluctant acceptance.

At one point in her retelling, Mark interrupted her and said, "I think I understand why it was hard for you to tell me. But I still don't understand why it was so hard for you to trust me."

Katie understood that Mark's trust had been bruised, like the first dent in a new car. No matter how good the repair, the memory of that blemish would forever remain.

Mark lay back on his elbows on the Murphy bed and bit his lip. "Tell me again why you decided to take the job with the foundation."

"Have you ever had to worry about money?"

"I live frugally. I've always worked and I've been fortunate enough to receive some support from my family. But the currency that's most important to me is trust. Without it, I don't think a healthy relationship is possible."

Katie put her hand on Mark's thigh. "You've been blessed. But I needed the money. Sexual assault is a bigger deal than I thought. Did I feel like an informant? Sure. But it was for a worthy cause. I helped a lot of students at the kiosk on campus."

As Katie prepared to leave the next morning, Mark approached her, took her things from her hands, and set them on the floor. He led her to the still-unmade bed and they sat. Mark put his arm around Katie and said, "I do love you, Katie. I'm thrilled to be reinstated and I don't know how I'll ever thank you."

"Thank Professor Wilson and Harriet Becker, the attorney."

Mark let out a sigh. "Our relationship caused a lot of turmoil."

Katie turned toward Mark and held his hand. "I still believe in us. I wouldn't change anything. I'd be more cautious with my photos, maybe." She let out a self-effacing chuckle.

Mark's blue eyes searched her face. "I got to ride my horse while I was home. It gave me a lot of time to think."

"Like when you first considered philosophy?"

"Right. But this time I thought about us. My career is important, but I think we're more important. I'm excited to get back to work. You've got a new job. Let's put this all behind us and move ahead."

"Oh, Mark, I'm thrilled you to hear you say it."

Katie hugged Mark and gathered her things. She stopped, wheeled around, and put them back down. She returned to Mark's tall figure, wrapped her arms tightly around his body, and passionately pressed her lips against his. He returned the kiss with enthusiasm. He regathered her things and headed down the stairs.

ON KATIE'S FIRST DAY OF WORK, her manager called her into a meeting with Detective Scott to discuss her desire to research sexual-assault cases. The manager was understanding, he said, so long as she followed Detective Scott's rules for handling the information. If a growing backlog of requests made it impossible to meet their stated policy of seventy-two-hour turn-around, then she'd need to stay for the day and focus on records requests. He'd then give her the next day off. Once the backlog was cleared, she'd be allowed to quietly search case files related to sexual-assault investigations.

Katie created a report of cases that had been closed. She was not allowed to review open cases. Documents in closed cases included an officer's case report with a written description of location and time of the stated offense, statute involved, and details about the victim and suspects. Depending on the nature of the crime and the subsequent investigation, other documents in the file might include any interviews with the victim and suspects as well as a list of property and evidence such as clothing, consent to search, sealed evidence bags, surveillance videos, buccal swabs (DNA) from suspects, forensically acquired phone data, and any supplemental notes from investigators. The final document was usually titled "Charging Review/Case Closure." Prosecutors were reluctant to bring formal charges unless their reviewing of the case files suggested that the testimony and evidence collected would sustain court proceedings against a higher standard than "beyond a reasonable doubt."

Katie limited her search to archived cases of up to four years old and those that involved victims who were from eighteen to twenty-two years old and were, or had been, students at the university. Although she suspected Drew's victims were likely sorority members, that wasn't a question that anyone normally asked or recorded. It took a couple of weeks to build her initial list of seven cases.

Most cases were difficult for Katie to read because of the graphic details, which often brought the cases to life, yet she found them interesting because they included the results of investigations, prosecutions, plea bargains, and sentencing.

In one case, a male student who was visiting Boulder from another university was partying with a female CU student. Per her testimony, they were both drinking heavily. She blacked out and woke up in a hotel room with the male. She believed she'd been assaulted. Witnesses told police that they'd seen the male carrying the victim from a party. He denied having sex with her, but the DNA evidence from a rape kit tied him to the crime. The assailant was charged with kidnapping and rape but later pled down to a rape charge and was sentenced to eighteen years in prison. He would be identified as a sexual offender for life.

Her review of another case from a couple of years earlier gave Katie chills because she found it eerily reminiscent of what had happened to Ava. From a grand-jury indictment, she read of an assailant named Smith who'd met his victim at a Pearl Street bar. During the encounter, Smith and the woman talked until the bar closed; he then offered to accompany her home.

The woman's roommate—who remembered her coming home with a man—noticed sometime after noon the next day that the victim's door was locked. She did not see her until later that night, when she checked her door and found it unlocked. The roommate told investigators that she'd found the victim naked on the bed. She was sweaty and appeared to have vomited, and she was having trouble focusing.

The investigators found a note in the victim's room (which prosecutors said was from Smith) that read, *I will wash your sheets for you love, see ya Saturday!* The investigators found signs that a cleaning agent had been used in the bedroom and bathroom.

Doctors at Boulder Community Hospital later determined that the victim had dangerously low blood sugar and was suffering from severe hypoglycemia, most likely due to an insulin injection. Prosecutors said Smith—a type 1 diabetic—not only used insulin but also had knowledge of its effects from working with his stepfather, who was an endocrinologist.

The victim did not attend the hearing, but a representative of the Rocky Mountain Victim Law Center read from a letter, written by the victim, in which she described her nightmares, trouble sleeping, and general loss of normalcy since the assault: "I miss being able to have fun. I miss the dreams of what I wanted to do with my life," she'd said. "He has changed me forever, and I will have to live with that every day for the rest of my life. I ask that you never let him be the same, either."

The assailant was found guilty of sexual assault with a deadly weapon, sexual assault causing serious bodily injury, and first-degree assault with a deadly weapon and was sentenced to eighty-three years to life in prison. He was also found guilty of two counts of second-degree assault and tampering with evidence. Katie hoped he would never walk the streets again.

The last case involved a match of DNA from a crime scene to DNA in the CODIS database; it didn't offer any help to Katie but was interesting nonetheless. The attack took place about three in the morning on a Sunday about eight years earlier, when the victim was riding her bike back to her apartment after spending the previous day with her mother. While passing the campus tennis courts and law school, she heard footsteps running behind her, and a man grabbed her and threw her to the ground. The victim fought her attacker, who overpowered her, stuffed her into the trunk of his car, raped her, and then left her beside the parking lot. The assailant gave her a deep cut on her hand with a knife and repeatedly threatened to kill her.

She later contacted a passerby who helped her contact the police, who took her to the hospital. Tests confirmed the sexual assault, and semen mixed with human blood was recovered from her clothes and body. The police collected those samples as evidence, and the victim provided them with a detailed description of her attacker, including his shaggy blond hair and heavily tattooed arms.

Although the police aggressively investigated the case and received more than a hundred leads, they did not make any arrests. The case remained unsolved for eight years, until a persistent detective discovered that the forensic exam from the night of her assault had never been tested. The police submitted the rape kit to the Colorado Bureau of Investigation, which found a match to a man who was in prison for another crime. The assailant was in his thirties and had a long criminal history. After a lengthy appeals case in which the defendant petitioned for prohibition of the DNA evidence and lost, the assailant was given three life sentences for kidnapping and rape. The DNA evidence showed that the chances of anyone but the assailant committing the crime were approximately one in sixty trillion.

"What are you working on?"

Katie was so engrossed in reading case files that she hadn't noticed a man walk up to her desk and sit on its corner. Habitually neat and well organized as she was, Katie didn't appreciate a strange man's ass being parked against her desk. "Doing some research," she muttered.

"You're that new part-time public-records officer, right?" The man wore a blazer over dress slacks. He was cute and well built, and appeared to be about her age. Katie wasn't sure from his comments what he had in mind, but it became obvious right away. She'd seen him working at a desk in the corner most days she was at work. She said nothing. "I was wondering if you'd like to join me for a cup of coffee sometime," he said at last.

Katie swiveled around in her chair. "Thanks, but I think I'll pass. My name's Katie." She didn't want to appear too cold, so she offered her hand.

"Nice to meet you. I'm Colin Richardson. You're that student who was written about in the paper recently."

He'd probably read about her in the news story and heard about her photos. "That's me. How can I help you?"

"I wondered if you needed any help getting settled in."

Katie thought for a second and decided he might be of assistance. "I do have a question. What do you know about untested rape kits?"

"We have a few. We're going to send them off to the lab. The state's about to pass legislation to provide funding for testing the backlog. Why do you ask?"

"I'm working on a special project for a former detective here named Scott. Do you know him?"

"Totally. He's a cool dude. A legend around here. Has one of the highest batting averages in the whole department."

"Batting average? Like baseball?"

"Yep. He has one of the highest percentages of cases closed with a successful prosecution. What's the project?"

"To understand why we have so many untested rape kits." She didn't want to give too much away, so she tried to change her story on the fly. "I'm planning on going to law school, and it's an interest of mine. I'm just curious."

"It's a controversial topic around here. If you want, I can take you to see where they're stored."

"Really? Can we go now?"

"Sure, come on."

Colin described his background as they walked. He began his career attending the police academy and then worked as a beat cop for several years afterward. He'd recently been promoted to detective in Boulder PD's criminal-investigation bureau. Among his duties as a detective were to conduct interviews, examine records, observe suspects' activities, and participate in raids and arrests. He routinely visited the records facility to do research.

Katie had been so shaken the night of Ava's assault that she could barely recall the exam procedure at the emergency room. So about a week earlier, to prepare for her job, she'd reviewed the nurse's guidelines to familiarize herself with how the exam was typically administered. The amount of information that was asked about and the evidence that was collected was exhaustive. The initial interview required a brief narrative of the assault, current physical state, and the use of alcohol or drugs before the event (including suspected "surreptitious drug administration"), followed by very detailed questions about sites of sexual contact, sites of penetration (oral, vaginal, and/or anal), what had done the penetration (hand, mouth, penis, and/or foreign object), sites where saliva might be deposited, sites where semen might be deposited, and if a condom had been used. Next, the SANE who administered the test would ask several questions about post-assault activity, including taking a shower or any other form of cleansing. It was no surprise to Katie that women thought long and hard about whether or not they should subject themselves to such invasive procedures.

The remainder of the guidelines contained instructions about collecting actual physical evidence, including using up to four swabs for each site (mouth, vagina, and rectum); collecting and labeling clothing, including underpants, even if the victim had changed after the assault; the use of a lancet for blood to obtain DNA; and examination of the victim's scalp, ears, neck, and eyes. She skipped over the section on genital examinations, since she remembered how the nurse had examined and swabbed Ava in a most thorough manner, and she recoiled at the anal exam, which specified using two swabs, each with a drop of water that was inserted one to two centimeters into the anus. Photographs were frequently collected during the process. She imagined, as additional punishment for a male perpetrator, that these examinations should be performed on him in a public setting. The student union would be a good choice, she thought, much like a Roman coliseum.

Katie and Colin arrived at a nondescript one-story building several blocks from the police station. Colin used his key card to gain access. A uniformed officer sat at a desk in the entryway and watched them closely.

After signing the visitors' log, Colin turned to Katie and said, "We'll walk down to the refrigerated facility where we store the kits. I can't let you in, but we can go look."

They followed the hall to a locked door covered with signs warning that the room beyond held materials that were subject to chain-of-possession restrictions. A thermostat outside the door indicated that the room's temperature was chilled to preserve laboratory samples. Colin switched on a light inside the room, and its interior became visible through a glass window in the door. Katie could just make out a wall lined with steel metal shelves, each appearing to hold about twenty kits. Each kit was in a small cardboard box about four inches thick—about the dimensions of a sheet of paper. She counted rows and estimated that the room had about 150 kits in all.

"Is this the total backlog of all the kits in Boulder?" Katie's review of the department's statistics indicated that around a hundred rape cases, both felony and misdemeanor, were reported each year, and they generally resulted in about ten arrests per year.

"Yes. Those that aren't sent to the state lab remain here, either until they've gone beyond the statute of limitations—ten years in most cases, at which time they're destroyed—or the victim releases the kit to investigators. Even then, some kits may not be submitted for testing if the rape was by a known assailant. In those cases, the only issue is whether the sex was consensual. If it was, then the investigator will typically conclude that the kit doesn't offer any useful information. A lot of the kits are listed under the name Jane Doe to protect people's privacy."

"What happens when a kit's tested?"

"The kit's sent to the state crime lab, where it's examined for biological evidence—usually DNA and saliva. If a DNA sample is found, then a suspect profile is developed and the data's uploaded to CODIS."

Katie interrupted, "Oh, right—I've heard of CODIS before."

"OK, good. It's a labor-intensive process; it takes about two years of training before forensic scientists can handle their own DNA casework. Once fully trained, each scientist can only complete testing on seven rape kits a month. That's one of the reasons for all the backlogs around the country. Analysts then use CODIS to compare the DNA profiles that are obtained from crime-scene evidence against DNA profiles from other crime scenes, convicted offenders, and arrestees. If the DNA profile from one of our rape kits matches a sample that's taken from another crime scene, then the cases may be linked in what we call a 'forensic hit.'"

"That gives you a potential suspect?"

"Right."

"Can't we go in and look around?"

"No. We can only retrieve a kit under the signed consent of the victim or the court. They're sealed, and we intentionally hold them here in the storage room, since they aren't technically evidence. The contents are the property of the person who's tested, and we're strict about protecting people's privacy. We use a formal chain-of-possession procedure for tracking these kits. Every time a kit moves out of possession of the hospital to this location, or to the lab, we require a signature."

Katie surveyed the room and shuddered at the thought of all the stories the boxes, secured with a signed seal, might tell. Law. Victims. Justice. She wanted to find the bad guys and put them behind bars. Why was sexual assault such a prevalent crime? She turned around. Colin seemed restless.

"Anything else?" Colin said as he switched off the light.

"I think I've seen enough."

They retraced their steps down the hallway and back to the front door. After Colin said good-bye to the officer on duty, they walked back to the records office. Katie thanked Colin and returned to her desk. She leaned back in her chair and contemplated what she had just seen. It was obvious that the untested kits represented just a small sample of the sexual assaults that occurred. Especially, as Detective Scott had mentioned, if she believed the statistic that seventy percent of all sexual assaults go unreported. She wondered if those untested rape kits held the answer to who else Drew might have assaulted. Unfortunately, unless she could get a court order or could find a victim who would be willing to file a complaint and have the kit tested, she wouldn't find the answer there. She needed to speak with Detective Scott again.

Katie decided she was done for the day and straightened her desk. She just wanted to go home and take a shower. While she was putting some things into her backpack, through an open window she heard a police car's engine rumble to life and its siren start to wail. She glanced outside and saw the car speed by and the sound of the siren fade into the distance. Katie closed her eyes and hoped it wasn't another assault.

KATIE FELT EXHAUSTED WHEN SHE RETURNED to work the next morning. Days spent reading police reports filled with sordid details of appalling human behavior had left her overwhelmed and disappointed. Her decision to pursue criminal law guaranteed that she'd have many more days like these to look forward to.

She walked into her office, put her things on her desk, grabbed her notebook, and headed to the cafeteria to meet Detective Scott. She planned to tell him about her job and to ask a few questions. He was sitting where they'd sat for their last meeting, a white porcelain mug casually gripped in both hands.

"Do you only have that one gray suit?" Katie enjoyed teasing him.

"I actually have two, but they're identical. I keep telling you I'm old-school. May I get you a cup of coffee?"

"Please." After the detective left, Katie opened her notebook and reviewed her notes.

He returned momentarily and asked, "How's the new job going?" He placed a full cup of coffee in front of her and a glazed donut on a plate. Katie smiled at his gesture.

"I'm learning a lot. Last week I did an interesting analysis of the distribution of gunshots fired across the county. Taught me a lot about the query system."

"Have you found time to look for any leads?"

Katie pulled her hair behind her ears and placed her hands in her lap. "Not really. I've found a couple of cases I still need to review. My biggest hope—gaining access to rape kits—seems improbable."

"Remind me why you think the rape kits are important?"

"If I'm correct that Drew has assaulted before, then I think other cases would have some similarities to Ava's: a victim who's an acquaintance, perhaps a student he'd met and coerced into bed through a mix of charm, alcohol, and drugs. Because the woman would be afraid of adverse publicity for herself, or for him, she'd be unwilling to press charges and prefer the experience to go away quietly."

"Why?"

Katie understood that he was merely testing her logic. "Because of the state of Ava's apartment after the assault. I'm sure he's careful, wears a condom, and doesn't resort to violence. Suppose a victim concludes that she's been assaulted. Then, alone, or with a friend, she might go to the hospital for an examination, just like Ava did with me. But after a couple of days and with a clearer head, she'll think things through a bit more and decide that the consequences of talking to the police will be too great. She'll convince herself that she's the one who made a mistake and will decide to avoid the hassle and embarrassment of going forward with a report."

"Sounds plausible. And you hope to find a rape kit from such an incident?"

"Correct. But they're locked up in a secure room with an officer who's responsible for access. With health-care-privacy laws, I can't even gain access through my role as a public-records officer. And I'm not ready for a charge of breaking and entering." Katie smiled, hoping he would know she was joking.

"What if you went about this from the other direction?"

"What do you mean?"

"What if you searched for victims who're still on campus or might have graduated and still reside here? There must be a way to reach women through social media. Didn't you say that you also suspect they might have been sorority members?"

Katie sat back and gently slapped her hands on the table. "That's a brilliant idea. I bet I could make some connections online. Most victims would likely seek support from their friends, and you know how rumors spread—especially with social media involved. There could be a large circle of people out there who might know people."

Detective Scott left to refill their cups. He returned to the table and stared out the window for a moment. "There's one aspect of this idea that worries me."

"What's that?"

"If you start poking around, word of your efforts will get out. I'm concerned that if Drew gets wind of it, he won't be happy. Didn't you say he threatened you?"

"Sort of."

"I'm sure he blames you for the investigation. Without you, there wouldn't have been a case."

"What do you suggest?"

"Be discreet. Keep a list of your contacts and conversations. In fact, keep a diary of what you're doing for me to review. You know you can call or text me anytime, right?"

"You've been very generous about that, yes."

"One more thing. Let's say you manage to identify another of Drew's victims: someone with an untested rape kit in storage who's willing to come forward. We'll need a sample of Drew's DNA. You've thought of that, haven't you?"

Katie again enjoyed the fact that he said "we." She said, "Let's worry about that when the time comes."

"I'll say this again. At some point, we'll have to get a detective involved. They prefer to operate independently. They'll hate that a young aspiring law-school student is doing their job for them."

"Got it." Katie stood, and the detective joined her. She wrapped a napkin around the donut to take with her. "Thanks for the donut."

Katie looked around the cafeteria and noticed Colin, the detective who had escorted her to the storage area. He sat by himself with a cup of coffee. His eyes were locked on hers.

CHAPTER 30
One Step at a Time

Following up on the idea she'd discussed with Detective Scott, Katie developed the same kind of profile she'd used during her search of criminal files of female victims who shared similar attributes. She then began to search the Internet, a task that was made easier by the existence of numerous social-media sites. She focused on women who were currently or had once been students of CU and were currently or had been members of a sorority. She found that sites that appealed to job seekers and hiring managers appeared to be the most popular and professional looking. To jump-start their careers, many undergrads developed and maintained résumés and listed their relevant experiences, such as serving as vice president of finance at a sorority, working as an undergrad research assistant, or even working part-time as a nanny. One student stated that she had researched and planned weekly science experiments, outings, and field trips for the children in her charge.

She built a list of names and contact information and wondered how best to write an inquiry that would sound legitimate and nonthreatening. She typed a draft.

Dear [name],

I'm a former University of Colorado grad student who will soon be attending law school. I'm currently researching the topic of partner sexual assault. I'm seeking to interview university women who have firsthand experience with this insidious problem on our campus.

My study is focused on women who were (or still are) undergrads during any of the past four years and are/were members of a sorority. Local law enforcement has approved my study, and I will keep our communications strictly confidential. If you or someone you know can assist me in my research, please contact me. To find out more about me, please request a link to my professional profile.

Katie knew she was stretching the truth with the "local law enforcement has approved my study" comment, but she could argue that it was at least sort of true. Besides, what was ethical in the pursuit of a legitimate result? Her wording was justified, as long as she didn't break the law; she suspected that lawyers often faced the same dilemma. She built a list of email addresses and prepared to send her message. After proofreading it a final time, she added her signature and sent the text. Fifteen women would soon receive a very sensitive request. She'd know soon enough how they'd respond.

Back at work, her considerable backlog of public-information requests kept her busy all morning. She decided to return to her apartment over lunch to go for a run. The warm February afternoon was the perfect temperature for a jog.

After an hour-long run around the Flatirons, Katie stopped back at her apartment and checked email for any responses to the query she'd sent. The first email she read came as a surprise, since she'd not thought about her negotiations with the university for a while. It was a note from Harriet Becker, who wanted Katie to schedule a meeting in her office as soon as possible and directed her to Becker's administrative assistant to set up an appointment. Somewhat alarmed, Katie wondered what Harriet was after.

She scanned other new emails and saw seven responses to her query. Two had been returned with bad addresses, a detail she noted on her spreadsheet. Two simply said they couldn't help. One encouraged her to "go get the bastards." The remaining three were more interesting. One was from a woman named Addison:

Hi Katie,

I graduated from CU two years ago and was a member of a sorority. I knew a lot of girls in the house who felt they'd been assaulted by an acquaintance. Fortunately, I never had that experience. I know it's common though. I'm happy to talk sometime. I live in Denver, so give me a shout.

Addison

Another was from a woman named Emma:

Katie,

I'm currently a student at CU, a senior, and am living off campus. I heard rumors about this happening to a friend who's a member of a sorority. I wouldn't want to talk about it unless she gave me permission. I'll check with her and get back to you.

Emma

That was exactly the kind of letter that worried her. Once someone talked with her friends about some former student named Katie who was asking about sexual assault, she would lose control of the conversation. It was what Detective Scott had said he was worried about. She wondered if she should have used an alias.

The last was from a woman named Bailey who simply wrote, "Please call me. I have something to say but won't do it over email." Katie dialed the phone number at the bottom of the message. A woman answered in a few rings.

"Bailey, this is Katie Russell. Thanks for replying to my email."

"Sure. How can I help you?"

"I'm doing research into sexual assault and trying to understand why women typically don't report it. I'm hoping to find women who fit that profile and who might be willing to speak with me about their experiences."

"I'll share my experience if you want. But I don't want my name used. Will you promise to withhold it?"

"Yes. I won't use your name unless you expressly give me permission to do so."

"OK. I'm a sophomore at CU, and I'm in a sorority. During my freshman year, I used to party quite a bit. I wasn't having sex, but I used to drink a lot on the weekends. I'd go to a lot of frat parties, and we'd just kind of hang out. One night, during the winter semester, I probably had too much to drink, because I don't really remember what happened."

"How do you know that anything happened?" Katie jotted down some notes on a page in her notebook.

The voice on the phone changed the subject. "By the way, how do I know you're legit?"

Katie had expected the question. "I guess you can't, really. You'll have to trust me. I can give you some references, though. One's an attorney, and the other's a retired Boulder police detective."

"Who's the detective?"

"Detective Alex Scott. He's still on their website. The attorney is Harriet Becker."

Katie heard the tapping of keys on the other end. "OK, I see both names online. You sound legit. So one night, I'm at a frat with some girlfriends. Late in the evening, I wandered off somewhere, and they started looking for me. They went upstairs and started checking rooms. They finally found me in a guy's room. I guess we were going at it. It's not like I was protesting or anything—just kind of going along. At least that's what my girlfriends told me. He stopped as soon as they barged in. They took me back to our sorority, and I slept for a whole day."

"It sounds like you were intoxicated. The rules are clear about that: if you were in a condition that prevented you from giving your informed consent, then what he did to you was sexual assault. Did you report it?"

"I thought about it. I was mad at myself for drinking so much and then mad at him for taking advantage of me. I didn't want to see him again. He texted me a few times, checking to see if I was OK. That was nice. But I was depressed for about a week. I seemed a bit off. In the end, I decided I sort of got what I deserved. Luckily, he'd used a condom. I did go to the hospital and got checked for STDs. I was fine."

"Was he an athlete?"

"No. Just the opposite. I think he was an engineering major. I remember thinking he seemed harmless. But in the end, it made me rethink my partying ways, and I became much more cautious. It really marked the turnaround in my behavior. Now, if I'm going to drink alone with some guy, I make sure that I know him well and that we both agree about where things are headed. I'm glad my friends came looking for me that day."

"Thanks for sharing your story with me. I promise I won't use your name."

"OK. Bye."

It was a start. She next replied to Addison, the recent graduate who lived in Denver, to inquire if she'd be willing to speak by phone. Since Katie still didn't have money to replace her car, she'd have to take a bus if she wanted to meet her in person. She'd wait to hear back from Emma, whom she hoped was seeking permission from her friend.

The next day, after work, Katie walked to Becker's law office at the arranged time. The attorney emerged into the well-appointed waiting room ten minutes later, and Katie could tell by the stern look on her face that something was up. After exchanging greetings, they walked to a conference room and sat down.

"You didn't tell me about taking a job with the police department."

"I didn't think it was important. I thought we were done with our negotiations and didn't think to mention it." Katie immediately felt defensive.

"You should have. I received a call from Stan Humphries. He said the university suspects that you aren't abiding by the terms of our agreement. They plan to withhold payment."

"What! Why?"

"Someone at the police department told him you're employed there and that you're reviewing past sexual-assault cases. They even claim you're working with Detective Scott. Is that true?"

Katie's heart began to pound. Once again, she was in a situation that called for her to be honest and forthright. It was time to abandon her past strategy of dodging difficult issues. In the firmest voice she could muster, she said, "Yes, I am."

"Tell me about it."

Katie described the responsibilities of her job, including her search and review of past sexual-assault cases. She also told her of Detective Scott's guidance and how she was only authorized to view documents; she could not copy or discuss them.

"That's all?"

"No. I'm also getting in touch with other university women. I hope to find another of Drew's victims: someone who'll come forward and assist in an investigation. But I've been doing that on my own time."

"I think what you're doing is dangerous. I get your interest in trying to bring the scumbag to justice, I really do. But you're out of your league. You need to talk to the police commander. Include Detective Scott in the discussion, and tell the commander about everything you're doing. Eliminate any suspicion. The fact that Humphries knows you're working there tells me that he knows someone inside the department who's talking. It's not surprising, now that you're an Internet celebrity."

Katie knew Harriet was referring to the tens of thousands of hits her story had received on the web since it was published. Fortunately, no one seemed to have found her email address, although she'd had to take down one of her social-media profiles because of the many crude messages she'd received. "OK. You're right. I should have told you."

"The next part isn't as easy. The university might try to claim you're in breach of the agreement and try to modify it. Or worse, they might try to invalidate it."

Katie looked down and frowned. She looked around the room and wondered how much of Becker's attorney's fees went to pay for such a nice office. "I don't care."

"What did you say?"

"I don't care. All I ever wanted was to get Mark reinstated. If they want to change the agreement, or not pay me, that's fine. I won't give up on my efforts to get Drew. I'm sorry."

"Are you kidding? Do you realize how much money we're talking about? Look, I know you're idealistic—it comes with your age—but you also sound foolish. Take my advice. Forget this whole thing with Drew and focus on your relationship with Mark. I've been divorced twice. Great relationships with decent men are hard to find. Don't let this one get away."

Katie stood and faced Becker. Her legs trembled slightly. "I'm sorry, but this thing with Drew is really important to me. Just get enough money to pay your fees. I'll continue to abide by the NDA, other than where it pertains to Drew. That's what I agreed to do."

"Katie, you're terribly naive."

"Maybe so, but it's time for me to follow my beliefs and do the right thing."

"I disagree, but I'll honor your request."

Katie left the office and stood outside, shaken by the conversation. She knew that any appearance of going after Drew, especially now that she was working for the police department, was bound to attract attention. Maybe Harriet Becker was right. She *was* all those things: naive, young, and idealistic. And she was also short on money. Her job in the police department barely covered food and rent. She wanted a glass of wine.

CHAPTER 31
Cards on the Table

Katie followed Becker's advice and requested a meeting with the police commander. The department's conference room was nothing like her attorney's well-appointed space. The commander's conference table, surrounded by plastic swivel chairs, looked like it had been fashioned from an old church pew, not the polished mahogany of Becker's office. The room did at least have an expensive-looking electronic whiteboard, and the high-resolution monitors suggested that the city used its facilities budget for technology, not for furniture.

The usually prompt Detective Scott had once again arrived before her. He was sitting in one of the plastic chairs and was engaged in an animated conversation with a tall man dressed in dark wool slacks and a white shirt. They both stood when Katie appeared. Detective Scott made introductions, and Katie shook hands with Commander Robert Bennett, whose warm smile and searching eyes put Katie at ease. Detective Scott was dressed in his usual gray suit. Katie wore a skirt and blouse for the meeting.

The commander said, "So, Ms. Russell, how's the new job going?"

"Fine, sir. I'm learning a lot."

"Detective Scott thought you would. He was very instrumental in our decision to hire you."

"He's been very supportive."

"He recognizes talent when he sees it. I certainly felt that way when he took me under his wing, years ago, when I was a young detective."

"You've known each other for a while?" Katie assumed as much based on their convivial interactions.

"Going on twenty years now. You might say he's like a father to me. I came up through the ranks, while Detective Scott here decided he didn't want anything to do with admin."

"I've never been too good at bureaucratic BS," the detective said with a laugh. "I'd rather be in the field than behind a desk writing reports. After spending a few months in retirement, I jumped at the chance to come back part-time as a consultant and let someone else worry about the paperwork."

"We now have twenty detectives in my department, and I'm lucky to have Detective Scott's guidance. So how can I help you, Ms. Russell? You called this meeting."

"Thank you. I wanted to explain my interest in some possible criminal activity."

"I believe you're referring to the university's star quarterback?"

Katie glanced toward a rather sheepish-looking Detective Scott. She remembered a favorite saying of her father's: "If you're playing a game of poker and you look around the table and can't tell who the mark is, it's you."

The commander said, "Detective Scott and I are testing you a bit. He's briefed me on your employment and on his recent investigation into the sexual assault you witnessed. He's been more circumspect in telling me about his involvement with the faculty investigation. I'm glad to hear it's been resolved."

Katie decided to enlighten them. "It's not completely resolved, actually. The university's Title IX coordinator called my attorney to complain that I'm not abiding by the agreement we negotiated. They're aware I'm investigating Drew and are concerned that I won't honor my NDA."

Bennett looked toward Detective Scott. "Did you know about this?"

"First I've heard of it. Did your attorney explain how they found out?"

Katie fidgeted as she spoke. "My attorney, Harriet Becker, believes Stan Humphries—the Title IX coordinator—has a contact within the police department."

Detective Scott and the commander glanced at each other again. The detective broke the silence. "I'm not surprised. Humphries knows some former associates in the prosecutor's office. With the articles in the paper and the photo that was leaked, I'm confident that a lot of people know about your employment here. Also, we asked one of our detectives to supervise your work. I think you've met him: Detective Colin Richardson."

Katie's face flushed. She needed watching? "Why?"

"We've entrusted you with access to some of our most sensitive data. We'd monitor anyone in your position during a normal probationary period. We're not singling you out, I promise. Colin's job is to review the documents you research to ensure that we're not releasing data that might compromise any ongoing investigations. So far, you've been doing an excellent job."

Katie directed her gaze at Bennett. She struggled to keep her emotions in check. "As I'm sure Detective Scott has told you, I'm applying to law school. This job has given me even more motivation to pursue a career in criminal law. Am I doing anything wrong?"

Commander Bennett leaned forward. "Katie, let's discuss your interest in quarterback Evans. Detective Scott briefed me about the facts of the case, including your testimony, the hearing, and the ultimate finding of his responsibility and the sanctions against him."

Detective Scott added, "I've told the commander about your idea to search for other victims. He thinks it has merit."

Commander Bennett said, "Right. Guys like this tend to reoffend. I agree that this likely wasn't his first assault. The idea you discussed with Detective Scott sounds promising. As a college-age woman yourself, we think you'll have greater success gaining victims' cooperation than we might."

Katie studied both men. "Are you suggesting that I have my job so that I can help you investigate Drew?"

Detective Scott's voice deepened. "Katie, you were hired because of our confidence that you'd do a great job. Your interviews and qualifications were all outstanding. Professor Wilson gave you a glowing recommendation. It's true we thought to enlist your help with this case, but I'm also concerned about your safety. You're a strong-minded young woman, and I worried you wouldn't give up your pursuit of justice just because I insisted. That's why I went to Commander Bennett."

Commander Bennett's response came across as a plea. "Katie, we want you to continue contacting other women with the appropriate profile. See what you come up with. But I do share Detective Scott's concerns about your safety. That's why we assigned Detective Richardson—for your personal security."

"To be my bodyguard?"

"Not exactly. We want you to inform him of any activity related to the investigation. If you ever want him to accompany you, he's available. He's what we call a security detail."

Katie wondered if security was his only interest. "OK, but just make sure he knows I have a boyfriend and that I'm not interested in anything else."

"I'll make that clear." Detective Scott's stern look made her think of her father.

Katie finally relaxed and leaned back in her chair. She looked at Detective Scott. "I'll help you."

"Excellent." Commander Bennett stood. "Katie, I'm happy that you're working in the department. I'm also pleased by your interest in criminal law. If you need help getting into law school, let me know." The commander left the room, and Katie and Detective Scott sat alone.

"Katie, I hope you don't feel blindsided."

"Ironically, I called the meeting to tell the chief about my activities. Sounds like he was one step ahead of me the whole time."

"Commander Bennett has a unique ability to ferret out the facts. Not much gets past him. He tries to anticipate events."

"I'd say he's had a good teacher. Come on. Let's go to the cafeteria. I'll buy you a cup of coffee this time."

KATIE WENT BACK TO HER APARTMENT, LEFT A message with Becker about the meeting with Commander Bennett, and checked email for any more responses to her query. Her new contact Emma confirmed that her friend had given her permission to discuss her experience. She suggested coffee that Saturday at a coffee shop in town. Katie sent a response, and they agreed to meet at ten. She'd also received a response from Addison, who agreed to a phone call and suggested late Sunday morning to talk.

Among her new messages were two more that had bounced back with bad addresses. Two more were new. One was from someone named Heather who declined to discuss the subject but wished Katie luck. Another was from someone named Claire, who was a senior and lived in a sorority. She'd discuss the subject if Katie would keep the conversation anonymous. Katie suggested coffee.

She now had four contacts with bad email addresses, three who were unwilling to talk, three who were active leads, and Bailey, who had spoken about an experience that didn't involve Drew. She hadn't received responses from four others. Katie was aware that some people would just ignore the email and not bother to respond. She spent the rest of the afternoon working on more sample LSAT questions.

WAITING FOR HER AT WORK ON FRIDAY MORNING was what seemed like a never-ending backlog of information requests. After two hours of work without a break, Detective Richardson—she decided to call him Colin—stopped by and again parked his ass on the edge of her desk.

"Hi, Colin. How about you pull up a chair and sit."

"Sure—sorry." Colin rolled an empty chair over from another desk and sat down. "I just wanted to say that I look forward to working with you. Let me know how I can help out."

"Did Detective Scott speak with you?"

"Don't worry. If I didn't know better, I'd think he was your father. He told me to keep my hands off."

"Good. Glad we understand each other."

"Tell me about your search for potential persons of interest. The commander and Detective Scott asked me to understand your plans so that I can assist if necessary."

"I sent emails to fifteen women I found through social media. I looked for current or past members of sororities on campus who either have recently graduated or are currently students. Since Drew's been on campus for four years—he redshirted a year—I assume he could have targeted women who are currently freshmen, or those who might've been upperclassmen when he was a freshman. I estimate his targets could span a period of six to seven years, but I think he'd lean toward women who are younger and less aware of the risks."

"Have you received any responses?"

"I have three active leads and haven't heard from four others. I may not. I'm meeting with one on Saturday and speaking with another by phone on Sunday. I'm still trying to set up a meeting with the third."

"Do you need any help from me?"

"Thanks, but I don't think so. Would you mind giving me your phone number, though, so I can contact you in case I do?"

"Sure. Here's my card. Feel free to call or text me anytime."

"Thanks. See you Monday." Colin stood and returned the chair to the empty desk. He smiled before he turned and walked away. Katie had a better feeling about him now. He seemed genuinely interested in the case and not just in hooking up.

Katie worked for two more hours and left work around one. That night she planned to meet Mark for dinner. It had been several weeks since their twenty-four-hour reunion at his apartment. She had a list of topics to discuss; foremost on her list was the conversation with Harriet Becker about the settlement agreement.

They met at a small Italian restaurant downtown. Katie summarized her meeting with the commander over eggplant Parmesan. As Mark ate and sipped his wine, Katie considered Becker's advice that she should simply forget about detective work and nurture her relationship with Mark. From what Katie had heard, once law school began, finding time with him would be harder than finding a frat guy who didn't think casual sex was a birthright. She decided to speak less of herself and more about Mark. "How are classes going?"

"Great. I'm teaching the philosophy and law class this semester, by myself this time. Professor Hatfield occasionally monitors my lectures, but she's given me total freedom to teach as I like."

"How's she treating you after the suspension? Did she say anything about us?" Katie had wanted to ask earlier but perhaps had held off because she was unsure of the answer she'd receive.

"She supports me. I think she feels the university's occasionally too PC. She doesn't believe college students need protecting as much as they need to learn critical-thinking skills. That's why she believes so strongly in the class. She's mentioned your presentation and paper several times, and she once made an unsolicited offer to write a statement to the dean to say that she hadn't observed any favoritism in my interactions with you as a student."

"That's a relief. That was one of the best classes ever. I'd hate to think our relationship somehow lowered her opinion of me. I was proud of my A."

"You should be. By the way, I hear the newspaper's going to publish a story about the investigation and its conclusion. They've tried to contact me for a comment, but I've refused. They won't mention your name."

"I know it's out there." Katie paused for a moment and drank some wine. "I want to talk about law school." She wanted to be completely open.

"Do you still want to go?"

"More than ever. But I'm worried about how it will affect us."

"By the time apart."

"Yes. I'm hoping I'll get into law school somewhere in Colorado. It'll be easier to spend time together that way."

Mark's face brightened. "I don't want to see anyone else." He smiled.

"Neither do I."

"Phew. That's a relief. You'll take the LSAT in June, right?"

"Yes. Then I apply to schools this fall. I should receive decision letters next spring, a year from now."

"We have lots of time. There's something else."

"What?"

"You should consider the best school possible. Don't settle for a regional school if you can get into one of the top programs. You have the skills for it. It sounds like you'll also have the money to go wherever you want."

"That might not be true after all."

"Why?" After Katie recounted her discussion with Becker, Mark said, "You really told her you didn't want the money? You'd give it up so you can go after Drew?"

"No more compromises. Remember your comment about acting morally?"

Mark placed his napkin on the table and leaned back in his chair. "Wow. Your sense of justice is admirable."

Katie got up from their small table and walked over to Mark's side. She leaned down, fully aware that nearby diners were watching. She grabbed Mark's jaw with her right hand and the back of his head with her left. She pressed her lips against his. When she finished, she simply said, "You're the best."

CHAPTER 32
Detective Work

Katie arrived at the coffee shop on Saturday morning and ordered a latte. She sat down near a window and soon noticed a diminutive female student with dark, shoulder-length hair and oversize eyeglasses enter the coffee shop and survey its interior. Katie assumed it was Emma and went to greet her.

After introductions, Emma went to order a drink while Katie returned to her table.

Katie studied Emma as she waited to order her drink. She stood calmly, occasionally checking her phone, and wore generic jeans and a leather jacket that hung loosely over a bulky sweater. Katie decided she should reconsider her stereotypes of sorority women, especially her bias that all sorority women look like blonde cover girls. Emma looked as wholesome and natural as any girl on campus.

Emma returned with a cup of tea and sat down before asking Katie a few questions about her research. Katie had become more comfortable with answering questions about her personal interest in sexual assault and her plans to attend law school, because her answers were truthful. Emma seemed satisfied with her answers.

"What about you?" Katie asked. "What's your major?"

"Accounting and finance. I've always liked numbers, especially when they have dollar signs in front of them." She laughed lightly and said, "You know, I still have a spiral notebook at home with entries I kept of all my babysitting earnings. Numbers have always fascinated me. I could recite the Pythagorean theorem by the time I was six."

"You won't have any trouble getting a job with that major. So, tell me about your experience with sexual assault."

Emma peeled off her jacket and hung it on the back of her chair. "It's a problem, especially with freshman women." She drank from her cup of tea and then continued. "That's when they're most vulnerable, and they're often unable to perceive risk. They're excited to be away from home, they feel invincible, and they're starting to really explore their sexuality. I think guys are fully aware of that and take advantage of the situation accordingly."

"Tell me about your friend."

"She was a freshman last year. I was a sophomore, and I sat on the rush committee. I liked her right off the bat. She came from a great family in Colorado Springs and was super sweet. She rushed our house in the fall. She always obeyed the rules, and everyone liked her. She was a guy magnet at all the frat parties—a fact I'm not sure she fully appreciated. I've never seen so many guys wanting to hang with one person. The term they used for her was 'wifey material.'" She made air quotes. "She usually brushed them off."

"What happened?" Katie jotted down notes as they talked.

"There was one guy who kept after her. I'd seen him with other girls in the house, at parties, or out dancing. Unlike my friend, those girls were more casual about hooking up. As the guys like to say, they knew how to 'get down.'" She made air quotes again.

"Have sex, you mean?"

"Right. They drank more than most and were gone lots of nights. You can't get in past the two o'clock curfew on the weekends, because they lock the doors. We try not to rush girls like that, but sometimes they slip in anyway." Emma paused as Katie scribbled in her notebook. "Maybe he liked the challenge. I don't know. But one time, he invited several of us to attend a house party. We arrived late, and it was a pretty typical scene: garbage-can punch spiked with alcohol, lots of beer, a pool table downstairs, dancing, and people smoking weed out back."

"A typical party, in other words."

"Right. So this guy comes up and immediately starts hitting on my friend. He offers her a drink, which she takes. He starts chatting her up, and he completely ignores me. I went to find a beer and ran into a couple of friends. While we're talking, I kept my eye on her. I didn't feel right about the guy. He struck me as trouble. Too good-looking. Too smooth."

"What did he look like?"

"Tall. Blond hair. Solid build. I think he was an athlete, but I'm not positive. Anyway, after I watched her for about fifteen minutes, she became animated. She laughed loudly and used exaggerated arm movements when she spoke. I even saw her spill her drink a few times."

"Sounds like she was getting drunk."

"That's what I thought. But it was hard to believe, since we'd been there less than an hour. I also noticed that the guy was placing his arm on her lower back and touching her a lot. Then I saw her put her plastic cup down and start wandering off, maybe looking for the bathroom. I intercepted her at the back of the house and asked if she was all right. She laughed and said yes and then proceeded to throw up all over the floor. I turned and looked for the guy and saw him slip out the front door."

"Do you think she'd been drugged?"

"I'm convinced she was. No doubt about it. She didn't have anything to drink before we left for the party. I know, because she was with me the whole time. In fact, I never did see her drink very much anytime we went out. Wasn't her thing, I guess."

"So what did you do?"

"I did my best to find some towels, and I cleaned up. Then I took her back to the house and put her to bed in my room. I stayed with her the whole night. She was better the next morning, but she seemed like she had a hangover."

"What about the guy?"

"I think he left her alone after that. She never said anything about seeing him again."

"So why do you think this story's important?" Katie was curious, since Emma hadn't described any sexual assault.

"Because I think it serves as a warning to college girls to keep an eye on their drinks and never take one from a stranger. That, and women should keep friends close until they really know a guy well."

"I'd say that's great advice. Thank you—and please thank your friend for me for sharing her story."

"Sure. You know, there is one more thing." Emma looked like she'd just remembered something.

"What?"

"About a month later, she was with another guy—someone from one of her classes, I think. They were walking through his dorm one night and walked past a room with an open door. My friend happened to peer inside and saw a guy at a desk, browsing through some photos on his computer. He'd viewed about four when he must have sensed that they were standing there watching him. He turned and said 'keep moving,' and then he got up and slammed the door shut."

"What was in the photos? Do you know?"

"They were of a guy sitting on a bed next to a woman wearing lingerie. They were like selfies. The girls were all smiles and seemed happy to pose. But the weird part was, the guy in each photo was the guy from the frat party. The girls were all different."

"Was he the guy in the room who slammed the door?"

"Nope. But I think he was a football player. Quite a few of them live in that dorm. And here's another thing. She recognized a girl in one of the photos—one of the girls I told you about from the sorority who liked to party."

Katie mulled over the information for a minute and took a sip of her latte. "Where's this girl now?"

"She's still a student. Moved out of the sorority at the end of last year and lives somewhere off campus now. Why, do you want to speak with her?"

"I'd love to. Do you know her name?"

Emma paused while she thought. "I'm pretty sure it's Amy Lewis, though I'm not sure how to contact her."

"I'll figure it out." Katie wrote down the name and tried to think of more questions. She couldn't. "Emma, thank you again for telling me your friend's story. Thank her for me, too. Tell her she did the right thing by sharing it."

Emma finished the last of her tea and set the cup on the table. "Women need to be careful," she said. "Sometimes I feel like we're at the zoo. If we throw ourselves over the fence into the tiger exhibit, we shouldn't be surprised if we get clawed."

Katie thought about the analogy. "Some people would demand a higher fence. But I think it's a better strategy to increase awareness and the threat of punishment until the day comes when fences are just a historical footnote—like segregated bathrooms."

Katie said good-bye to Emma and walked back to her apartment. She logged onto her laptop and searched for the story Mark had warned her about. She was happy to find that it wasn't on the front page.

ASSISTANT PROF CLEARED OF CONDUCT VIOLATION

BOULDER, COLO. — Assistant Professor Mark O'Connor has been cleared in a University of Colorado investigation into allegations of a prohibited amorous relationship with a graduate student. The university released a statement: "Our investigation concluded that the relationship started after the professor had completed his official supervisory responsibilities in a graduate-level class, at the end of the semester. Therefore, there was no policy violation." The professor has been fully reinstated. This newspaper continues to withhold the name of the student to protect her privacy.

During the investigation, a nude photo of the graduate student was received by this paper. We chose not to publish the photo as a matter of journalistic policy, although the stolen photo was reportedly leaked to several online websites that traffic in scandalous and explicit photos of movie stars and public personalities. Neither the university nor the professor was available for comment.

Katie, against her better instincts, scrolled down to some of the comments at the end of the story. She hesitated, because they were typically mean-spirited or written with an obvious lack of intelligence. Most, she knew, were written by trolls who had nothing better to do with their lives.

The first one simply read: *Hey professor, I saw the photo. Well done. You're the man! She's a babe.*

Another one, from a woman, was equally tasteless: *Mark, if I sign up for your class, can I get extra credit for research in your bedroom?* It included an emoticon of a smiley face with a wink and a kiss.

The next, solidly in the mean-spirited category, was the last one she could stomach: *We pay these professors high salaries to teach at one of the most beautiful college campuses in the country, and what do they do—seduce our children. Shame on them.*

Katie tossed the laptop onto her bed and decided on a long walk followed by an early night.

THE NEXT MORNING, KATIE AWOKE AND STARED out her window and saw that it was snowing heavily. Rivers of white flakes cascaded down from an amorphous sky. After a moment spent admiring the snow, she turned on the baseboard heater, pulled her notebook from her backpack, and located her notes in preparation for the phone call with Addison. Once she had coffee in hand, she inserted her earbuds and dialed. After introductions, Addison asked Katie a few questions she had anticipated about the nature of her interest in sexual assault. Once Addison seemed to be satisfied with Katie's responses, she began her story.

"I graduated last year and now live in Denver, where I work for a PR firm. Something happened my senior year while I was vice president of new-member services at my sorority, and I think it's relevant to your research. My role was to organize new-member programs and to work with the junior council. As part of my duties, I arranged the big-sister and little-sister pairings."

"I'm aware of the tradition," Katie said. She knew that each new member was matched with a big sister, who would act as a mentor throughout the new-membership period. The new member was called a "little." These bonds tended to continue throughout college, she'd heard, and they often developed into long-lasting friendships.

"We had a new pledge that year who seemed more naive than most. I decided to become her big sister. I made sure that she was fully integrated into the activities of the house and guided her involvement in some of our philanthropic activities, like raising money for the YWCA—that kind of thing. Even though she was very attractive, she didn't date much. She was sort of shy."

"What was her name? Do you mind telling me?"

"I'd rather not say."

"That's fine."

"Early in the fall semester, after she'd moved into the house, one of the frats had a mixer. I couldn't go because I was working on a research project for one of my classes at the time, but I made sure my little sis went with a group of other girls. Late that night, around midnight, I heard a few of them return to the house. Some of them went to bed, and others just hung out downstairs. Around one in the morning, I went to check on my little and didn't find her in her room, so I went downstairs and asked some of the girls who'd gone with her if they knew her whereabouts. They said she'd met a guy at the party and left with him, but no one knew where she'd gone. I scolded them for not staying with her. We try to keep an eye on our younger members while they're learning the ropes of college life."

"What happened?"

"I went to bed and sent her a text. I didn't get a reply. I was concerned. Then, around four a.m., she called my phone, hysterical. She was saying things like 'I woke up in his bed' and 'He raped me.' I finally got her to calm down enough to tell me where it had happened. She wasn't sure, but she thought she was walking on University Avenue when a passing car spotted her and called the police. The police came and immediately took her to the hospital. I jumped out of bed and drove there myself. She looked so fragile when I saw her lying on the examination table wrapped in a blanket. I felt sick. Over the next several hours, a nurse examined her and performed a sexual-assault exam. Do you know what that is?"

"Yes—a rape kit."

"Right. After she was through with the exam, a police officer tried to ask her a few questions, but she refused to answer them. She just kept saying that she wanted to go home. She asked me to make sure her parents didn't find out. After she was released from the hospital, I took her back to the house and put her to bed."

"Did she ever report it?"

"No. After she'd gotten some sleep and calmed down for a day, we spoke about it. She could only remember that she'd danced with a bunch of guys, but one more than the others. Some of the other sisters who were there described him as tall, blond, and very good-looking. She vaguely remembered talking to him on the back deck. Said that's when she started feeling really out of it. The next thing she remembered was waking up in his bed, several hours later. She freaked out, grabbed her clothes, and ran. It was cold that night, too. The nurse was worried about hypothermia."

"Did she have any more interactions with the police?"

"Yeah, early the following week. She told them again what happened, but she refused to identify the guy or file a complaint. I think she was afraid of him and wanted the whole thing to just go away. Her parents are very conservative. Her biggest fear was of them finding out."

"She must have been terrified."

"She told me she couldn't imagine anyone doing that to her. She was trusting. We only talked about it a few more times. She was clearly depressed. I convinced her to get counseling at the student medical center, which I think helped. At least she finally decided to tell her parents."

"Then what happened?"

"She withdrew from school at the end of the fall semester and moved back home. She took the next semester off and then enrolled at a different college the following year. We still stay in touch, and I've spoken with her a few times. It was probably my saddest experience at school. I felt like I'd really let her down as her big sis. I've blamed myself ever since for not going with her that night."

"Don't—you shouldn't blame yourself. Wow. That's a horrible story, though. I'd like to meet her."

"What do you plan to do with the information?"

Katie had wondered the same thing. Might the man have been Drew? He certainly fit the profile. "I'm not sure yet," she said. "How do you think your friend would react if I chose to investigate her experience?"

"She'd want assurance that she could trust you and that it would be worthwhile. I sense that she's finally getting that horrible experience behind her. It might just open up an old wound."

"It sounds to me like she was traumatized, and I don't blame her. I hate that men do this. But I also believe that what compounds the harm is, like you said, naively hoping that it will just go away somehow. In most cases, it doesn't just go away. These men will continue to offend. If we can get proof of what happened, do you think we could convince her to come forward?"

"Maybe. I think it really depends on the progress she's made healing. She also needs to get the support of her parents."

"Have you met them?"

"Yes. Nice couple. Very serious. I think they attend church regularly. I suspect her desire to minimize what happened starts with them. They're second-generation Latinos, and she's the first in the family to attend college. You'd not only have to convince her, you'd have to convince them, too."

"Will you help me?"

"What, convince her?"

"Yes." Katie recognized that Addison's little sis had trusted her. Maybe she could help convince her little sis of the virtue of Katie's desire to hold Drew accountable. Katie truly believed that this was the healthiest, though certainly the hardest, way forward for everyone.

"I will."

Katie was thrilled. "Thank you. That's great. First I'll review the police report." Then it hit her: she may have already reviewed the report's summary. It described a girl who'd been picked up on University Avenue who refused to release her sexual-assault exam and was unwilling to consider any legal proceedings. Just to be sure, Katie asked Addison for the girl's name. "I promise that until she agrees to go forward, I'll only use it to locate the report."

"Natalie Garcia."

Katie thanked Addison and promised to get back in touch later in the week.

After the call, Katie wasted no time in calling Detective Richardson. She left a voice mail and made a pot of tea. The scene on the street below her living room window looked like it was from an animated film: the river of snow continued to streak from the sky in a blend of white and gray. Her favorite tree, a conspirator in her trip to Durango, stood mostly bare except where inches of snow had piled up on its wider and more substantial branches. She glimpsed tiny clusters of dormant buds, vigilant against the winter and awaiting spring and their transformation into new shoots. She felt affinity for that tree. Her phone rang.

It was Colin. Katie told him about the phone call with Addison, the woman named Natalie Garcia, and the case file that she'd once read in the police archives. Colin hadn't heard of the case but said he'd stop by the office later in the day to see what he could find. They agreed to meet on Monday when Katie arrived for work.

CHAPTER 33

A Breakthrough

olin was seated at Katie's desk when she arrived for work in the morning. "The case file you mentioned is stored in the archives," he said.

"Let's go."

The archived records were stored in the same building as the rape kits. Katie shivered at the memory of her first trip there with Colin, when she'd seen the roomful of sealed boxes, each with trauma inside. It was a memory so vivid she would never forget it, like the time her father cried or the sound of Justin's coffee mug smashing on the kitchen floor.

Colin filled out the required paperwork, and a clerk returned ten minutes later with a legal-size file folder. Colin penned the required signature, and they took the folder to an empty desk. The file's table of contents included a preliminary-findings report prepared by the prosecuting attorney's office, an incident report written by the officer who'd located Natalie on University Avenue the night of the assault, a report from another officer who'd visited the sorority a week later to interview Natalie, and separate interviews with Natalie and Addison. Katie and Colin took turns over the next hour reading through the contents. The prosecuting attorney's findings were almost apologetic.

We have an ethical obligation to evaluate all incidents of sexual assault and determine whether we are able to meet the burden of proof at trial. Occasionally, there will be issues that develop with a witness where we conclude we can't reach that legal threshold, and we have an obligation to close an investigation before charges are filed.

Katie understood that Natalie was the witness and that her refusal to cooperate had left the prosecutor's office with no other choice but to close the case. The remaining reports and statements seemed to corroborate the details Addison had provided during her phone call.

Colin laid the last of the documents on the desk and looked up at Katie. "What do you think?"

"Looks pretty much as Addison described it."

"I agree. The second police report mentioned the exam at the hospital and stated that a rape kit had been filed under a Jane Doe, pending Natalie's consent to release it. Since she didn't consent, I assume it's still in storage."

"And we can't touch it."

"Nope. Not without Natalie's signed release or a judge's order."

"Can we confirm that it exists?" Katie wanted some assurance that if they went to the trouble of gaining Natalie's support, they would actually have a chance of securing useful evidence.

"We can find out."

"How?"

"When we store kits anonymously, and without release by the person who's been examined, we use a system to identify the kit. We use a preliminary report number of 99999. Then we fill in the last name of the victim as that report number, and 'Unknown' becomes the victim's first name. We use the victim's date of birth as the date of the exam, we always list race as unknown, and we list the location as 'community at large.'"

"Then if we know Natalie's date of birth, we can confirm that the kit exists somewhere in the storage room?"

"Right. And the DOB's listed on the contact form. You're getting pretty good at this. Forget law school—become a cop!"

Katie assumed he was joking. "Thanks, I'll take that as encouragement." Katie turned back to Natalie's statement. "You know, there was something I read here that Addison didn't mention."

"What's that?"

"In her statement, Natalie said that one of the last things she remembered before waking up in her assailant's bed was something he did."

"You mean the photo?"

"Right. He insisted that she put on a piece of jewelry and then sit down next to him on the bed. She complied, and he took a photo. She recalled only wearing underwear at that point. That was the last thing she remembered." Katie slid her chair back, stood, and then slowly paced around the table. "I don't recall her describing the jewelry."

Colin reread the report. "No, she didn't."

Katie stopped and stared at Colin. "The dorm room!"

"What dorm room?"

"Yesterday I spoke with a woman named Emma. She told me a story about a student in her sorority who was walking through a dorm one night and saw a guy, in his room, looking at photos of women on his computer. The student watched this guy look at about four similar photos. The guy in each photo was the same, but the women were all different. Each of them sat next to him on the bed in various types of lingerie."

"Sounds like it could be the same guy."

"It must be." Katie looked at her watch. "I need to get to work. Can you determine if the rape kit's in the storage room?"

"Sure."

"Also, any chance you can find an address for me? A student named Amy Lewis. She lives off campus somewhere."

Colin gathered up the reports and prepared to return them to storage. "Sure, I'll see what I can find."

"Can I call you after work?"

"Sure. Talk to you then."

Katie returned to her desk and was tempted to start searching for Amy Lewis herself but decided to let Colin do it. She was way behind on her records requests.

AFTER WORK, KATIE SLOWLY WALKED BACK TO HER apartment, a thousand threads of detail spinning through the loom of her mind. She didn't want to jump prematurely to any conclusions, but the profile of Drew was becoming clear. Could he really be capable of assaulting so many women? She knew that to accept that conclusion would mean to step out of innocence and face true depravity.

She stopped walking and looked skyward. Saturated hues of deep blue stretched across the horizon, unfiltered by clouds. She closed her eyes and let the strong rays of the sun penetrate her skin and warm her soul. Spring was on the way—a time when life is reborn. If she peered much further into Drew's soul, she reflected, she may well need to be reborn herself.

Back inside her apartment, Katie opened a window and unpacked her things. She thought to go to the laundromat and start a load of clothes. She moved from room to room in search of dirty ones and to fold any strewn-about but clean clothes. She'd learned by watching her father how the seemingly humdrum activities of daily life always proved to be more meaningful and consequential in retrospect and how living alone could be restorative in its own way. But overall, she still desired to have someone of constant character in her life. Someone like Mark.

She hauled the bag of clothes down the block toward the combined laundry and pub, a convenient place she'd discovered after her Christmas trip home. Once the washing machine started to churn, she went into the pub to get a beer. While it was being poured, she retrieved her phone and called Colin.

He sounded excited. "The rape kit's in storage. Looks like we can contact Natalie. How do you want to proceed?"

"I should speak with Addison and get her advice first. Her parents will need some hand-holding. A request from you, in your position as detective, would be more credible."

"I agree. I also found the address you wanted."

Katie jotted it down. "Thanks. I think I'll drop by later and see if I can catch her at home. I hope she'll talk with me."

"Let me know how it goes. See you tomorrow."

While the clothes were drying, Katie got out her laptop and updated her spreadsheet. She hadn't received any more responses and concluded that she probably wouldn't. She did have one more lead to contact: the senior named Claire who'd requested that their conversation remain anonymous.

LATE IN THE AFTERNOON, AFTER RETURNING HOME with clean clothes and several completed LSAT practice questions, Katie bundled up and headed back outside. Amy Lewis's address was five miles away. She took a bus, then walked a few blocks to an older-looking two-level building that appeared to contain eight apartments. She rang the buzzer for Amy's unit and was pleasantly surprised when the door began to open but then was startled when one of its hinges sang like an annoyed cat.

"Hi. I'm looking for Amy Lewis?" Katie eyed the girl behind the half-opened door, dressed in yoga pants and a sweatshirt.

"Who's asking?"

"Katie Russell."

"Come on in. Amy's upstairs studying. I'll go get her." Once they were inside and the door had creaked closed, the woman headed up a stairway.

Katie took a seat on a worn sofa and noticed a couple of beer bottles on a counter in the kitchen. She also detected a faint smell of pot in the air. She wondered if the bottles had been left out after the night before or perhaps had been consumed more recently. She soon heard the muffled steps of both girls coming down a carpeted stairway.

Katie rose. "Hi, I'm Katie Russell. I used to be a grad student here at CU, but I've decided to switch to law school."

"Hi," Amy said. "Why are you looking for me?" Katie had anticipated this question and hadn't come up with a convincing answer, so she remained silent for a moment. "Let's sit," Amy said.

Katie returned to her spot on the sofa. "I've been researching ways in which women can avoid sexual assault, especially younger students, since they seem more prone to danger. That led me to sororities. I've spoken with many women who've told me some pretty scary stories."

"So why are you talking to me? I've never had anything to do with sexual assault."

Katie studied Amy's face, which was free of makeup and radiant with natural beauty. It was late in the afternoon, and she looked tired. "A woman from your sorority named Emma gave me your name."

"Oh yeah, I remember her from last year. She was fun. Pretty straight, but still fun."

"Well, she thinks you might've dated a guy I'm trying to find. He's a good-looking athlete. Blond guy." Katie sensed that her story was going nowhere.

"Well, sounds like my type. But who I date is none of your business."

"I agree. But here's the deal. Someone saw you in a photo with this guy. You were sitting on a bed next to him wearing only lingerie."

"Whoa. Who saw that?"

"Another girl in your sorority. She was walking through a dorm and saw a guy looking at photos on his computer. She recognized you in one of them."

"That creep. I remember that night, when he told me what he wanted me to do. I told him no way—I didn't want my photo out there. He promised he wouldn't post it or anything. I believed him."

"What did you mean he told you what he wanted you to do?"

"Look, I like guys. I don't mind admitting it. I figure I'm only in college for four years—my parents hope so anyway—and I might as well have as much fun as I can while I'm here. I'll settle down some day, but for now, if I find a guy I want to fuck, I don't see any reason to waste time just hanging out."

Katie was surprised by her forthrightness. She almost admired it. "Did you fuck this guy for long?"

"No, unfortunately. We only lasted about a month. I think I slept with him the first night we met. It was at a frat party. He knew what he was doing, too. He had the body of an Adonis. But after about a month, I could tell he was getting bored and ready to move on. That was OK with me. I was ready for a change myself."

Katie couldn't imagine having such a cavalier attitude about sex. "All right, so what was it he asked you to do?"

"Look, what are you going to do with this information? I don't want to get him into any trouble. Of course I'm pissed that he posted a photo of me, but I don't think he's a bad guy." Amy suddenly got up and went to the kitchen and returned with a beer. "Want one?"

"No, thanks. To be honest, I'm not so sure he isn't a bad guy. His name's Drew, right?"

"I'd rather not say." Amy sipped at her beer. "Why, what do you think he might've done?"

"I think he goes after women. Nothing wrong with that, of course—consensual sex is fine. But I suspect he often uses drugs or alcohol to get his way."

"'Yes means yes,' right? He never had to do that with me."

"I understand. But some girls might not be so..." Katie searched for the right word; *easy* wouldn't do "...like-minded. What did he ask you to do?"

"Before we had sex that first night, he asked me to strip down to my bra and panties. I gladly did. But then he did something I always thought was a bit weird."

"What?"

"He asked me to put on a pearl necklace. It was beautiful. I could tell it was expensive."

"Did you?"

"Sure. Once I had it on, he sat on the bed next to me and took the selfies. I liked them. I have to say, seeing myself sitting there in my underwear with a string of pearls around my neck? I looked hot. After that, we really went at it. It turned me on."

Katie suddenly wished she'd accepted that beer. She could use a drink. "Other than that, he was like any other guy?"

"Pretty much. Way better-looking, though." Amy took a sip. "I've probably said too much. I don't want you repeating this, OK? He didn't do anything to me. If you find out that he assaulted someone, well, that's between them. I want to stay out of this."

"I get it. You've been a big help. I don't need to share our conversation."

Katie left the apartment and took the bus back downtown. It was nearly five thirty, and she really did need a drink now. She decided to walk over to the Bohemian Biergarten. It had been a while since she'd been there. It was time for a return visit.

She found an empty table and sat down. After ordering a pint, she pulled out her journal and started writing down notes. She found it hard to believe that only six months had passed since her first visit to the bar. So much had happened since then. It was hard to digest it all. Was life always this crazy? Her thoughts turned to Mark. She admired how focused he was about teaching and how confident he was in his goals. Yet her future seemed unknowable. She recalled times in her life when things seemed simple, like playing tennis when she was in the zone and every shot seemed perfect. Or swimming, when her stroke count was low and her speed fast. She even remembered an oral final as an undergraduate, when she knew her subject so well that not a single question could throw her off. All those efforts seemed easy. She wanted her relationship with Mark to feel that way.

Her beer arrived. As she sipped it, she recalled her conversation with Amy and how different she was from most of the girls Katie knew. Healthy? Maybe. Maybe not. Amy certainly had her own confidence about where her life was headed. The picture Katie was building of Drew was getting complicated. Maybe that was the nature of this type of serial rapist: one who can be both charming and cunning and doesn't need to resort to violence. What drove him? He could, and apparently did, have almost any woman he desired. What made him tick?

Katie finished her beer and penned some final thoughts. *I want to be normal. My life now seems anything but. I don't want a boring life, just a normal life. Shared with someone. Doing good in the world. Finding my place.* She finished by sketching a tree branch: a leafy springtime branch on the tree outside her window, with a bird singing a morning song. She even included a few notes on a score leaving the bird's beak: "Here Comes the Sun." She hummed the old Beatles song as she packed up her notebook and headed home.

CHAPTER 34
Perdóname, Por Favor

Katie and Colin were assigned an unmarked police cruiser from the motor pool and drove from Boulder to Pueblo in a little over two hours. Katie admired the front range of the Rockies while Colin concentrated on driving. She read an online entry on Pueblo on their way and learned that the city in the southern part of the state, with a population that was about forty percent Latino, was known for its many immigrants. Some people called it Steel City because of the large steel mill in town. Its crime rate was higher than the state's average, she read, and its cost of living was lower. It was one of the poorest cities in the state.

A few days earlier, Colin and Katie had briefed Detective Scott and Commander Bennett on Katie's conversation with Addison about Natalie Garcia and their subsequent review of her case file. Bennett subsequently gave Colin permission to contact Ms. Garcia in a meeting that Katie facilitated through Addison. He also promised to contact the original detective on the case, as a courtesy, and inform him of his approval to reopen the investigation.

In her phone call to Addison, Katie explained that she and Colin wanted to meet with Ms. Garcia and examine her willingness to release her rape kit for testing. Addison agreed to the introduction, and Katie spoke with Natalie, who originally declined but then agreed to a meeting at her family's home in Pueblo. Colin would present an official request to Natalie's parents.

Katie tapped nervously with her fingernails on the passenger window as they pulled up in front of a modest and carefully maintained row home. It reminded her of old photos of postwar bungalows she'd seen in her

Western history class. The photos portrayed the nation's economic boom after World War II. The small home's front porch was adorned with colorful hand-painted pots. After they ascended a short flight of stairs and arrived on a porch, the front door opened for them. From behind it stepped one of the most beautiful young women Katie had ever seen. She had a smooth, olive-skinned face with dark almond eyes. Her body was accentuated by long, thick black hair pulled forward over her shoulder and cascading down her left side. The plume fell just short of her waist. She saw a simple gold cross hanging from a chain and resting on top of a starched white blouse. In that moment, any doubts Katie had about Drew's moral turpitude transformed into total contempt.

"Please come in. I'm Natalie."

Katie and Colin followed her into a living room. "These are my parents, Mr. and Mrs. Garcia."

"Buenos días," Colin said. He offered his hand to the older gentleman seated on a sofa next to his wife. Colin added in perfect Spanish, "*Encantado de conocerte.*" Katie was impressed by his skill.

The man said something in response that Katie didn't understand.

Natalie looked at Colin and said, "My father doesn't speak English. I'll translate for him. He said, 'It's nice to meet you, too.' My mother understands perfectly." Natalie offered two chairs for them, left the room, and returned shortly with two glasses of hibiscus tea.

Colin thanked Natalie for the tea in Spanish and then took a sip. He switched back to English and stated that he was a detective from the Boulder Police Department and that Katie was his assistant.

Colin turned to Natalie. "Ms. Garcia, have you spoken with your parents about our request?"

"Yes. They're very concerned."

"May I ask why?"

"They struggled along with me as I was dealing with the aftermath of the assault. It was hard on me, but it was particularly hard on them. They have a lot of pride. They believe that what happened to me has brought shame to the family."

Katie listened as Natalie repeated what she had said, in Spanish, for her father. He listened politely, grew animated, and nodded his head back and forth. He then said spoke rapidly.

Natalie translated. "He says, 'I watched my daughter suffer terribly for what happened to her. She's the first in our family to go to college. I worried about her being so far away from home, and then this happened. She's a good girl. And now she can't sleep at night, because some criminal violated her.'"

Colin spoke again, in English. "I'm terribly sorry for what's happened to your daughter, Mr. Garcia. She's suffered more than I'll ever know. But I also believe the right thing to do is bring this criminal to justice."

After Natalie's translation, she and her father spoke to each other in Spanish. Katie thought it interesting that Natalie's mother had yet to say anything.

"My father said he only wants it to be over. I'm now attending school in Colorado Springs, at a good private college there. It's expensive, but I received a scholarship, and the cost isn't much more than the cost in Boulder. I'm getting good grades, and I feel like I'm getting back to some normalcy. My parents sense it, too, I think. They're worried I might suffer emotionally from any legal proceedings."

Katie decided to speak. "Natalie, tell your mother and father that I have a friend I believe was assaulted by the same man. She wouldn't come forward, so now the man is free to assault again. That's what these men do. If we don't stop him, he will continue. Please help us put him in jail where he won't be able to harm any more young women."

Natalie translated for her parents again. Then they got into what seemed like a heated discussion. When they stopped, Katie could see tears begin to form in Natalie's eyes. Natalie dropped to the floor next to her father and took his hands in hers. With tears flowing, she sobbed, "*Perdóname*, por favor." She wrapped her arms around his waist and hugged him.

Mrs. Garcia finally spoke, in excellent English. "Natalie is asking for his forgiveness. She knows he has suffered greatly and lost honor in the eyes of his family. That is everything to him. What is it you want us to do?"

Colin said with urgency in his voice, "Mrs. Garcia, we want your daughter's written permission to perform lab tests on the contents of the medical evidence that was collected in the hospital the night of her assault. I believe it's our best chance to obtain some credible evidence against the man who assaulted her. Please help us send him to jail."

"Will my daughter need to testify?"

Colin was hesitant with his response. "Most likely. But if the evidence is strong, and his attorney believes a plea bargain is preferable to trial, then perhaps not. But you should assume that she'll be called to testify as a witness."

Natalie and her parents talked some more in Spanish; Natalie then returned to her chair and turned to Colin and Katie. "My father's reluctant, but my mother convinced him that it's the right thing to do. We agree that I'll help you."

At that point, the last thing to do was obtain Natalie's signature on the consent form to authorize the state crime lab to examine her rape kit. Once Colin had tucked the signed form safely inside his briefcase, they thanked the Garcias and began their drive back home.

Katie couldn't believe her rush of her emotions. "Does success like this always feel so good? That was incredible. We're going to get him. I'm sure of it."

"Slow down." Colin's tone was serious. "Let's not get too far out in front of reality here. We just took a huge step forward, but we don't even know if we'll find anything in the rape kit."

"I feel confident we will."

"Well, now you know the highs of this work. But I warn you, the lows can take you to the opposite extreme. When you lose a case, or a bad guy gets away because of a stupid mistake you made, it can take you to dark places. But it's the wins that keep you going. For most professionals in this business, it can be addictive."

"I get that. Our experience with Natalie was incredible. But now we have to see it through."

"You got it."

A THREE-WEEK WAIT FOR THE COLORADO BUREAU of Investigation to test Natalie's prioritized rape kit seemed as agonizing as the wait for a college acceptance letter. Everything depended on finding a reliable sample of DNA. Katie continued her work at the police department and completed an interview over coffee with Claire, her last active lead.

Over lattes, Claire described an experience from spring break two years earlier. She and several other sorority friends had vacationed in

Cancún. Katie was aware of its reputation as a place to party with fun, sun, and occasional trouble. The drinking age was only eighteen, so alcohol tended to flow freely. Once Katie heard the location, she knew the story wouldn't be useful to her investigation. She listened politely nonetheless.

Claire said she and her friends had had too much to drink one night and ended up in the condominium of several guys from a college in California. Katie couldn't help notice that a lot of these stories included the words "too much to drink." Katie had heard just about enough when Claire confessed that she had woken up in a bedroom with two guys, both snoring away.

"And you think that was sexual assault?"

"Well, I hadn't planned on having sex with two guys at once. I'd never done that before."

"Have you done it since?" Katie asked, a bit perturbed.

"No. But they shouldn't have taken advantage of me."

"But you weren't forced, right, and you didn't try to stop them?"

"I was afraid for my safety. I didn't want to say no."

"Had they given you any reason to suggest that they were violent or wouldn't take rejection well?"

"No. They were very friendly. The next morning, we all went out to breakfast. We still stay in touch."

Katie couldn't believe she was serious. "Well, thanks for sharing your story. You may not have liked the outcome, or maybe you did—I can't tell. But I don't think there's a jury anywhere that wouldn't accuse you of bad judgment instead of finding two guys guilty of assaulting you, especially guilty beyond a reasonable doubt. Just be more careful next time, or at least be honest with yourself about your actions." Katie thanked her for her time and left the coffee shop.

THE DAYS PASSED SLOWLY, AND KATIE KEPT her focus on a routine of working on records requests in the morning and on LSAT practice in the afternoon. Her exam was scheduled for June, and she'd signed up for an eight-week preparation course through April and May. Now it was almost March, and the weather was getting warmer and the days longer. She got out for some longer runs.

Another loose end that Katie wanted to tie up was the status of her settlement agreement with the university. She called and left a message for Harriet Becker with a request to call her back.

During the lull, Katie also met with Mark for coffee a couple of times. During one of their conversations, she described her progress in finding another one of Drew's victims and the satisfying experience she'd had in Pueblo that had reinforced her interest in going to law school. She also explained her reluctance to visit him at the Old Main building due to a sense of notoriety that made her feel self-conscious. Mark said he understood but emphasized that whenever she felt ready, she was welcome in his class anytime.

Finally, exactly three weeks after the kit was submitted, the lab issued its report directly to Commander Bennett. He subsequently called a meeting of Detective Scott, Detective Richardson, and Katie in his conference room on Tuesday morning.

Bennett began once everyone was seated. "I know you've anxiously awaited the lab results from Ms. Garcia's rape kit. I've handed out copies of the findings, but let me go over the highlights." Katie watched Colin flip through pages of the report, no doubt looking for the DNA section. "The report concludes that the patient did have GHB in her bloodstream at a level that would cause intoxication. Depending on when the dose was administered, it's possible that it could've been enough to cause incapacitation. That's an important legal distinction for the prosecutor."

Katie immediately realized that his reference to a prosecutor implied that DNA was present and that charges would be filed. She tried to suppress her glee.

"Second, no vaginal semen was present (although a condom was likely used). Third, there was no indication of any bruising or cuts. It does not appear that Ms. Garcia struggled with her assailant."

"Hard to struggle when you're passed out," Colin pointed out.

"Fourth, no likely samples of DNA were found on her clothing. Other than her own hair, no foreign hair samples were found, although a deposit of dried semen was found on Ms. Garcia's body. The attending nurse hypothesized that the assailant might have gotten excited and discharged an amount onto her leg prior to affixing a condom. She said she'd observed this in other cases. By the time the act was completed, the ejaculate would have dried and escaped detection. Fortunately, Ms. Garcia had not showered before the exam."

Detective Scott jumped in with the obvious question. "Was it positive for DNA?"

"The sample was tested and it returned a positive DNA profile, and there isn't a match in the CODIS database. We're in business." Bennett's fingers pulled at his chin.

Katie beamed at Colin. "I knew it."

"I suggest you all take your time to read through the report. It's unfortunate that Ms. Garcia was so hysterical and intoxicated the night of the attack that she wasn't able to recall the location of her assault. I reread the case file, and when she was first picked up on University Avenue, she mentioned that she'd walked from somewhere close to the campus. Anyone know where our suspect's living?"

Colin said, "He's renting a house with a couple of guys up off Baseline, near the Flatirons. Nowhere near the campus."

"The assault could have occurred anywhere," Bennett said. He looked at Detective Scott. "Now we need to get a sample of DNA from the suspect."

The detective said, "Can't we obtain a search warrant and go swab him?"

Bennet replied, "I spoke with the criminal prosecutor this morning. She prefers that we get a sample on our own."

Katie was incredulous. "Why? We have a witness who will testify that he assaulted her. And he was found guilty of sexually assaulting Ava."

Bennet replied, "What we have is a reluctant witness who hasn't even identified the suspect. We'd want to perform a lineup first—a step that Drew's lawyer would likely discourage, short of an arrest warrant. And Drew was found 'responsible' in a university hearing, not in a criminal proceeding, for nonconsensual sexual intercourse. We haven't even been allowed to see his file at the university. And we have a few other issues, too."

Detective Scott added, "Let me guess. She doesn't like the risk."

Bennet said, "Correct. And I understand her position. If we obtain and serve a search warrant, then Drew and his attorney will know where we're headed. As we saw with Natalie's kit, it takes time to get lab results. Drew's lawyer will no doubt use that delay to run interference every step of the way. Plus, Drew might become a flight risk or even try to intimidate our witness. No, she wants to get her ducks in a row first, and I don't blame her. It's a high-profile case with the university's star quarterback. She'll back us a hundred percent if we get matching DNA."

Katie said, "Great, more preferential treatment for a university athlete."

Colin said, "We'll get him. So how are we going to get his DNA?"

"I'll do it." Katie's face went tight.

Detective Scott blurted out, "You're going to get Drew's DNA? How?"

"I haven't figured that out yet, but I have some ideas."

Bennett narrowed his eyes. "Ms. Russell, I don't see how I can allow it. If you were a sworn officer of the department, maybe, but it feels too risky."

Katie had expected pushback. "I understand, but who's better able to get a sample than me? I'm of student age, he knows me, and I suspect he might be attracted to me. Whatever we come up with, I'll just meet him, get a sample, and get out. And if Detective Richardson is supporting me, I'm confident I can avoid any risk. Remember, as far as we know, Drew's never been violent with a victim."

"Detective Scott," said Bennett, "you've known Ms. Russell longer than any of us. What's your opinion?"

"Well, from what I've seen, she's observant and very bright. I believe she'd sense trouble and understand when she was in danger. But I'm concerned that she's never had any self-defense training. I'd want Colin nearby whenever an operation was under way if we went through with this."

Bennett said, "I'm skeptical, but she makes a good point about fitting the right profile to coax him into giving up a sample. I'd like Ms. Russell and Detective Richardson to come up with a proposal. Let's meet back here again tomorrow and hear what they come up with. Until then, don't approach him. Anything else?"

Everyone around the conference table remained silent.

"OK, see you tomorrow, same time." Bennett got up and left the room.

Detective Scott clasped his hands together and stared at Katie. "I'm not a fan of this. You've had no training."

"Colin and I will work on a plan. I promise we won't take any unnecessary risks. I'm confident that together we can avoid trouble. Besides, since I was the one who got this whole thing started with my testimony last year, I'd like to be the one to finish it."

"Fair enough. But I won't recommend anything until after I review your plan."

Katie returned to work and agreed to meet Colin in the afternoon. She found it hard to concentrate on records requests back in her office. All she could think about was how to obtain a DNA sample from Drew. A glass he'd drunk from? Perhaps sweat from a towel? She'd read that the Seattle police had successfully sent a known offender an official-looking letter stating that he'd won some prize money. They'd included an envelope for him to lick before he returned his confirmation. They got his DNA.

KATIE AND COLIN MET AFTER WORK AT A coffee shop and found a quiet corner table. "I'm having a hard time coming up with anything clever," Katie said. "Nothing very inspired, anyway. Maybe I could arrange to meet with him, and when he isn't looking, grab a glass he's used."

"If you approach him, won't he question your motives because of your role at the hearing? He'll be very cautious, even paranoid. He's shown that he knows how to be careful by the way he cleaned Ava's apartment after the assault. How do you think he'll respond if you try to contact him?"

"I don't know. But I did come up with one idea."

"What's that?"

"The night I first met him, he was with another football player named Desmond."

"The one you thought he fought with? I've read Detective Scott's report."

"Right. I think we kind of connected. After he was hurt in a football game, I got in touch with him. I dropped off a card and some flowers."

"You think he might be open to meeting with you?" Colin scrunched up his face.

"I'm pretty sure he would. If so, I'd try to find a logical reason to get together with Drew."

"Like what?"

"I don't know."

"Well, I haven't thought of anything better. You'd get him to a place where he drinks from a glass or a cup, and then you secretly take it? Sounds like a long shot. Where would you do this?"

"How about my apartment?"

"No way. Too dangerous. I think you need to choose a public place, like a bar or coffee shop. That way I can be watching in case anything goes wrong. He doesn't know me, so he won't recognize me. I can just blend in. What's the full name of the other football player? I'd like to run a background check on him."

"Desmond Baker. He's a strong safety."

"All right. It feels weak to me, but let's take it to the boss tomorrow. Don't do anything before then."

"I won't. I promise."

CHAPTER 35

The Plan

Katie and Colin met with Commander Bennett and Detective Scott the next morning as requested and presented their seemingly weak plan. After the short meeting, Katie returned to her desk. She crossed her arms and bounced her foot on the ground while she replayed their conversation in her head. Her role didn't seem very original, but no one had come up with anything better. So long as Colin was present during any operations, they were authorized to proceed. Her first step was to contact Desmond.

She failed to find his email address in her files or through a subsequent search of social-media sites. She recalled her trip to Desmond's apartment to drop off the card and flowers after his football injury, though, and soon found his home address. She ripped a blank page from one of her notebooks and wrote, *Hi Desmond, just wondering how you're getting along. I'd like to buy you coffee and catch up sometime. Text me.* She included her phone number. Later that afternoon, she walked over to his apartment and stuck it inside his mailbox. She decided not to knock.

The next day a text arrived: *Coffee would be great. Good to see you. How about the place on Pearl Street?*

She replied: *Sounds good. How about six tonight?*

After Desmond agreed to the time, Katie called Colin to let him know of the meeting. He planned to arrive by five thirty and reminded Katie not to acknowledge his presence inside the coffee shop.

Katie strolled into the coffee shop and quickly spotted Desmond's imposing figure seated behind a table. He was so out of proportion to the furniture that he appeared to be sitting in a first-grade classroom. She sat in the chair opposite his.

"Thanks for meeting me," she said. "How're you feeling?" Katie took a bottle of water from her bag and set it down on the table.

"Good, thanks. The doctor says I'm fully recovered now. Thanks for the card and flowers you gave me last fall."

"I was at the game when you got injured. It looked horrific." In her peripheral vision, Katie noticed Colin seated at a table along the back wall. He appeared to be reading a book.

"I was sort of surprised to hear from you. I didn't think you'd want to have anything to do with me after the hearing." Desmond leaned back in his chair and fingered his coffee.

Katie found his features surprisingly soft. "It's been a strange experience, that's for sure. Looking back, I feel bad about the whole thing." She caught herself repeatedly twisting the fashion ring on her finger.

"Bad, why?" Desmond's brow wrinkled.

"I don't know. I mean, it's clear that you didn't have anything to do with it, and then you got hurt in that football game. That didn't seem right to me."

"Let me tell you somethin' about that game. I didn't get hit because I fought with Drew over Ava."

"What do you mean?" she asked. His comment was contrary to what he'd testified in the hearing.

"We fought over you."

"What?" Katie's mouth went dry. She took a sip of water.

"I just made it up, about him wantin' me to have sex with her. We decided it was a believable story and it would keep me out of it. Drew knew he wouldn't be benched, anyway. The coach had already told him that. But that's not how it really went down."

"I don't understand."

"He wanted you that night. He thought you were hot—the older-woman kind of thing. He wanted me to help him. I was always his wingman."

Katie stared at Desmond and tried to read his face. His direct eye contact and stable speech pattern made him seem honest. Maybe this was the opening she needed. "Drew wanted me? Really?"

"Yep. I told him it was a stupid idea. You struck me as way too smart. I knew you wouldn't put up with his bullshit."

"And you fought over that?"

"Right after you left. He wanted me to go down to your apartment and convince you to come back upstairs. Ava was already out of it, so he figured we'd just all party. I refused. He got angry, sayin' he expected me to do what I was told. I didn't like that, so I hit him. That's when he knocked over the chair, fell against the dresser, and cut his head open. I left right after that."

Katie was startled by his revelation. She could easily recall the sight of blood on the dresser and struggled to regain some composure. "He retaliated in that football game by having you hit?"

"It was an old high school friend he used to play with. He was on the opposing team that day. Probably returning a favor."

Katie decided to go for it. "Do you think Drew would meet with me?"

"Why would *you* want to meet with him?" Desmond asked, slightly tilting his head to one side.

"Because I think I owe him an apology. I know I got him into a lot of trouble. Now I'm wondering if I might have made a mistake. He and Ava used to date, so maybe having sex again that night wasn't that big of a deal. Besides, I didn't know he liked me." Katie struggled to sound sincere.

"I think you're asking for trouble. You almost cost him his career, and that means everything to him."

"I don't see how a friendly drink could hurt. How about if you come along? I'd feel better if you were there. He might, too."

"Katie, I kind of like you. But if I were you, I'd stay away from him. If you want me to ask him, I will. Besides, I know he wants you even more now."

"Why do you think that?"

"Because he found your photo on the web. He was impressed. Now he calls you the one who got away."

Katie set her jaw. "You know, Desmond, I feel exactly the same way." She gave him a superficial hug and hurriedly left the coffee shop. She didn't want to risk being seen with Colin. While walking back to her apartment she noticed how tight her shoulders had become. Once she was home she called Colin.

"What did you guys talk about? "You looked surprised a couple of times."

Katie recounted the details of her first meeting with Drew inside Ava's apartment and then summarized the written testimony Desmond had provided at the hearing in which he claimed that Drew had attempted to coerce Desmond into having sex with Ava in order to gain his silence. Katie then reviewed the conversation with Desmond at the coffee shop, including his new version of what had happened that night. "I think he was telling the truth."

"Or, he could be walking you into a trap with Drew. Do you really want to go through with this?"

"More than ever."

"So now what? Wait and see if you hear back from Desmond or Drew?"

"I'm sure I will."

"OK, let me know."

Katie spent the next few days trying to concentrate on work. That was hard enough, but trying to practice LSAT questions was nearly impossible. Finally, two days later, on Friday, she received a text message from Desmond: *Drew said he'd like to meet. How about Saturday night, around seven, at the Sink? I'm coming too.*

Katie tapped back: *See you there.*

She'd only been to the Sink one previous time. It was a favorite college bar located in the Hill area of town, located near campus. It seemed like a reasonable place to meet. Katie and Colin agreed on the same strategy as before. Colin planned to arrive early and keep a watchful eye. Concerned as he was about the presence of two large football players, he also arranged for two officers to be on standby in case anything happened that he couldn't handle.

The night before the meeting with Drew, Katie invited Mark over to her place for dinner. It was the first time she'd cooked for him. She made a simple bowl of spaghetti and meatballs. Over plates of food and cabernet, she shared her plan to meet Drew at the Sink while Colin would remain undercover and ready to assist if necessary. She tried to sound confident but suspected that her anxiety was obvious.

It was also obvious that Mark wasn't comfortable with the plan. "Can I come along?" he asked.

"I don't think that would be wise. If either of them recognize you, they might get suspicious and bolt. Drew's seen my photo, and I bet he's followed the story. He probably knows your identity. It's not a good idea. Remember, Colin will be there."

"Will you call as soon as you're out of there?"

"I promise."

While she was washing dishes after dinner, her phone rang. Her hands were wet and soapy, so she asked Mark to answer it. Her phone had been on the dining table; when Mark picked up, she could hear his side of the conversation from her location in the kitchen.

"This is Mark O'Conner." There was a pause. "She's here, but she's busy right now. May I take a message?" Another pause. "Sure, I'll tell her."

Mark reappeared in the kitchen, and his eyes were quizzical. "It was someone named Joan. She said it's time to come meet the family."

Katie stared at Mark and tried to suppress a broad smile. She then pinched her thumb and index finger together and ran them along her lips to indicate that she wouldn't say a thing.

They spent the rest of the night watching a movie in Katie's bed. It was the first night Mark had slept at her place.

CHAPTER 36
Undercover

Colin entered the Sink through the front door and made his way toward the back of the restaurant. He found a table for two up against a wall in a darker part of the dining area. He hadn't been there long when he saw Drew and Desmond saunter into the room and sit in a booth a couple of tables away. They were even larger than he'd imagined. He focused his attention on his phone and tried to seem disinterested in anything else. He texted the two uniformed officers sitting in a patrol car out front to let them know that he was in position and that the players had arrived. It wasn't long before he saw Katie walk into the bar and join the two behemoths.

KATIE ARRIVED AT THE SINK ABOUT TEN MINUTES late so that Colin would have plenty of time to get in position. It wasn't hard to spot the two football players seated toward the back of the dining room when she walked in, but she didn't see Colin on her way to their table. Her stomach felt slightly queasy as she slipped into the booth next to Desmond and across from Drew, but she relaxed a bit when she finally noticed Colin sitting at a nearby table in a dark corner. He had a beer in front of him, and his eyes were focused on his phone.

Drew said, "Nice to see you, Katie. After all these months."

She sensed he was analyzing her, searching for clues. "Good to see you too, Drew. Like I told Desmond, I feel like I might owe you an apology."

"That's nice," Drew said with a smile, "but it's hardly necessary. No harm, no foul. I kept playing football. Besides, it was good for me to write that paper for school. Made me appreciate a woman's perspective better."

A waitress walked up, and Katie ordered a hard cider. Drew and Desmond were already halfway through their beers. Katie thought Drew looked radiant. His teeth were perfect. It was obvious why he had an easy time with women. Now that she had the opportunity to view him up close—unlike their first meeting in Ava's apartment or later at the hearing—she was better able to appreciate his rugged good looks. She even felt some attraction, although the response disgusted her.

Katie's drink arrived. She took a sip. It was very dry, almost salty tasting. "I know that Ava cared for you."

Drew got a hurt look on his face. "Let's not talk about her." Katie noticed Drew thrusting his chest out and spreading his elbows wide.

Everyone silently worked on their drinks. The waitress put a bowl of popcorn on the table.

"I hear you dropped out of school?" Drew had a slight sneer on his face as he said it.

"Let's just say I had my own issues with the administration." Katie hoped to evoke some empathy based on an obvious similarity between their experiences.

"From doing your professor, that's what I heard," Drew said. He and Desmond both snorted.

"Hey, what I do in my own time is none of the school's business," she said with a laugh she hoped didn't sound too fake. "Especially if it doesn't harm anyone else."

"Why can't I argue the same thing?" Drew asked, staring at her. "Ava and I were on our own time. It didn't affect school for either one of us, did it?"

Katie had asked for that. She forgot for a second that her relationship with Mark was consensual while Drew's was an unforgivable exercise in assault; still, she knew to lie. "I think that's why I might owe you an apology. Now that I've experienced my own issues, I think I can see your point. Can I ask you a question about something else?"

"Sure."

"Why the horrific hit on Desmond at the football game? You guys seem pretty tight."

Drew smiled. "I just wanted to remind him of what he should say at the hearing." Drew bumped Desmond on the shoulder. Desmond's face remained expressionless.

"But he didn't testify at the hearing."

"Right." Drew's smile turned to a wicked grin.

"Hmm." She decided to change the subject. "Next year's your senior year, right? Will you go through the football draft after the season's over?"

"Hell yes. My coaches think I'll get drafted first or second round. Desmond will, too."

"I know the football team owes its success to you, Drew." Katie noticed Desmond frowning at her comment.

"It's a team sport. We all worked together to achieve that championship." Drew and Desmond high-fived.

The conversation paused again while they drank. Katie looked around the room. The paintings on the walls reminded her of stoner comic books, bold and colorful. She laughed out loud as she read some of the inscriptions. "I hear Robert Redford used to work here."

Desmond asked, "The actor? Here?"

"Yep. And Barack Obama visited a couple of times. I saw his photo near the door on the way in."

"You still with your professor boyfriend?" Drew asked, his smile still wicked. "Is he any good?"

Katie laughed so hard she almost sprayed cider out her nose. "Good, he's—" She stopped herself just short of saying *amazing*. "He's fine. He's also a good friend."

"Well, if you ever get tired of him, I'm ready to step in."

"I'm sure you are." Katie looked around the table. The guys' beers were empty. She wondered how she could get Drew's glass. She took another sip from her own. Maybe they could order another round, and she could follow the waitress as she carried away the empties. Katie again felt Drew staring at her. She decided to go to the restroom; first, she drained the rest of her cider. "How about you guys order us another round. I'll be right back." Katie slid out from her side of the booth. A few steps away from the table, she tripped on her first step into the hallway. She looked down and saw the culprit: an uneven floor runner that led toward the restrooms.

FROM HIS VANTAGE POINT, COLIN THOUGHT THE conversation between Katie and the football players seemed normal until he detected a flash of anger pass over Drew's face. Colin studied Katie. He watched her eyes roam over the colored drawings on the walls and ceiling. She laughed a couple of times. He didn't remember ever seeing her look so jovial before. The conversation continued for another five or ten minutes. Katie finished her drink and got up from the table. Colin assumed she was off to the bathroom. He noticed her trip on a rubber mat that led into the hallway. Her stumble was slight, but he'd noticed. After five more minutes, Drew got up from the table and headed in the same direction. Colin figured he was probably headed for the men's room.

INSIDE THE BATHROOM, KATIE LOOKED IN A MIRROR. Her face stared back at her above a sign reading EMPLOYEES MUST WASH HANDS. She thought she looked OK. Her eyes seemed normal. She walked past a condom dispenser hanging on the wall and entered a stall. She locked the door, put down the seat, laid down a paper liner, and sat down. She put her head in her hands and wondered why she felt sort of off. She was a bit light-headed—happy, really. She thought back to her laugh at the table. She felt as she might after a night of drinking, not just one drink. She'd watched her glass the whole time. There was no way Drew or Desmond could have put anything into it. She got up from the seat and flushed the toilet, as if she'd done something. After exiting the stall, she went to the sink and washed her hands. She tried to dry them under an ineffective blower. Her hands were still damp when she left the restroom and stepped into the hallway. From her left side, a strong hand grabbed her arm and pulled her toward the back of the bar.

In a matter of seconds, she was out the back door and into an alleyway. Drew nearly dragged her toward a set of solid wood-plank steps that rose alongside the exterior of the building. She saw a landing with a door at the top.

"Get up the stairs."

Katie stumbled several times on the way. When they reached the landing, Drew unlocked the door with a key and swung it open. He gave Katie a shove toward the inside of the room, and she fell on top of a bed. Drew then switched on a lamp on a nightstand and locked and chained the door. "Welcome to my clubhouse."

Katie looked around the small room. It contained a desk with a laptop on it, a small refrigerator, a door that led to what she assumed was a bathroom, and a wardrobe. Other than that, it was empty. No coverings on the bare wood floor. She could make out muffled but boisterous-sounding voices penetrating from the bar below. The comforter she lay on was worn and stained, and she noticed a few rips. When she tried to get up from the bed, Drew pushed her back down.

"Look, don't fight. You're the one who asked to meet me. Care for another drink?" Drew opened the refrigerator and pulled out two beers. He opened them and offered one to Katie.

"No, thanks." She watched Drew take a long drink from his. Katie began to feel really buzzed. And she had to contain the urge to laugh. It was the oddest sensation.

Drew reached down and started unfastening the belt on his jeans. "Take your clothes off. I want to see what you've got."

"I'm not taking my clothes off."

"Yes, you are. Do you want me to have Desmond come up and help?"

BACK IN THE BAR, COLIN WORRIED ABOUT KATIE. She had been gone way too long. He got up and walked past the table where Desmond now sat alone. He found the bathroom and walked inside. A young woman was alone at a mirror applying some lipstick. "I'm with the police. You see another woman in here a minute ago?"

The woman gave Colin a quizzical smile. "Nope, just us in here. You lost? You can hang around if you like." Her smile suggested that she'd had a few drinks.

Colin checked both stalls. Empty. He left the restroom and returned to the table where Desmond had been sitting, but Desmond was gone. Colin thought for a second. He hadn't seen either Katie or Drew after they'd walked toward the restrooms. He stared at the table and noticed three empty glasses. He pulled an evidence bag from his pocket and a latex glove. He quickly put on the glove and picked up the glass from Drew's position on the table and placed it inside the plastic bag. Then he headed to the bar, which was Saturday-night loud. At the servers' station, he managed to get the bartender's attention. He almost had to yell.

"Hey, have you seen a couple of football players in here? I'm looking for a tall, good-looking blond guy."

"Nope," he said. "Lots of football players come in here. And they're all pretty good-looking."

Even with the smug response, Colin detected just a hint of worry on the bartender's face. He pulled out his police badge and shoved it in his face. "I'm with the Boulder Police Department. You should tell me if you know anything about this guy." He pulled a photo of Drew from his pocket and held it next to his badge. "It's important. Tell me now, or I'll charge you with obstruction." It was a bluff.

"Oh, that football player. Drew Evans. Yeah, he has an apartment above the bar. That's where he takes all the girls."

"How do I get there? Is there a door out back?"

"Go past the restrooms. There's a door that leads to the alley. You can't miss the stairs on the left."

Colin called the two backup officers. "They're in a room up above the bar. Access is from behind the building. I'll meet you in the alley. Hurry." Colin ran toward the back of the bar and past the restrooms. He found a large metal door and slammed his hands down on its long-bar handle. He threw the door open. To his left he could see a wooden stairway.

IN THE APARTMENT ABOVE THE BAR, KATIE wondered what had happened to Colin. Why hadn't he followed her? She felt dazed, but she knew she had to stall for time. "I don't think we need Desmond." Katie smiled and hoped to convince Drew that she'd cooperate. "I think I'll have that beer after all." Katie recognized that she was starting to lose it. What was happening to her?

Drew handed her the other beer. "Good thinking. Now take off your clothes."

Katie took a sip from the bottle and put the beer on the nightstand. Her hands moved slowly as she struggled to unbutton her white blouse. She normally found it difficult to work buttons because of the crooked finger on her right hand; now, with her impaired motor skills, she found it almost impossible. She suddenly regretted wearing one of her nicer bras: the black Italian lace design. As she got to the last button and peeled away the blouse, she could dimly hear Drew letting out a grunt of appreciation.

Drew pulled off his jeans and shirt as he watched her undress. He stood in his boxers and a T-shirt imprinted with the football team's logo and leered at Katie as she struggled with her clothes. Without a hint of respect, he said, "Now your pants."

Katie's hands lacked coordination, and she struggled to unfasten the button on her pants and lower the zipper. Getting them off her legs was taking an eternity, and she was fearful that she might pass out. When she finished, she saw that Drew had taken off his shirt and was now standing in only his boxers. He crossed his arms and leered at her.

Katie had never seen a man's body as perfectly chiseled as Drew's. She momentarily admired his physique, which confused her. She had a vague thought about GHB and wondered if he'd managed to slip her some of it somehow. What was happening to her? "Why are you doing this? You know you can have any woman you want."

"Here, put these on." Drew reached into the desk drawer and pulled out a small blue box. He tossed it on the bed next to Katie.

She had the vague feeling that she would know what was inside. She opened it and saw a pearl necklace. "I don't think I can," she mumbled. "You'll have to do it for me."

Drew leaned over Katie. Her body wavered on the bed while his hands fumbled at the back of her neck. His touch repulsed her; she could still sense that. When he'd finally closed the clasp, Drew stood back and admired his work. "Perfect. You look beautiful."

Katie struggled to focus. She put her hand to her neck and felt the perfectly shaped pearls.

Drew reached down and retrieved his phone from his jeans on the floor. He sat down on the bed next to Katie and put one arm around her back. He pulled her close. With his other arm, he held the phone out as far as he could and took several photos of their bodies pressed together.

Katie couldn't stop smiling. She tried. She hated to give him the satisfaction.

When Drew finished taking the photos, he released his arm from around her. She fell back onto the mattress and sensed that she'd be unable to sit up if she tried. She watched him toss the phone back on top of his jeans. He returned to the desk and reached back into the drawer. Katie watched him pull out a condom.

Drew held it in his hand while he took another gulp of beer. Katie watched helplessly as he used his teeth to rip off the top of the packaging.

Just as he put his beer bottle down on the desk, Katie thought she heard a knock on the door.

DOWN IN THE ALLEY, TIME SEEMED TO CRAWL as Colin waited for the other officers. Tires skidded on loose gravel as the unmarked patrol car came to a stop at the bottom of the stairs. Two officers jumped out. Colin handed the evidence bag to one and told the other to follow him. He led the way up the stairs and took them two at a time. When he arrived at the top of the landing, his heart was pounding from the adrenaline. He knocked on the door but didn't wait for a response. He lowered his shoulder and smashed against the door's solid panel with all the force he could muster. Pieces of wood frame exploded inward as it burst open. Colin fell forward and into the room. He caught a glimpse of Katie lying on the bed as he fell to the floor. She was nearly naked. "You bastard!" he yelled.

Drew grabbed him, and they struggled on the floor. Katie screamed. Colin momentarily feared that Drew might use his superior strength to push him back through the doorway and over the railing. The trailing officer entered the room and joined the fracas. Together, they managed to subdue Drew and fastened handcuffs to his wrists.

Colin searched for a blanket and covered Katie's mostly naked body. He read Drew his Miranda rights and, assisted by the other officer, escorted the scowling quarterback down the stairs and toward the patrol car. Colin smiled as he watched Drew's head strike the metal doorframe a few times as the officer pushed him into the back seat of the car. After Drew was on his way to jail, Colin requested that the other officer stay behind and secure the crime scene. Colin collected Katie and her things and drove her to the hospital as fast as he could.

CHAPTER 37
Pearls

Katie opened her eyes and struggled with determining time and place. The room around her was dark other than some dim light that was streaming in through an open door to a hallway. On her left, she spotted Mark asleep in a chair. His shoulders were wrapped in a blanket, his hair tousled, and his breathing deep. She could hear the familiar chirps and chimes of medical equipment monitoring her vital signs. With a sense of familiarity, Katie realized that she was again in a hospital. Groggy and thirsty, she reached for a plastic cup and took a sip of water from a bendable straw. A nurse entered the room.

"How are you feeling?"

"Tired, but OK."

"The doctor says you're doing well. You're here for observation. He'll stop by later this morning. I expect he'll discharge you soon."

Mark began to stir. He opened his eyes and looked momentarily confused until he saw Katie. "Hey. You're awake."

The nurse left them alone. Mark walked over to Katie's bed and sat down on the edge.

Katie said, "I just woke up. How long have you been here?"

"Since around midnight. After I didn't hear from you, I called Detective Scott. He gave me a quick description of what happened, and I came right away."

Katie struggled to remember the events from the evening with Drew and Desmond. "Where's Colin?"

"He went home. He got roughed up a bit."

"Tell me what happened."

"I think it's best if Detective Scott does that. He said he'll be in later this morning. I only have bits and pieces."

"Where's Drew?"

"He's in jail. It's Sunday, so I expect it will take him some time to make bail."

"Good."

Mark lay down next to Katie on the bed. Within minutes, they'd both fallen back asleep.

A couple of hours later, the nurse returned and turned up the lights. Katie stirred and felt Mark's body next to hers on the bed. She prodded him softly with her elbow.

"Detective Scott is here to see you. Shall I bring him in?"

"Sure." Katie sat up, and Mark returned to his chair.

The affable detective walked in and stood next to the bed. She was happy to see that he was wearing the same rumpled gray suit. She tried to smile, but her dull headache made it difficult. "Good morning, Detective Scott."

"You OK? You put a scare into all of us."

"I'm fine. What happened last night?"

He summarized Colin's version of events, from his arrival at the bar to his delivery of Katie to the hospital.

"My memory isn't very clear. I vaguely remember Colin bursting through the door at one point. Most of it seems like a dream."

"I'm not surprised. We don't yet have your blood tests back, but I'll be surprised if you weren't drugged. Other than that, you appear to be fine."

"I think Colin arrived just in time. Drew would have raped me if he hadn't." Katie stared at the foot of the bed and wrapped her arms around her flimsy hospital gown. "I felt out of it so fast. How did he do it? I watched my drink the whole time."

"He must have had help from either the bartender or your waitress. We'll question them later today. One of them must have spiked your drink."

Katie tried to recall more details. She put her hand to her neck and felt that it was bare. "Was I wearing pearls when I arrived here last night, or was I dreaming that?"

Detective Scott stared at her, seemingly confused by the question. "We can ask the nurse. Why?"

Katie found it hard to think. She closed her eyes. More details slowly clicked into place. Suddenly, eyes wide, she sat up. "I've seen them before."

"Seen what before?" The detective looked up from his notes.

"The pearls. Ava was wearing them in a photo I saw the first night I went to her apartment. On her corkboard was a photo of her together with Drew. She looked beautiful. Wore a tight black dress with a pearl necklace. Where are my things?"

Detective Scott left the room to go locate a nurse. When he returned, he went to the closet and retrieved a garment bag. "The nurse said all of your things should be in here. They normally collect everything when you're admitted to the ER." Detective Scott lay the bag on the bed.

Katie pulled down the bag's zipper, rummaged around in her belongings, and removed a paper bag. She dumped its contents onto the bed. Out fell her phone, her wallet, keys, and a string of pearls in a clear plastic bag. She removed them from the bag and rolled them between her fingers. They were radiant. Touching them felt almost sensual. She guessed they were expensive. Katie was confident they were the same pearls that were in the photo she'd seen. "I'm sure these belonged to Ava."

"Do you think that's significant?"

"I don't know. I'm sure it has something to do with Drew, though."

"We'll submit them into evidence. I plan to get over to the jail tomorrow morning and observe a detective interviewing Drew. He'll ask Drew about the pearls."

Katie stared at Detective Scott. "Could I come?"

"No, that's out of the question. It would be prejudicial to any formal proceedings for you to witness the interview with the prime suspect in a crime that was committed against you. Colin could attend, though."

Katie stared down at the pearls. "OK. I'm not sure I'm up to it anyway. A few more minutes, and Drew...I'm not sure I could see him now."

"I understand. When this is all over, I recommend that you and Mark consider counseling. I'm sure the doctor will tell you the same thing. I've seen situations like this leave some emotional scars." He turned to Mark. "Katie's going to need your support. She's suffered through a traumatic event."

"She knows she has it." Mark took Katie's hand.

"I'll let you rest. We'll talk more tomorrow. I'll let Colin know about the interview."

"Detective, I have one more question. Did you get a sample of Drew's DNA?"

"We have a beer bottle we recovered from the apartment and Drew's glass from the table in the Sink. Colin was brilliant to collect it before he went to find you."

Katie smiled. Her night of terror had been worth it. She closed her eyes.

LATER THAT AFTERNOON, THE DOCTOR STOPPED BY and, after a quick examination, permitted Katie to go home. As Detective Scott had predicted, the doctor recommended that Katie contact a therapist to discuss the likelihood of post-traumatic stress from the assault. Mark took Katie to his apartment and let her sleep the rest of the day.

On Monday morning, Colin attended the interview with Drew and watched from behind a one-way mirror with Detective Scott. Drew and his attorney were seated in metal chairs at a metal desk bolted to the floor. A video camera on a tripod stood ready to record the interview. The two detectives stood next to a third detective named Lewis who would conduct the interview. Drew's attorney insisted he be present, which would necessarily limit the scope of the conversation. Drew had already been Mirandized upon arrest and therefore wasn't required to answer any questions at that point in the investigation.

Detective Scott looked at Colin. "Are you sure you want to be here? You don't have to watch."

"I know. I'll never forgive him for what he almost did to Katie. I need to see this. What will happen to Drew after the interview?"

Detective Scott spoke calmly, as if it were commonplace. "He'll be arraigned later today and charged with a felony. Then, he'll likely make bond and be released. Within thirty-five days, he'll have a probable-cause hearing, where the prosecutor will present enough evidence to convince the judge that there is at least a probable cause that the crimes he's charged with did in fact occur. It's highly unlikely that Katie would have to testify at that time. If the judge agrees that charges are warranted, then Drew will be bound over to circuit court for trial. Because we don't have her blood tests back yet, the initial charge of attempted sexual assault could be amended later as a higher-level felony. And a charge of kidnapping is a possibility. Ms. Garcia would be a separate charge. But for that, we first need a positive match with Drew's DNA."

"Katie's involvement won't be over for a while, will it?"

"I'm afraid not. We'll try to make it as easy as possible for her, but she'll have to face him in a courtroom sooner or later."

"Will Drew be able to approach her outside the courtroom?"

"The prosecutor will request a no-contact order on Drew's release bond. I'm confident the judge will grant it. Then Drew can't legally contact her."

Detective Lewis spoke up. "I need to get started." He left the room. Colin watched through the one-way mirror as Lewis reappeared in the interview room and took a seat at the metal table opposite Drew and his attorney. The detectives could hear their conversation through a speaker.

"Mr. Evans, I'm Detective Lewis. I'd like to ask you a few questions." Detective Lewis put a file folder on the desk and switched on the video camera.

"Detective Lewis, I'm Landry Clarke, Mr. Evans's lawyer. I've instructed Mr. Evans not to respond to any questions. You can't force him to have this conversation."

Drew said, "What do you want to know?" He sat back with an open posture and appeared relaxed.

"I told you not to say anything." Clarke put a hand on Drew's forearm. Drew brushed it away.

"Last Saturday night, you had drinks with Ms. Katie Russell and Mr. Desmond Baker at a restaurant called the Sink. Is that correct?"

"Yep. No law against that, is there?"

"After drinks, did Ms. Russell accompany you to your apartment above the bar?"

"Don't answer that."

Detective Lewis continued. "Why did Ms. Russell accompany you to your room above the bar?"

"She wanted to have some fun."

"Did Ms. Russell say anything that would suggest that she'd agreed to join you willingly?" Detective Lewis looked down at his notes.

"Hey, it was her idea to have drinks with me that night. She'll tell you. She asked *me.*"

"Ms. Russell has stated that you asked her to remove her clothes. Did she?"

"Willingly."

"Then you took a photograph of the two of you together. Have you done this with other women?" Detective Lewis removed an eight-by-ten-inch photo from his folder and placed in on the desktop. Even from his vantage point behind the mirror, Colin could see the image: Katie sat on a filthy bed next to Drew, wearing only a bra and panties. A string of shiny pearls adorned her neck.

"Don't answer that." Clarke stood and walked behind Drew's chair. "Don't answer the question."

"I take a photo like that with every woman I sleep with." Drew crossed his arms and looked smug.

"There's something about those photos I don't quite understand," Detective Lewis said. "Why did you ask her to put these on first?" Lewis reached into his suit pocket and pulled out the string of pearls. They were enclosed in a sealed clear-plastic evidence bag.

Drew's demeanor changed immediately. His smugness was replaced by anger. "Those fucking pearls!"

"Are they special in some way?" Detective Lewis asked, staring calmly at Drew.

"I gave those to Ava. I don't come from a wealthy family like she does. I borrowed money from my father. It took a lot of my savings to buy those pearls. Five thousand dollars. And she threw them at me. Screamed that it was over."

"When did that happen?"

"Last year. I'd slept with one of her sorority friends. She found out about it and got angry. She doesn't understand men. Just because I was in a relationship with her didn't mean it was exclusive. She didn't see it that way."

"And she broke up with you."

"And she thought she was so perfect. Beautiful. Smart. Came from a powerful family in Denver. I know she loved me. I never would have made it through my freshman year without her help."

"And you were angry."

"No one breaks up with me. I can get any girl I want. Until her."

"Did you take photos of yourself with other women while they wore the pearls you'd given Ava? The ones she threw at you when she broke off the relationship?"

"Someday I'll show her what I do. I want her to feel the pain I felt."

"Detective Lewis, I insist. End this interview." Drew again brushed Clarke aside. The attorney sat back down.

"One more question, then I'm done. Why do you need to force women to have sex with you?"

Drew leaned forward, smirking now. He pressed his hands into the desk. "Because the ones who don't want me, the ones who play hard to get—" he paused for emphasis with a tap on the desk "—they're the ones who turn me on." He laughed as he stood up. "The easy ones? I can have them any time I want."

Detective Lewis stood, too, and switched off the video camera. "Thank you, Mr. Evans. See you in court."

Colin stared in disbelief. He screamed at the mirrored window. "Yes means yes, you bastard!"

A uniformed officer entered the interview room and escorted Drew back to a holding cell, with Clarke following behind. Detective Lewis gathered his things.

Colin hurriedly left the room. He wasn't sure how much to share with Katie about the interview and Drew's comments. One thing he was sure of was that it was a good thing Katie hadn't been there. Drew would have enraged her.

THE PROSECUTING ATTORNEY PLACED A CALL TO COMMANDER BENNETT about the same time the interview with Drew was over. She explained that she'd reviewed the Evans file and that it was important they meet right away. Bennett invited her to his office.

After the prosecuting attorney finished her summary of the state's case against Drew, Bennett wasted no time rounding up Detectives Richardson and Scott. Fifteen minutes later, they arrived in his conference room wondering what was up.

Bennett looked somber. "We have a problem." He nodded toward the prosecuting attorney. "Tell them."

"We have to let Mr. Evans go."

"What!" Colin shot up out of his chair.

"Let me guess," Detective Scott said. "Exigent circumstances?"

"The arrest Saturday night was unlawful." The prosecuting attorney's scowl signaled her disappointment. "Colin, even though you saved a woman from being raped, you had no probable cause to break into the apartment."

"But I knew she was there with Drew. He was going to assault her. I had to stop him."

The prosecuting attorney shot back, "You *suspected* she was up there and you *suspected* he was going to assault her. But mere suspicion can't support a finding of probable cause for a warrantless arrest. Mr. Evans was arraigned earlier this afternoon. He's out on bond with a stipulation that he not contact Katie. Evans's attorney, however, rightly mentioned the questionable nature of the arrest. I plan to drop all charges prior to the probable-cause hearing. Attempted sexual assault while the victim is incapacitated is a serious felony. But if we failed to enter his premises lawfully, then I have no choice. The only reason I haven't dropped charges yet is because I want to keep the no-contact order in effect. His probable-cause hearing is scheduled for three weeks."

"But he's a known rapist. If we knew that Katie was with him, then wouldn't we have probable cause to suspect he'd reoffend?"

"He's never been convicted of a crime in court, only in a university hearing that resulted in a finding of responsibility for nonconsensual intercourse. Because we suspect he *might* be in a room with an at-risk female doesn't prove that a crime is being committed. Exigent circumstances require that a reasonable person believes that entry was necessary to prevent physical harm to an officer or other person, destruction of evidence, escape of the suspect, or something else that would thwart legitimate enforcement efforts. Maybe if Desmond or the bartender had told you that Drew intended to drug and rape Katie, then you could have proceeded. But the bartender's comment that Drew had a room above the bar wasn't sufficient."

Colin's body slumped in his chair. His gaze fixated on the center of the conference table.

Detective Scott asked, "Did you even knock and announce yourself before you busted through the door?"

Colin shook his head. "I knocked." His gaze remained unfocused.

An awkward silence filled the room.

Commander Bennett broke it. "Colin, I'm sorry about this. Given a choice between rescuing Katie and following the letter of the law, I'm not sure what I would have done."

Colin turned his attention toward the prosecuting attorney. "What about the evidence?"

"We'll have to return everything we confiscated from the apartment."

Detective Scott asked, "Did you have a chance to look at the phone and the laptop?"

"We did. The phone contained photos of Katie and Drew that were taken that night. On his laptop we found over thirty photos of him with various women. All of them wore lingerie—tops, bottoms, or both. All were next to him on a bed and wearing pearls."

Colin's face turned crimson. "Next you're going to tell me we can't even use the beer bottle from the apartment."

"Correct."

"Katie risked everything, and we get nothing?" Colin spread his hands, pleading.

"Not so fast. The glass you took from the table remains admissible. Drew left it behind. That's known as abandonment." The prosecuting attorney finally showed a slight smile.

Colin wasn't placated. "But any charges from Saturday night are now gone? We can't get him for attempted sexual assault, or kidnapping, or drugging Katie?"

"I'm afraid not."

Detective Scott said, "We interviewed the bartender and the waitress. They denied knowing anything about a drug being added to Katie's drink, though I don't see any other explanation for it. The blood test came back positive, showing Katie had GHB in her system. But we have no evidence to indicate how it got there."

The prosecuting attorney said, "Now we wait for the test results from Drew's glass and see if we get any usable DNA. If we do, and if it matches the DNA from Natalie Garcia's rape kit, then we're back in business."

Colin said, "What about Desmond? He must have known that something was about to happen that night."

"He might have been involved. None of the photos suggest he was complicit in any sexual assaults. Realistically, the photos only suggest consensual activity between Drew and the women. Hard to tell about the drugs. Desmond might have known. First things first. Let's get the DNA sample. If we get a match, then we can sit down and have a conversation with Desmond. It won't take much to make him a cooperating witness once he knows Drew's going down."

The conference room again went silent. Colin placed his elbows on the table and rested his face in his hands. A few minutes later, he looked up. "I want to be the one to tell Katie."

Commander Bennett said, "I think you should. Take Detective Scott with you. I know she trusts him. Thanks to her, we're going to get this guy."

"Colin, I'm sorry." The prosecuting attorney closed her file and left the room.

THE FOLLOWING DAY, AS BENNETT HAD SUGGESTED, the two detectives met Katie in the department's conference room and explained the legal challenges that Drew's arrest posed. Katie was shocked to learn that the prosecuting attorney planned to drop all charges. How could they release someone that dangerous? It was a quick lesson in arrest warrants and probable cause. As Katie listened, her emotions advanced from disbelief to anger and finally to resolve. Later on, when she thought back to that moment, Katie would recognize that that meeting marked the apex her educational transformation—she would absolutely pursue a career in criminal law. Colin's quick action had saved her from falling victim to a despicable act. It was impossible to feel disappointed by his failure to execute a clean arrest.

After the meeting, Katie walked hurriedly to campus, oblivious to most everything around her. It was her first visit to Old Main since last semester. She went straight to Mark's office and found it locked. She went downstairs to the philosophy department and asked for Professor O'Connor's class schedule. The printout showed he was in the same classroom where she'd taken the philosophy and law class. She bounded up two flights of stairs and ran to the classroom door. She saw Mark through its glass window, standing behind a lectern and facing his students. When he turned toward the whiteboard to write, he saw her and subtly nodded.

Katie paced in the hallway for fifteen minutes while the class finished. The sounds of chairs sliding on the floor and students gathering their things signaled when it was over. As the students filed from the classroom and into the hallway, Katie slipped past and went straight to Mark. She gazed up at his face and wrapped her arms around him. Katie felt the stares from the students as they headed out the door.

Mark returned the hug and bent down and kissed her longingly. He broke away and locked his eyes on hers. "I love you."

CHAPTER 38
Justice

Over the following weeks of March, while waiting for the results from the lab test of Drew's beer glass, Katie continued her work on public-records requests. With her research into acquaintance rape over, the job became more routine. It was one step away from boring. Although she learned a lot from reading the requested documents, and the steady paychecks were great, she planned to ask Commander Bennett for a job with more responsibility. She'd wait until after she'd completed the LSAT exam. He'd seemed generous and sincere when he'd offered to help her, and she planned to find out how. Over coffee and an occasional donut, she continued her friendly conversations with Detective Scott. He became a second father to her. She liked to tease him. He liked to show her off.

When the written results finally arrived from the lab, Commander Bennett called a special meeting of the two detectives and Katie. Katie sat impatiently at the conference table with the others while they waited for Colin to arrive. She studied their faces and could detect an almost whimsical twinkle in Bennett's eyes, perhaps in a signal that the tests had come back positive. The success of her efforts depended on it.

Colin finally strolled in—looking surprisingly carefree, in Katie's opinion—and Bennett began his summary. "The beer glass Colin collected from the table in the Sink was found to have Drew's fingerprints and DNA. The DNA matched the sample that was taken from the dried semen found on Natalie Garcia's leg: a sample that had been stored in a Jane Doe rape kit for over a year."

Katie and Colin leaned together and fist-bumped each other. The commander then launched into a serious pep talk about the benefits of teamwork and adherence to the letter of the law. Katie suddenly heard a commotion at the back of the room and swiveled around in her chair. Bennett's administrative assistant rolled in a cart with soft drinks and a large sheet cake on top. Most of the on-duty detectives and staff followed her through the door.

Bennett stopped his impromptu comments as the group gathered. When everyone was in place, he said, "Katie and Colin, I thought we should celebrate your success. Congratulations on a job well done."

A round of applause broke out. Katie joined Colin, and they stood next to the cake. Katie smiled at the frosting-designed caricature of Batman and Catwoman, complete with *Kapow!* and *Crime Fighters* written in icing on top. Katie's smile widened even further when she noticed that "Katwoman" was spelled with a *K* and that the image of the dark-haired heroine in a black cat suit looked exaggeratedly voluptuous. That damn photo. The name "Colin" was below Batman, and "Katie" below Katwoman. Katie started to tear up. She smiled at Colin through watery eyes while Bennett vigorously shook their hands.

Two days later, the prosecuting attorney dropped all charges stemming from Drew's attempted assault of Katie in the apartment above the Sink. She then immediately filed new charges for the sexual assault and kidnapping of Natalie Garcia. Drew was again released on bail with a no-contact stipulation for Natalie. The prosecuting attorney said to Bennett that she was confident the probable-cause hearing would be straightforward. It was. The trial was originally set for September, six months later. Drew's attorney requested a continuance so that his client could play football in the fall. The motion was granted, and the trial was rescheduled for January the following year. Drew would play his final season.

Once Drew was charged the second time, Detective Lewis brought Desmond Baker in for questioning. When the officers who were sent to pick him up explained what they wanted, he agreed to go along willingly. Detectives Lewis and Scott questioned Desmond in a regular conference room, one decidedly more pleasant than the interrogation room behind the one-way mirror they'd used with Drew.

Detective Lewis began the questioning. "One of your teammates, Drew Evans, has been arrested and charged with sexual assault. Since drugs were present and the victim was unable to give her consent, Mr. Evans has been charged with a felony. It's a serious matter."

Desmond looked worried. "What do you want with me?"

"We're wondering if you might know anything about it."

"I don't know nothin'."

"We're aware you were present with Mr. Evans in the Sink several weeks ago. Are you aware that he attempted to rape someone that night?"

"I'm not surprised. I told her to stay away from him. I didn't know what he did. Look, are you chargin' me with somethin'?"

"Not at the moment, no. We're primarily interested in Mr. Evans. Unless you're an accomplice."

The giant football player scowled. "Look, I know what he does, but I've never been a part of it. I've kept my mouth shut, but I never participated in any of this."

"Why'd you keep your mouth shut?" Detective Lewis asked, exploiting the opening. "Didn't you worry about women getting hurt?"

"It's Detective Lewis, right?"

"Right."

"Detective, football is all I got. If I don't get into the NFL, I'll be back to gang life in Compton, pronto. My life ain't worth shit back there. Football's my way out."

"Did Mr. Evans threaten you to gain your silence?"

"It's like the marines, Detective Lewis—unit, corps, God, country. Same with football. Team comes before everything. If I don't protect the team, I don't get no playin' time. No playin' time, no pro draft. I don't like Drew Evans, but he's one hell of a quarterback. The man knows how to win. I need him to survive."

"Are you aware that Mr. Evans regularly uses drugs to rape women?"

"I heard rumors."

"Do you know if he used any that night in the Sink or had help from the waitress or the bartender?"

Desmond's eyes widened at the question. He looked away. "Maybe."

"If you had knowledge, would you be willing to testify against Mr. Evans?"

"Why would I?"

"Because he's a bad dude, and we're going to lock him up for a long time."

"I want to talk to a lawyer."

With that request, Detective Lewis had to immediately end the conversation. "We're done for now. Thank you, Mr. Baker. We'll be in touch. In the meantime, I think you *should* contact a lawyer."

KATIE STARTED HER LSAT PREPARATION CLASS AT the beginning of April. A week after her sessions began, she received a call from Harriet Becker. "I hear you got your guy."

"I helped."

"You did more than help. From what I hear, they never would've located the other victim and convinced her to testify without your efforts."

"It felt like the right thing to do."

"How's the LSAT coming?"

"I take it in June."

"You'll do fine. I spoke with the university about your settlement."

"Will they pay you?" Katie recalled Becker's dismissive lecture when she told the attorney that she just wanted to walk away from any money beyond what was necessary to pay Becker her fees.

"Yes. They have a problem on their hands with Drew. They also recognize your celebrity status as the student who helped apprehend a dangerous criminal. The university concluded that they'd have a PR bonanza if they embraced you. Consequently, they amended their offer."

"I can't imagine."

"I told them of your plans to attend law school. They'd like to see you remain at the University of Colorado. If you're admitted, they'll give you a full scholarship. You'll need to pay room and board, but they'll cover all tuition, books, and fees. They also agreed to pay me. And they offered to give you a lump sum of a hundred thousand dollars."

"It seems generous."

"It is. I'd take it. You still need to maintain the NDA about everything but Drew."

"I will."

"I'll let them know. How are things going with your professor?"

"Great. I'm never going to let him go. Bye, Harriet. And thanks."

A COUPLE OF WEEKS LATER, AFTER THINGS had quieted down on the case, Mark and Katie took Colin out to dinner. Over pizza and beer, she tried to assuage Colin's lingering guilt over the night at the Sink. He remained devastated by the improper arrest. He said that having charges dropped because he'd screwed up was the most embarrassing moment of his law-enforcement career. Katie pointed out that it was because of his quick thinking that they'd gotten the beer glass into evidence. Thanks to him, she'd told him, all the women Drew had assaulted would finally see justice done.

Despite the somber discussion, by the time dinner was over and after a few more beers, Colin was in better spirits. They began to laugh and speak of less weighty topics. Colin joked about stories from inside the department, and Mark told funny tales about some of his students in the classroom. After Colin said good night and left the restaurant, Katie sensed that she'd made a good friend. Boulder had come to feel like home. Katie and Mark stayed behind and finished their beers.

Mark leaned back in his chair. His jaw went tight. "Can we talk about the night in the Sink?"

Katie's gaze flicked up from the table. "Sure, if you want."

"The counselor cautioned me to go easy. PTSD is a real concern. You've been through a lot. You could have been raped."

Katie crossed her arms. "I'm aware of that."

"Was it wise to put yourself in such a risky position?"

Katie tightened her arms around her chest. "We shouldn't talk about this right now."

"Now that I've found you, I can't imagine being without you. If you pursue a career in criminal law, you might face these kinds of dangers again."

"I helped bring a criminal to trial. Isn't that worth the risk?"

"It's the risk that bothers me."

Katie stared at Mark. What was his point? Her pride in apprehending Drew exceeded her anguish over the near-rape. What if Drew had successfully penetrated her? Had Colin arrived five minutes later, he would have. "I did take risks. We believed that with Colin and two policemen present, nothing bad could happen. We were wrong, and I was lucky. I'm sorry if I frightened you. Isn't it the result that counts? If I *had* been raped, would you feel differently about me? Is that it?"

Mark let the question sit there for a second. "I've thought about it. I'd love you regardless. But if you'd been raped, I'd want to kill Drew. I've never felt such anger toward anyone. I don't like it."

Katie understood. "You have my word. I promise to be careful. But I need you to understand my passion for law. Since I arrived in Boulder, you've shown me what it feels like to love and be loved. Our relationship's everything to me. But I also want to make a difference in this world. Beyond loving you, I now have purpose. I've achieved some balance. I won't turn back."

THE FRIDAY AFTER HAVING BEERS WITH Colin, Katie borrowed Mark's car. She still hadn't replaced her own. Once she received payment from the university, it would become her top priority. She simply told Mark that she had an errand to run. After walking to his apartment to pick up the car, she drove back to her own and ran inside. She returned with a plastic clothes basket and a clean towel. After putting them inside the car, she knocked on Ava's door.

The door opened, and Katie said, "Come on, let's go. I'm late."

"This is going to be so much fun."

They got into the car, and Katie drove north out of town. Their destination was twenty miles away. It was a perfect day to drive. The sky was clear and the sun warm. Katie loved Boulder weather.

Half an hour later, Katie pulled the car off the highway and followed a gravel road for another couple of miles. She turned into the driveway of a sprawling ranch-style home and pulled to a stop next to a small barn.

"Aren't you excited? I am." Ava beamed behind oversize sunglasses that covered a large part of her face.

The girls walked up to the porch of the main home and rang the bell.

An older woman, her gray hair perfectly combed and pulled back in a ponytail, opened the door. She wore faded blue jeans, a flannel shirt, and a leather vest. "Ready to pick up your boy?"

"Joan, this is my friend Ava. I can't wait to see him again."

Katie had started the process months earlier. Right after Mark was reinstated at the university. When Joan had called her at her apartment, Katie fretted that Mark might have guessed her plan. But he hadn't.

Joan said, "Well, let's go get him."

Katie and Ava followed her to the barn, where Joan rolled open a large hanging door. Inside was a metal pen layered with sawdust and full of golden retriever puppies. A female golden wagged her tail and watched the girls closely as they approached her litter.

Joan said, "That's him, the one toward the back. Playing with one of his sisters. He has an orange ribbon tied around his neck."

Katie watched the small puppy tug on the ears of a littermate. Katie walked over and reached down inside the pen. She gently coaxed him away from his sister, delicately grasped him with her thumbs under his front legs and her hands wrapped firmly around his sides, and lifted him from the pen. He hung completely limp and studied her through large brown eyes highlighted by long blond lashes. She brought him in close. He licked her face. She'd heard people talk nostalgically about the sweet smell of puppy's breath. She inhaled deeply. It was the sweetest fragrance she'd ever smelled—one to add to the list of things she'd never forget. He was adorable.

"He's yours now. You read all the books, right?"

"I think I'm ready to take care of him."

"Remember, these puppies are like family to me. If you ever decide you can't keep him, or no longer want him, you agreed in your contract to return him to me. It doesn't happen often, but I'd rather care for him myself than see him go off to an uncertain fate."

"You have my word."

"Congratulations. I can tell you'll take great care of him. Call me anytime if you have questions. Make sure you have your veterinarian check him out within a week to make sure he's doing OK."

Katie gently placed the puppy inside the clothes basket on top of the towel and put the basket in the back seat next to Ava. Ava spoke to the puppy in soft, loving tones the whole way back to Boulder. He cried off and on, no doubt missing his family and fearful of his new surroundings.

Since it was Friday, and in what had become a routine, Katie planned to spend the weekend with Mark. She couldn't wait to surprise him. She spent an hour at her place after returning from the breeder getting ready. The puppy stayed in the basket inside her apartment while she packed her things. He whimpered occasionally, but not as much as he had on the drive home. He kept a watchful eye on Katie as she moved around and put things into her bag.

After putting everything into Mark's car, Katie drove to his apartment with the puppy in the passenger seat beside her. Even though she'd found a way to loop the seat belt around the basket to secure it, she'd never before felt more cautious driving and obeyed every stop sign and traffic signal along the way. She thought of new parents and how cautious they must feel when they drive their babies home from the hospital for the first time.

Katie arrived on Mark's porch with her bag around her shoulder and the laundry basket firmly gripped in her hands. She rang the buzzer and waited, her smile so wide it hurt.

Mark called out, "Come on up!"

She waited, unable to open his door, and in a moment heard his footsteps come down the inside stairway. The latch released, and the door swung open. Katie watched his face absorb the surprise. She remembered a previous surprise and a similar look of pure joy on his face. He stared at the puppy with wide eyes.

"Who is this little guy?"

"He doesn't have a name yet. I got him for you."

Mark beamed. He reached in and picked the puppy up and brought him in close. The puppy began to lick and nibble on his face.

"Hey, that's my job," Katie said with a laugh.

"He's precious. Come on. Let's take him upstairs."

Mark took the puppy up the steps, and Katie followed with her bag and the basket. They sat down on the floor opposite each other with their legs crossed and watched as the puppy tripped and stumbled his way around the space between them.

"I can't believe you did this."

"I loved the story you told about raising puppies as a boy. Getting this little guy seemed like a great way to tell you how sorry I am for the pain I've caused you."

"You have nothing to apologize for." Mark leaned in and kissed her. The puppy climbed up into his lap, and Mark broke off the kiss and looked down. The puppy rolled over on his back and let Mark rub his pink tummy. "What shall we name him?"

"What do you think of Wilson? We could honor a professor we both admire who encouraged me to go to law school."

"That's brilliant. Wilson is a great name. But we have a problem." Mark's eyes sparkled.

"Oh?"

"Wilson's going to need more space and a backyard. We should find a new home. A place for all of us."

"You serious?"

"We've been together almost six months. I think we should live together. Wilson's the perfect excuse."

Katie grinned. "I'd call Wilson the perfect gift."

The End

ACKNOWLEDGEMENTS

I thank everyone who contributed to this book. It's a long list of generous people who, over the course of two years, have made a significant impact. They include a prosecuting attorney from the sex crimes unit in King County, who explained the challenges of gaining a conviction in a sexual assault case; a recent graduate of the University of Washington, who helped me better understand daily life for women on today's college campuses; and a practicing chief criminal deputy prosecutor who ensured my legal proceedings were accurate. Multiple test readers, ranging in age from eighteen to seventy, gave me their valuable and unvarnished feedback. An editor once said, if one person has a concern, it might be based on their own interpretation. If several have the same concern, then you have a problem.

Lastly, thanks to two editors who helped polish the manuscript and make it shine. Through many revisions, Yes Means Yes now stands on its own, and readers will judge whether I successfully captured this difficult and critical issue in a way that is interesting, compelling, and authentic.

ABOUT THE AUTHOR

Steven Wells has written three books, all self-published. His first book, Ginger's Story, was written as a short first-person narrative about the challenges of raising a daughter through high school as a single dad. Narrated by Ginger, the daughter's golden retriever, the short and poignant story tells of a family torn apart by divorce and healed through the love of a dog. As a single father, Steven followed the lives of his young daughter and her friends through college and into young adulthood. Now that they have graduated from college, this cohort of women has exposed Steven to many of the issues that young women face today. His next two books, Killer Cuvée and Harvest Homicide, are "wine mystery" novels about a fictional winemaker in Walla Walla, Washington, who becomes embroiled in murder mysteries. Both books are written with an abundance of factual wine-making knowledge and educate readers about life in a small winery through the telling of suspenseful stories.

A former executive at Microsoft, Steven also served as the board chair of the Microsoft Alumni Foundation. His efforts have helped steer the foundation's grants of $750,000 to Microsoft alumni and their numerous philanthropic efforts. His experience with the foundation has involved Steven in some of the world's greatest challenges, including disaster relief, health-care delivery, illiteracy prevention, juvenile-incarceration advocacy, and climate-change activism. Many of these issues share a common element: they affect women disproportionately.

Steven's educational background includes a BS in engineering from the University of Colorado, Boulder, which he chose for the location of Yes Means Yes. He received an MBA from Seattle University, a degree in wine production from South Seattle Community College, and a certificate in nonfiction writing from the University of Washington. Steven can be reached at www.stevenmwells.com.

www.ingramcontent.com/pod-product-compliance
Lightning Source LLC
Chambersburg PA
CBHW071126200626
46817CB00018B/2277